ᐅᑭᐢᑭᓯᐎᓇ ᐅᑭᒫᐎᐢᑵᐤ ᑭᐦᐁᐤ ᒥᑎᓯᐘᐩ

The Memoirs of Miss Chief Eagle Testickle

ᐅᑭᐢᑭᓯᐏᓇ

ᐅᑭᒫᐏᐢᑿᐤ

ᑭᐦᐁᐤ

ᒥᑎᓯᐘᐩ

THE MEMOIRS

OF

MISS CHIEF EAGLE TESTICKLE

A TRUE AND EXACT ACCOUNTING OF THE HISTORY OF TURTLE ISLAND

VOL. ONE

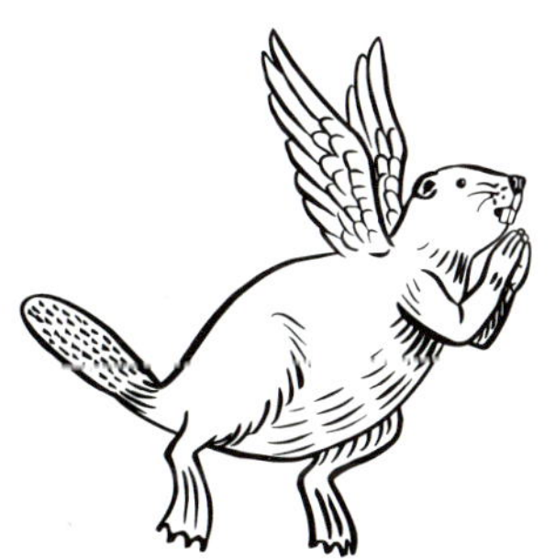

KENT MONKMAN & GISÈLE GORDON

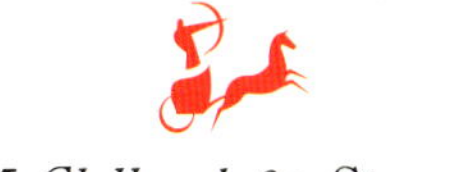

McClelland & Stewart

Hardcover edition published 2023
Trade paperback edition published 2025

McClelland & Stewart and colophon are registered trademarks of Penguin Random House Canada Limited.

Library and Archives Canada Cataloguing in Publication data is available upon request.

ISBN: 978-0-7710-2281-4
eBook ISBN: 978-0-7710-6123-3

The authors wish to thank the Ontario Arts Council and the Canada Council for the Arts for their support.

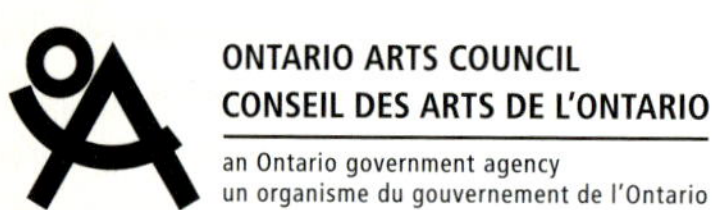

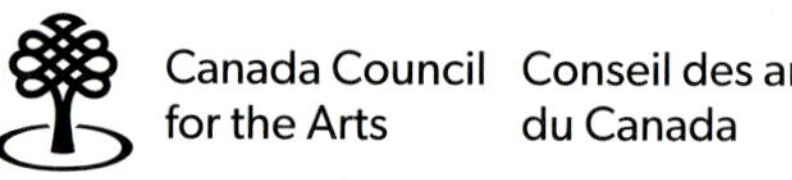

Book design by Andrew Roberts
Front cover art: Kent Monkman, *The Trapper's Bride*, 2006, Acrylic on canvas, 28 in. by 20 in.
Back cover art: Kent Monkman, *Resurgence of the People*, 2019, Acrylic on canvas, 132 in. by 264 in. Collection of the Metropolitan Museum of Art.
Typeset in Adobe Caslon Pro by M&S, Toronto
Printed in India

McClelland & Stewart,
a division of Penguin Random House Canada Limited,
a Penguin Random House Company
www.penguinrandomhouse.ca

1 2 3 4 5 29 28 27 26 25

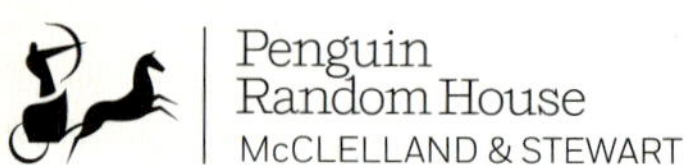

For all the ancestors who were
once children, all the children
who are our future ancestors,
and all the children in our lives.

Gisèle would like to name her
greatest teachers, her children Carson,
Miyoteh, and Keewetin, who give us
faith in the future every day.

ᒫᒪᐚᑕᐢᒋᑫᐏᐣ

Author Introduction *viii*
A Note on the Use of Cree *xi*
Preface by Miss Chief *xii*

A Star Is Born 1
When I Dreamed What Was to Come 23
My First Encounter with a Newcomer 33
The Massacre of Our Beaver Relatives Foreshadowed What Was to Come 39
The Newcomers Had Much to Learn 49
Many Trappers Sought Freedom in Our Forests 61
I Summoned My Admirers to Honour Me 77
The Time When Many Nations Came Together 85

CONTENTS

The Painter Who Could Not See 97

When I Travelled to the Newcomers' Homelands 109

Our Ways of Seeing Were So Different 129

Return to miskinâhk-oministik 141

My Intercourse with the Crown 147

I Learned That They Would Steal Everything 161

To Help My People I Made Mischief with the Newcomers' Leaders 179

Notes 193

Acknowledgements 237

Cree Language Glossary 241

ᑮᑳᐧᐩ ᐆᒪ ᐁᑲᐧ ᐊᐄᐧᓂᑭ ᐆᐦᐃ

INTRODUCTION

All stories start somewhere.

Our connection to Miss Chief began when she first appeared in Kent's painting *Artist and Model* in 2002. Since then, she has evolved and come into her own in the many works of performance art, installations, collaborative writing, and films we've made together. As she grew, she guided us, allowing us to tell her story, nudging us to learn more to tell it the best way we could. If we have not honoured her as we should, we ask her forgiveness, for we would never want to let her down.

Miss Chief led us here the long way. What began as a friendship over changing oil and tinkering with our mid-70s Honda motorcycles with other artist friends in Toronto in 1990 turned into thirty-plus years of partnership and collaboration. Kent is Swampy Cree, a member of Fisher River First Nation in Manitoba. He grew up mostly in Winnipeg, close to his Cree father's extended family, including his great-grandmother, Caroline Everette, and his grandmother, Elizabeth Monkman, a survivor of Brandon Residential School. Gisèle is a settler who moved to these lands as a child from the UK. After three decades of bouncing ideas off one another, our lives and families are now intertwined.

This story begins with the paintings. Kent's paintings of Miss Chief became our storyboard to flesh out her story. Some of the paintings confront difficult truths head on, some are sexy, many are tongue in cheek.

They are all drawn from Kent's personal experience of Cree culture and worldview as a Two-Spirit Cree cisgender man. We have made over a dozen projects translating the visual vocabulary and deeper context of Kent's paintings into films, performance, and installation projects. This book is an extension of our longer collaboration, continuing the story in what is, for us, a new medium.

We are grateful to many people for their assistance, but will save most of those thank yous until this tale is done. There are a few, however, that we need to thank up front. Like many descendants of those who went to residential "schools," Kent did not grow up as a Cree speaker. Before our tale begins, we'd like to honour and acknowledge the four brilliant minds who were generous enough to agree to be our main advisors on this book. Their combined knowledge and insights on the wisdom, kindness, and playfulness embedded in Cree language and culture made this book possible:

Dr. Keith Goulet, Nehinuw (Cree) from Cumberland House, who has been one of our most important teachers for the past two decades—we are deeply grateful to him and the wîcihitowin he and three generations of his family have shown us. He grew up trapping, fishing, and hunting, and is a scholar of Cree oral history, with a PhD in history on land dispossession and the Cree concept of land. The depth and breadth of his knowledge of Cree language and its connection to land and history is immense;

Floyd Favel, nêhiyaw (Cree) journalist, playwright, essayist, theatre theorist, and Cree cultural practitioner, Curator of the Chief Poundmaker Museum and Director of the Miyawata Culture Association from Poundmaker Cree Nation, is a long-time friend and collaborator whose unique artistic perspective and mâtinamâkêwin have been invaluable, hilarious, and inspirational to us both;

Dr. Belinda Daniels, award-winning nêhiyaw educator from Sturgeon Lake First Nation whose PhD dissertation is on nêhiyawêwin (Cree language) reclamation in her home community. Belinda is one of our Cree teachers—her nikwatisiwin and her help with incorporating profound concepts in a respectful way was invaluable;

And our dear friend, fluent Cree and Michif speaker, director, producer, screenwriter, and actor Gail Maurice from the village of Beauval. She helped us solve complex story problems with inspired solutions, encouraged us with her enthusiasm, and was often our muse, for, like Miss Chief, she radiates sâkihitowin with a generous dose of mischief.

Without their guidance, ideas, editing, consulting over dinners, campfires, teas, and many phone and zoom calls, we would not have been able to tell Miss Chief's story as it needed to be told. Over the past five years, their advice, feedback, ideas, and encouragement transformed and guided this memoir. They connected us with other knowledge keepers and shared family connections to open insightful, transformative conversations. Their commitment and passion to seeing us through this project was invaluable. Their opinions reflect a fragment of the diversity of thought from community to community, and also within communities.

This is a story by two artists on a path of exploration and discovery. If we have made mistakes with our Cree knowledge or the shared histories of these lands, they are ours alone.

A NOTE ON THE USE OF CREE

Cree is an oral language that is not standardized. It has multiple dialects; we use the Plains Cree Y dialect and mostly follow the most common Cree written spelling system of Standard Roman Orthography (SRO), which does not capitalize words. We made an exception in response to a request from our publisher to capitalize the Cree proper names of people in the book in order to help non-Cree speakers. In cases where we are quoting from Cree speakers we also kept their dialects and spellings, which are not always Y dialect SRO.

We are grateful to the expert help and generosity of Dorothy Thunder, Miriam McNabb, Solomon Ratt, and Bill Cook for helping us with translations and correcting our many mistakes in Cree. If errors remain, it is entirely our fault.

My name is
Miss Chief
Eagle Testickle
and I come
from the stars

Let me start at the beginning. Miss Chief Eagle Testickle nitisiyihkâson êkwa ohci niya acâhkosihk, my name is Miss Chief Eagle Testickle and I come from the stars. I will tell you an âtayôhkânis, a little sacred story. It is the story of this land. It is my story, and the story of my people. But it is also your story, for we are all relatives. It is the story of where we have come from. And perhaps where we are going, although that part is up to you. It is not our way to tell you how to behave, yet we may show you the way. Though perhaps it's better for you to listen to what I say, not to what I do, and some good may come of this after all.

ᓂᐦᑖᐃᐧᑫᐤ ᐊᒐᐦᑯᐢ

A Star is Born I

kayâs, a long time ago, there was only the dark fog and the one sound, a low hum that cycled through the universe. *I* was there, of course, but not in a way that you would understand.[2] After some time, the forces of light and dark joined together to become the great goodness, Kisê-manitow, the Great Spirit, who created all things, including us, the oldest beings. Kisê-manitow sent out a thought into the universe, which became the first acâhkos, the first star. I was still elemental; you would think of my form as hydrogen, but I was so much more. The beginning of everything was here, including you.[3]

My experience of time is different from yours. After a while, Kisê-manitow formed Grandfather Sun and Grandmother Moon, those that you see in the sky today, and also askiy, this planet you call earth. Kisê-manitow brought the elements—fire, water, air, and earth—and from these were made the land we stand on, the rock, the mountains, valleys and plains, the oceans, lakes, and rivers.

My elder siblings, the sacred beings, were created next. Wîsahkêcâhk,[4] I call him nistês, my elder brother, some of you call him trickster, but he is much, much more. piyêsiwak,[5] the thunder beings, were there, and also my dear friend and sister/brother Mistâpêw, who some of you call Sasquatch. There were others there, including those who do not wish to be named, and those who should not be named.

You haven't brought me tobacco, blankets, horses, not even a pack of chewing gum, so I cannot tell you the whole story. I cannot tell you about Kôhkominâkêsîs, Grandmother Spider, or acâhkos iskwêw, Sky Woman, but I can reveal enough for you to understand my story.[6] What I can tell you is that after my elder siblings, the âtayôhkanak, the spirit beings, came to be, there was one more legendary being created, one most people don't know about. That being was me. I am Miss Chief Eagle Testickle, and this is my story.

This tale was written on the rocks so far back in time that the people have long forgotten how to read them,[7] but listen, and I shall tell it to you now. I came from pakonî-kîsik, the hole in the sky that connects this

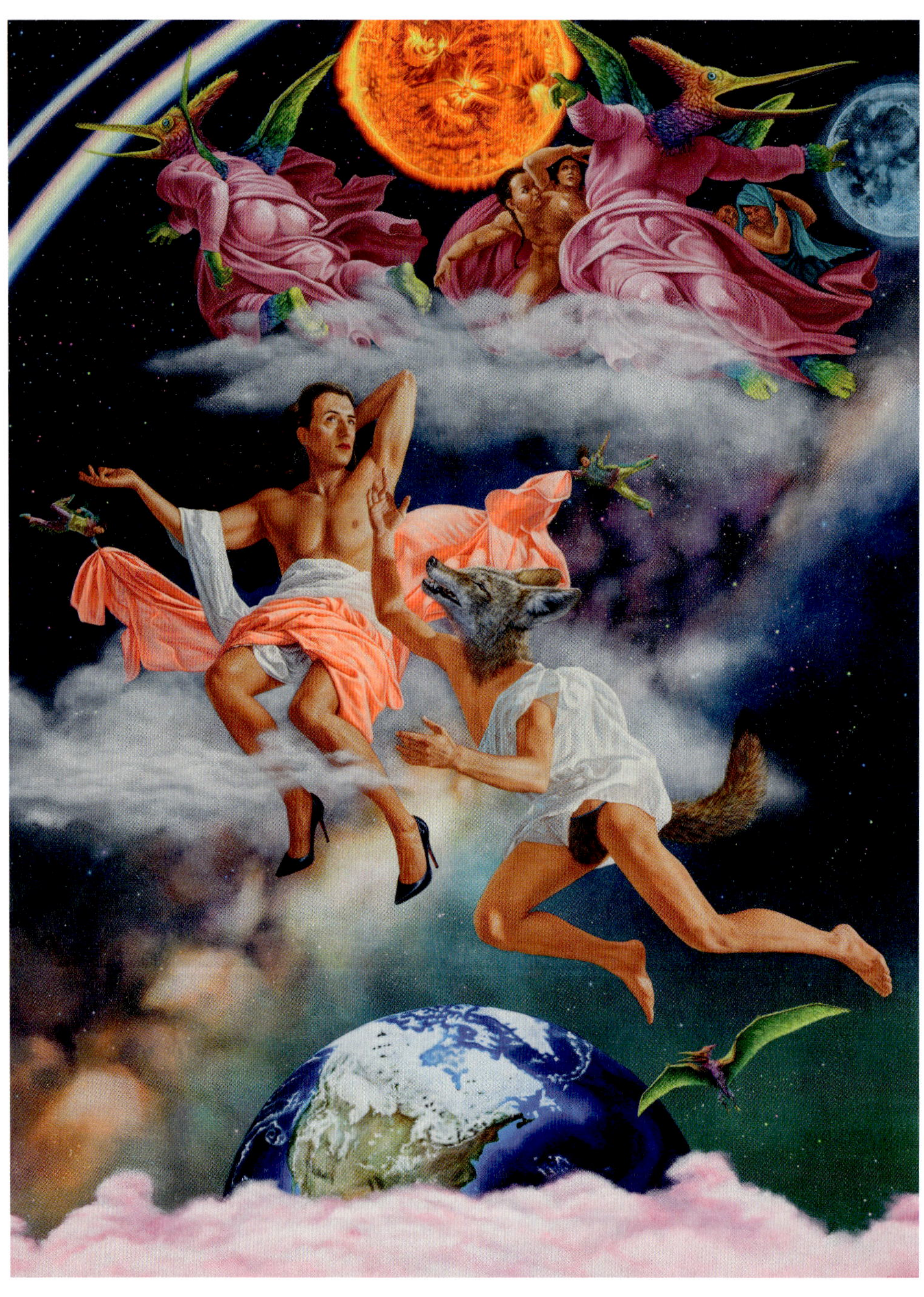

I shone so brightly with ***acâhkosak****, the stars.*

I Come From pâkwan kîsik, the Hole in the Sky, 2022. Acrylic on canvas. 108 in. x 81 in.

world to another behind the Seven Sisters, the place Wîsahkêcâhk points to in the winter sky—what some of you call the Pleiades.[8] It is a place without what you understand as dimension, but it contains your past and your future. You can only fully comprehend it in your dreams.[9]

Kisê-manitow sent me blazing down to askiy, leaving a glittering pink trail in my wake,[10] transforming me as I fell. My form shifted from gas to cloud, to rain, soft kimiwan sprinkled with cosmic dust. As I hurtled to earth, I laughed, sending shock waves of sound rolling in all directions. A blur of new sensations coursed through my newly forged body. Emotions flooded through me in sharp focus one at a time and then all at once, blurred and packed in incomprehensible layers. New feelings tumbled over one another—the shock of physical awareness, primal delight and wonder, and an overwhelming feeling of love for all of creation.

I was now a being with senses, an external shape with bones, skin, muscle, and cells full of nipiy, water, carrying positive and negatively charged ions that danced within me. Every sense in my new human body was firing as I experienced them for the first time. The wind howled in my ears and my skin glowed hot. The pressure of the atmosphere sparked off my golden-brown skin as I plummeted to earth. From all four directions the winds came, working together to slow my screaming, smouldering descent, but still I sparked, glowing ever brighter until my black hair began to singe and smoke.

I opened my mouth to scream my first human sound, but before I could, a great shadow flew before me. Kisê-manitow had sent kihêw, the great eagle, to further slow my descent. The air shrieked apart as the leader of the winged ones cracked the molecules aside with his mighty wings. He flapped again and enfolded me against his breast, my body relaxing into his cool feathers.

I arched my back to press myself into his sternum, which felt so exquisitely hard underneath the softness of the downy surface. kihêw looked me in the eye and gripped me harder with his razor-sharp talons as he

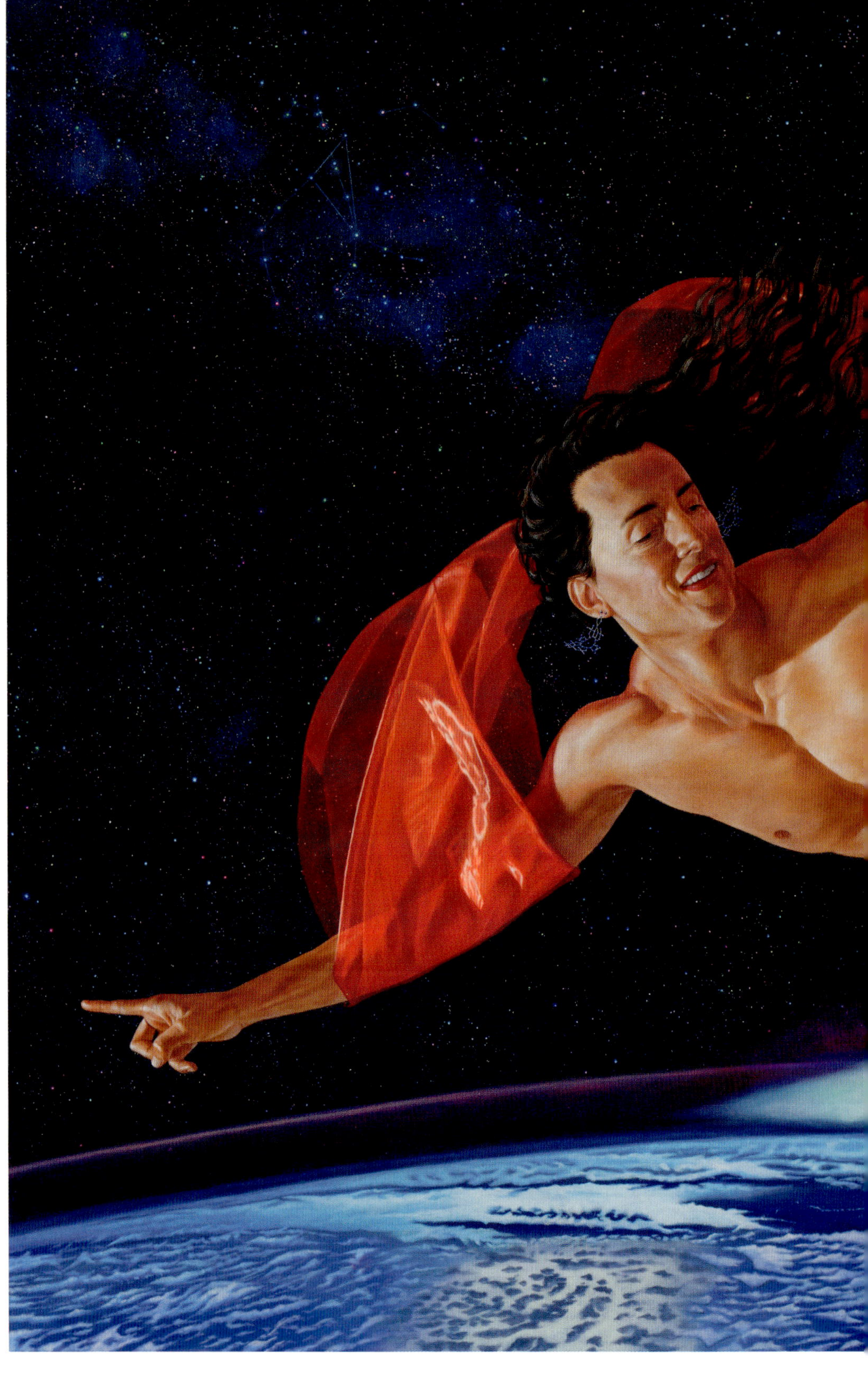

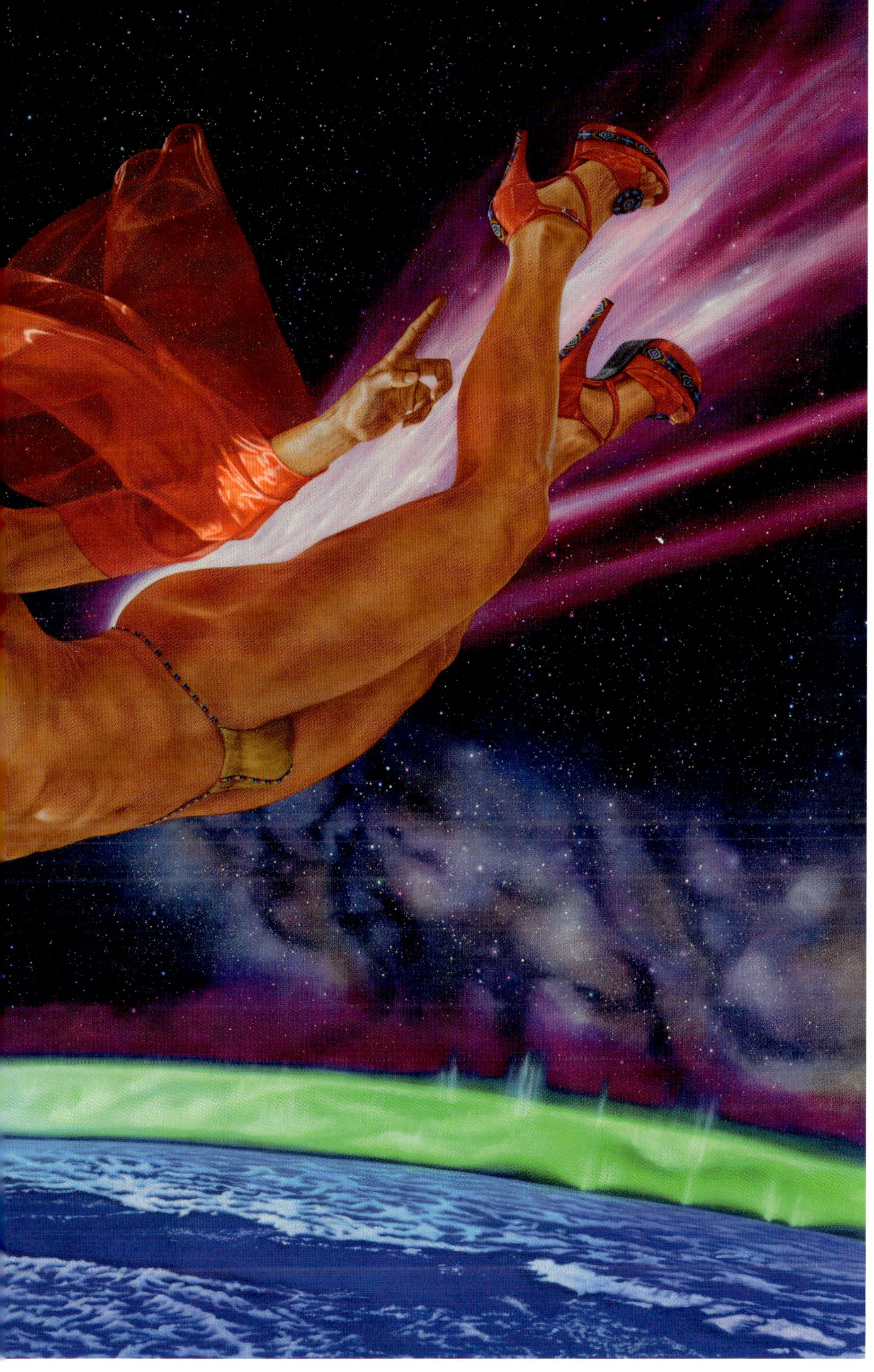

As I hurtled to askiy, confusion and fear gripped my new faculties, but underneath I felt joy burbling, finding its way to the surface.

We Are Made of Stardust, 2022. Acrylic on canvas. 81 in. x 108 in.

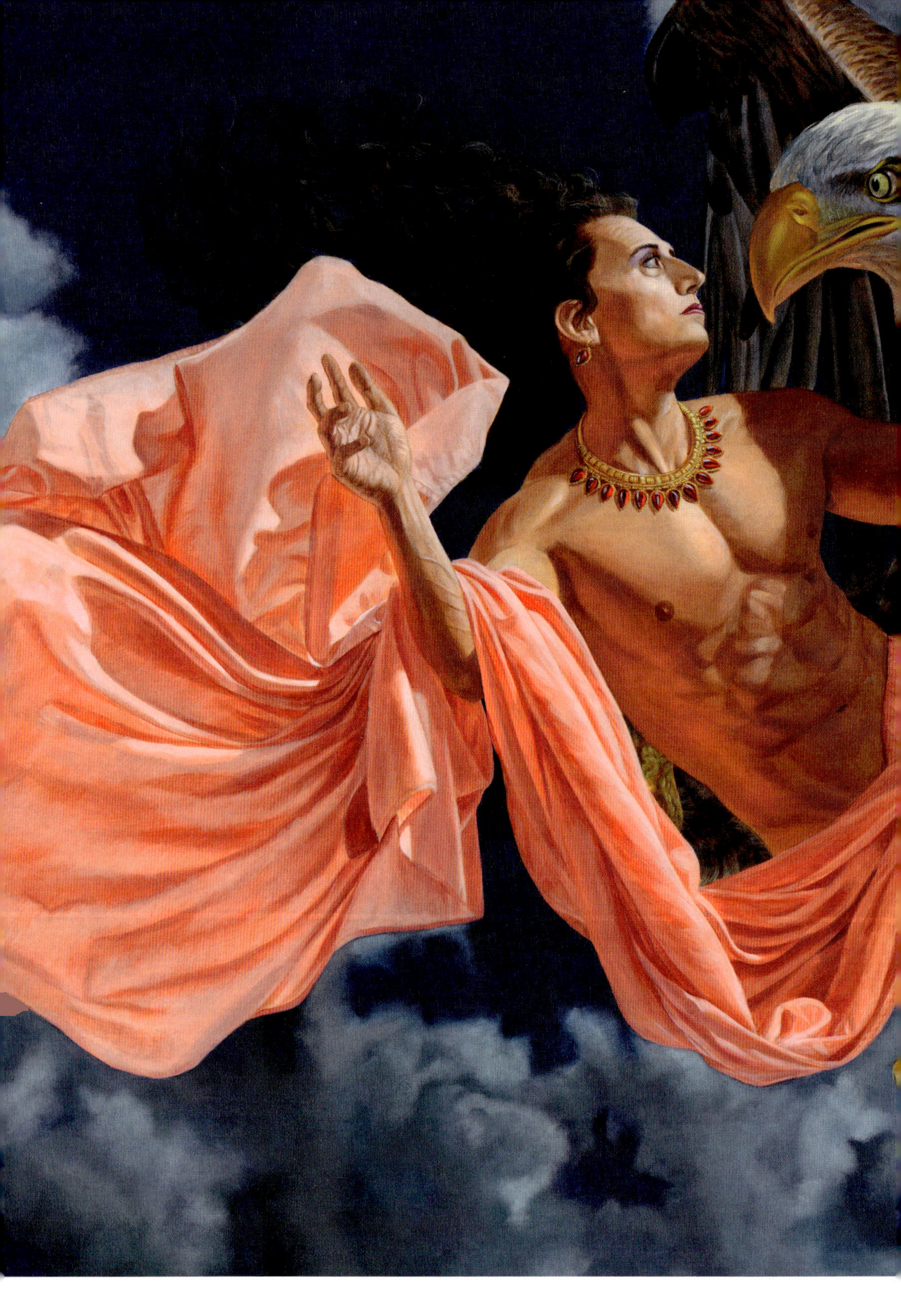

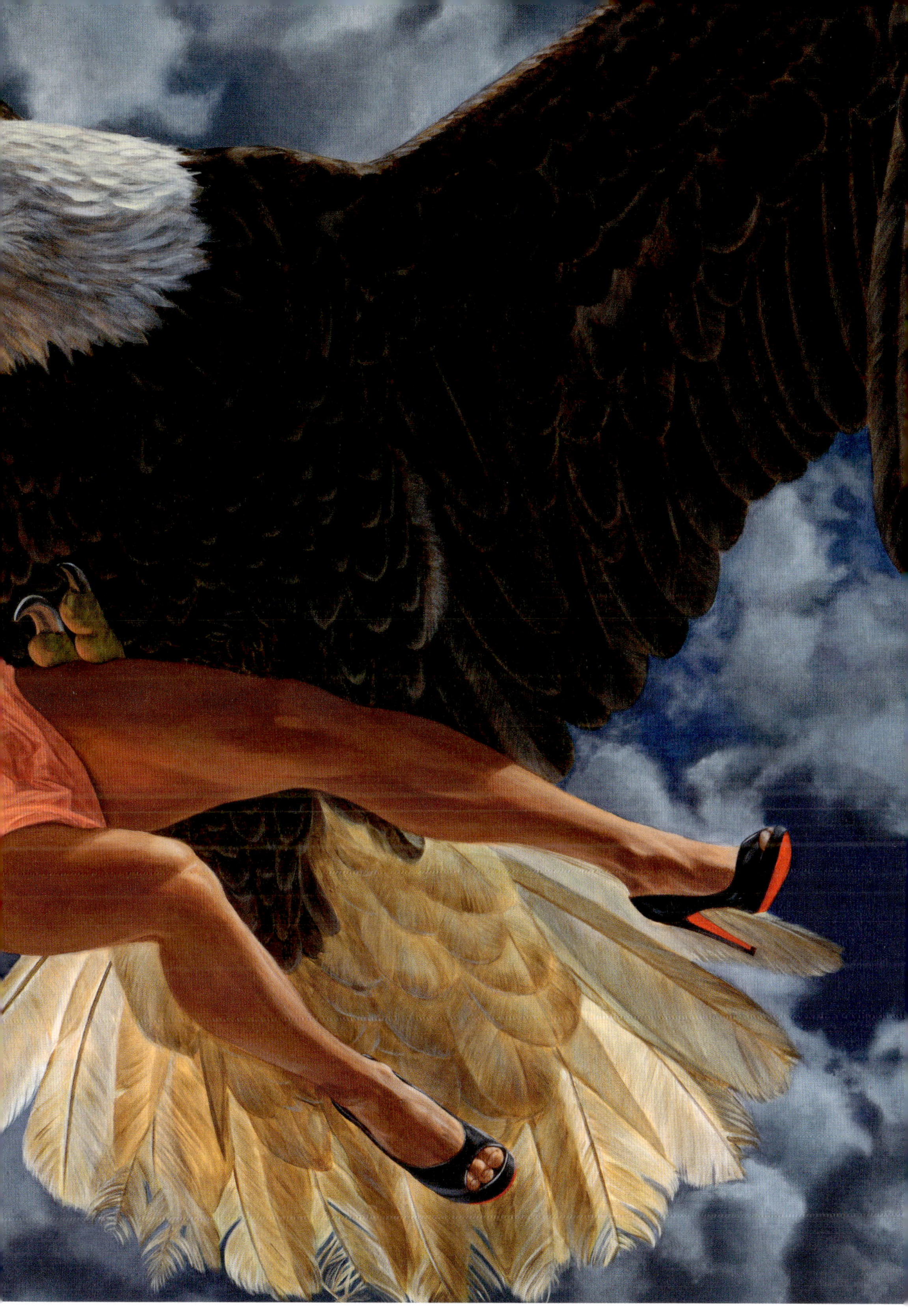

Everywhere my body connected with his, I felt new pathways burn to my brain and my loins until I became aware of another part of my body, rock hard, with intention all of its own.

Being Legendary, 2018. Acrylic on canvas. 48 in. x 72 in.

spread his wings ever wider. Everywhere my body connected with his, I felt new pathways burn to my brain and my loins until I became aware of another part of my body, rock hard, with intention all of its own. Things were getting more and more interesting.

"Do not get distracted from your path," kihêw admonished me, seeing the desire clearly in my eyes. "We each have our role. I have been sent to tell you that there will be beings in the future, two-leggeds, who require our assistance. You are to live with them, learn their ways, hold their stories and become legend with them as they go through the times of great change that will come with visitors from across the seas. Above all, you must love them, and with this love, this sâkihitowin, keep them on their right path, for they are weak and will need our help."

I could barely hear kihêw over the roaring of the atmosphere streaking past us. And, oh yes, I *was* thoroughly distracted. This tugging upon my body, emotion, and thought gave way to a new feeling. Desire. kihêw's sharp talons released a little and, afraid that I might slip, I instinctively plunged my hands into the warm, downy space between kihêw's legs and grabbed the first thing I could reach: the weighty balls that hung there so invitingly. kihêw's yellow eyes widened as he glowered. "You are mischief!" I could barely hear him. "Your game with the eagle's testicles!" With the deafening roar, what I heard was "You are Miss Chief, your name is Eagle Testickle!" I gazed into his eyes with great pride. It was kihêw himself that had given me my spirit name!

Heat spread upwards from my loins as part of this new body swelled and began to throb with a delicious ache. kihêw glared at me fearsomely, which only intensified the burning pull in my groin. The tension was exquisite; I reveled in it as we hurtled to askiy, my new home. I looked again at kihêw's eyes; they had softened, and now held an invitation. I smiled to myself. Yes, I decidedly liked it here.

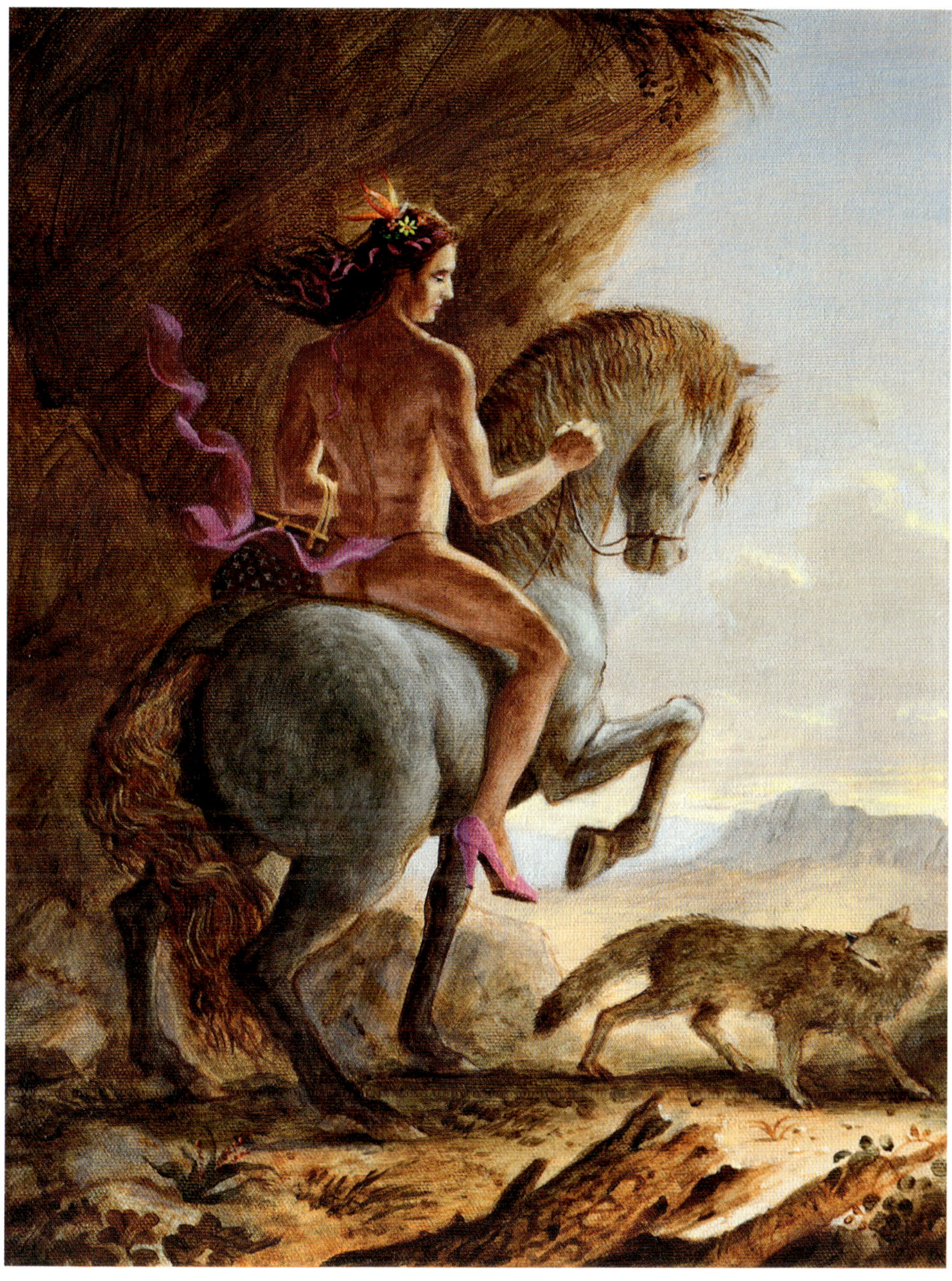

Time passes differently for us than for you—eons passed, but we did not count them.

Untitled, 2010. Acrylic on canvas. 11 in. x 14 in.

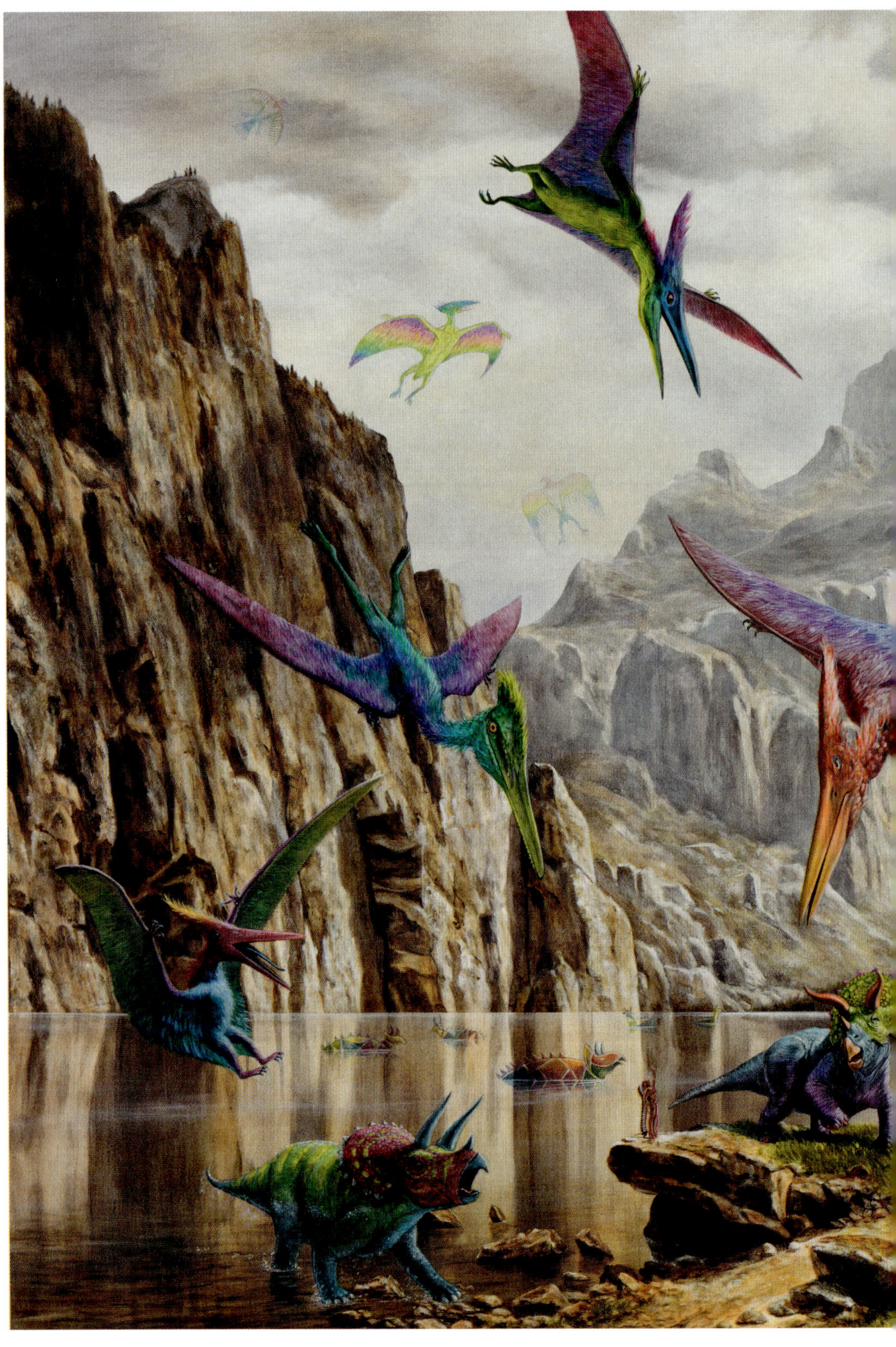

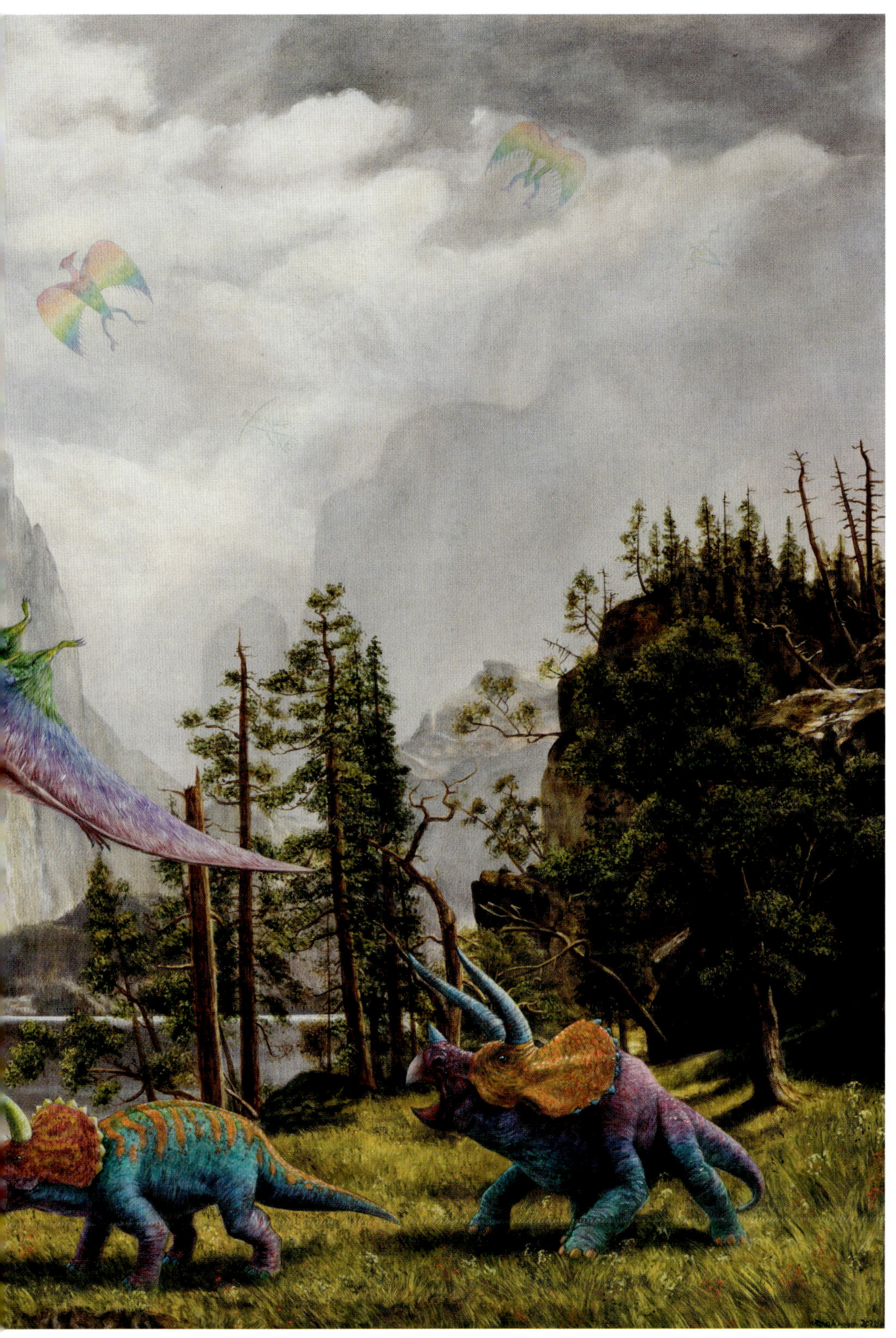

Many years from now, our peoples would find the bones of these giant creatures under the earth.[11]

Battle of the piyêsiwak and the misipisiwak, 2022. Acrylic on canvas. 51 in. x 72 in.

kayâs, a long time ago for you human beings, before the other spirit beings went into hiding, they helped prepare me for the times that were to come. The fiery mountains worked and slept, the great land masses moved, the ice sheets came and went. Smouldering tips of volcanoes belched smoke through the roiling waves under blackened skies streaked with lightning from the ceaseless battles between the piyêsiwak, and those old, old creatures the misipisiwak, great underwater lynx, and the giant beaver, mistahimisk.

Back then, the ground trembled as the giant buffalo,[12] mistahipaskwâwi-mostoswak, massive beyond imagining, pounded the land flat in their search for new grazing grounds. The great bears, the misi-maskwak, still roamed the earth, and all beings knew how to speak to one another. The ancient horses, the very small ones, would let us ride them if we knew how to ask. Sweetly, of course, for they were like cats and only did as they wished.[13] But we âtayôhkanak, us legendary beings—curmudgeons, divas, and tricksters, supernatural all—we mostly kept clear of each other unless, of course, we were making love, for we each had the power to cause the other great harm, and one could never tell what kind of mood our siblings were in.

The one I was closest to was my spiritual elder sibling Wîsahkêcâhk, the most powerful of all of us âtayôhkanak. He helped Kisê-manitow make the world. mwêstas, later, when the human beings were created, Wîsahkêcâhk was the one who gave ninêhiyawak, my Cree people, Kisê-manitow's laws to guide their actions in the ways of wâhkôhtowin, kinship, with all our relations—the four-leggeds, the flyers, the crawlers, the swimmers, the plant beings, the rock beings, and nipiy, the water. His assistance to those nêhiyawak would be, naturally, entirely in his own way.

Kisê-manitow gave me many gifts—the gift of shifting my shape, the gift of travelling fluidly through the web of space and time, and the gift of being both male and female and a multitude of spirits beyond gender together in one body. Some human beings, when they came, would also have this gift. It was my role to help human beings love one another, as I love all of creation, for we are all in wâhkôhtowin together. Some of their ahcâhk-iskotêwa, or soul flames, burned brighter than others, but they were all beautiful to me. Kisê-manitow had also given me special gifts to convince other creatures to do my bidding, tools I would need on this earth in my dealings with the human beings. I waited impatiently for them to arrive, for I loved to love and I loved to play.

One day, as we walked under the dappled shade of the poplars that sang to us as their leaves fluttered in the wind, Wîsahkêcâhk touched my cheek gently and told me about the times of trouble and great hardships that would come with the arrival of pale, hairy-faced humans on large wooden boats from across the sea. "When those ones come, starving and in thin rags, they will take much, and much will be lost. We will help the human beings remember what they will need to remember." He smiled and traced his finger along my lips. "I have my ways, you have yours." I kissed his salty finger as I held his gaze, for although all of us ätayôhkanak enjoyed our amorous adventures, Wîsahkêcâhk loved to tease me that I enjoyed them most of all. It was, after all, my nature, and had he not encouraged me?

Seeing a look in my eyes that he knew all too well, Wîsahkêcâhk gently turned my head to look intently into my eyes. "It will be difficult for you. You will witness the human beings suffering a great deal, and you will love them too much, but you must let them find their way on their own. We will help them remember what they need to know, and they will endure."

I nodded, not yet understanding all he was telling me, but yes, I would love them as kihêw had also instructed me, for I was built for love. As if hearing me aloud, Wîsahkêcâhk pulled me down beside him and we sat on the mossy log, nuzzling each other for a while. I turned to him, mouth slightly open, expecting the same delicious mingling of

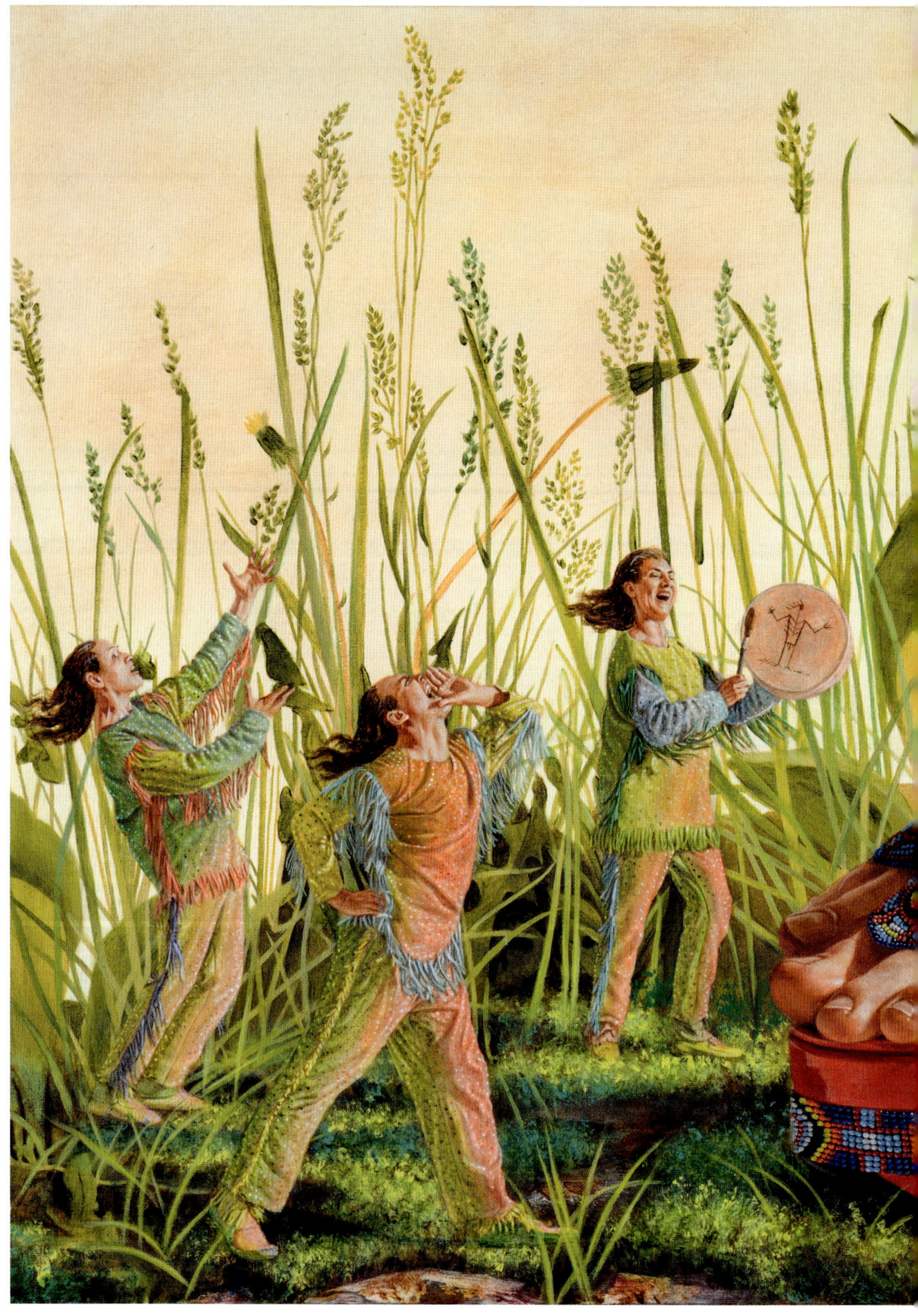

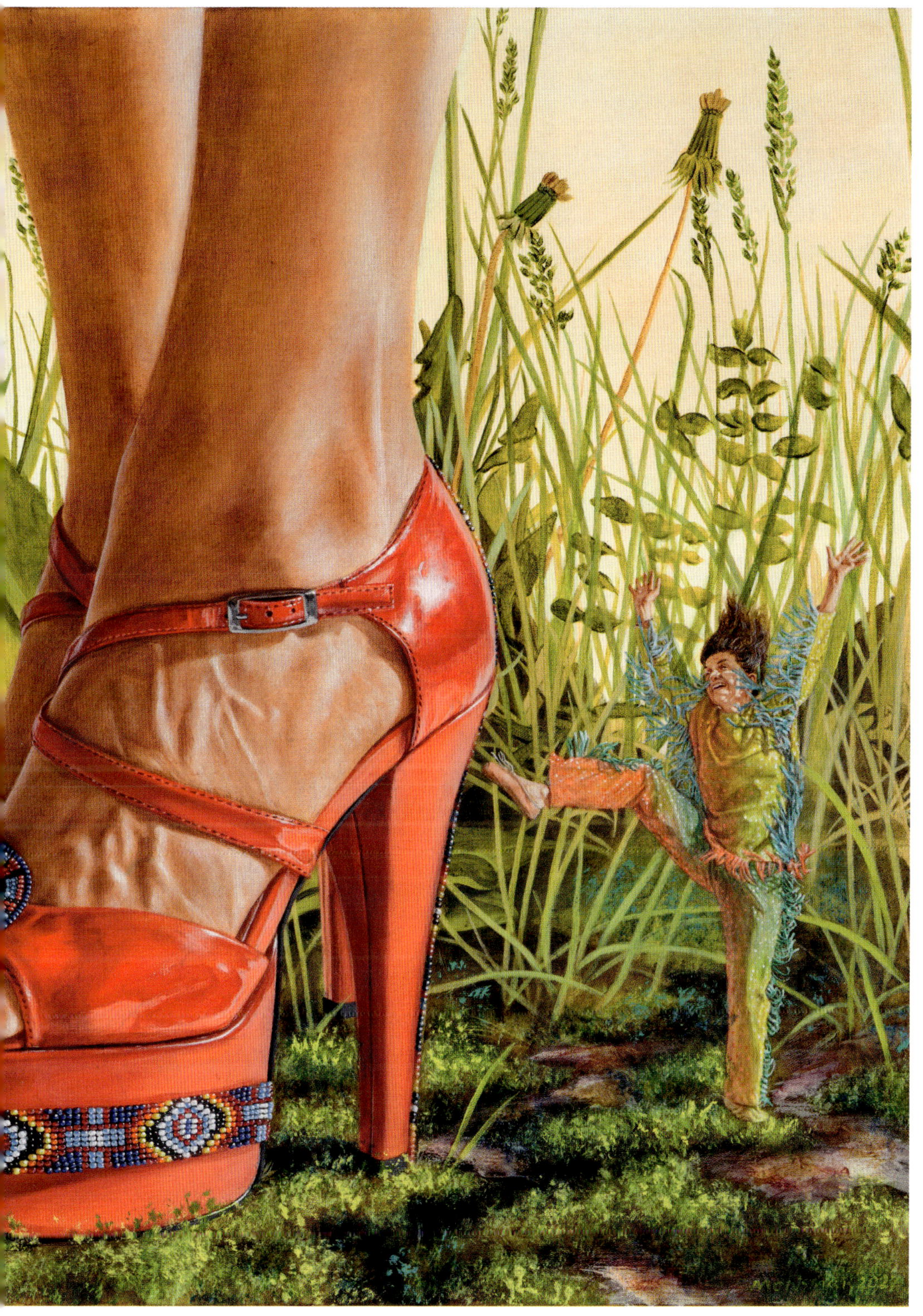

The mêmêkwêsiwak, the little people, and Mistâpêw, Sasquatch, had not yet gone into hiding, although they showed themselves only on their terms.

Compositional Study for They Walk Softly on This Earth, 2022. Acrylic on canvas. 24 in. x 36 in.

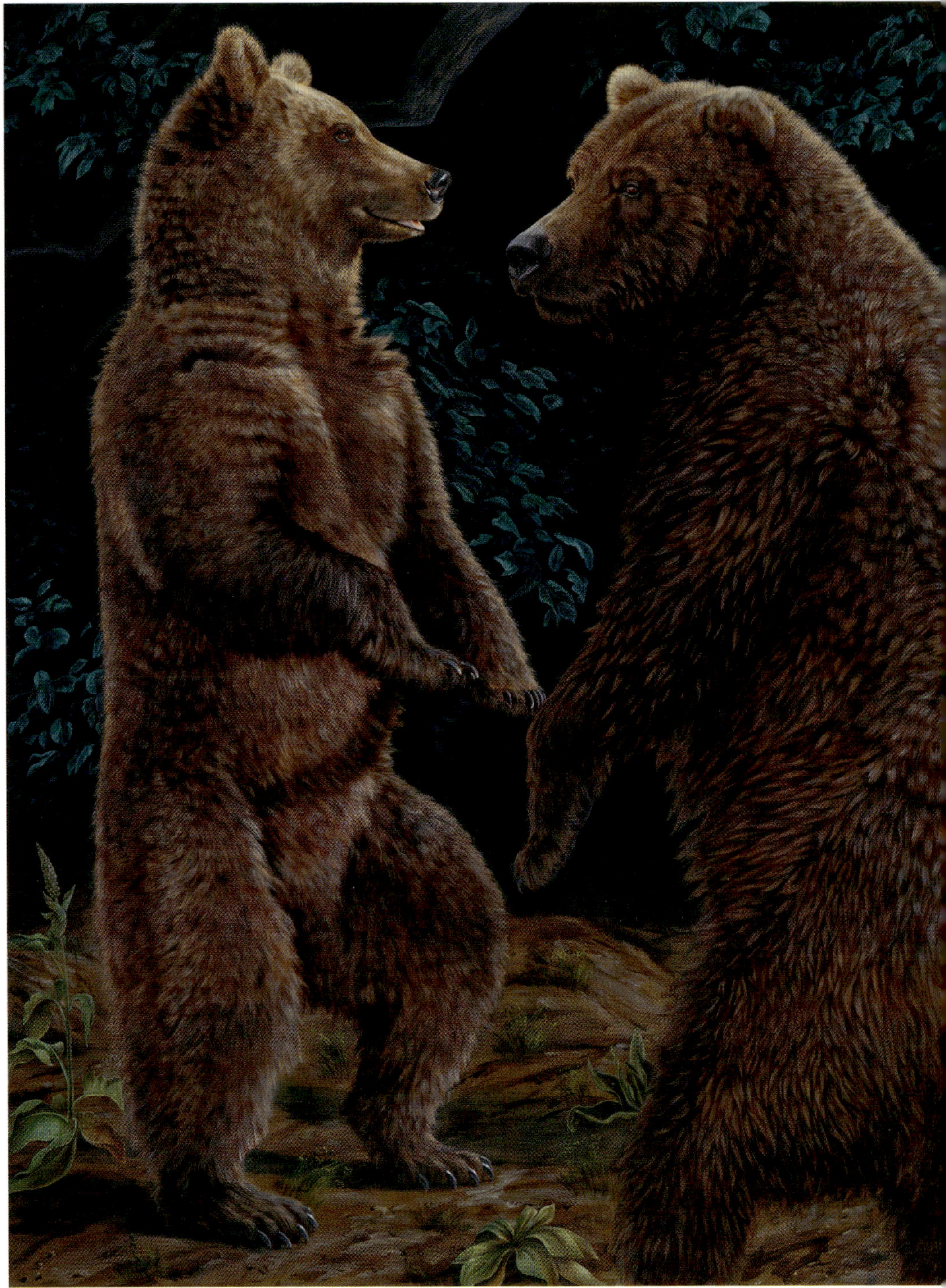

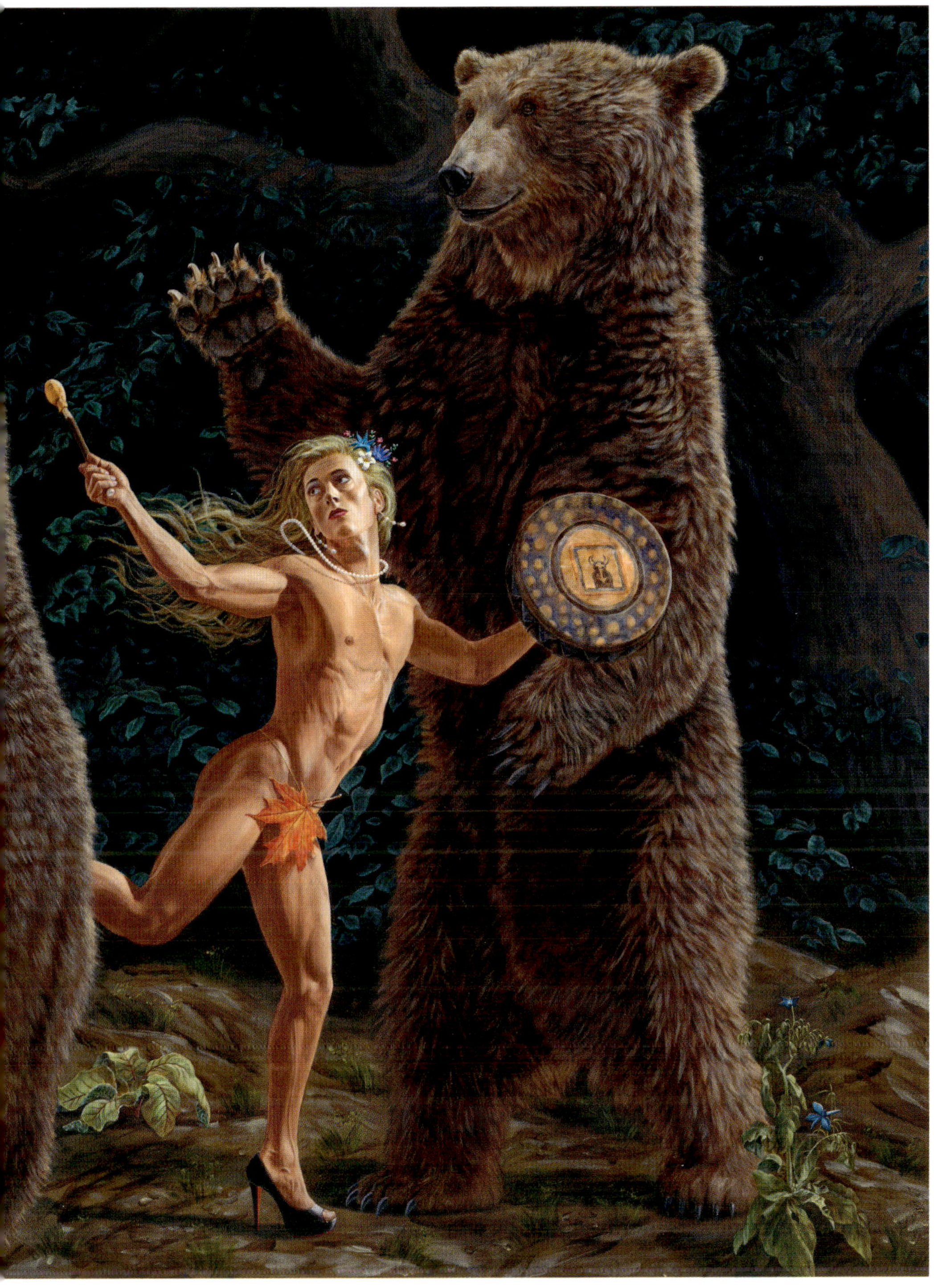

While the misi-maskwak did not have Wisahkêcâhk's power, they knew many things, including how to play.

The Three Bachelors, 2018. Acrylic on canvas. 84 in. x 132 in.

our physical and ethereal forms that was so irresistible, but just then Wîsahkêcâhk spied some ducks. He licked his chops and loped down the hill without turning back.

I did not follow—I had my pride, after all. He was a capricious sort anyway, and only good company when he wanted to be. When he wasn't in the mood for something, or it wasn't his idea, his temperature shifted like a summer storm, and his temper was formidable. When he didn't want to be found, he could dampen his soul flame so that I could not find him. Brilliant, kind, and sometimes unutterably foolish, he was the best lover I'd ever had. Although his quicksilver temperament often rankled me, he was the only one of my many supernatural lovers who could match me. One of our lovemaking sessions could last for weeks, both of us shifting form, body, and spirit until we merged in an ecstasy so violent it shook the eyeballs into the back of my head. But when he wasn't being seductive and interesting, he could be insufferable. We were too much alike to be together for long without crossing one another. And the farts! Never had I smelled something so vile.

I lay back on the log, absorbing the power of askiy, the cool moss prickling my warm skin, and I listened to the murmurings of the spruce trees that surrounded me. Plant language was the sweetest and most delicate, humming all through the tangled twisted roots in the vast network underground.

The giant bears, the misi-maskwak, were some of my most beloved companions. While they did not have Wîsahkêcâhk's power, they knew many things, including how to play. I could also trust them not to misguide me for my own instruction, or their own amusement, as Wîsahkêcâhk sometimes did. The misi-maskwak taught me how to manage my powers in this physical world—my uncanny ability to attract any living being to me, for example, for we all are spirit clothed in skin. All of us living beings have Kisê-manitow's ahcâhk-iskotêw inside us, making it possible to do wondrous things.[14] The misi-maskwak gave me gifts of medicine, laughter, joy, and pleasure to help me survive the dark times that were to come. Each maskwa introduced me to their unique ways of seduction and corporal delight, of which I was, of course, a most quick and eager student.

I threw myself into my task of exploration with abandon, helped by lovers of all genders, four-leggeds, winged ones, swimmers, crawlers, plant and rock people. Form and sex were, of course, no barrier, as many of us were shapeshifters in the ancient times. Enmeshed in one another's feathers, fur, skin, or scales, we would transform at the point of no return together, oft-times barely touching, for our unions were of mind and ahcâhk-iskotêw. Some encounters were fleeting. Others lasted a night, a day, and another night as I pulled their energy deeper into mine, intensifying my power, slowing down time, quenching their desire and revelling in the exquisite heights and complexities of pleasure that my human form allowed. It was one sweet, sticky, salty, bliss-filled blur.

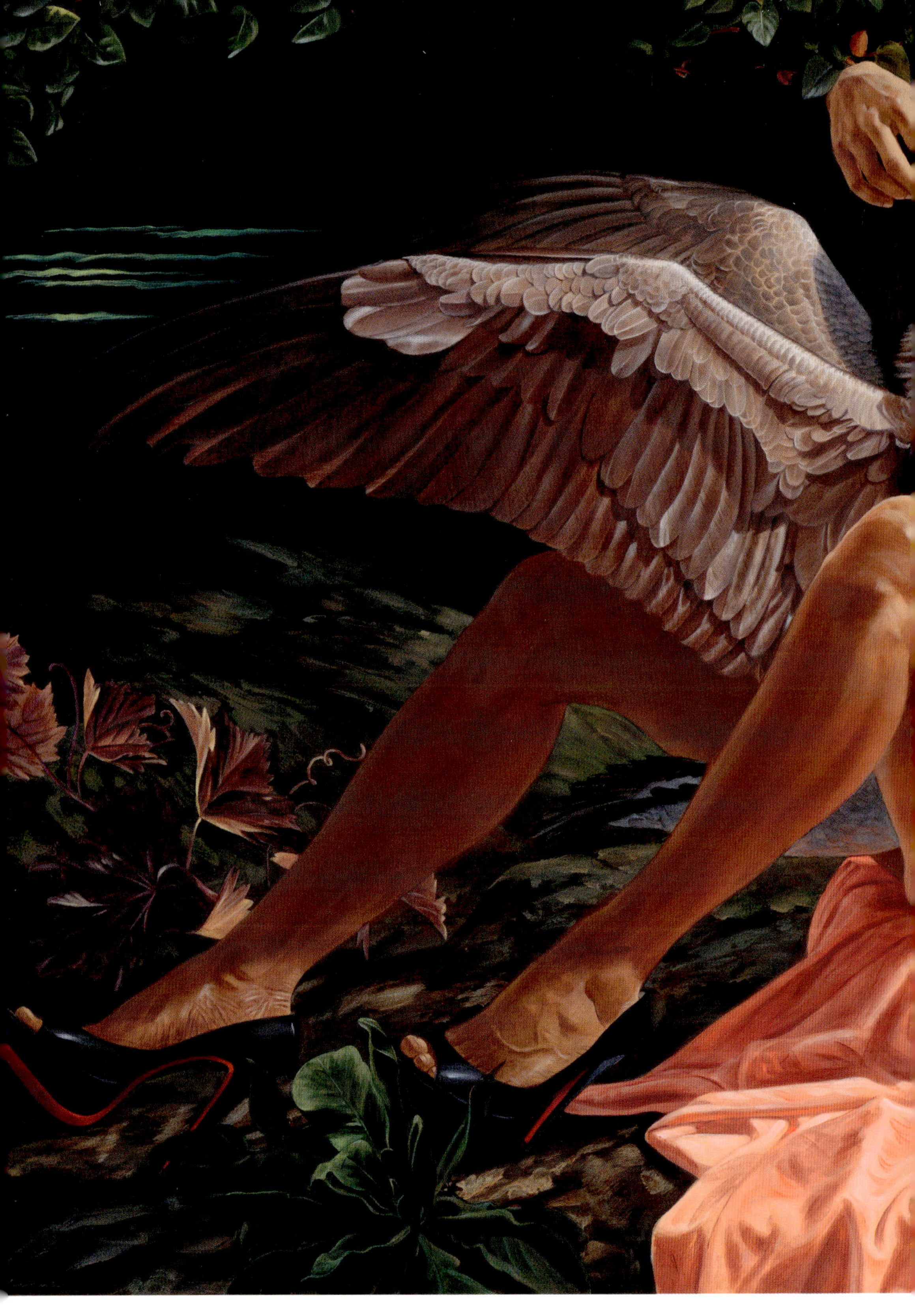

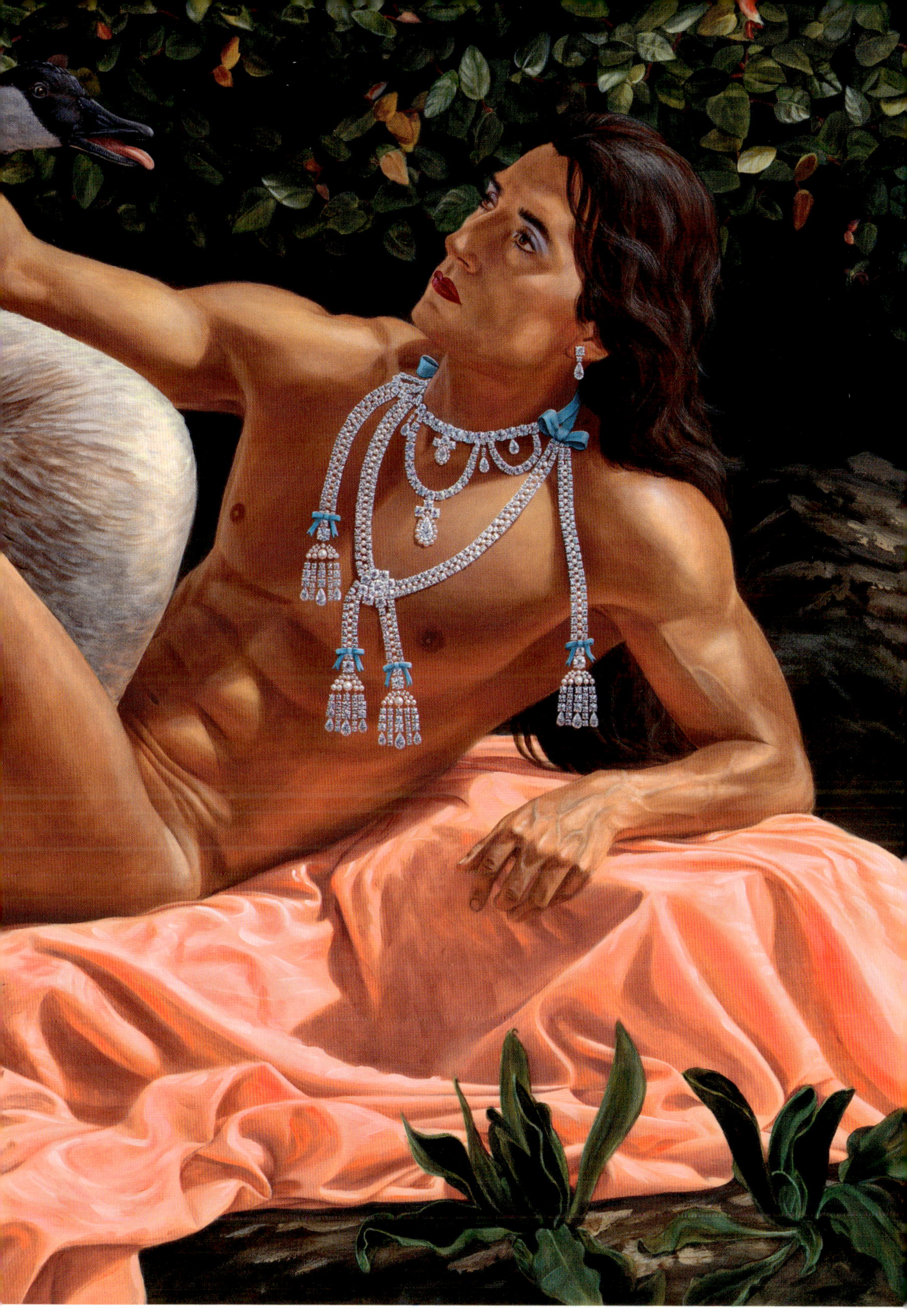

I threw myself into my task of exploration with abandon, helped by lovers of all genders, four-leggeds, winged ones, swimmers, crawlers, plant and rock people.

The Affair, 2018. Acrylic on canvas. 48 in. x 72 in.

ᑲᑮ ᐸᐚᑕᒫᐣ

ᑮᒁᐩ

ᑭᑲ ᐯ ᐃᐢᐸᔨᐠ

When I Dreamed What Was to Come

After a long while, the harmony between all creatures began to fray. Over time, many had begun to forget love, kindness, and the laws of wâhkôhtowin. All was descending into chaos and conflict. Kisê-manitow had warned Wîsahkêcâhk that it was his role to ensure peace, but his attention, as it was often wont to do, had wandered. 'Tis true, I could be held partially to blame, although truthfully, Wîsahkêcâhk needed no help to be distracted.

So it was that Kisê-manitow summoned the piyêsiwak, who rained down black sheets of water and flooded the world. Everything disappeared under the huge dark waves. All were subsumed but Wîsahkêcâhk, one otter, one beaver, and one muskrat, adrift on a raft.

As I slipped through the surface of nipiy, into the deep dark below, I focused my energies, shifting my molecules until their composition and form became liquid. I sighed, merging into the dark expanse of the sea. Every ripple, current, and wave resonated in me simultaneously as a symphony of feeling and sound merged into another sense that I cannot describe to you, because it is outside the realm of human experience. I drifted with the waves as tipiskâwi-pîsim, the moon, rose and fell many, many times, the weight of the water pressing in on each molecule, cool and fluid, expanding and contracting with the tides.

At one point, a misipisiw, a great lynx, the most powerful and feared of the water beings, swam by, her enormous tail making huge currents beneath the sea. I shielded my presence, for I was a lover, not a fighter, but I felt a commotion deep below, and heard terrible sounds. The misipisiw had many enemies, and as long as conflict prevailed, the waters would not recede.

Time passed, elongated and compressed. I felt sublime detachment and allowed myself to sink deeper and deeper, falling into mamahtâwisiwin, tapping into the great mystery.[15] All other sensation faded away as I heard the four winds calling to me under the water and felt the particles of the sunbeam infuse my current state of matter and permeate my life force with a vision—or was it the future? It is often so hard to tell. Some parts of what I saw cannot be shared, but some I will tell you now, for this is your story too.

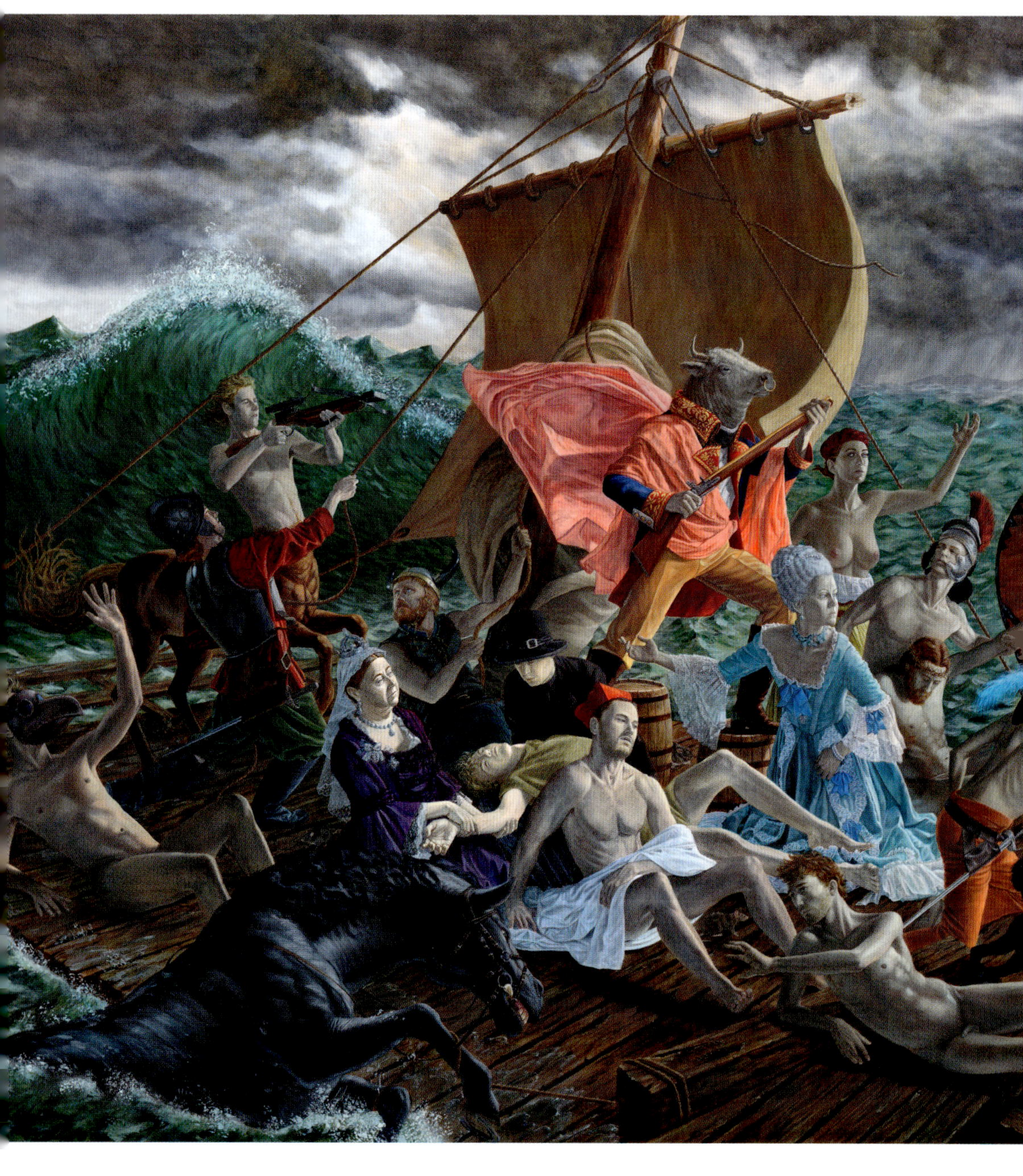

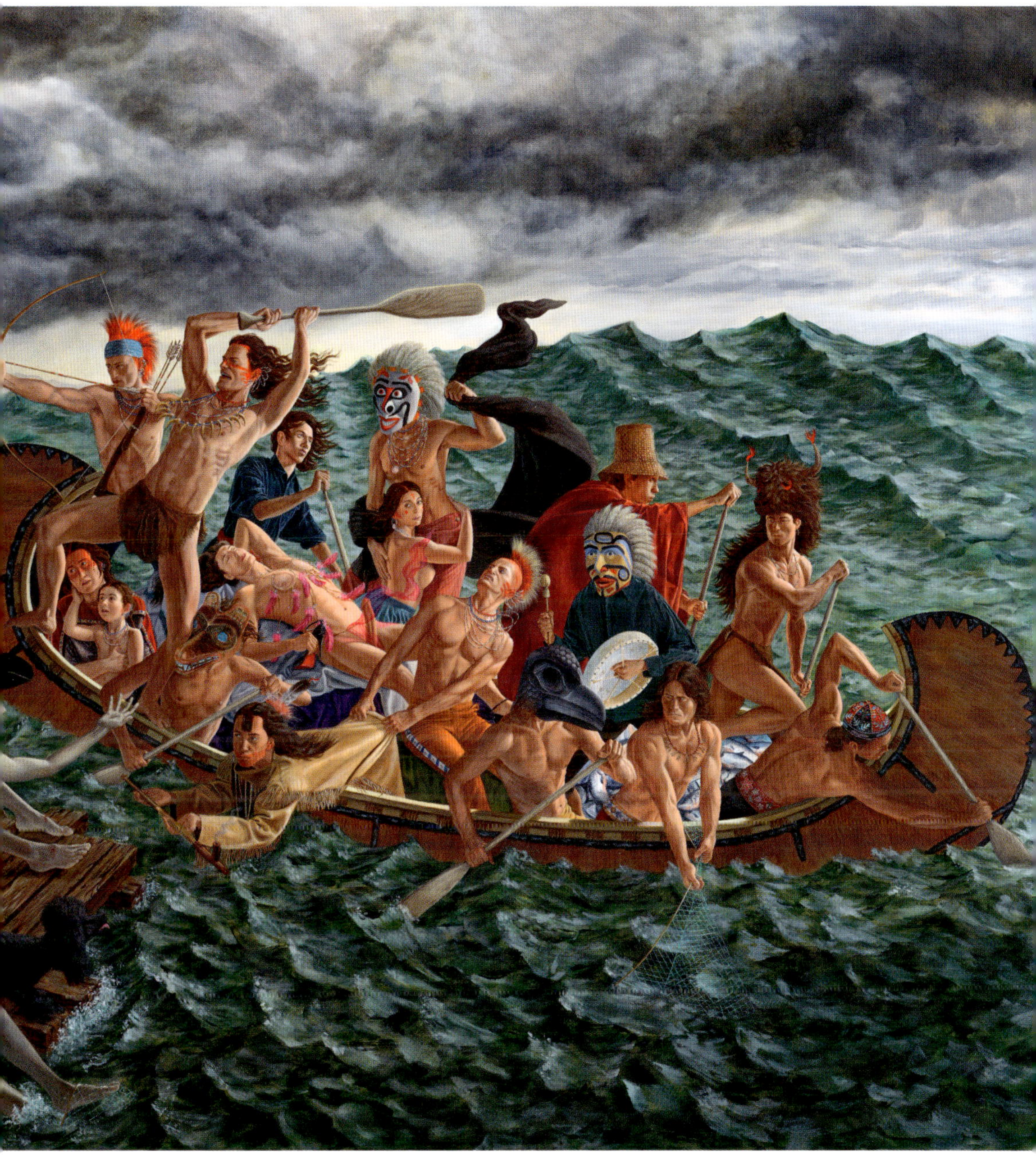

In the dream, my sleeping figure stirred, but could not seem to rouse to warn my people.

Miss Chief's Wet Dream, 2018. Acrylic on canvas. 144 in. x 288 in.

I was asleep in the centre of a large canoe, surrounded by the two-leggeds who would become my people. With us in the vessel were their ancestors, and their children yet to be born. I had seen these ahcâhk-iskotêwa in other visions or travels through time. They were from the many nations of miskinâhk-oministik, these lands created on the turtle's back[16]—some, of course, were my lovers.

Together, they propelled us through the stormy sea. Their musky scent mingled with the spray from the ocean glistening on their rippling shoulders and powerful arms as they leaned into each wave. Their grunts of exertion and exclamations aroused me as I dreamed within my dream. My diaphanous loincloth fluttered like a flag from nicimasowin, my erection, as the violent winds whipped the turbulent water into towering waves. Black storm clouds had obscured kîwêtin acâhkos, the north star, and tipiskâwi-pîsim, and far in the distance, piyêsiwak were shooting streaks of light across the horizon.

I heard the groans and creaks of another vessel close by. I wanted to wake up, but was unable to move. Cries of distress came from the other boat, answered by shouts of "awas, go away!" from my people. The two-leggeds in the other boat did not look well—their skin was pale, almost blue. I saw them as they truly were, ghosts starving for sustenance much deeper than physical nourishment. Desperate and lost, some were half-beast. They had hair on their gaunt faces and their bones poked through their skin. Their presence boded ill. I was both asleep and awake, as we âtayôhkanak can be in many states and times, and felt the danger but could not wake fully. Their leader sat calmly, tending her sickly subjects, surveying us as if we were hers, although she and her people would surely die if my companions did not come to their aid.

I was finally woken from my vision by the movements of a tiny muskrat desperately trying to reach the surface of the water, his frantic paddling rippling through my being. I gently pushed a wave under his exhausted body to buoy him. He hesitated in surprise, then resumed his furious paddling until he reached the dark outline of elder brother's raft. I saw

Wîsahkêcâhk's arm reach down to pull him up, heard muffled shouts from above nipiy's surface, and slowly felt the waters begin to recede.

I sighed and shifted my form again, sinking my toes into the muck that was newly exposed. I reached down, grabbed it, and inhaled deeply, breathing in the rich smell of askiy and the beginnings of new life. The earth rose to meet the sky once more—fresh, fecund, and full of possibility.

The beings of creation were granted one more chance by Kisê-manitow. The world was created on the turtle's back. asiniyak, rocks, plants, and animals—Wîsahkêcâhk made it anew. On it he placed the winged ones, the four-leggeds, the crawlers, the swimmers, and the two-leggeds—the iyiniwak, the human beings, including the ancestors of my own people, the nêhiyawak. The human beings were weak, so Kisê-manitow asked the animals and some of us âtayôhkanak to take pity on them and help them.

The paskwâwi-mostoswak, buffalo, agreed to feed, clothe, and care for them; the amiskwak, beavers, promised to help feed and clothe them; and many other animals offered to help the pitiful human beings. In return, the two-leggeds were to give thanks and not take more than they needed. Wîsahkêcâhk and I had agreed long ago to help them, each in our own way. Kisê-manitow created for them medicines to help them heal their bodies, minds, soul, and spirits, and gave them their most important gift, the gift of tâpwêwin, truth, and kitimâkêyihcikêwin, compassion—the most humble and brave amongst them would have these gifts buried deep inside their hearts.[17]

It was a time of renewal. My human form was once again ensnared in the burdens and delights of instinct, emotion, and desire, but I had a task to do, so I shifted my focus to helping the beings learn how to live in wîcêwâkanihtowin, partnerships, once more. I had honed my powers of sâkihitowin, love, with eons of experience and exquisite lessons from lovers of all forms, so I would begin with that.

Loving these newly formed creatures was no challenge—all forms of love were important, of course, but I took particular delight in the sensual possibilities of the human form. I told myself that this would help me in the times to come, but to be truthful, if I had to be (mostly) confined within the slow, limited skin of a human being, this research afforded me sensation that came closest to reaching the intense interconnectedness I felt when I was amongst the stars and in mamahtâwisiwin. My research was broad, unbiased, and in-depth.

I loved being with ninêhiyawak and learning how to live amongst them as a human being. They lived in unbroken kinship with the land, hunting the four-leggeds that roamed the Plains with their finely crafted stone tools.[18] I kept a finely hewed arrowhead tucked into my scarlet loincloth. I loved the way it felt in my hand, or against my body, and it reminded me of their skill. My people knew how to read the stars and understood much more about how the universe worked than the human beings to come ever would. I loved watching them learn from the rock beings, the plant beings, and us, the âtayôhkanak. I loved playing with them, but most of all, I loved telling and listening to stories with them, for âcimowina, stories, make us who we are.

When the great ice engulfed miskinâhk-oministik,[19] they needed my help to hunt the giant animals: the short-faced maskwak, the mammoths, the mistahi-paskwâwi-mostoswak, and the enormous amiskwak. When we sat around the fires in the lodge through the dark winters, laughter echoed through the camp as the hunters regaled us with their exploits, acting out their greatly exaggerated prowess. They gasped at my stories of even-larger creatures who had roamed the earth long before the creator had even made the nêhiyawak. They loved to hear the âtayôhkêwina, the sacred stories, especially the story about when the piyêsiwak destroyed the misikinêpik, the underwater monsters, to protect the nêhiyawak.[20]

When the ice receded I showed them the remains of the great creatures in the rocks. I listened as the knowledge keepers retold these stories to their children and grandchildren, drawing pictures on the rocks of us âtayôhkanak. I had many special friends amongst the adult human beings, but I played most with the hard-bodied hunters—there was so much laughter in those times. After embracing strenuously for much of the day, we would stretch our naked bodies on sun-warmed rocks together, feeling with bliss our connection to askiy.

I knew that when the pale sickly newcomers I had seen in my vision finally came to these lands, my work would begin, for everything would change—but how, and how much, was uncertain. My people were many, and all around us was abundance.

A few times over the ages, I felt something, a ripple in the pattern of wâhkôhtowin. I made enquiries through my winged, four-legged, and plant friends, and learned first of the visit to the southern shores from seafarers from the islands in the east,[21] then incursions on the northeastern shores by hairy-faced men from northern lands across the ocean. But these visitors did not stay—these were not the newcomers of my vision.

One day, wanting to understand more of these newcomers, I gently pinched the web of time to peer forward. The stench, cacophony, and wreckage I saw filled me with dread. I pulled back into my present, aching and nauseous. The land in the days to come had been scraped bare. My people were sick, their numbers reduced, things were wrong. I could not bear to go forward in time to see this, not yet. I knew that I would be in that time soon enough. Until then I would love my people and build up my strength to face what was to come. I looked around me, surrounded by strong healthy people on these rich lands. I could not imagine how those pale sickly people who would arrive in the future could ever be a threat.

Many years later I woke up from an uneasy sleep. They were near. Many of our peoples would help them, as would I, for that was my nature, but askiy began to feel different. The strands underground connecting all plant life quivered at different frequencies. It was subtle at first, a change in how the wind tasted, the grasses strangely quiet, but layers of disturbances kept coming through. kihêw and maskwa confirmed it. It had begun.

One late afternoon, during a portage, I startled a strikingly handsome young warrior. I could tell he was Kanien'kehá:ka, Mohawk, by the way his head was shorn, the hair gathered on top carefully groomed with vermilion and festooned with beads and ribbons. He fumbled for his weapons when he saw me because he was far from his own territory. I quickly signed in the language we used that was universal in these territories that I came in peace from nêhiyânâhk territory. He flashed a broad smile of relief, showing perfect white teeth, and signed back that I was not one of his known enemies. His body language relaxed and he pulled a plump young wâpos, rabbit, from his canoe, indicating we could eat it together. When I drew close enough, I spoke to him in his language, for tongues are as one to us âtayôhkanak.

He introduced himself as Atonwa and I asked him for news, especially of the newcomers. He told his story in stages while he made his camp. He was slow and careful; I watched his large hands and thick fingers, and could already feel them on my body. I had seen in his eyes that he had thought the same. We sat close enough that I could feel the heat of his body on my skin as I built a fire and he skinned the wâpos. After he roasted it over his fire, he offered me some, feeding me the tastiest morsels with his fingers. As the cold night air settled in, we sat closer to the fire, shoulders touching, and he recounted what was happening to his people.

He told me that, in his territory, newcomers were unsettling the great law of peace[22] and making preposterous claims. One of the hairy-faces, Jacques Cartier, had claimed the territory of Atonwa's people for his king, a so-called leader who had not even come to lead his people. Atonwa told me that O'seronni'ón:we[23] traders had founded a nation they called Québec on their territory and that one of them, Samuel de Champlain, had made allies with the enemies of his people: the Omàmiwininiwak,[24] Wendat, and Innu.[25] He told me he was worried that, with alliances shifting so quickly, the Haudenosaunee Confederacy might not stand.

I told him about my dream of the two vessels, and he stared at me for a long while without speaking. Then he looked into the fire and told me about the Tekeni Teiohate wampum belt treaty made between the Ratiristón:ni[26] and the Haudenosaunee; the wampum belt represented the two nations travelling on a parallel course in the river of life, never interfering with each other.[27]

"They have useful items for trade, and some of them are alright—they have become my friends—but by being here, they are changing everything," he said. "It's all happening too fast. They undermine our alliances, threatening even those made under the great tree of peace, and they bring with them a terrible sickness. I watched almost everyone in my family die. Even our most powerful healers could do nothing to save them from these new illnesses invading our shores."[28]

I stared at the fire, respecting his loss. He stayed silent for a very long time. Then Atonwa said that he must continue on early in the morning. This territory was shifting, and he did not feel safe here. I could see pain in his handsome dark eyes, and that he longed for the comfort a warm body could provide. I felt his pain and wanted to lighten the terrible burden of it. I moved closer, wiped one tear from his dusty cheek and pulled my blanket aside to reveal my interest to him as a question, and I caressed his bare leg with my foot. He pulled his loincloth aside, revealing his answer.

Atonwa reached over and wrapped his thick fingers around the back of my neck and pulled me in for a long, deep kiss. I could feel the sadness of his ahcâhk-iskotêw. The oils from the wâpos meat were on his lips and the vermilion paint from his hair smeared as he kissed me. We made love all night under the stars, crashing against his grief with the act of life, and finally collapsed under my paskwâwi-mostos robe. When I awoke, he was gone. The only traces of him were the streaks of vermilion on my face, thighs, and balls.

ᓂᐢᑕᑦ

ᑲᑮ ᓇᑭᐢᑲᐘᑊ

ᐅᐢᑭ ᐅᑭᔫᑫᐤ

My First Encounter with a Newcomer

For a long while, things were relatively peaceful. The newcomers' presence could be felt, but they were still far to the east. The human beings—the two-leggeds—were in wâhkôhtowin with the four-leggeds, crawlers, swimmers, flyers, the land and waters. We had miyo-pimâtisiwin, the good life, but that is not to say that there was no conflict. We are talking about human beings, after all.

Change was coming, so I stayed close to my people. The poplars whispered of the newcomers, their tinkling voices warning us to take heed. They were coming closer, changing our world as they moved west. I slipped ahead in the timestream to see what was coming for myself. It was too much—the cacophony, the land unrecognizable, nothing smelled or sounded the same. I retreated to the moment I had come from as quickly as I could. Even for us sacred beings, travelling too far forward or back is a risky thing, and it was one of the few things I did only in moderation.

One late sîkwan, crisp spring morning, Pîsim and Kistahkisiw, two nêhiyaw hunters with whom I was intimately acquainted, brought in the first newcomer that I would see with open eyes. They had come across him when trading amiskwayânak, beaver pelts, where the two big rivers met. Pîsim told me this one was âkayâsiw, English. He said there were also many wooden boat people who spoke another language, French—our people called these ones wêmistikôsiwak. Both these newcomer nations came to our lands from their settlement, Montréal, so we called them môniyâwak.[29] This young one had followed Kistahkisiw and Pîsim around and learned enough of our language to beg them to take him with them.

He called himself Danny. Just as I had seen in my vision, his skin was very pale, almost transparent with a blue tinge. His hair and the soft golden fur all over his body shone in the sunlight, but his eyes were uncannily translucent, like ice, lacking the warmth and depth of the deep brown eyes to which I was accustomed. But unlike the newcomers I had seen in my vision, this one's nature was sweet, and his ahcâhk-iskotêw was bright and clear.

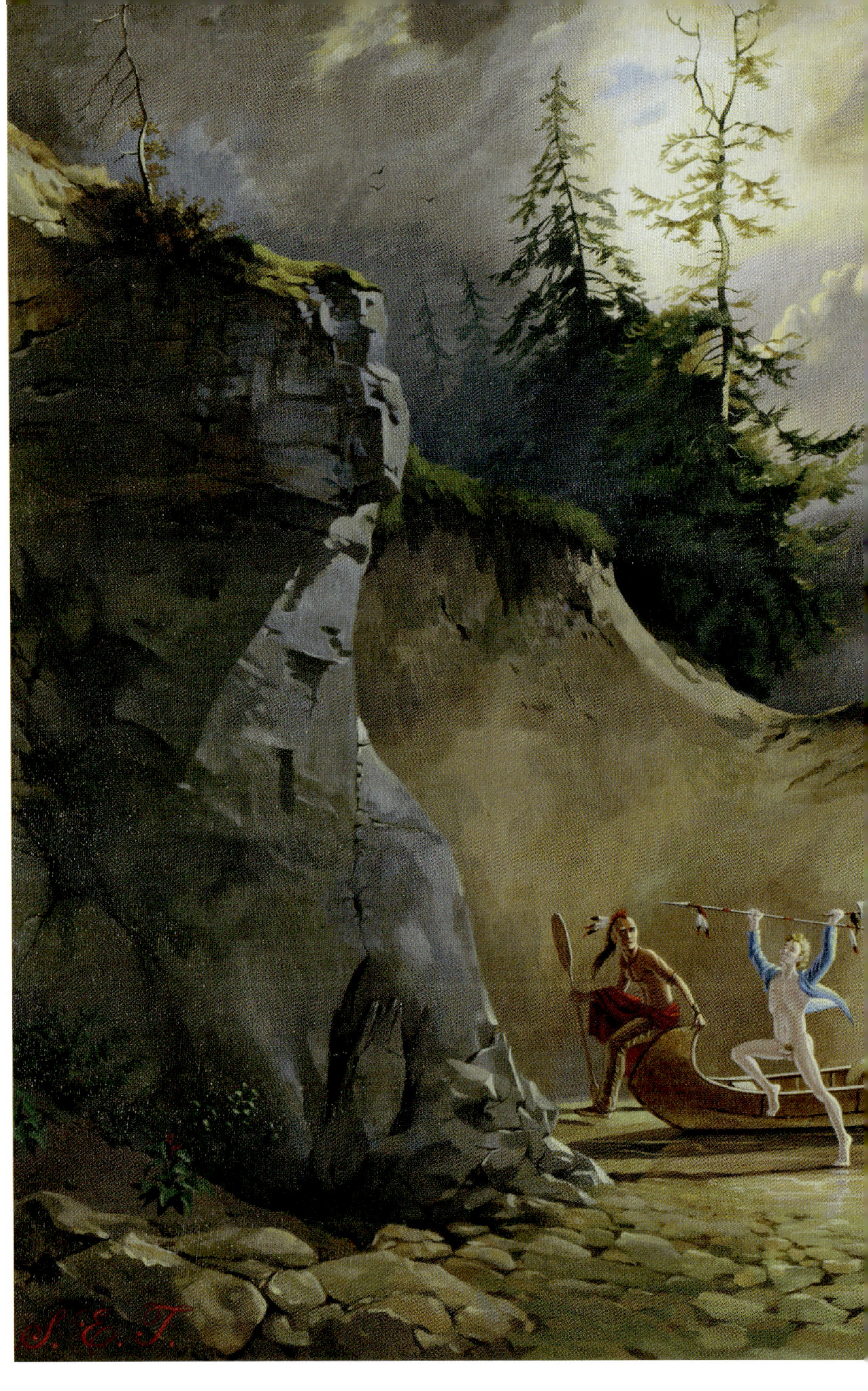
S. E. T.

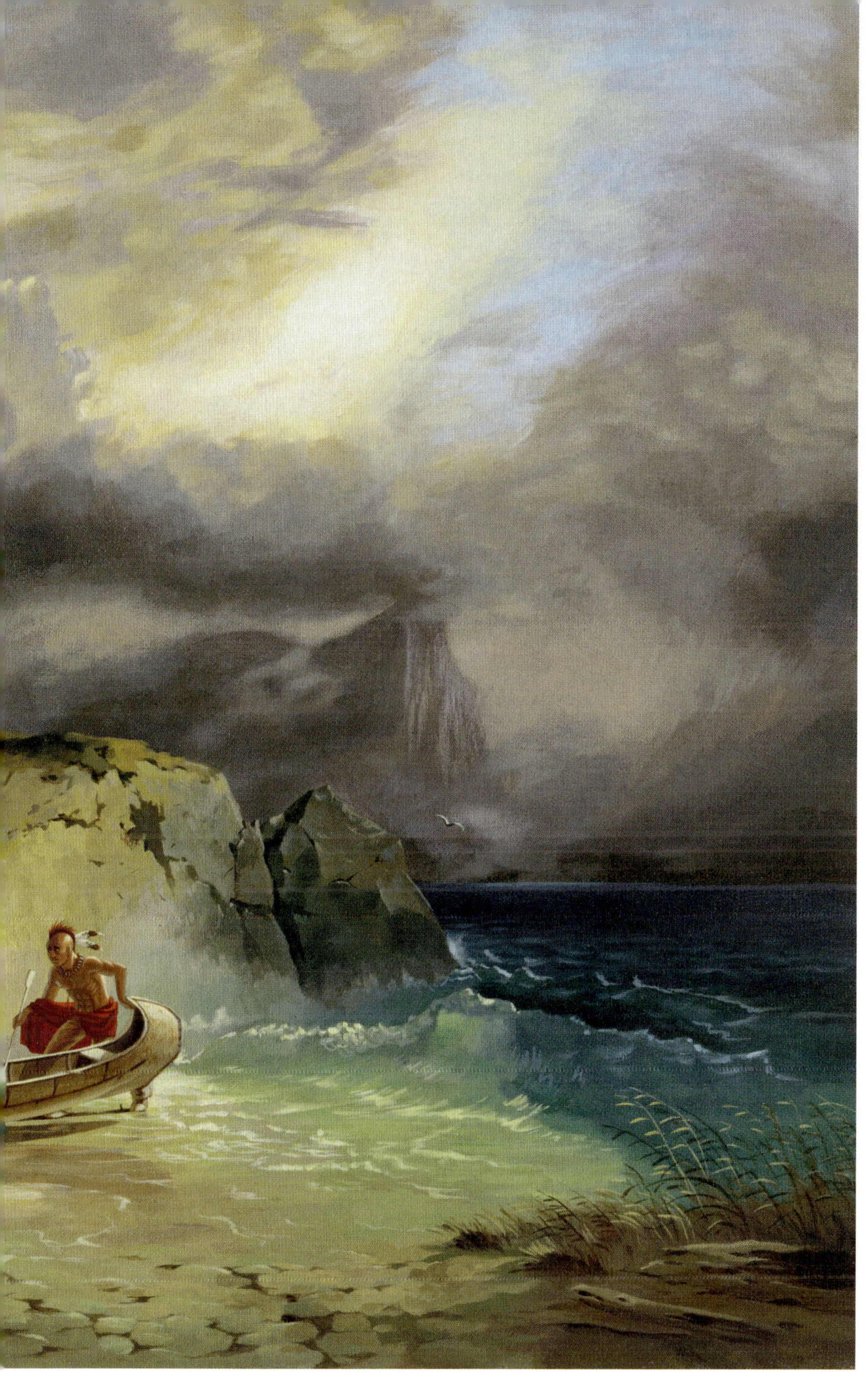

The newcomers had much to learn and I had much to teach them.

The Rape of Daniel Boone Junior, 2002. Acrylic on canvas. 18 in. x 24 in.

Kistahkisiw and Pîsim laughed as they told me that his aversion to violence made him unable even to watch us hunt. He delighted in all he came across, and although he was thoroughly helpless without others to take care of him, his eyes shone as those of one who was intoxicated by the land. He talked too much without listening, mostly about his own opinions, to the great amusement of Pîsim and Kistahkisiw, who indulged his rudeness, treating him with the patience they would grant a very young child.

The four of us spent many happy days camping by a river not far from the big water we knew as wînipêk, but which Danny's people called James Bay—fishing, trapping rabbits, and revelling in one another's company. Danny was eager to learn about physical love, so I assisted Pîsim and Kistahkisiw in indulging his every curiosity about the mitakay, penis—how it felt to have more than one inside his smooth round bum and hungry wet mouth. He gave himself to us—ê-nânapwêkinât—as we folded him over and over into different positions, until we all collapsed in a tangle of smooth brown limbs intertwined with golden furred legs.

As we lay holding each other, catching our breath, Danny talked of how in our societies he saw the liberty he, as a poor man, did not have in his grey-skied, gold-obsessed homeland across the sea. He told me a most astonishing tale of how his leader, their king, had granted a small group of men calling themselves "The Company of Adventurers of England Trading into Hudson's Bay" a huge section of land that included the territory of my people, and indeed a good portion of miskinâhk-oministik![30] The very idea of this was absurd, as though human beings could "give" what was not anyone's to give!

Land cannot belong to anyone. We were in wâhkôhtowin with it and all the other beings who shared it with us. It was not only against our laws, but also shameful to keep things for ourselves. For us, respect was earned from how much we shared or gave away, not how much we tried to take and hoard for ourselves. Pîsim and Kistahkisiw teased Danny, for all these tales seemed preposterous, but I listened carefully.

As Danny shared stories of what was happening in the east, I became increasingly uneasy. He told us that the outcasts of his people, rather than the best, had come here on the ships: the destitute, the criminals, the damaged, the dregs of his society.[31] People who had nothing in their homelands, those who wanted to hide, were now coming by the hundreds of thousands. As they moved west, building fortified settlements along the way, they took the trees, the amiskwak, and as much as they could from askiy. Danny also told us of those sent here in bondage from his land in lifelong servitude,[32] and people who had been captured elsewhere and brought to these lands in chains.[33] The horror of it turned my insides cold. I had felt some of this bleakness in my vision and the quick glance into the future. I asked Danny many questions so that I might prepare for what was coming.

We spoke together of the Beaver Wars, a generation of conflict involving Danny's people and our nations, allies, and enemies in an ever-changing landscape of dominance in the fur trade, which was causing much upheaval and damage to long-standing alliances, wîcêwâkanihtiwina. We discussed the Wendat Confederacy, devastated by môniyâw diseases, and how its people were leaving their homelands. I remembered the conversation I had had with the handsome Kanien'kehá:ka hunter Atonwa not so very long ago and his worries for his people, the rivals of the Wendat. The Haudenosaunee Confederacy had endured, but what further trouble lay in store for them, and for us all?

Pîsim sat up in disgust, throwing his leg over mine and Danny's, and interjected, revealing how he had witnessed the newcomer traders plying the trappers with a dark liquid before trading in the pelts of our cousins the amiskwak began. The resulting disorientation and befuddlement naturally increased profits for the traders.[34] If unsuccessful, the traders had other ways of tricking or cheating our people, who were becoming increasingly dependent on the new trade goods. We had always adapted to new technologies. Some change was beneficial, but at what cost?

Despite the warm body heat of my sprawling companions, I was filled with a cold, creeping sense of foreboding. The changes I had foreseen were already here.

ᑲᑮ ᔾᐋᐧᓈᒋᐦᐃᒋᐠ
ᑭᑕᒥᐢᑯᐋᐧᑰᒫᑲᓂᒥᓈᓇᐠ
ᑮ ᐄᐧᑕᑑᒪᑲᐣ ᐆᐟ ᐆᒪ
ᑲ ᐄᐧ ᐃᐢᐸᔨᐠ ᓃᑳᓂᕽ

The Massacre of Our Beaver Relatives Foreshadowed What Was to Come

Time for us âtayôhkanak works differently, but it was perhaps several human generations after my time with Pîsim, Kistahkisiw, and Danny that I found myself back lying on the same smooth asiniy the four of us had enjoyed with such sweetness. My drawings depicting the copious permutations of our encounters would remain there for many generations, etched in the surface of the rock.

For a long time now, I had been hearing the mîtosak, the trees, whispering that the balance was changing. Tendrils of alarm had been sent through their root systems from forest to forest.[35] This sense of foreboding had been making me uneasy. I allowed the worry to melt away as I felt the warm radiance of kîsikâwi-pîsim, the sun, infuse my naked body, penetrating through me, deep into asiniy. The low sweet hum of askiy throbbed exquisitely, coursing through every part of me as I sank into sublime surrender.

A loud smack of a beaver tail on the water cut short my pleasure. I sat up and heard a quieter splash close to shore. It was followed by another splash and then another. I carefully got up and concealed myself behind a misâskwatômin—saskatoon berry—bush and waited. My stomach growled at the thought of stewed amisk in a misâskwatômin coulis, with a side of watercress and chestnuts—I gave thanks to Kisê-manitow for sending my next meal without me having to look for it. Pulling back my bow and arrow, I aimed at a young amisk swimming to shore. Strangely, he swam straight towards my hiding spot in the misâskwatômin bush and collapsed on a rock in front of me, his breast heaving with exhaustion.

Startled, I lowered my bow. Suddenly several more beavers, young ones clinging to their mothers' breasts and old ones helped along by others, swam to shore and threw themselves on the rocks next to him, exhausted.

In the distance I could see yet more amiskwak arriving, an aquatic caravan of several desperate amiskwak families. I sat quietly waiting as a large clan of exhausted beavers collected themselves and huddled together, shivering. The little ones whimpered and trembled as they clung to their mothers.

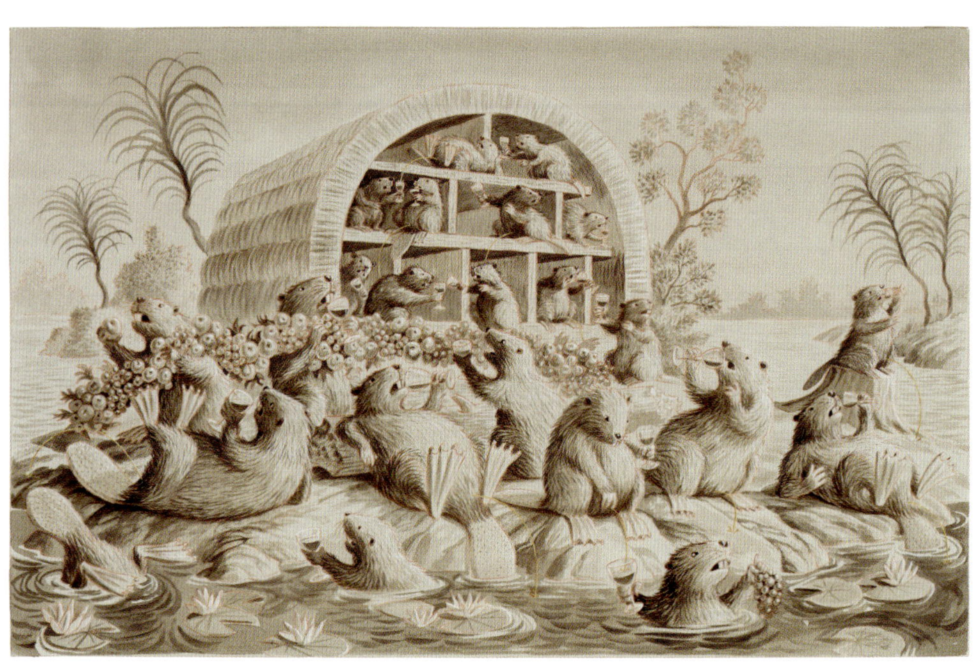

The amiskwak had lived in plenty since the time of the giants; their lives were bountiful, full of leisure, and they never went hungry.

Study for Beaver Bacchanal, 2015. Watercolour, gouache, and gold acrylic on acid free watercolour paper. 22 in. x 30 in.

As the bedraggled amiskwak busied themselves collecting poplar saplings, resting, and feeding their young, I laid down my bow, returned the arrow to my quiver, and slowly stepped out to reveal myself. There was an audible gasp as the amiskwak panicked, eyes wild with fear, and threw themselves into the lake, disappearing underwater with a splash of their tails. The kêhtê-amisk, elder beaver, was too slow. Fear and resignation in his face, he held his ground and bravely began singing his death song.

I sat down on the rocks, and with my calm slow movements and quiet body language I could see the kêhtê-amisk begin to relax. He sighed heavily and looked over at me warily until his bleary eyes recognized me, for I had known his ancestors—the mistahi-amiskwak—kayâs, long ago. The amiskwak were an ancient people. They were a vast nation that spread across miskinâhk-oministik from coast to coast. In the east they lived in opulent multi-tiered lodges and had bustling villages that numbered in the millions.[36] The cedar waxwings and blackbirds had taught them how to harvest fermented âhâsiwimina, juniper berries, and the misâskwatômina from the many lush forests that surrounded their lodges, and make wine from them. Their lives had been bountiful, full of leisure, and they had never gone hungry.

The kêhtê-amisk signaled with a slap of his tail that I was no threat. After a few moments, the others began to cautiously return to shore. I asked him to tell me the news of their nation, and what trouble they were fleeing. When his clan had all gathered around, he told me his story.

One day, the kêhtê-amisk recounted, strange pale men with a sour smell and fur on their faces had appeared on their rivers. They had sticks of metal that sparked and smoked with terrifyingly loud bangs. The men hid jagged metal jaws by the entrances to the amiskwak lodges, which would clamp onto their legs so they would either drown or be bludgeoned to death. With those weapons the men killed the amiskwak in numbers that were not to be believed. “They broke open our lodges and slaughtered entire families, taking only our hides to trade and leaving our bodies to rot, with no thanks or offerings to our spirits.”

I nodded. His trembling voice did not lie. This was one of the most serious wrongs that could be committed—ohcinêwin, the breaking of laws against other beings—for the amiskwak, like the other animals, had promised to help the humans if they respected them and took only what they needed. Our peoples had used all parts of the beaver: their meat for stew; their amiskowêsinâw, castor gland oils, for medicine; and their pelts for our robes. The newcomers were treating the amiskwak not as a relative who provided for the people, but as a commodity for trade. This grim commerce had upset the natural laws of the land. The kêhtê-amisk took a ragged breath, and whispered very quietly, "It's a massacre."

The kêhtê-amisk told me that this trade was continuing to pit many of our nations against each other.[37] "We have seen them fighting in war after war, murdering each other with the killing sticks." He described the recent terrible fighting by the big lakes—bloody conflicts with horrific outcomes.

"We were once so numerous no one could imagine we could disappear, but our nation is almost gone from Kaniatarowanénhne. Our once towering lodges and thriving villages are now no more than ruined husks on the rivers and lakes. I, and what is left of my family, are the only survivors from the area that was once our paradise."[38]

I felt sickened. From what kêhtê-amisk was telling me, the balance of mâmawi-wîcihitowin, all beings helping one another, was disintegrating. I had been hearing similar things from the salmon: the newcomers had taken massive catches of giant cod off the eastern coast shores of miskinâhk-oministik, depleting them to the extent that they could no longer replenish themselves.[39] Wave after wave of the newcomers were brutally pushing our Beothuk and Mi'kmaq relatives out of their territories[40] and sending ship after ship sailing back to Europe piled high with dried cod.

"These newcomers from across the seas have stripped everything bare. They have killed all the beavers in their home nations, and now they are doing the same to us—not to feed their families, but to scent themselves and decorate their heads with hats that do not even keep the heads of those

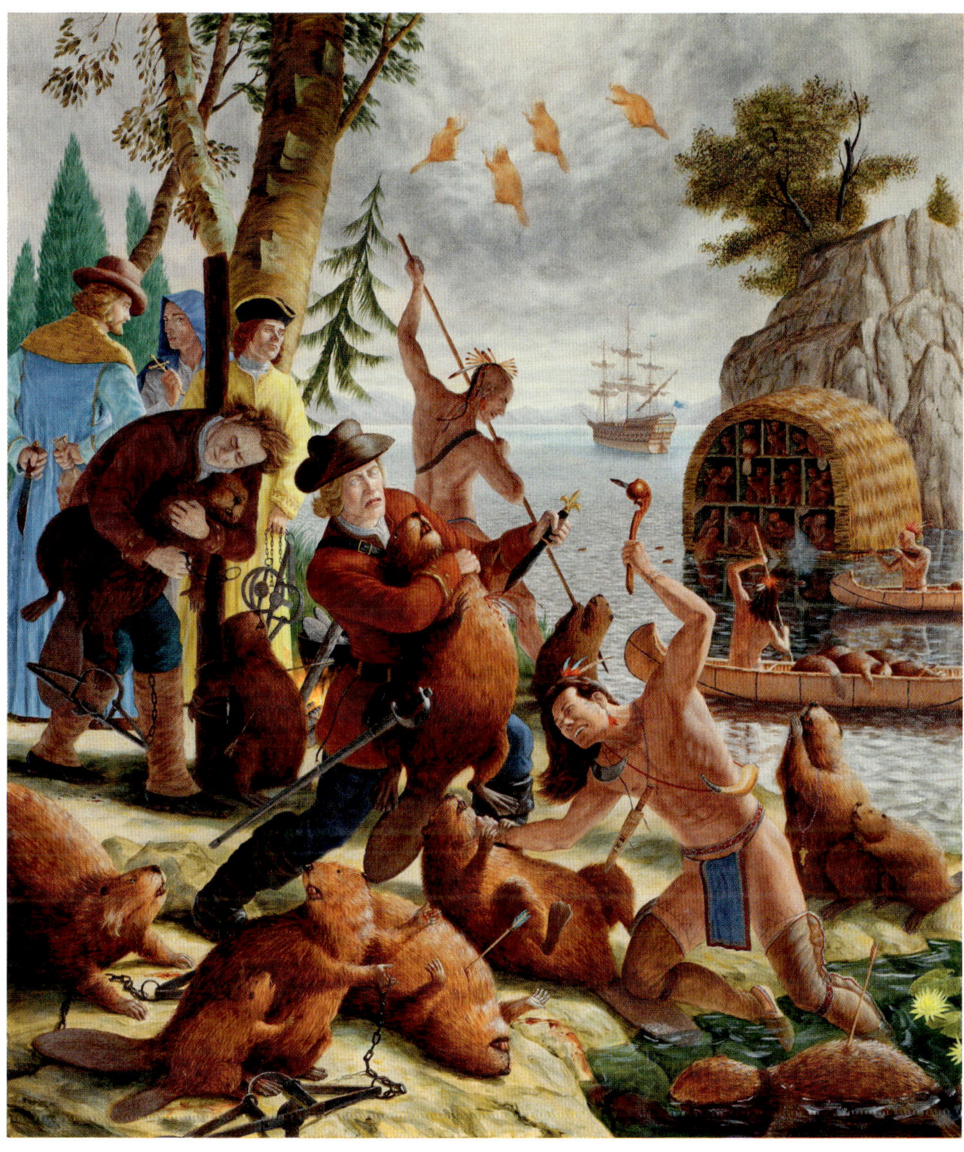

The old amisk choked and whispered in a broken voice, "It's a massacre."

Les Castors Du Roi, 2011. Acrylic on canvas. 96 in. x 84 in.

who wear them warm. We gave our word to Kisê-manitow we would help the human beings of this land, but wîcihitowin, supporting and helping each other, is not being respected. The hairy-faces act as if they have no relations. We have lost so many relatives, not only of our nation, but the trees and the fish,[41] and your nations too. They are a plague upon us, devouring all in their path.[42] Those of us who are left, all we can do is hide."

kêhtê-amisk wiped his eyes and cleared his throat. He began singing, softly at first, then gathering power until his beautiful lamenting melody cut through the forest in his coarse quivering tenor. I could not hold back my tears when I saw every one of his clan weeping openly as kêhtê-amisk's haunting ode to their homeland echoed across the lake. When he finished, his last note hung high in the air above the stillness of the water. The cry of a mwâkwa, a loon, answered back, echoing in emptiness.

kêhtê-amisk cleared his throat and said they had to keep moving further west. They didn't feel safe. He gave a few weary instructions to the families, and within a few minutes the clan of beavers slid into the water and were gone.

I sat quietly on the rock and thanked Kisê-manitow for sending this message to me. I wept for the amisk Nation. I wept for all of our nations, because if the amiskwak were in danger, it would not be long before nêhiyawak and all our kin on miskinâhk-oministik would be suffering in equal measure.

What did these newcomers want so badly that they would slaughter whole nations for it? I sighed, for I knew a visit to their settlements to attempt to comprehend their ways was in order, but I could not move. I felt my younger brother's grief deeply, the weight of loss that had already befallen so many, but more so the crushing foreboding of the loss yet to come. I felt the absence of millions. So much would be lost, not only to the metal firesticks of the newcomers, but to their most deadly weapon, misi-omikîwin. Smallpox and other diseases would carry nine out of ten of our people to the river of spirits, ahcâhko-sîpiy. Tears rolled down my face, but I could not lift my hand to brush them away.

To gather strength and seek guidance, I lay back down on asiniy and allowed myself to merge with it. I felt my heartbeat slow down to the point of seeming to be stopped, my movements imperceptible to all but the plant nations. In mamahtâwisiwin, the deep peace of the interconnectedness of all spirit washed over me and I opened my eyes. For me it was but moments, but for the human beings, as so often happens with our different experience of time, a generation or more had passed. I was ready to meet the newcomers where they were. I would go east.

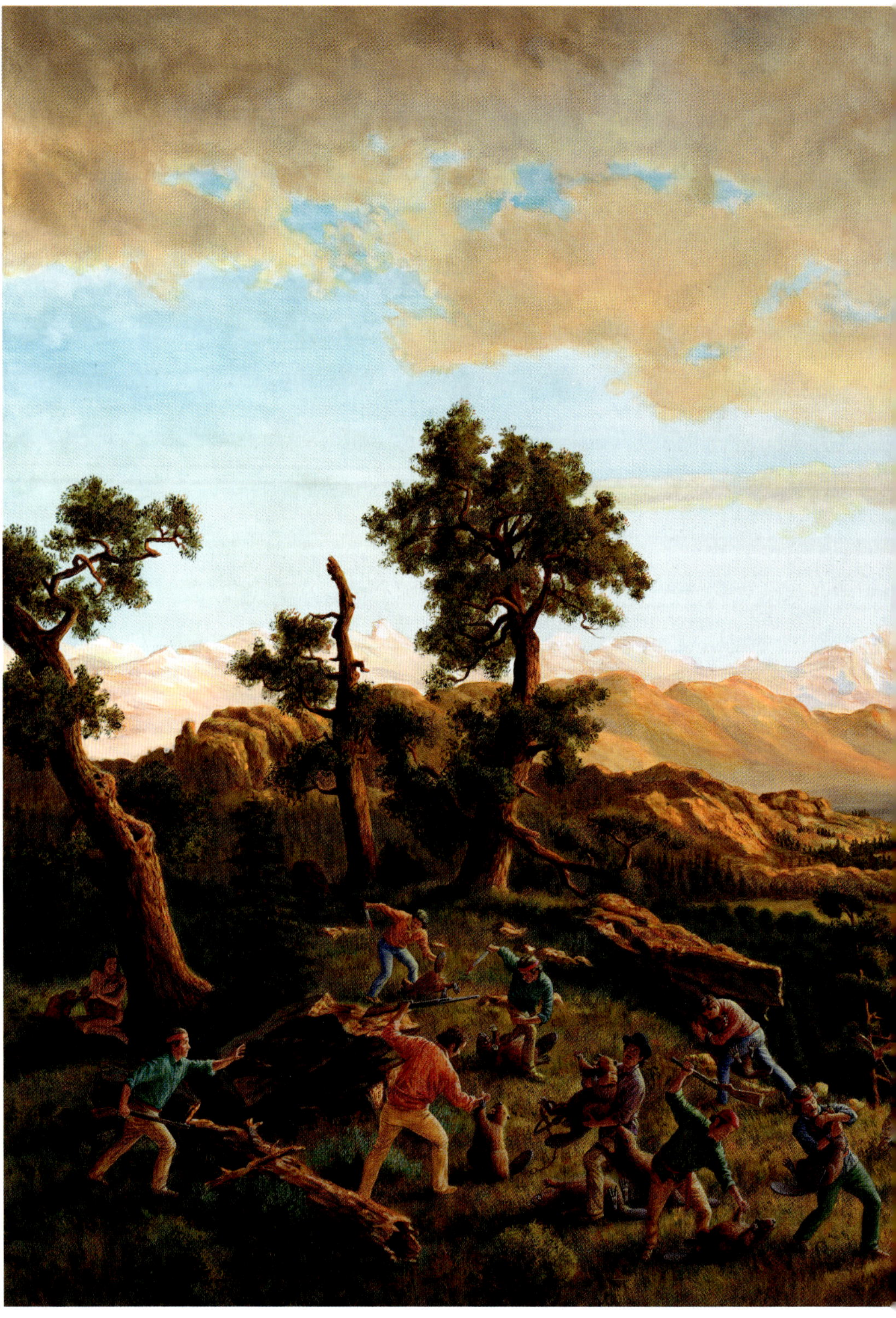

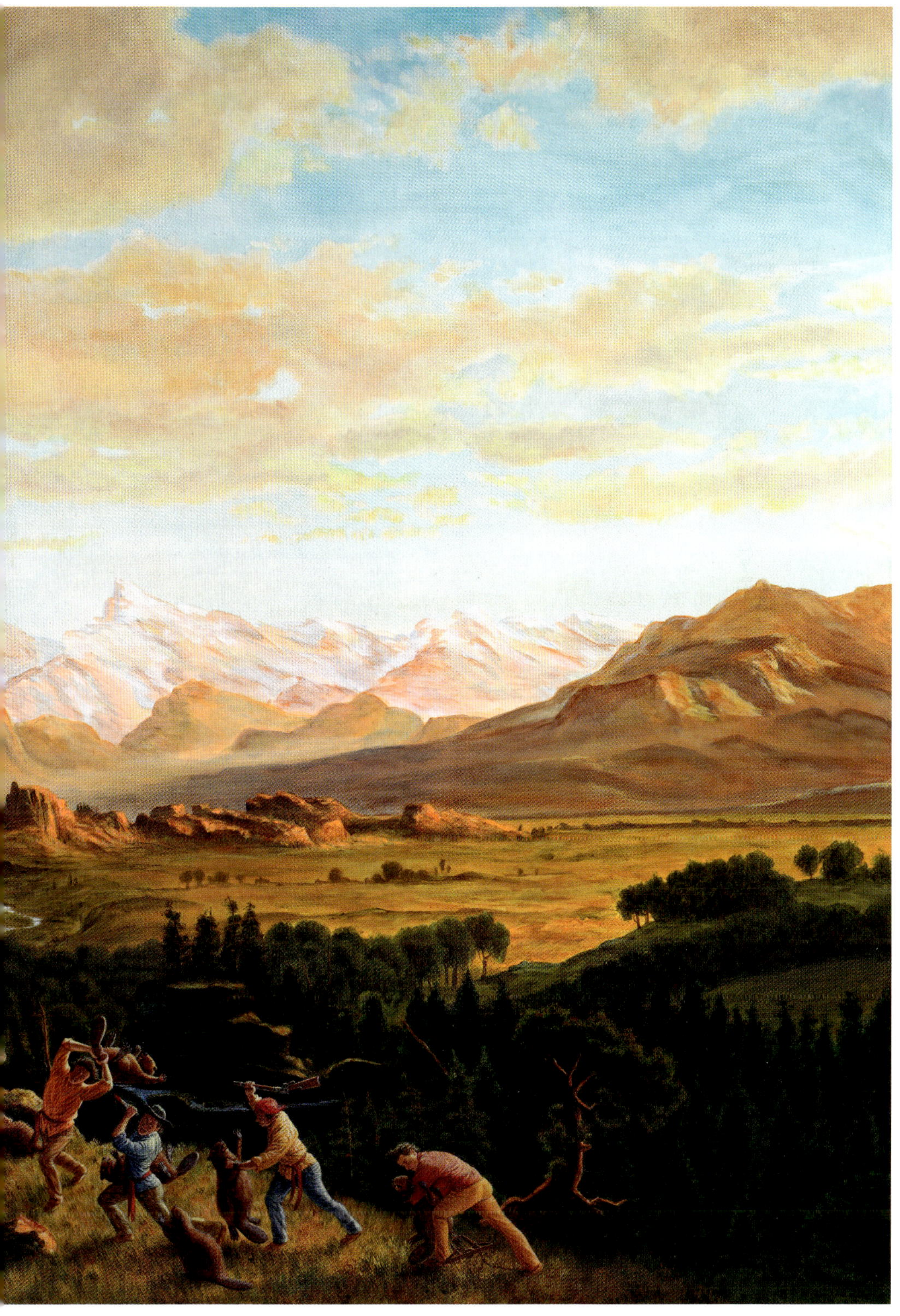

After the newcomers had driven their own amiskwak to the brink of extinction, they came for ours, slaughtering our relatives for fashion, riches, and land.

Massacre of the Innocents, 2015. Acrylic on canvas. 72 in. x 102 in.

ᐅᐢᑭ ᐅᑭᓰᑫᐘᐠ

ᑭᓵᐱ-ᒥᐢᑕᐦᐃ

ᑕ ᑭᐢᑭᓌᐦᐋᒫᑯᓯᒋᐠ

The Newcomers Had Much to Learn

I began my journey east towards the môniyâwak settlements on foot. With each step, vibrations from the roots and soil travelled up my shiny black heels. askiy told me what I needed to know. By now, the newcomers had spread across miskinâhk-oministik in all directions, setting up their colonies and taking what they could carry out of our lands with the efficiency of ants. For us, trade had always been important, but now it dominated the land. The pelts of our relatives the amiskwak remained their main currency—a dozen pelts bought a rifle, to kill more of their amisk nation—but the meat and hides of the buffalo nation, the paskwâwi-mostoswak, would soon become the next great commodity to be carelessly expended by the môniyâwak on miskinâhk-oministik.

Along the way, I listened to the murmurings of the forest beings, the forest, the mîtosak, and the smaller plant beings. They told me that new creatures and microbes had entered the soil where the newcomers had settled in the east, that the plants were changing and the paskwâwi-mostoswak who nurtured the earth with their gifts were greatly diminishing.[43] I felt a twinge of fear, but did not want to believe what I knew to be true. I tried to convince myself that the paskwâwi-mostoswak were safe, for they had been here in their giant form long before the human beings.[44] Our powerful sisters and brothers numbered in the tens of millions. When the herds moved, they spread across the prairie to the horizon, taking many days to pass.[45] They were everything to my people. We honoured them, for they were our medicine.

When I crossed through the great forest, along the river's edge I called the mêmêkwêsiwak to me. Like all the sacred beings, they were my kin—small, but not to be underestimated. The little people normally loved to laugh, but were now sombre, clambering on me half-heartedly, with none of their normal glee.

We walked in silence past an abandoned village, the only sound the tattered prayer flags blowing in the trees. One of the mêmêkwêsiwak tugged on my earlobe, gesturing for me to look up, and I saw an

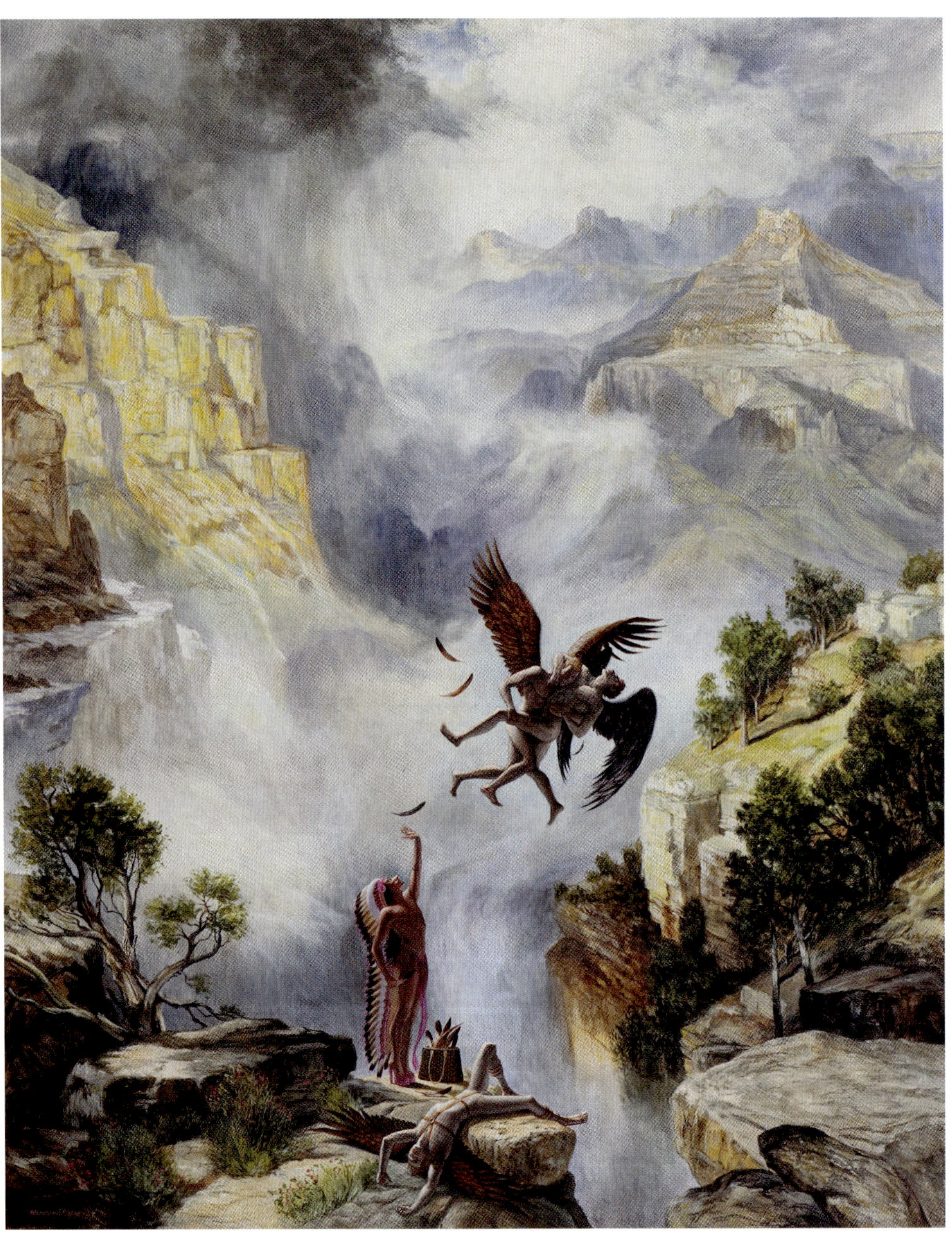

These ôskitakosinokîsikowak are not what you think they are.

Kiss the Sky, 2010. Acrylic on canvas. 59.5 in. x 47.5 in.

oskitakosinokîsikow, a newcomer spirit being, fly above the treetops carrying a môniyâw spirit to their heavens. At times, these beings appeared as balls of light, but this one was in human form, with wings as wide as clouds. I understood that many of all nations were dying of this terrible curse the newcomers had brought to our lands, misi-omikîwin.

It was the time of tears. misi-omikîwin raged through our nations with great violence, sparing only the very lucky few.[46] I witnessed my people lying unable to care for their children, dying where they fell with no one left to bury them. I buried more than I could count, crying with rage and sadness for my strong beautiful people laid to waste by this cruel disease. For our peoples, it would be the first, but not the last, apocalypse of so many ahcâhk-iskotêwa being extinguished.

I cried for weeks, grieving the stories that would never be passed down, the songs now silenced that had contained wisdom thousands of years old, the ceremonies that cared for askiy, and the love and laughter that would never be heard again. The mêmêkwêsiwak stayed quiet, honouring the depth of my mourning. I took solace from their presence, but could not speak to them. They understood.

The trees whispered to me, calming my spirit, and the lichen under my feet gave me strength, for great power comes from connection to askiy. I found a kind of peace by slowing my metabolism and sense of time down, that I might better connect with them. I would need their strength in the time to come, so I lay on askiy and drifted into mamahtâwisiwin, tapping into the great mystery.

One tree-lifetime later, I emerged from the forest, transformed, and continued on my way as a kêhkêhk, a hawk. Soaring high above the Plains, catching the eastern wind currents when I was able, I could still see vast dark clouds of paskwâwi-mostos herds. I let myself believe that maybe the plant beings had been mistaken. But I knew deep inside it was more likely the môniyâwak had not yet travelled this far in great numbers.

---

mwêscasês, a little later, I was back in human form, continuing east on a pony I had coaxed to take me on my journey. When the newcomers returned our equine relatives—the ones we had last seen on this continent when they were still small—to miskinâhk-oministik, we gratefully received the mistatimwak again, although the horses had changed over the thousands of generations they had been away. Larger, faster, and of softer natures, they transformed our Plains peoples. We became Horse Nations.

I had stopped to collect some of the feathers dropped by the oskitakosin-okîsikowak for a new robe when I came upon a pitiable sight. On a rocky ledge overlooking the river, a tall, thin figure was clearly struggling, unsure whether to jump to his doom or cling to the rock. I could not clearly sense his ahcâhk-iskotêw—it was so dim as to be non-existent.

As I regarded him, I noted a Black Robe from one of the newcomers' new villages approaching further along the path. He looked in the wretched man's direction, hesitated, and moved on. A moment later, I saw a long-bearded trader come towards the wretched môniyâw, but as he came closer, he seemed to start, then turned his head, and hurriedly continued on his way as well.

I still had little experience with the môniyâwak and did not yet understand their ways, but I could not fathom why this wretch's fellow countrymen would walk past, abandoning the poor soul to his fate. But there was no time to ponder. The sad fellow staggered back, lost his balance, and with a loud splash, fell headlong into the river. Flailing and sputtering, he surfaced and made his way to the shore before losing consciousness on the bank. This scattered the mêmêkwêsiwak, who favoured the banks of rivers and lakes and, always curious, had come to watch what would happen next.

I quickly dismounted my pony and hurried over to assist him, my pink heels sinking into the muddy shoreline. As I approached I was able to regard him properly. Underneath his sodden clothes, I could see the man was still fairly young, lean and muscled, with strange cuts on his skin—not

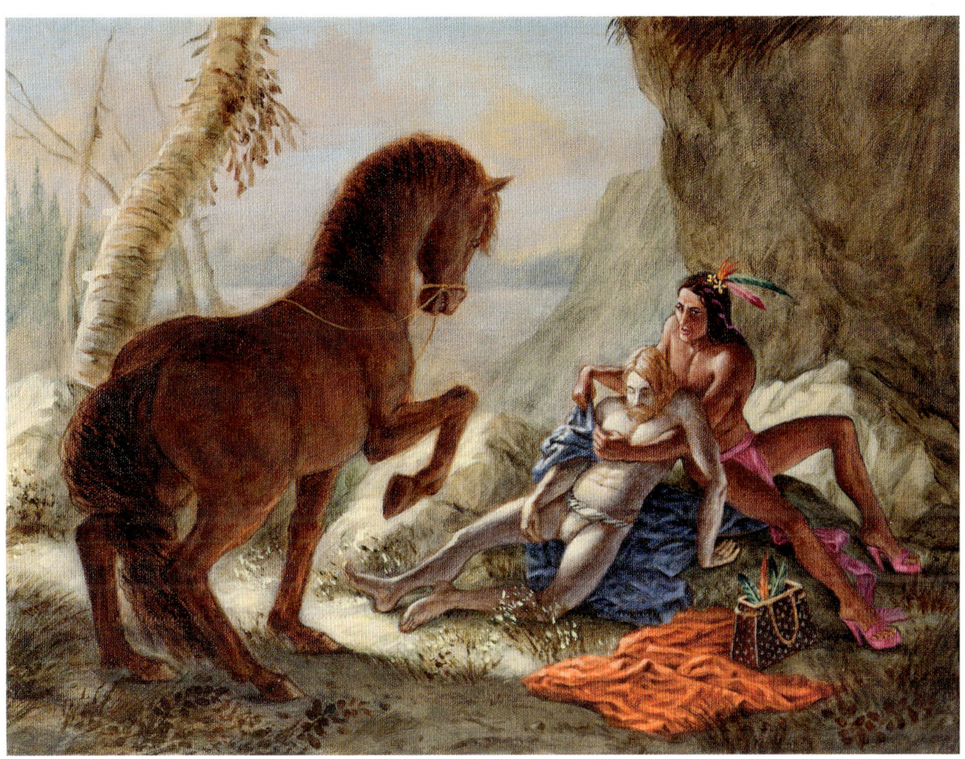

"Whatever ails you," I told the desperate wretch as I stroked his forehead gently, "it cannot be so dire that you must defile the sacredness of your life."

The Good Samaritan, 2010. Acrylic on canvas. 14 in. x 11 in.

a bad specimen if it weren't for the dark yellow pall to his skin that I learned later was the mark of the chronic opium-eater. He had the same sharp, stale odour many of these visitors had, but layered with the scent of fear, desperation, and excessive drink.[47]

I held him in my arms, although he was hardly aware of my presence. Even in this close proximity his ahcâhk-iskotêw was barely existent. He abruptly regained consciousness, retching and coughing, his eyes unfocused, and I wiped the vomit from the edges of his mouth.

His babbling was incoherent, showing derangement of mind and great nervousness, but I was able to make out bits and pieces: "My captain, my friend, my companion . . . punished, I will burn for eternity, my soul . . . I cannot bear the torture without you, my friend, my captain."[48] He began to shake violently, so I wrapped him in my blankets and held him until he stopped shivering. Eventually he was able to tell me his name. I heard something like Merry Weather Loo-wis, which sounded strange to my ears, so I decided I would call him Môci-kîsikâw, Happy Day.

He nestled into me, murmuring, "My friend . . . no more . . . perfect . . . union," and something else that I couldn't catch. He kissed my shoulder, which I naturally reciprocated, my hot full lips pressing on his cold thin ones. He recoiled in horror. "No, it's a sin!" Too soon, then.

I wondered what laws the môniyâwak had, if any, about taking one's own life? For our lives were given to us by the Kisê-manitow and not ours to take away.

"Whatever ails you"—I stroked his forehead gently—"it cannot be so dire that you must defile the sacredness of your life."

He barely registered my words. Turning towards me, desperation in his eyes, he began his jumbled, tearful confession. "She found the journal . . . threw me out, said I'd never set eyes on him again," he sobbed.[49]

"Who will you never set eyes upon? Your captain? Your friend?" I asked, trying to make sense of his sad tale.

He nodded despairingly. "I experienced a longing for him so violent . . . my united force of reason and religion was scarcely sufficient to enable me to resist those impetuous passions . . . I was rendered like unto a beast, furious and headstrong . . ."[50]

"What difference does it make who you love?" I asked, for I could not comprehend his distress.

In fits and starts, interrupted by much sobbing and self-deprecation, he told his story.

He had travelled with his companion, who was named Clark, to explore the western reaches of this land under the orders of their nation's leader. They were led and protected by a Newe[51] woman known to the Nuxbaaga[52] as Sacagawea.[53] She had helped them as they made their way through what Môci-kîsikâw called a country "on which the foot of civilized man had never trodden."[54] What strange illusions these môniyâwak had! For these lands were well populated[55] by the Nations of the Numakaki,[56] Nuxbaaga, Wahzhazhe,[57] Tsétsêhéstâhese,[58] Apsáalooke,[59] Sahnish,[60] Newe, Séliš,[61] Niimi'ipuu,[62] Sqeliz,[63] Mamachatpam,[64] Wanapum,[65] Waluulapam,[66] Watɬlala,[67] Očhéthi Šakówiŋ,[68] Ñút^achi, Jiwére, Báxoje,[69] Kathlamet, Wahkiakum,[70] Skilloot,[71] Nehalem,[72] Tlatskanai,[73] Multnomah,[74] Piikani,[75] Nakoda,[76] Umo^{n}ho^{n},[77] Chaticks si Chaticks,[78] Gaigwu,[79] Hinono'eino,[80] Aaniihnén,[81] Kiikaapoi,[82] Pan'akwati, Schitsu'umsh,[83] Wasco,[84] Ita'xluit,[85] La'k!elak,[86] Sts'ailes,[87] Atfalati,[88] Ql'ispé,[89] Guithla'kimas,[90] Stl'pulmsh,[91] Ksanka,[92] Kuitsch, Siuslaw,[93] Hanis,[94] Qwulhhwaipum,[95] Wusi,[96] Liksiyu,[97] Imatalamłáma,[98] Palus,[99] K^{w}ínayɫ,[100] Siletz,[101] Wyam,[102] Kaw,[103] Pó^{n}ka,[104] oθaakiiwaki,[105] meškwahki·haki,[106] Ndee,[107] Nʉmʉnʉʉ,[108] Núuchi-u,[109] Kitikiti'sh,[110] Anishinaabe,[111] Lenape,[112] Sawano,[113] Kalapuya,[114] q^{w}idiččaʔa·tx̌,[115] and many more who hunted and travelled through this territory.

As he described their journey, I remembered having seen some of their party's travels along what the Nuxbaaga called the Awathi, or Canoe River,[116] when I went to visit some of my kâ-wâsihkopayicik friends, the ones who shine.[117] We had seen a dozen boats and canoes and thirty or more travellers, most of them môniyâwak, save for the one we knew to be Sacagawea, the baby she carried on her back, a few Métis guides, and a kaskitêwiyiniw hunter who was one of the best shots I had ever seen.[118]

Despite the best efforts of their guides, we heard from all they had met that these unwelcome guests had ignored the protocols of these lands, offending and upsetting delicate wîcêwâkanihtowin, alliances and trade partnerships, wherever they went. Sacagawea saved them from annihilation more times than they knew.[119]

From my visions, I knew that these môniyâwak would bring others, and those others would bring wars, destruction, and sickness behind them. I had warned my brothers and sisters to vanish[120] and had sent my maskwak, the grizzly bears of the forest, to line the shores of the river and scare off the môniyâwak from landing close to where the people lived.[121]

Not all of the people had heeded my warnings. Seeing Sacagawea and her baby, the Sahnish, Numakaki, Niimi'ipuu, and Chinook had welcomed and cared for the newcomers, and some had even had such intimate relations that now there were children born of these encounters living along the river shores.[122] As Môci-kîsikâw continued his sad tale, I chuckled grimly to myself about how, after my initial thoughts about driving his people away, now I was caring for this "explorer." Maybe there was a reason he had been brought to me?

Môci-kîsikâw described how he and his companion had lived intimately, away from the company of their thirty-odd men. He told me how they had their own tent, and would share a whisky together every evening, and much more, and yet more after this love-addled wretch was accidentally shot in his lean and lovely buttock.[123] It seems that the tender administrations of medicinal attention to that area by his sensitive companion had been very healing indeed, and with some extra laudanum for the pain, and much whisky consumed by both, they had finally allowed their relationship to blossom in a physical sense. Stroking him now, I felt the scar tissue across his tight and responsive rump.

"No, no!" he cried. "I shall rot in torment for transgressions already committed." What he meant by that, I could not comprehend. With my

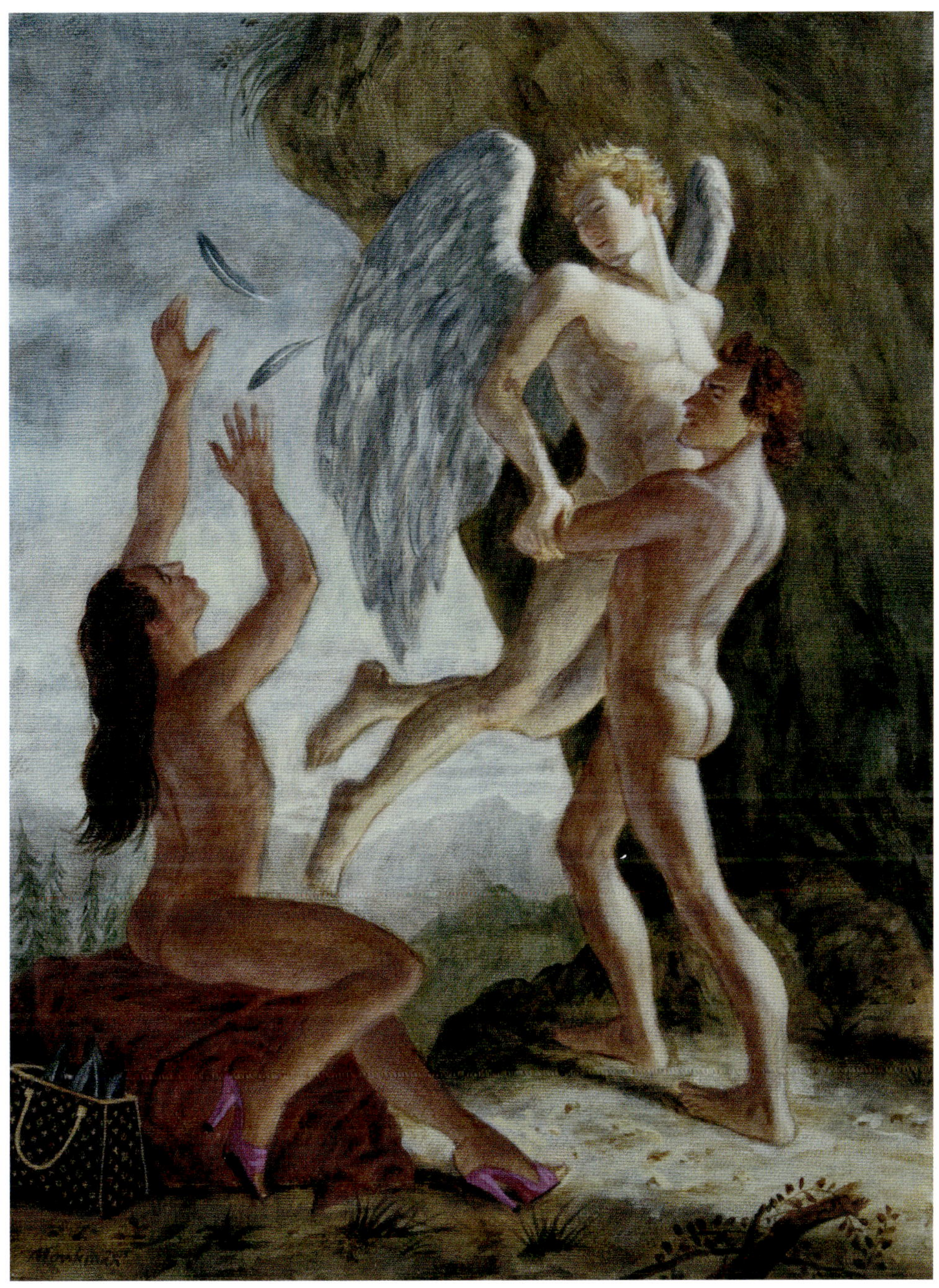

Still somewhat delirious, he asked, "Are you an angel, sent to warn me against not succumbing to further perversions?"

Two Spirits, 2011. Acrylic on canvas. 16 in. x 12 in.

hand gently caressing his scarred buttock (my hand which he, by the way, did not remove, despite his protestations), I could see his hard âpacihcikan, tool, ê-makwayikihkâtêk, filling his pants with a bulge, under the blanket—giving me a truer answer.

What strange thinking was this, that pleasure between two creatures who desired it could be a sin? What kind of people had laws that created so much anguish for what was natural and beautiful? Surely, they had confused Kisê-manitow's laws. I asked him, did he not see that this was the cause of his distress, not his lover's rejection?

Still somewhat delirious, he asked, "Are you an angel, sent to warn me against not succumbing to further perversions?"

"Firstly," I answered, "I would never warn anyone against seeking consensual adult pleasure, and secondly, those beings you call angels, I have known them for a very long time. These oskitakosinokîsikowak are not what you think they are. They sometimes help, but you may not understand why. I prefer their feathers for my adornment above all others, but trust me, your concepts of goodness and sin are lost on them, and be assured, they do not hesitate to take pleasures where they find them."

I tried to explain how each living thing contains balance, how we live in pêyâhtakêyimowin—taking care of each other and being respectful of each other—with all living things. I told him there are many genders and that love, sâkihitowin, is for all beings. He would not hear my words and began trembling and whimpering again. Poor man, perhaps he was still drunk or under the effects of the poppy.

"Listen to your heart and ahcâhk-iskotêw, young man. You have nothing to fear from loving your captain. If the desire is mutual, seize it, embrace your nature, and allow yourself to feel the heights of experience that you are now denying. Your ideas of how things can be just one thing and not another do not fit our world. Across our land, in every nation, you will find others like yourself. Indeed, among your own countrymen you will find yourself in good company, although your societies do not yet seem to understand the flexible nature of desire as ours do.

"Come, Môci-kîsikâw, to my next honour dance. I will invite some of your countrymen so you will see that what your heart tells you is true, and not at all strange. Many of my nîcimosak, my sweethearts—young and old—will dance to honour me and the moments they have spent with me. You may recognize some; others, such as our supernatural beings, may be strange to you. But these are my kind, and we gather and cavort when we can. Bring your captain and be free to love him without fear in this fine and varied company. You will see that you are not alone, and in the times of your people's past and future, your desires were, and will be, embraced. To truly live, we need to experience miyawâtamowin, joyfulness."

He eventually calmed, whether from my words, exhaustion, or the effects of the poppy and the whisky, I knew not. I fed him some misâskwatômina to recover his strength, took him on my pony back to his people, then sent word to his captain to come and fetch him.

ᒥᐦᒉᐟ ᐅᑖᐸᑫᐧᐊᐧᐠ
ᑮ ᑲᑫᐧ ᐋᓴᐋᐧᐸᐦᑕᒧᐠ
ᑎᐱᔨᒥᓱᐃᐧᐣ
ᑭᓇᐦᒋᒦᒥᓂᐦᑲᐧ

Many Trappers Sought Freedom in Our Forests

Many seasons later, the amiskwak were moving further and further west, hunted relentlessly by the trappers and the traders and clerks who followed them, building ever-larger forts and towns with the new wealth. This môniyâwak trade now included paskwâwi-mostoswak, for their hides and, more particularly, for their meat—which, when mixed with berries and lard, became pimîhkân, pemmican, the fuel upon which the fur trade depended.[124]

The return of the horse had changed my people's and all the Plains Nations' ways of defining our territories, our ways of warring, and, most importantly, our ways of hunting. We could now move fast enough to match the paskwâwi-mostoswak's pace, and our best riders were some of the swiftest on the prairies. But the newcomers were also hunting paskwâwi-mostoswak, and the môniyâwak brought more guns, and more conflict.

Late one night, under the cool light of tipiskâw-pîsim, I walked amongst my siblings, the paskwâwi-mostoswak. The matriarch turned her massive, shaggy head towards me and grunted, blowing great clouds of cool air from her black nostrils, and she nuzzled my chest, catching me off guard and almost knocking me over. I reached up and placed my hand on her warm neck, sighing as I communicated my concerns to her. "Yes, it is true, our nation is in grave danger. What we once thought impossible is happening now." She spoke to me of their fear. We both looked at tipiskâw-pîsim for a very long time. The balance of pêyâhtakêy-imowin was shifting.

Our lands, and all that grew and moved on them, were being used as pawns in a game of commerce. The two largest môniyâw companies trading in furs—the English Hudson's Bay Company, controlled from London, and the North West Company, based in Montréal—were warring with each other over control and access to the fur trade. The British agents of the Hudson's Bay Company stayed in their forts, forcing the trappers to come to them. The North West Company's French-speaking voyageurs travelled with their agents deep into the bush to meet the trappers inland—journeys that would be impossible to make without pimîhkân.[125] The

English and Scots agents of the Hudson's Bay Company were discouraged from openly marrying our women,[126] although many had country wives, such as myself, but more on that debacle later.[127] The French-speaking agents of most of the other fur trading companies (including the North West Company), on the other hand, freely intermarried with our women, depending on their knowledge of the land and powerful kinship ties.[128] Their descendants, the âpihtawikosisânak, the half-sons, soon grew to become a distinct nation: the Métis Nation, Otipemisiwak.[129]

Our Métis kin had joined us in the Iron Confederacy, the hunting, trading, political and military wîcêwâkanihtowin that centered around the fur trade. This alliance included my people, the nêhiyawak, the Nakoda, the Nakawē,[130] and others.[131] When the Hudson's Bay Company and Lord Selkirk began the illegal and uninvited (like almost all such colonies were) settlement of his displaced Scots kinsmen on our lands surrounding mihkwâkamîwi-sîpiy, the Red River,[132] he was given aid by Chief Peguis, who, practising otôtêmihtowin, our way of openness to others, friendship, diplomacy, saved the unprepared settlers from starvation[133] and, even though they were not invited guests, made a wîcêwâkanihtowin with them to share the lands of his people.[134]

Having learned nothing from the generosity of Chief Peguis, the Red River Colony governor—the short-tempered, arrogant Scotsman, Miles MacDonell—acted in a way I would soon come to see as typical amongst these newcomers. As winter approached and more unprepared settlers arrived, MacDonell issued the Pemmican Proclamation on behalf of another Scotsman who was only thinking about his own big ideas about our lands, Lord Selkirk. Instead of nikwâtisowin êkwa mâtinamâkêwin, the sharing and generosity that was the way of our lands, Selkirk and the Hudson's Bay Company outlawed the removal of food and pimîhkân from the Red River Colony. They said it was to feed new settlers coming in, but really they hoarded the stockpiled pimîhkân to cut off the supply to their bitter rivals, the North West Company, guaranteeing conflict with the Métis fur traders and trappers who depended on pimîhkân, and thereby setting in motion the actions that would lead to ever-worsening warfare.[135]

When the Métis fur trader and leader Wappeston[136] took a large party of warriors to bring pimîhkân to the rival North West Company despite the ban, Hudson's Bay Company officers tried to stop them. Twenty men died in the battle, but Wappeston and his men walked away with some brief economic freedom and a moment that sparked their identity as the Métis Nation.[137]

My friend Chief Peguis intervened to protect the remaining settlers, who moved with their nêhiyawak allies to the safety of the Hudson's Bay Company stronghold at Norway House.[138]

I felt the beginnings of the trouble I had foreseen. Unsettled, I dreamed one night of a green-eyed, ginger-haired bellicose fool who brought an even more particular ill wind to my people, but when I woke, I could recall only a fragment; the full meaning eluded me. I rolled over in the mossy cedar-bough bed I had made the night before, gaining focus from askiy beneath me. I took out the ancient arrowhead I had carried for so long and pushed it into the soft earth.

Fighting was not my way. Wîsahkêcâhk had long counselled me that it was not my place to prevent conflict, only help the human beings find their own paths. I remembered what Danny had told me about those who were sent here from Europe being their broken ones, their cast-offs, those who had committed crimes and done terrible things in their home communities. But I had to believe that there were also good ones, who could eventually understand the deeper significance of the otôtêmihtowin Chief Peguis and so many others had shown them. I decided I would use whatever means necessary to get close to other môniyâwak so I might show them our ways—and perhaps, if they proved open, a little more. I wanted them to understand our responsibility to live in conscious

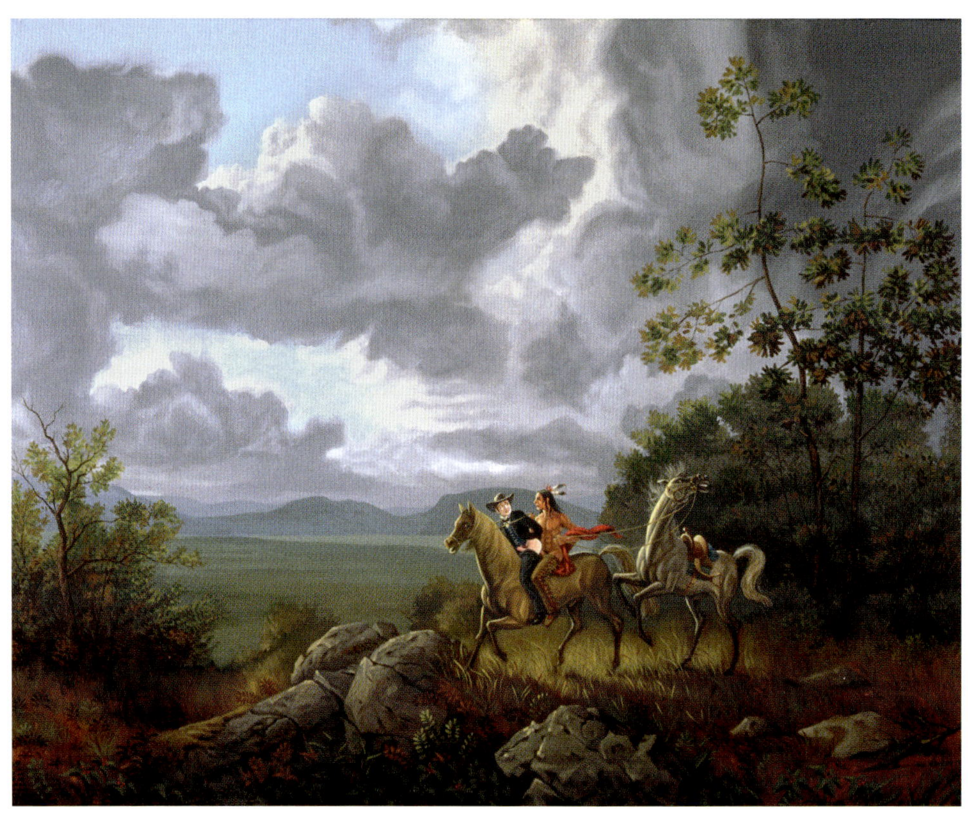

We rode my horse to a special place, one where there was teaching within the rocks.

Red Man Teaches White Man How to Ride Bareback, 2003. Acrylic on canvas. 16 in. x 20 in.

connection with the land and living things in a way that creates and sustains balance—miyo-pimâtisiwin, the way of living beautifully[139]—so they could live in harmony with my brothers and sisters, the land and all living beings.

On a late summer day, with the crackling promise of a storm in the air, and thunderbirds, piyêsiwak, in the distance, I spied a fine young môniyâw specimen, a trapper, on his way into town. I could tell at a glance that he was one of the many who were drawn to a life far from the prying eyes of his regular society.

He was grimy, with matted hair, his smell a mixture of smoke, moose hide, and maleness that I always found intoxicating. He had the starved look of someone who'd been in the bush for a long time, and I thought that perhaps he might appreciate some sport before going on his way. I spoke to him with my most alluring voice, suggesting he take a pleasurable detour with me.

The lively fellow was young and inexperienced, but didn't need to be asked twice, for he had not set eyes on another soul for many months and was eager for some conversation and kindness. We rode my horse to a special place, one where there was teaching within the rocks. There we enjoyed a fine afternoon under the late summer skies. Afterwards, we collapsed in the tall fragrant grasses, basking in the sweaty afterglow of our tryst. I rolled over and stroked his hairy chest, wrapped my arms and legs around him, and inhaled the sweet, pungent scent of our congress.

Our muscular bodies still entwined and radiating heat, I whispered to him that otôtêmihtowin was not limited to human beings. "Do not take more than you need," I said, kissing him tenderly. "Respect all creatures and also the land. Tell your people." He nodded, assuring me that he would, but I was not convinced he had understood, so I kept spreading the word in the way I knew best.

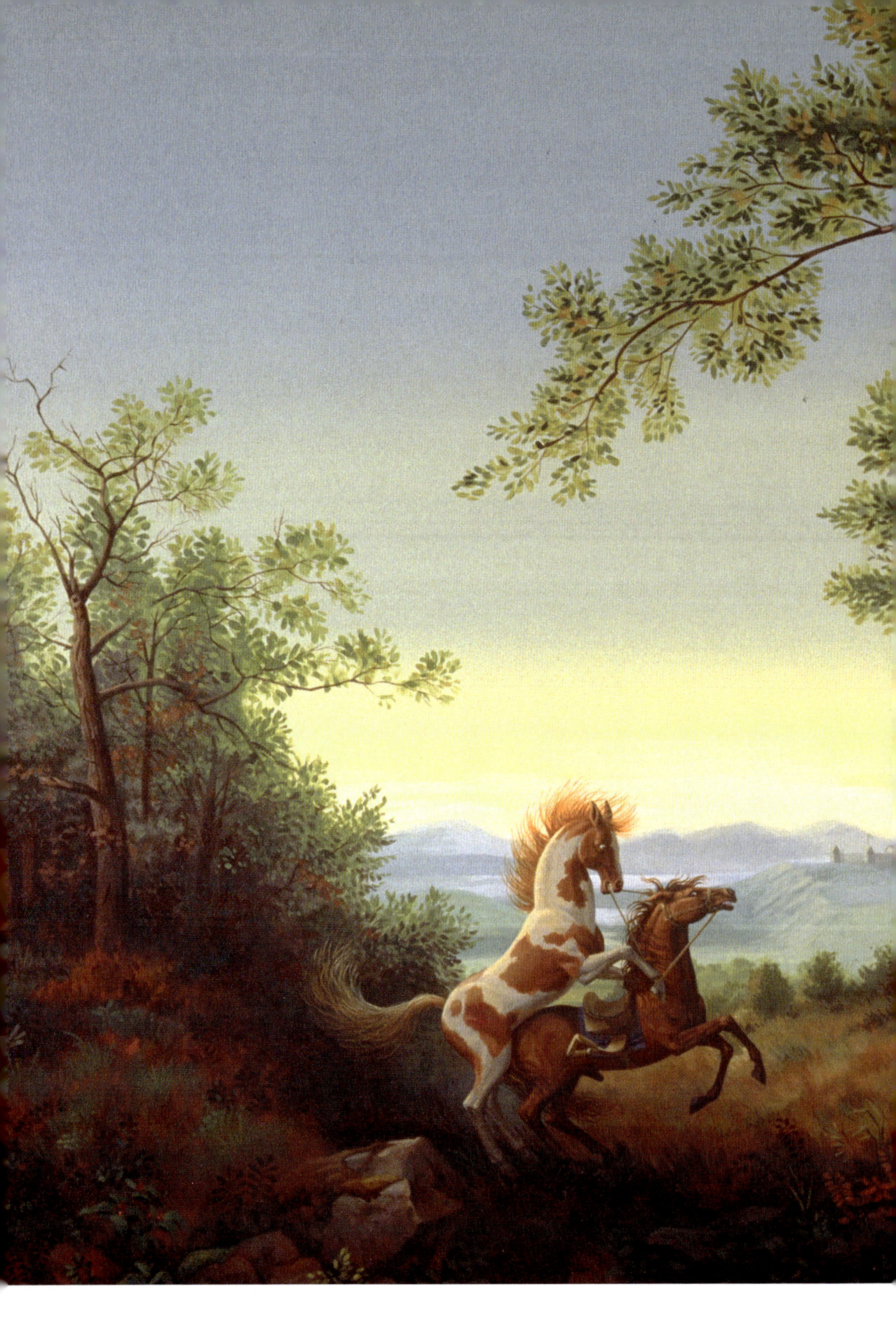

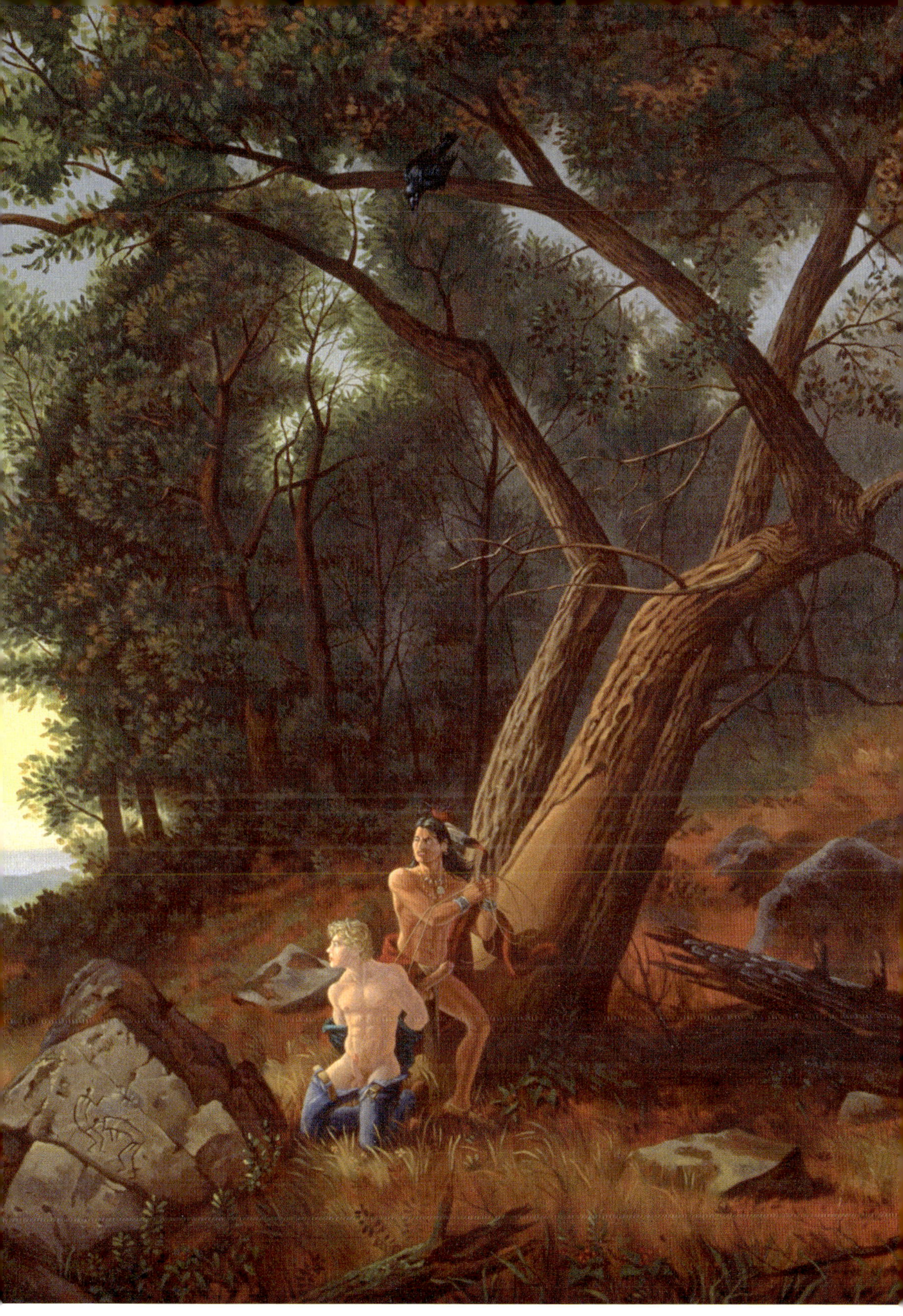

As more môniyâwak trickled, then flooded, into our lands, my edifying encounters with them likewise increased.

Fort Edmonton, 2003. Acrylic on canvas. 24 in. x 36 in.

As more môniyâwak trickled, then flooded, into our lands, my edifying encounters with them likewise increased. There was an abundance of trappers seeking freedom in our forests from the persecution and hangings they would face from their "civilizations" out east, or back in their home countries, simply for loving who they loved.[140]

They were so broken and disconnected from miyo-pimâtisiwin. Pitiful and with ahcâhk-iskotêwak so dim, until our encounters, some of them were barely aware that they were alive.

They would experience a personal awakening, often crying out in much more than physical ecstasy as they were transported by the release of years of pent-up desire. I too felt the rush as their spirits expanded, growing ever brighter. For both young and old, I had opened a door to their tâpwêwin. Some were euphoric and revelled in a freedom heretofore never experienced, but some recoiled from me immediately after our climaxes, their countenances darkening with the heaviness of the same guilt I had seen consume Môci-kîsikâw as they kneeled, hands clasped, anxiously murmuring about laws they had broken. I did not understand their religion of the cross, which did not allow them to be who they were. I thought they too should accept with humility how Kisê-manitow had made them, for there is no shame in loving.

"Go home," I would say to them. "This place is not for you, not unless you are going to live by the laws of this land." Some laughed, not understanding that we nêhiyawak belong to this land, as do all of our relatives here on miskinâhk-oministik. A few, however, grew serious, taking me in their strong arms and telling me they would try to understand, or they would leave, if that was my wish.

I sought to reach more of their kind so that they might more widely spread their new understanding, but these delectable trappers with their pent-up desire and hardened forest edge were isolated from each other, spread out to ensure they would not trap over one another's territory. It was an irksome business to travel through wetlands, dense bush, and over the mountain ranges for this sweet instruction, but I endured. Then one fine spring day, I received the gift of inspiration.

A trader in town had told me of a small group of trappers camped to trade over the next ridge. I thought I might visit them to see which ones would be open to my stern message and sweet persuasions. I found them late in the afternoon, swimming naked in the clear mountain lake. Amongst the rough and burly men was a more refined and perfumed gentleman—tall, with a white buckskin jacket, tight tartan trousers, and a wide-brimmed hat, who commanded a large caravan with many supplies, and horses, and handsome young men. I could tell by the gay manner and ease with which he comported himself that he was also of the persuasion I preferred, although not conflicted about it as so many of his people were.[141] Certainly if I could gain his influence he might assist in the enterprise I had in mind.

Before I could approach this gay Scotsman, I became aware of a brown-haired môniyâw in his party, strangely attired in what, perhaps to him, approximated our manner of dress, who was intently following me with his gaze. He approached me and handed me a small card that said "Geo. Catlin, Esq.", with the word "Lawyer" crossed out and "Artist" written over it in very fine handwriting.[142]

"I am an artist of distinction," he said, introducing himself with an astonishing lack of manners and humility, "and soon I intend to undertake my life's mission: to capture the noble nature of real Indians in authentic portraits. I would very much like to paint your likeness for posterity."[143] His tone was presumptuous and ingratiating, and he waited expectantly for my answer.

"Perhaps, someday," I said distractedly, eyeing a broad-shouldered, almond-eyed beauty with long wavy hair, clearly the Scotsman's consort, who was splitting wood. The artist took my vague, noncommittal answer as assurance, however, and eagerly pumped my limp hand as he told me to seek him out once he had acquired the funds for his "arduous undertaking."[144]

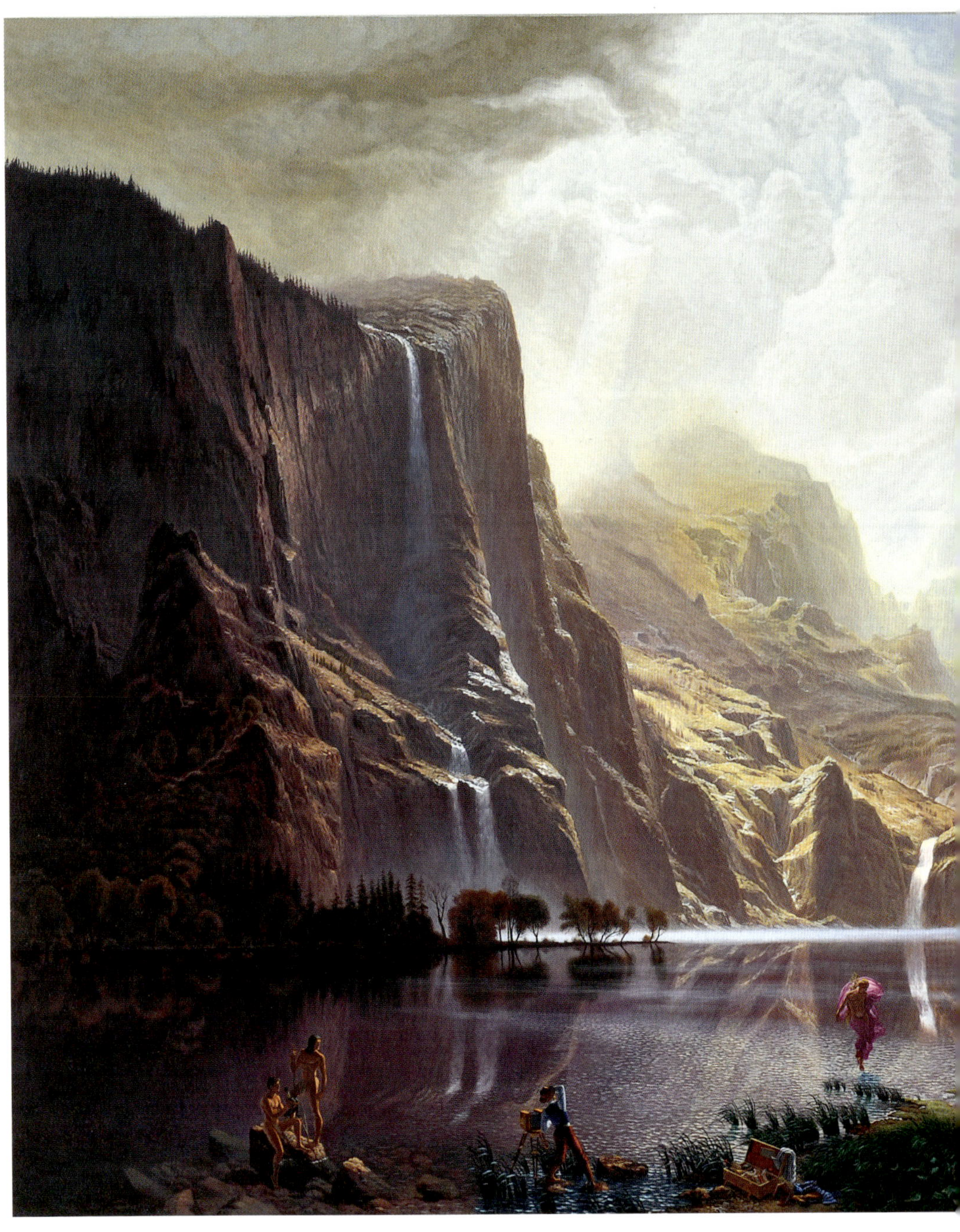

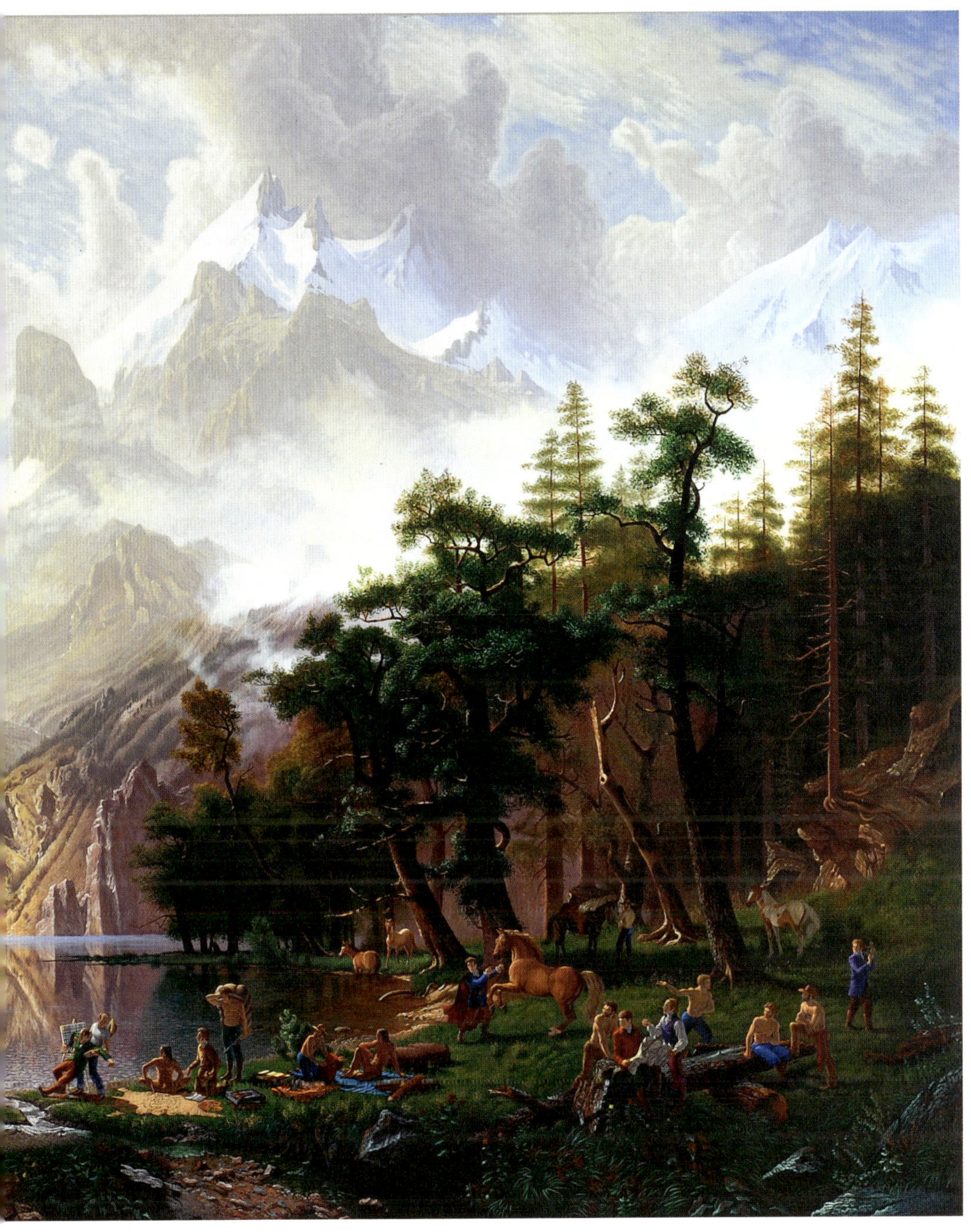

These men came from a culture of exploitation, judgement, and strife. I would teach them about our laws of sâkihitowin, love; kisêwâtisiwin, kindness; and kistêyihtamowin, respect for all beings.

Trappers of Men, 2006. Acrylic on canvas. 84 in. x 144 in.

I turned my back to Catlin and faced those to whom I actually wished to speak. Raising my voice so the Scotsman and everyone gathered near me could hear, I declared, "I propose in two moons' time a gathering along the Seeds-kee-dee Agie, in the lower foothills of Newe territory." I had selected a place rich in furs and food, which the trappers called Henry's Fork. We could pitch our tents on the banks of the river. "Gather your pelts! I will invite the fur companies. You can do your trading without having to go all the way back east. I shall call it a Rendezvous,[145] in honour of our trapper friends from New France. To launch this Rendezvous, we shall have a celebration. âstam, come"—I motioned to the trappers—"come join us in the foothills in the wâwiyêsiwi-pîsim, the full moon, of paskowipîsim, the moulting moon."

Those in attendance did not hesitate. They whooped and hollered, firing their guns in agreement. It would be easy trading for them—they could avoid the long and dangerous trip back to their trading posts and were sure of a wild and raucous time. These men came from a culture of exploitation, judgement, and strife. I would teach the newcomers amongst them about our laws of sâkihitowin, love; kisêwâtisiwin, kindness; and kistêyihtamowin, respect for all beings, including the beaver and the buffalo. They could take only what they needed, no more.

The dapper Scotsman approached me and bowed deeply. "M' lady, allow me to assist this excellent venture," he offered. "If you will permit it, I would be honoured to supply bountiful food and drink and other essentials for this endeavour." I took him up on his offer and together we made plans for a gathering of love and liberation, the likes of which had never been seen.

---

mwêscasês, in paskowipîsim, mid-summer, I travelled over asinîwaciya, the Rocky Mountains, by horse with the gay Scotsman, who enthusiastically told me he was an exceedingly rich lord by the name of William

Drummond Stewart. We were joined by Stewart's lover Antoine, whose almond-shaped hazel eyes and long wavy hair had so caught my attention a few months before. He was the son of a nêhiyaw-iskwêw, a Cree mother, and a French father, and he would be the principal hunter for our group.[146] He was known for many days' ride in all directions as one of the best Métis buffalo hunters around. Normally a fellow of fine disposition, his temper however, when aroused, was uncontrollable.[147] The traders gave him a wide berth so as not to inadvertently provoke him, but Stewart hung on Antoine's every word, eagerly embracing his ways and views.

The journey over the asinîwaciya to our Rendezvous location at Seeds-kee-dee Agie was arduous and slow, but the time passed pleasantly enough in the company of my new friends. Stewart was by far the most animated European I had yet met. He was a keen study, and greatly interested in our laws and sympathetic to our situation as he was not a fan of the English, whose many incursions upon his own country he recounted often, with great historical detail.

"Be wary," he warned. "The sassenachs are here to make everything theirs. They did it to us, and they'll do it to you." I nodded grimly—I was witnessing the beginnings of what I had seen in my visions now play out before me.

One night, about midway on our journey, I lingered by the fire flirting with some of the young trappers. It was a clear, warm night. A gentle breeze cascading down from the mountains kept the mosquitoes at bay. Those sitting close to the flames had removed their outer garments; as they reclined, the firelight danced on their skin, which glistened with a sheen of sweat, and their body hair shone like Danny's gold fur. The Newe, Núuchi-u, and Pan'akwati men lounged on their blankets, splaying their bare legs open suggestively, pointing at the trappers with their lips, sharing private jokes, and teasing each other in sign language. The sexual tension around the fire was palpable, as one young trapper sang plaintively in his crisp baritone, plucking his banjo.

Stewart had gone to his tent, and returned to the campfire in his nightshirt with a small flask, now a bit tipsy from the champagne he had brought. He asked if he might take my hand—I smiled and walked with him to his tent as the men around the fire chuckled and murmured knowingly. A coal oil lamp threw the shadows of two intertwined figures on the wall of the tent. When I opened the flap, I saw Antoine, naked, wrestling on the cot with one of the hairy blond trappers, their clothes strewn all about. Stewart stepped in behind me, letting his body brush against mine ever so slightly. With a soft tug, I let my gossamer loincloth drop to the floor, releasing nicimasowin that was now as big as that of a mistatim. We would ride all night, or as my lovers and I liked to say, ê-wâpanitêhtapit. This was the first of many similar nights with different groupings along our journey. There were many tents in our caravan and I visited all of them.

I had travelled this route a month earlier to offer gifts and ask permission to cross the lands of the Newe and to camp along the riverbank. I had followed the protocols of the territory so that we might travel undisturbed, unless of course we were visited by some who also wished to taste this exotic revelry. Stewart and I set up camp with William Ashley, owner of the Rocky Mountain Fur Company, and his trader William Sublette, whom the Newe called Cut Face because of the scar on his chin. Also with their company was Jim Beckwourth, known as the Gaudy Liar—a handsome kaskitêwiyiniw, Black trapper, now a free man and married into the Apsáalooke Nation, who called him Nan-kup-bah-pah.[148] A gifted storyteller, Beckwourth's tall tales—told with great dramatic effect, and more than a little enhancement—rivalled even mine.

One by one the trappers converged on our camp nestled in a rolling valley with stands of lodgepole pine, subalpine fir, Engelmann spruce, Douglas fir, and quaking aspen. The forest provided firewood, good hunting, and much space for trappers' tents, tipis, mirth, songs, dancing, shouting, trading, running, jumping, singing, racing, target-shooting, yarns, frolic, with all sorts of extravagances that white men or "Indians" could invent.[149]

Many of the trappers who made the journey to our Rendezvous were from William Ashley's company, but trappers from other companies also converged on our camp. We were joined by French Canadian and Haudenosaunee trappers who had until recently been employees of the Hudson's Bay Company. They had been happy to get away from the tyranny of their former master, George Simpson,[150] but since his company had merged with their former rival, the North West Company, to form a near-total monopoly,[151] the prices they were paid for furs had fallen. The trappers had become disgruntled by the new owners' haggling and been lured by the better price offered by the American traders. I was now offering them something much more.

I noticed the absence of one I had hoped to see here—the tormented soul I had pulled out of the river, Môci-kîsikâw. I had promised him that one day I would invite him to experience the natural pleasures of his true nature, and the love available to him if he could open himself to it. I had wondered if he would come with his captain. I searched through the vibrations to connect with his ahcâhk-iskotêw but could not sense him.

A while later, an oskitakosinokîsikow, newcomer spirit being, sent me a message that they had taken Môci-kîsikâw home after he had laid himself down on a mostoswayân, a buffalo robe, and, consumed by self-hatred, fired a gun into his own chest.[152] I was saddened to hear this, but the oskitakosinokîsikow told me not to grieve him, as Môci-kîsikâw was finally able to experience the natural pleasures of his true nature on the other side. I would be sure to tell other tormented souls like him not to fear what awaited them there.

ᓂᑮ ᑌᐹᐧᑖᐊᐧᐠ
ᐊᓂᑭ ᑲ ᒥᔦᐧᔨᒥᒋᐠ
ᑕ ᐯ ᒪᓈᒋᐦᐃᒋᐠ

I Summoned My Admirers to Honour Me

Before we began the Rendezvous, I wished to celebrate the spirit of love that was my nature with my own form of honour dance. I opened my soul flame wide, let it burn bright and drifted into the realm outside this world of flesh and bone, shifting through time and space, to transport my human and fellow âtayôhkanak lovers of many nations and origins. Through the vortex of love, I pulled all those who desired me from my past, present, and future to pay homage to love in all its forms—and, of course, to me.[153] Somewhere in the background I noticed the môniyâw, Catlin, who called himself a painter—his attraction to me had caught him up in the slipstream with all the others. I did not mind, for all were welcome.

All around me were my friends who love whomever they want, niwîcêwâkanak pikwâwiyak kâ-sâkihâcik,[154] my friends who live however they want to live, niwîcêwâkanak pikwîsi kâ-isi-wîkicik,[155] and the ones who shine, kâ-wâsihkopayicik.

The ground vibrated as the drummers beat out a rhythm that echoed for miles throughout the valley. My lovers began to arrive in singles and in groups, laying gifts of blankets, furs, meat, adornments of precious shells and silver at my feet.[156] They swirled around me and threw themselves into the dance, their feet pounding the grass flat, their lust and admiration concentrated on me. I breathed it all in deeply, absorbing their sensuality and energy, letting it intermingle with mine and revelling in the exquisite pull of their desire. Wîsahkêcâhk was there, of course—like me, his soul is made for love, and he never misses a good party. He glanced at me with a smile as he entered the circle. I raised my eyebrows in query, and followed his pointed lips to our dear friend/sister/brother, the deliciously furry Mistâpêw. For no matter how varied Wîsahkêcâhk's tastes might be, he would always choose them, or me of course, over other lovers, but I was much distracted.

Now numbering hundreds strong, my lovers drummed and danced, pushing in tightly around me. I could feel the heat from their torsos pressing against my back, their hands wandering over my waist, stomach, and

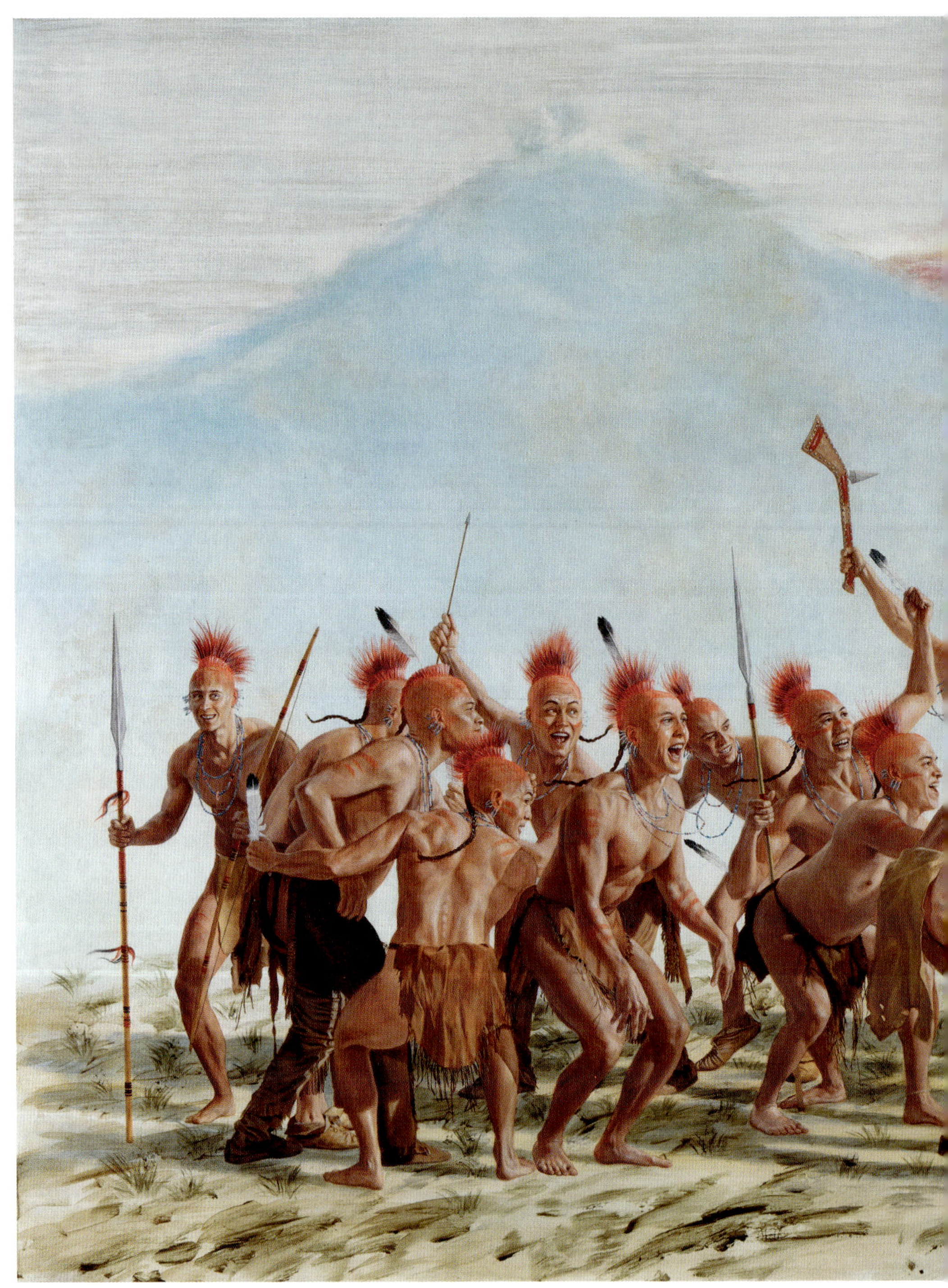

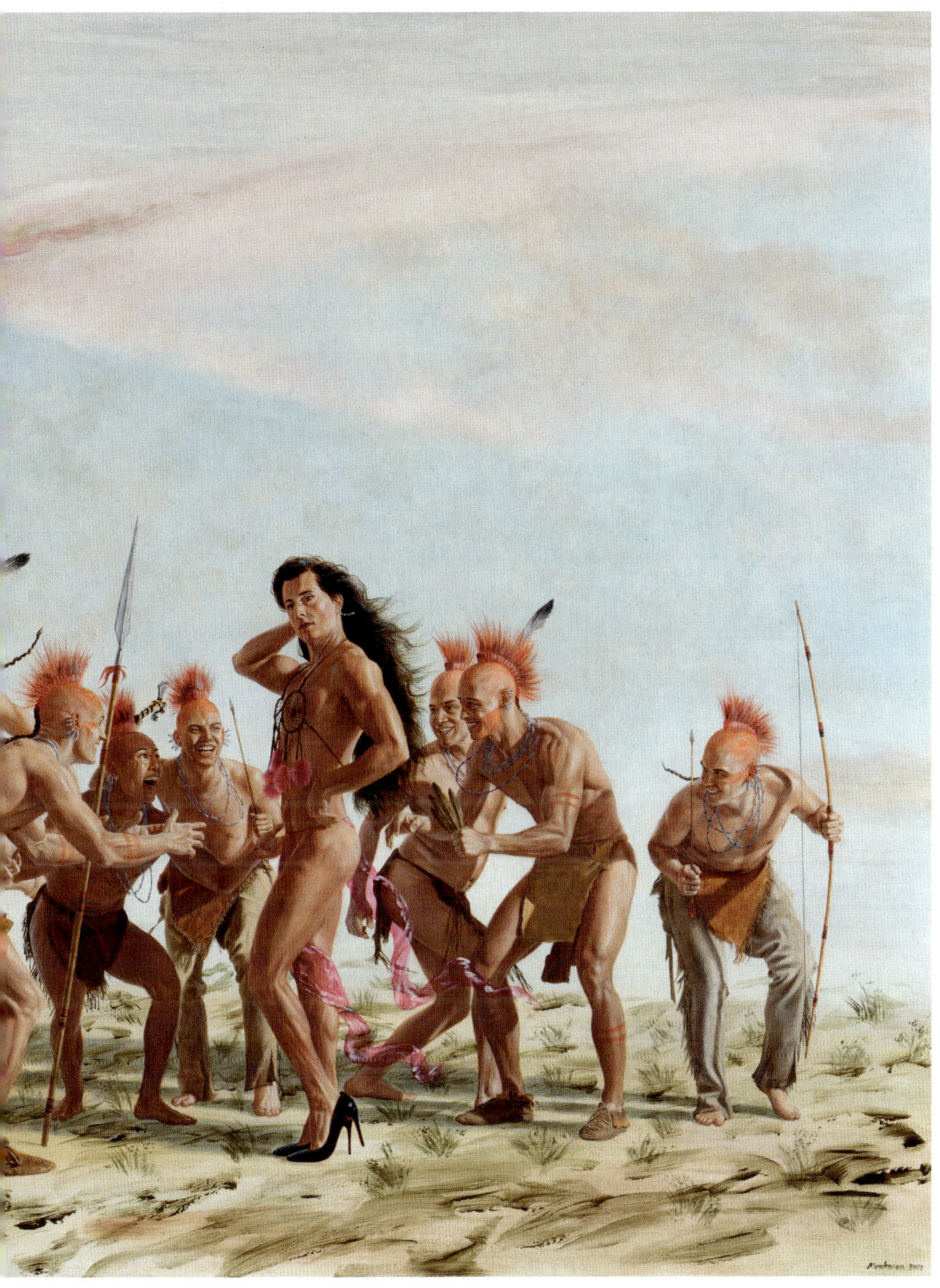

Through the vortex of love, I pulled all those who desired me from my past, present, and future to pay homage to love in all its forms—and, of course, to me.

Honour Dance, 2020. Acrylic on canvas. 60 in. x 94.25 in.

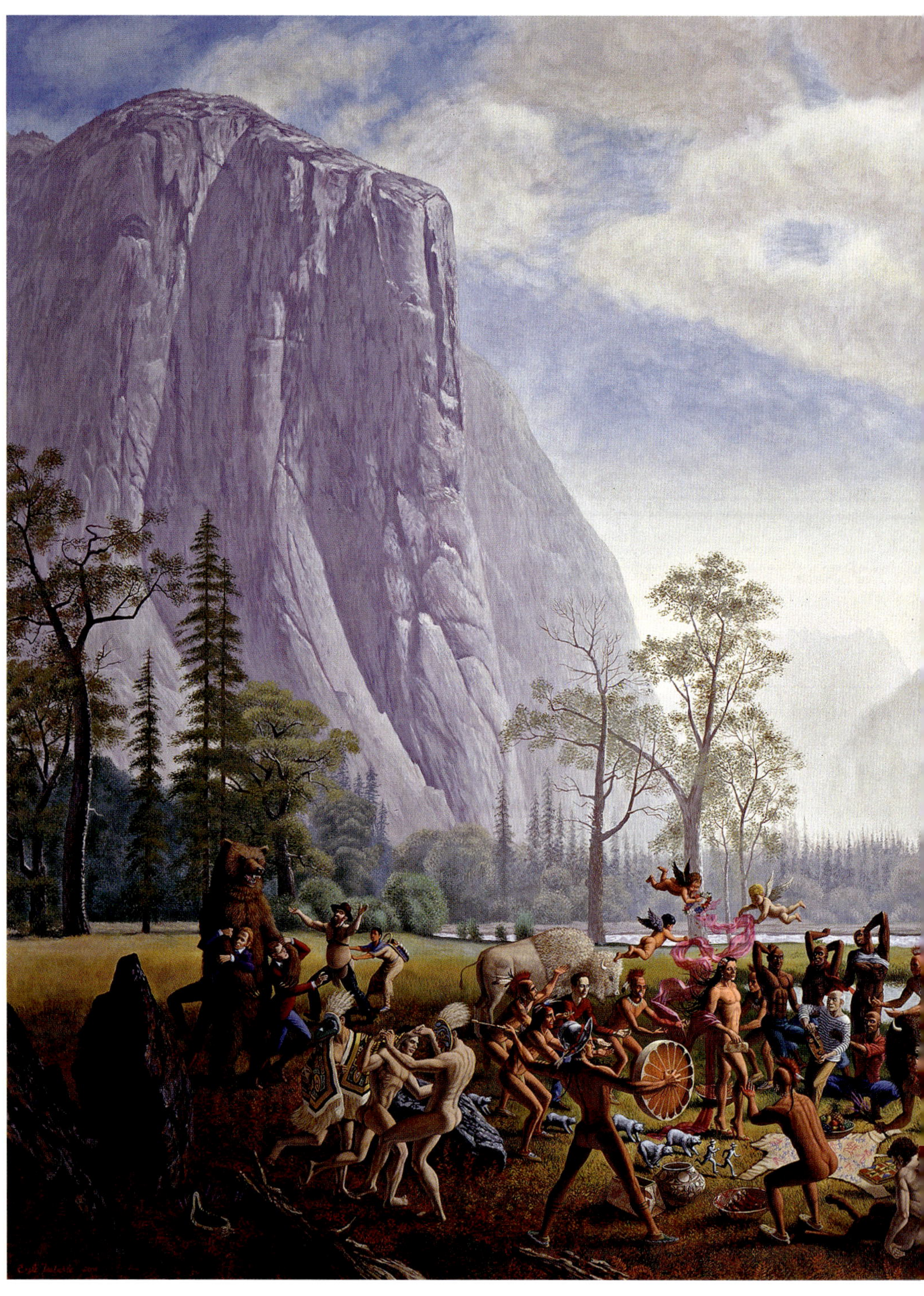

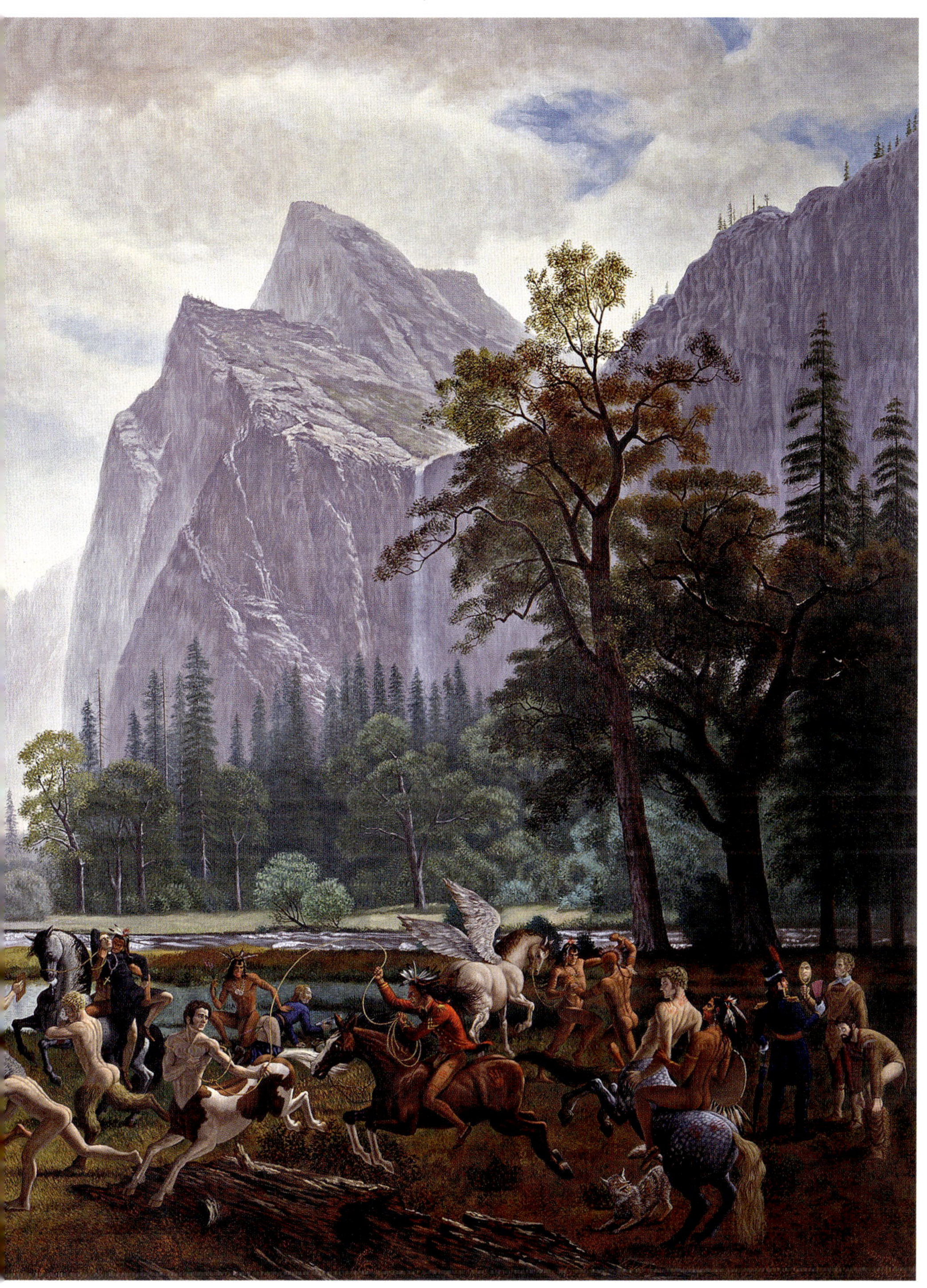

All around me were my friends who love whomever they want, niwîcêwâkanak pikwâwiyak kâ-sâkihâcik, my friends who live however they want to live, niwîcêwâkanak pikwîsi kâ isi wîkicik, and the ones who shine, kâ wâsihkopayicik

The Triumph of Mischief, 2007. Acrylic on canvas. 84 in. x 132 in.

thighs as I ground my ass against the hardness swelling inside one breechcloth and the furry softness of another. As a bright melody from a young Métis fiddler, the handsome Thierry, rose above the thunderous beat in the musky warm air, my suitors, now a throbbing mass of muscle and sweat, whooped as they cleared a circle around me.

I took the cue to begin my solo dance for them. Arching my back, I teased their eagerness with my hips and eyes. Lips parted slightly, I exhaled and tossed my head back, flinging my long raven locks in joyful miyawâtamowin to the pulsing drumbeats. When I reached my moment of climax in the dance, I extended my arms to those closest to me and pulled them into the centre of the circle that they might share in the shuddering pleasure with me amidst the near-deafening whoops, whistles, and cheers of adulation. Adrenaline pumped through my veins, and I danced for hours.

Late in the darkness of night I felt the warmth of a furry tall body grinding against me. I instantly recognized the pungent peaty smell of sweet Mistâpêw. They had adorned themselves with garlands of wildflowers, and ribbons and pendants of cowrie shells tied to their matted dreadlocks bounced on their chest as they danced even closer to me. I could feel their heavy warm breath on my neck. My hand felt tiny in my sister/brother's thick paw as they led me out of the crowd and into the cool darkness of the bushes, scattering the hundreds of mêmêkwêsiwak who, to avoid being stepped on, had been dancing at the perimeter of the clearing.

Grunting, Mistâpêw pulled my hand to the wetness between their legs. I gently pushed into the heat of their mitâhkay, teasing them until they moaned again. Almost the height of two nêhiyaw nâpêwak, Cree men, they towered over me, even in my heels. They pulled my face to their furry wetness and lifted one leg and braced it on a fallen tree. The musky scent of wet fur, mingled with the sweetness of the blooms, pine needles and juniper and wet earth, overwhelmed me as I pleasured them with my tongue. They clutched the back of my skull, threw back their head, and thrust their groin into my face, releasing a shower of ejaculate down my face, neck, and body as they let out a low guttural growl that echoed through the forest. I steadied myself against a sturdy tree and bent forward, allowing their wetness to drip off me. They grunted and crashed away into the bush, snapping branches and leaving me gasping. Encounters with other âtayôhkanak always left me shattered, in the very best way.

ᐁᑯᐢᐱᕽ ᑲᐦᑭᔭᐤ
ᑲᑮ ᒫᒪᐏᐸᔨᒋᐠ
ᐃᔨᓂᐘᐠ

The Time When Many Nations Came Together

After bringing in the spirit of miyawâtamowin with my honour dance, the festivities of the Rendezvous commenced with much joy and laughter.

About three hundred horses and one hundred souls had now set up camp and were beginning to visit one another and trade. They were mostly men, for that was Stewart's inclination, but I loved all my people, so I had also invited my sisters and those of every gender, for we did not draw lines around such things.

Amongst my strong and beautiful sisters were Niska, Minôsis, and Kimiwan. They kept me humble, for if I should let my ego show, even for a moment, Niska was quick to tease me. Kimiwan would help me remember the other side of every argument, and Minôsis could make me laugh, no matter how choleric I might be feeling. They never let me forget who I was and I loved them all the more for it. They had told me of emptiness they had seen in the môniyâwak, how the pale men were starved for compassion and love, and how the resulting vacuum was filled with acquisition and competition.

The newcomers sorely misunderstood our women and their freedoms. Sublime in their sensuality, grounded in the land, my sisters and other women had come to the Rendezvous to play, without shame. Our women were, as always, our earth and centre.[157] Some came alone, some with their partners—we embraced all.

The fur company supplied free whisky—their tactic to get the trappers befuddled so they could pay them little for the pelts, but charge them exorbitantly for the tobacco, coffee, and other goods to which the trappers were becoming accustomed.[158] It was not my concern if the môniyâwak traders and their people consumed the whisky, but I was saddened to see some of our people partake, for my visions had shown what destruction osâmipiy, drinking, abuse of the mind, would wreak. It broke my heart to see that damage already starting.

When the commerce was done, we feasted, and one by one, we began to feel out the partner with whom we wished to frolic. Stewart, Antoine, and I had already enjoyed many nights together. I was curious for new

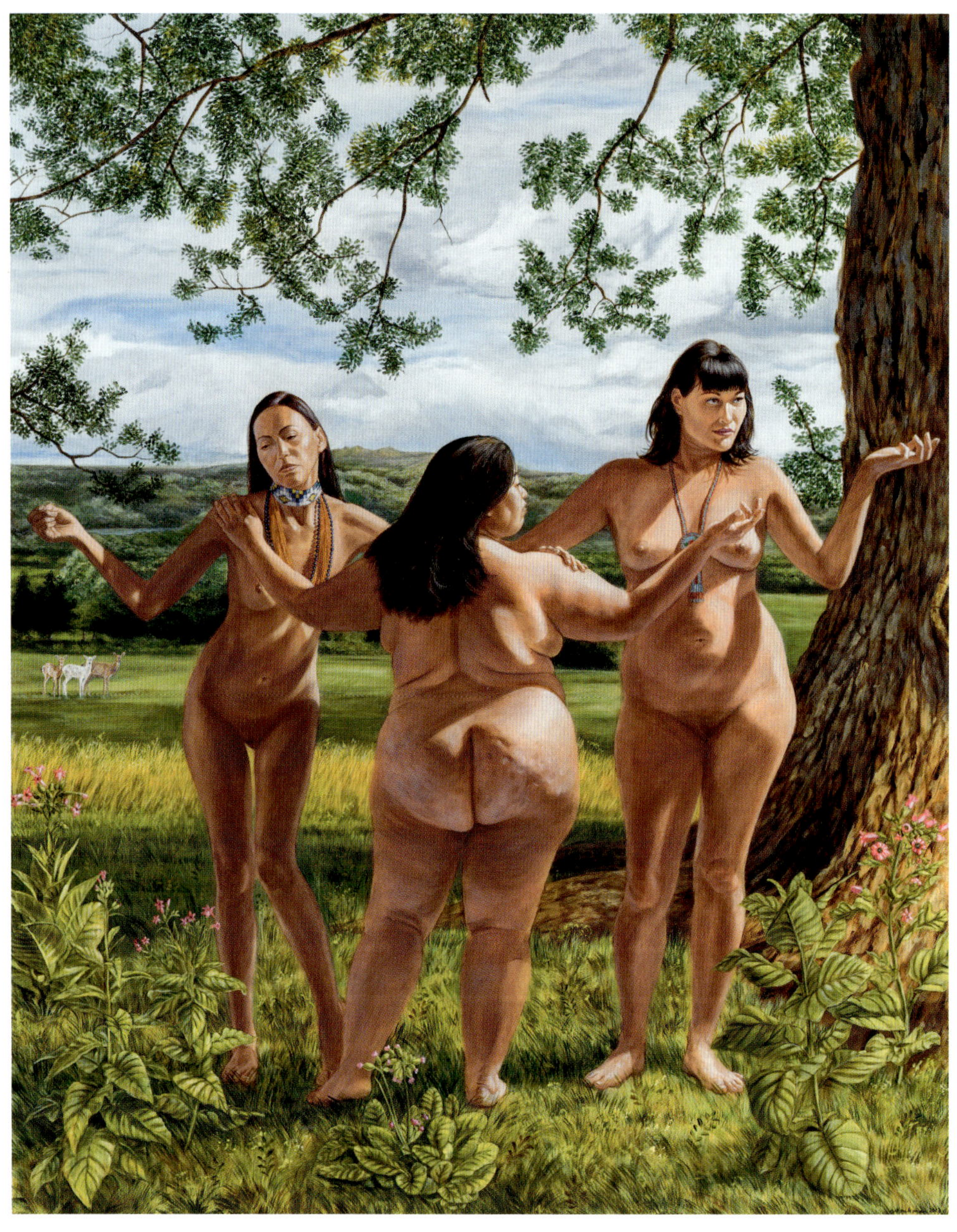

We danced together among the medicines, for I loved my sisters dearly, and they cared for me always.

The Three Graces, 2017. Acrylic on canvas. 60 in. x 48 in.

things, as always, and not much interested in the company men. I had tried a few in my diligent attempts to spread the messages of nikwatisowin êkwa mâtinamâkêwin, the sharing and caring that is fundamental to living in a good way on these lands. But they did not listen, so I soon grew tired of their pallid appetites and their stiffness in all the wrong places.

The free trappers were my favourite lovers—they were a magnificent mix of those who did not fit in any society; the Métis; the Newe, Núuchi-u, Pan'akwati, Apsáalooke, Niimi'ipuu, and Salish traders who wished to live a different way; Africans who were living new lives on the fringes of society;[159] and my dear kindred spirits, my friends who love whomever they want, niwîcêwâkanak pikwâwiyak kâ-sâkihâcik, and my friends who live however they want to live, niwîcêwâkanak pikwîsi kâ-isi-wîkicik, for our ways of loving were all-encompassing.

All were hardened from the bush, but styled each to his own design, some with hats made of their hunting trophies—coyote heads, wolf tails, bear claws—and others wearing ornaments of trade—silver, glass beads, feathers, bells, and all manner of prettifying trinkets.[160] They were full of mirth to be with so many gay creatures of their kind far away from the prying eyes of those who would denounce them. I coaxed many of this motley, merry group to the river to scrub the lice and ticks off their skin and clothing, and readied them for delights to which they were not yet accustomed.

Stewart gaily organized all manner of races and competitions: shooting contests (most likely to show off his shiny new Manton rifles), tomahawk throwing, horse racing, wrestling, and various exploits that involved exhibitions of skill and daring, often conducted in the silk and velvet Renaissance clothing he had brought from Paris expressly for this purpose.[161] At night I would watch the mêmêkwêsiwak sneak around camp and collect the gifts some of us would leave for them, and any coins and shiny trinkets that had tumbled out during the revelry. They were shy of humans but loved all that sparkled.

Stewart, with his endless energy for revelry, had set a tone of extravagance and indulgence on his side of the camp. He had seemingly

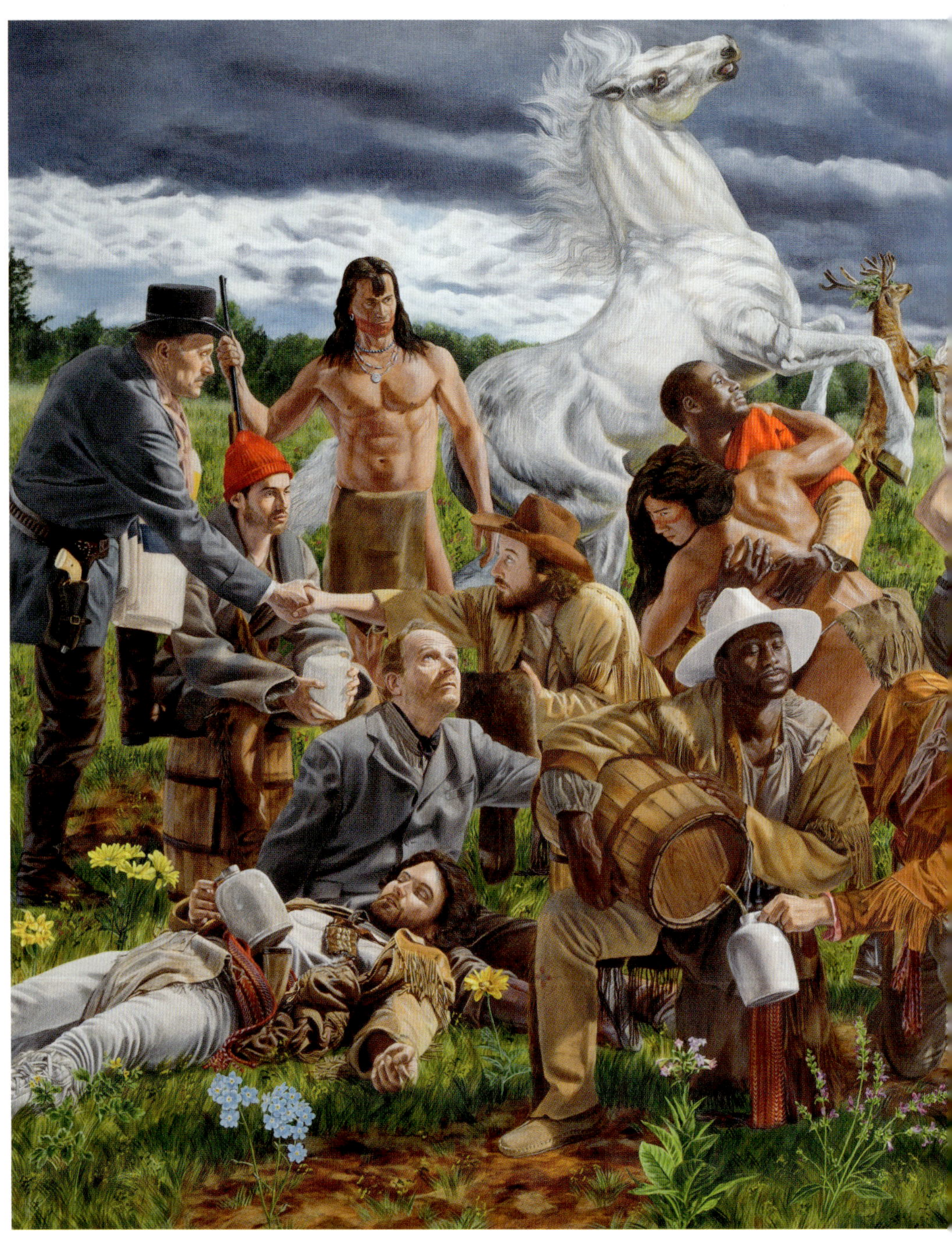

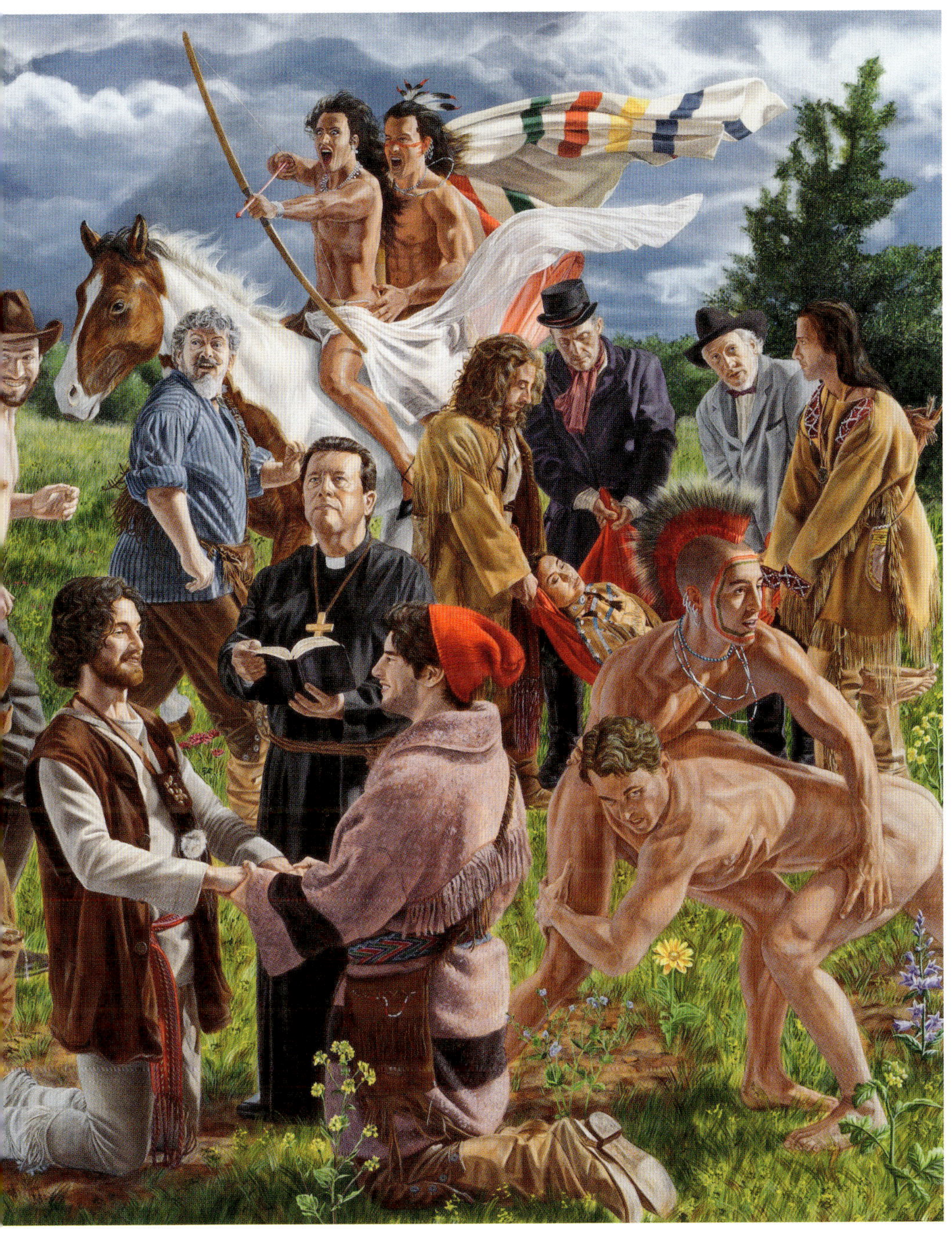

They were full of mirth to be with so many gay creatures of their kind, far away from the prying eyes of those who would denounce them.

Wedding at Sodom, 2017. Acrylic on canvas. 72 in. x 120 in.

unlimited supplies of luxurious delicacies that he would lay out on white monogrammed table linens with silverware and crystal glasses, pulling one after another from the lavishly gilded leather trunks he travelled with.[162] Many of the rough-edged trappers, including Stewart's sweetheart Antoine, loved the theatricality of it all, and it aroused in them a sensitivity and playfulness that I was deeply drawn to.

The artist that Stewart had hired to document his journey, Mr. Miller, was often wide-eyed and embarrassed by the abandon with which the men around him indulged their inner impulses. His paintings captured the boisterous and raucous energy of the journey, but on Stewart's strict orders he was forbidden to paint the physical expressions of love that were ever-present in our camp. For it was still a hanging offence in his homeland, and Stewart was no fool.[163]

When things became too belligerent, I would ride through the gathering, shooting arrows of love hither and thither, dispelling the conflict and laughing at the joyful mayhem that replaced it. By the end of the week, amidst much chaotic revelry, I had tasted over a hundred different flavours of woodsmoke, tobacco, and coffee on the tongues of those who were willing. I had spread the ways of our people and sated my desires with lovers of all genders from all the nations present, gently showing them the many ways that love could be expressed for all creatures—including rock, plant, animal, and earth—for these concepts were strange and new to those who had grown up in the narrow confines of an English world.

One night, I had a harrowing vision, which I hoped was merely a dream. Through a confusion of memory, I saw a beautiful sister ailing with a disease brought with the very blanket she was being carried on. misi-omikîwin had returned and was spreading further west with the newcomers—sometimes by their conscious hand—continuing to scorch our lands with its terrible death.[164] When I awoke, only a fragment remained and was soon banished from my mind by my dismay at Stewart's liberal doling out of the brown firewater favoured by his nation—iskotêwâpoy, whisky—amongst my people. When he did not listen to my

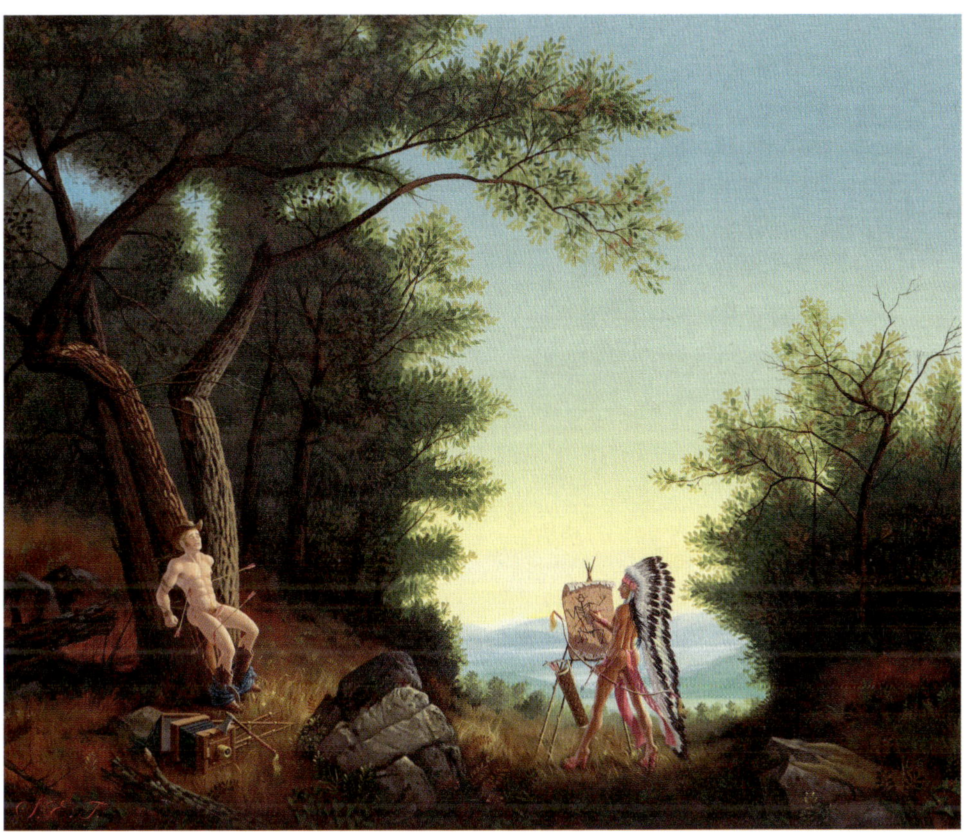

While Miller documented our journey through his gaze, it amused me to paint another narrative of my own. My portrait of Stewart depicted him as a specimen of his "race," as Catlin and so many others had painted us.

Study for Artist and Model, 2003. Acrylic on canvas. 20 in. x 24 in.

OVERLEAF: *I had spread the ways of our people and sated my desires with lovers of all genders from all the nations present, gently showing the many ways that love could be expressed for all creatures—including rock, plant, animal and earth—for these concepts were strange and new to those who had grown up in the narrow confines of an English world.*

Gender Splendour, 2021. Acrylic on canvas. 48 in. x 60 in.

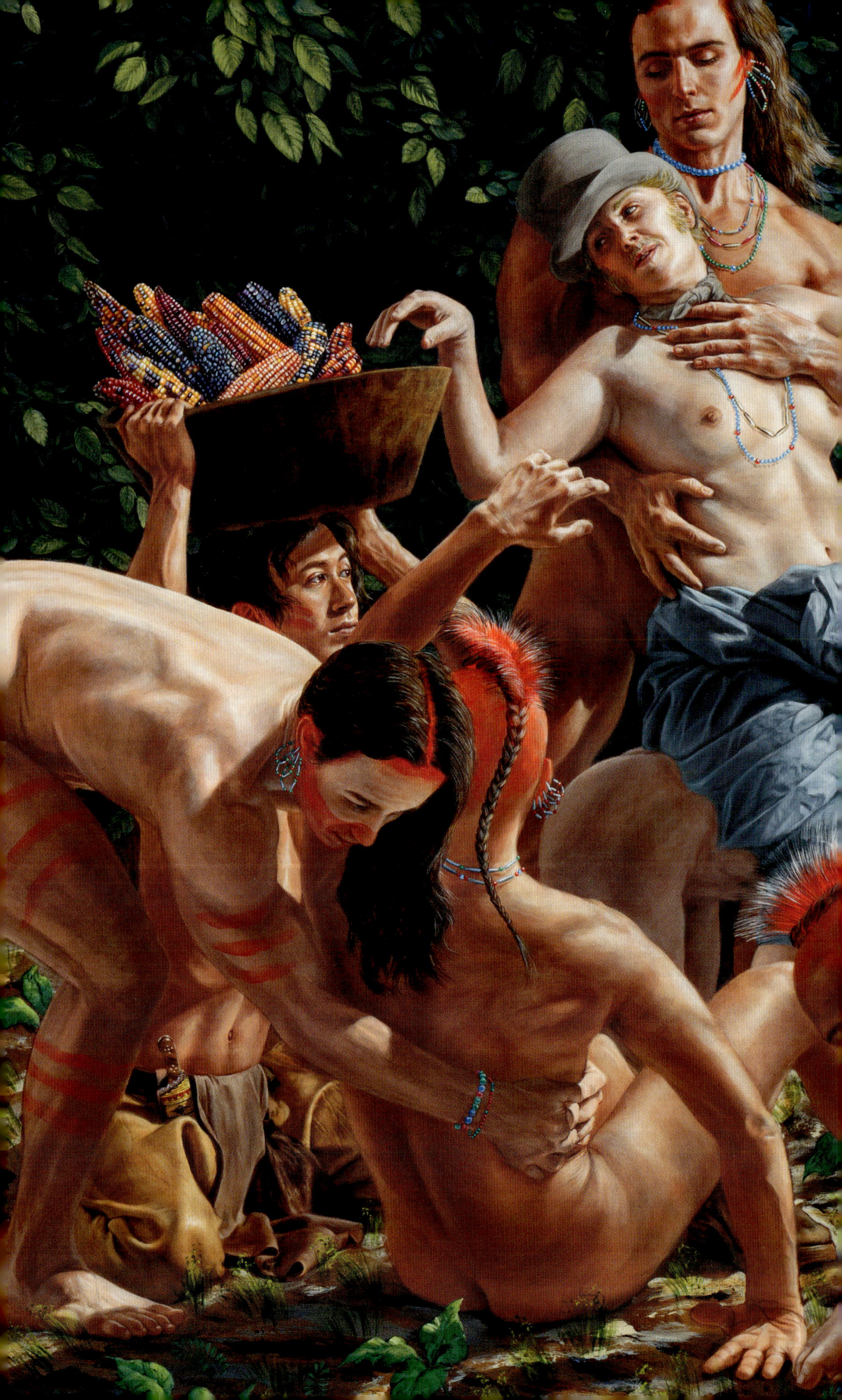

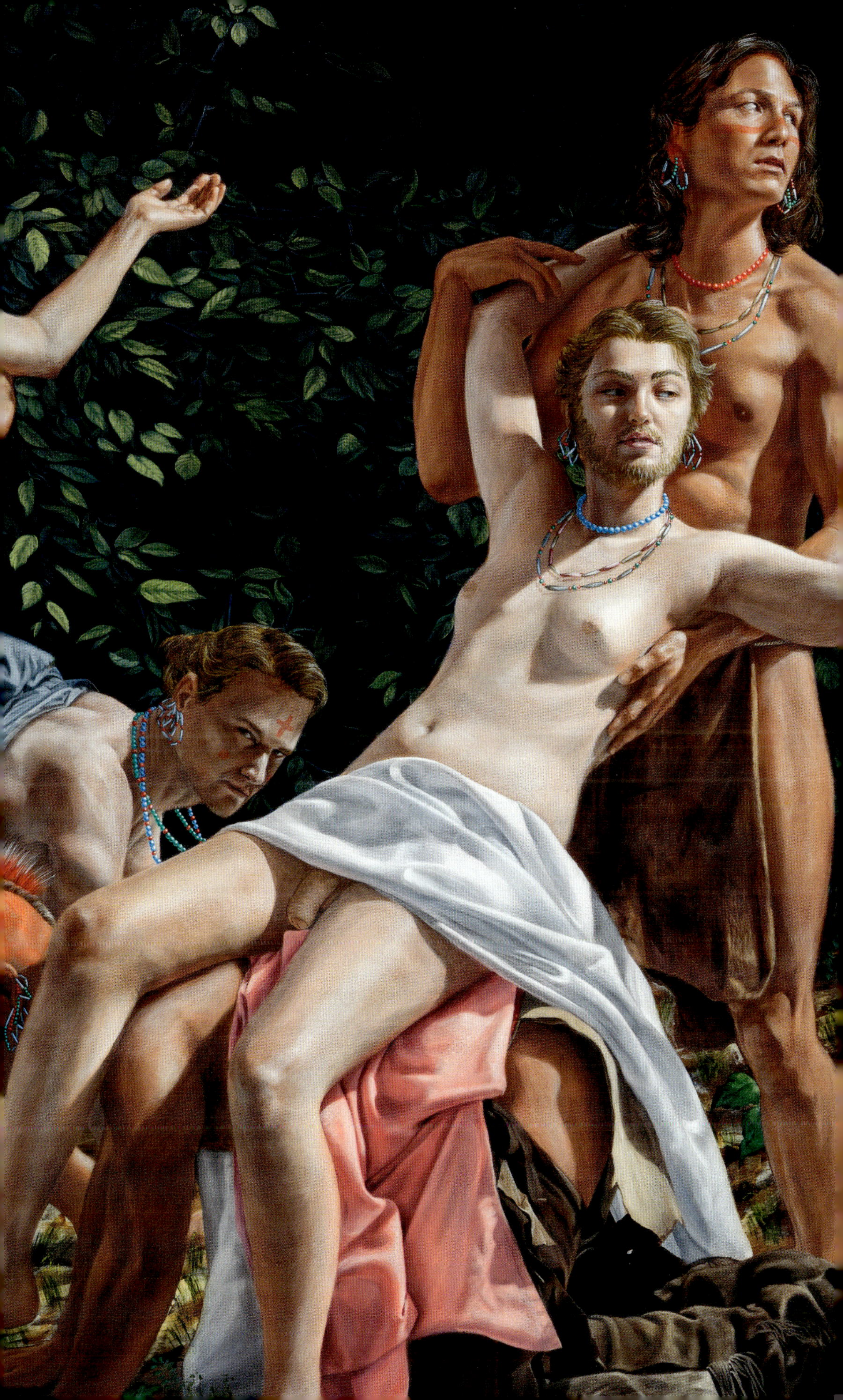

demands that he stop, I smashed the remaining bottles and that was the end of it.

Many of the traders seemed to be open to what I whispered into their ears over the weeks we spent together. From all but a few of my most intractable lovers, I managed to elicit promises and pledges, often moaned in the most heated moments of passion, to practise manâcihitowin, mutual respect for the land and original people. I felt I was gaining ground here at the Rendezvous. New understandings were formed between our people and theirs. The exploration and play between us opened doors that let other, more lasting ideas take hold. The ease with which all of our ways of being had always been accepted in our societies was astonishing to the môniyâwak amongst us.

Our people had a lot to teach theirs about themselves and their true natures. Stewart had already learned we were free to be drawn across vast chasms of cultural and societal differences, curious about each other's bodies, minds, and spirits. The smooth skinned hunters did not restrain themselves from embracing the hairy chests of their trapper counterparts. They had much to say that did not involve words.

Some of our number wished to seal their unions more formally, so we held our own weddings. I myself married, for the week anyway, the lover I most enjoyed: Ned, a sweet, strong trapper whose only pleasure was in giving me pleasure. He, more than the rest of his môniyâwak kin, had truly listened to my teachings, and the scorching heat of our ahcâhk-iskotêwak burning brightly together warmed many hearts around us. We left the dregs of the revellers behind, too enamoured with one another and the newness of our love to notice the foreboding darkness of the gathering piyêsiwak above.

My honour dance and the Rendezvous had been healing for my nit-ahcâhk, my soul. I was able to put aside, for a while, the worry and concern that I carried with me. In small numbers, these newcomers could be kind, and some seemed to understand how to live. But underneath many was a lust for power and sôniyâw, money, that was not our way. I knew that unless it was checked with mutual respect, kistêyimowin, it could bode ill for all humans and living things. Even land should fear them.

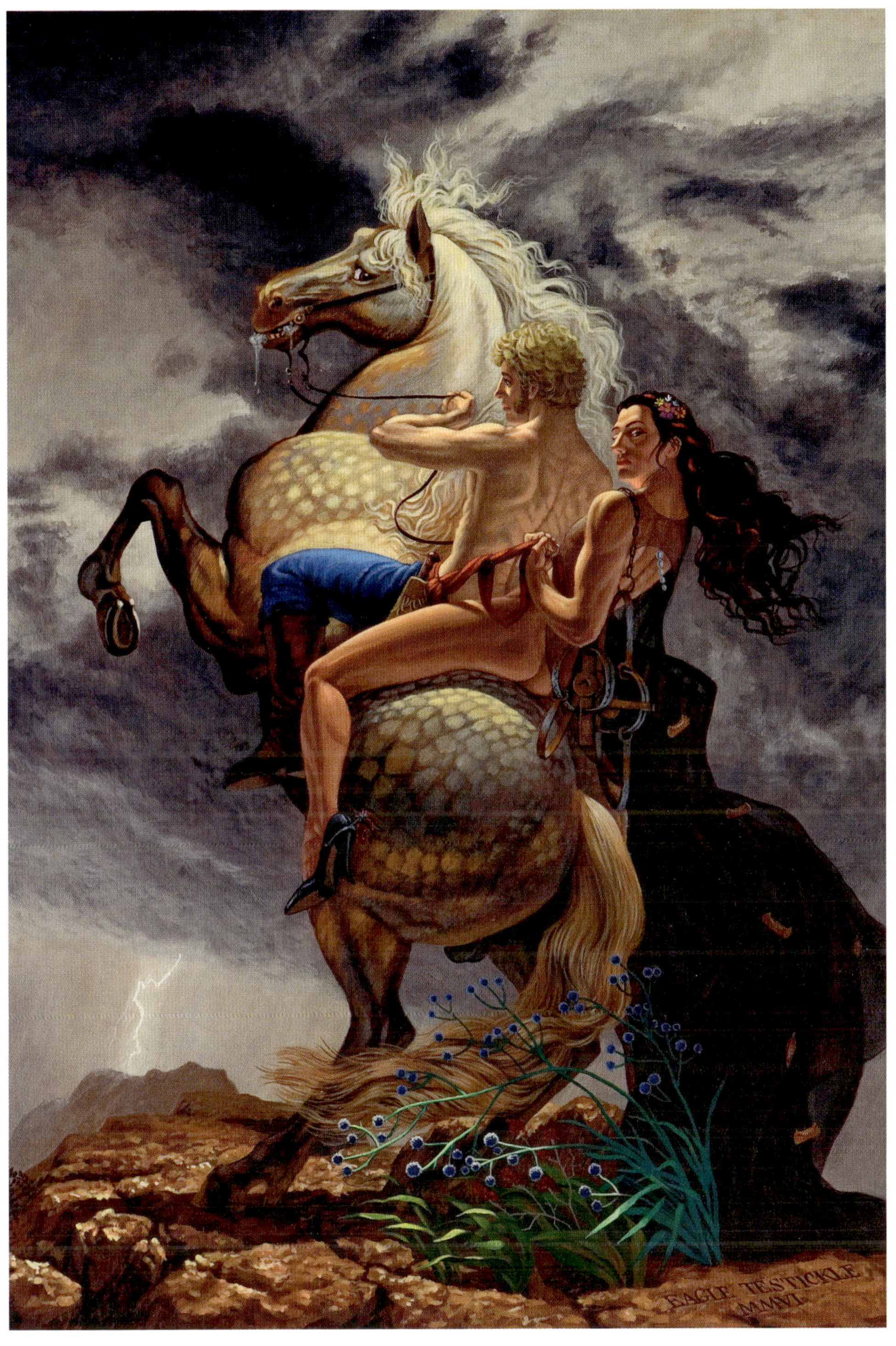

We left the dregs of the revellers behind, too enamoured with one another and the newness of our love to notice the foreboding darkness of the gathering piyêsiwak above.

The Trapper's Bride, 2006. Acrylic on canvas. 28 in. x 20 in.

ᐅᓯᐯᑲᐦᐃᑫᐤ

ᐄᑳ ᑲᑮ ᐚᐱᐟ

The Painter Who Could Not See

The Rendezvous gatherings continued for many years, growing in popularity with the trappers, traders, and my own people; most were somewhat more staid, although not by much. At the last such one I attended, the artist George Catlin found me again, his sketchbook and easel in hand as always. "How magnificent to see you once more!" he enunciated loudly in his continental baritone, clearly for the benefit of others within earshot. "You are simply one of the most ravishing and exquisite creatures that I have ever been fortunate enough to lay eyes upon!"

He brazenly thrust upon me a small charcoal sketch of my countenance that he claimed was a fair and just monument to the memory of my lofty and noble self;[165] it was not quite terrible, but he had not captured my best side and I eyed him appraisingly, wondering what it was he wanted from me.

"When I first met you some years ago, I had no idea of your exotic talents for dance," Catlin proclaimed, almost breathless. "But seeing you dance, your unbridled sensuality was extraordinary! I have a small painting that I made from memory, of your splendid performance, that I wish to show you one day. As I have said before, I would very much like to capture your likeness in oils if you would agree to pose for me."

There was no point in explaining to him that my dance was no performance, but a connection to pimâtisiwin—life—itself. My eyes had wandered off Catlin and his crude sketch and were now undressing the variety of fine-looking kâ-wâsihkopayicik, hairy trappers, and lithe hunters who, having heard Catlin's pompous declarations to me, had gathered around us to watch. Now that he had an audience, he amplified his entreaties to me, his flattery sounding scripted and well worn. "You are," he said, "without a doubt one of the most ravishing and exotic creatures that I have ever been fortunate to lay eyes upon on this continent of North America! Perhaps you could meet me in Mandan country, at the Numakaki village, Mitu'tahakto's, the First Village of the Mitutanika Numakaki? I will be studying some splendidly attired authentic specimens who I have heard still groom themselves in the primitive customs of their forebears. I will use my magic to capture you on canvas and make you look astonishingly authentic, as only I can do!"[166]

Make *me* look astonishingly authentic? As only *he* could do? I tossed my long hair back, and with one hand on my hip, turned to my people and said quietly in nêhiyawêwin, "I will use my magic to capture your amiskosis, little beaver, with nîtakay, my penis, and make you look astonishingly authentic, as only I can do!" Catlin grinned widely, unaware, as usual, that the joke was on him.

The hubris of this atimocisk! Did this dog's ass presume he could begin to capture the intricacies of our clothing, designs, colours, bead- and quill-work, passed down through generations, and fathom the depth of their meaning, much less be the arbiter of what was authentic for my people? It was as Kistahkisiw and Pîsim had said—the môniyâwak were like children, they had no concept of miyo-wîcêhtowin, getting along with others.

"I shall consider your offer. I do have some friends I like to visit there," I replied coolly, winking at the kâ-wâsihkopayicik, letting Catlin know that his hubris was out of place here. It was clear that he had not been taught about humility and kistêyimowin, mutual respect; perhaps he had no relations. But I had been thinking of visiting my Numakaki niwîcêwâkanak pikwîsi kâ-isi-wîkicik for a while and, to be honest, my vanity could not resist the thought of having my likeness painted, even by such a narcissist as this Catlin.

"Can I count on seeing you there then?" Catlin beamed as he rode off, waving his hat at me eagerly.

I nodded, feigning disinterest. "Perhaps."

Catlin held some curiosity for me. What was this magic that he said he possessed? Could these paintings hurt or help my people? I could also use this opportunity to teach him something about tapahtêyimisowin, humility, and kistêyimowin, and perhaps a few other lessons as well involving nîtakay. I thought of my fashion-forward friends, the Dandies, kâ-wâsihkopayicik, in the Numakaki village, whom he wanted to meet.[167] Always adorned in the most meticulous and opulent manner, many of them had attended the Rendezvous and had snagged me or been snagged by me after the dance. What splendid models they would make for this boastful pretender, if only he could do them justice!

mwêscasês, I made the journey with my Numakaki friends back to their village. I brought with me the new robe I was making from the feathers of the spirit beings that had followed the newcomers here, the oskitakosin-okîsikowak. I would indulge myself in one of the weaknesses I had honed from my time with humans—vanity—and make a grand entrance. With some shame, I do confess that I allowed Catlin's lavish flattery to triumph over my better judgement. I had put his lack of understanding of our peoples and our ever-evolving modes of dress out of my mind, musing instead on how spectacular a portrait of me could be.

When we arrived at Mitu'tahakto's a few weeks later, I bid my companions pause so that I could drape myself in my now-completed robe. The oskitakosinokîsikowak feathers shimmered in the sunlight, their iridescent hues accentuating and revealing the most curvaceous parts of my body. The robe draped, flowing slightly, over the rump of my favourite dappled palomino pony, given to me by one of my lovers. The palomino pranced, stepping high with pride, her mane adorned with the same magenta ribbons that decorated my hair. I had arrived.

Whoops and exclamations rang throughout the village as my friends ran to meet me—the exquisitely attired and lavishly adorned kâ-wâsih-kopayicik sparkling at the front of the excited crowd. The children of the village raced around them to reach me first. They shrieked with joy as I dismounted and threw four of them over my shoulders. Everyone exclaimed as I encouraged them to feel the softness of my robe, and they chattered excitedly about all that had transpired since my last visit. Neighbouring villages had been pushed out by the newcomers, and there was much concern about what might impact their village next. The fort beside them brought more hairy faces with each month.

I settled in at the lodge of one of my lovers, touched up my face, and slid into the sexiest high-heeled and intricately beaded moccasins I had with me (one can never travel with too many pairs), and set out to visit some of my old friends with a few of the kâ-wâsihkopayicik in tow. As I walked towards the centre of the village, I saw in the distance a figure painting at an easel, but could not at first make him out. As I approached, I realized it was the painter Catlin, dressed, for some reason, in the garb of an oθaakiiwaki warrior.[168] He looked up from his painting at the sound of my footsteps and beamed when he saw me, then strode forth to greet me.

"What a spectacular sight you are in this magnificent robe! What species of fowl is this to create such a dazzling effect?" Like so many of his kin, Catlin's lack of humility prevented him from speaking in normal tones—everything was announced in his booming stage voice for the entire village to hear. He caressed the feathers without asking my permission. Oblivious to my stern frown and his own deplorable lack of manners, he smiled broadly, bowed, took my hand and kissed it.

"These are oskitakosinokîsikowak feathers, dropped from the skies by your very own spirit beings, Mr. Catlin. Not unremarkably, it is my exceptional talent and vision that has fashioned this stunningly beautiful robe," I said, removing my hand from his and wiping Catlin's spittle off on my robe. How fortunate that I had received the teachings about humility and kistêyimowin, and was not prone to boast as he was.

"I consider myself an amateur ornithologist," he said, "but I have never seen such feathers! While your manner of dress is perhaps contaminated by European conventions,[169] I would be most pleased to assist in attiring you more accurately in the style of your ancestors—who, once formidable, are quickly disappearing from these trackless forests and vast plains.[170] The style of your gown is perhaps European in origin or influence, but rest assured I have many costumes and vestments that I have procured in my distant voyages to the villages across this continent of your cousins, the Hidatsa, the Cherokee, the Siksika[171]—you can wear one of these more authentic beaded buckskins, madame!"

"Eeeeeeee!!!!" exclaimed my friends, who had followed close behind me. Their shock at his disrespect to our individual traditions, and my particularly personal and unstoppably flamboyant style, pierced the air.

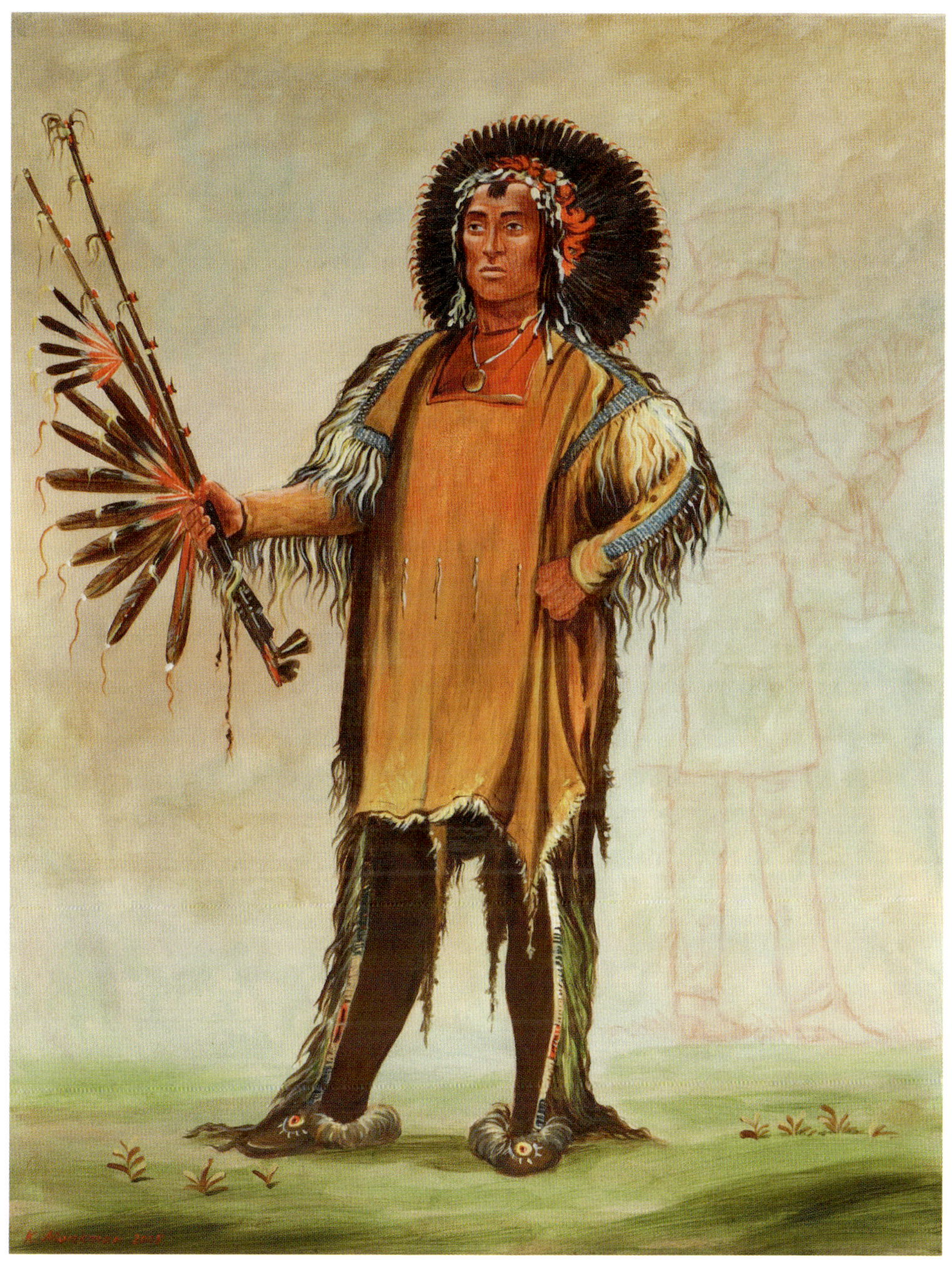

As the chief's image took shape on the canvas, I observed how Catlin had captured the likeness but not the spirit of his subject.

Ha-Na-Tā-Nu-Maūk (Wolf Chief, Head Chief of the Tribe) with Indian Beau 8,566, 2008. Acrylic on canvas. 28 in. x 22 in.

He was now painting Chief Ha-na-tá-nu-maúk, Wolf Chief, Head Chief, who invited me to sit and watch the process along with the rest of the village gathered around to observe.[172] Despite my ruffled feathers, I leaned in to observe as well.

As the chief's image took shape on the canvas, I observed how Catlin had captured the likeness but not the spirit of his subject. As we watched, my friends told me more about how the newcomers were pushing our peoples out. They told me that back east, the yat'siminoli[173] were being pressured to leave their lands by the government of the new country the newcomers had claimed to the south, the United States. I had heard that, last year, the Chahta[174] had been forced to do the same and had been subjected to a gruelling march west out of their homeland. Catlin, with utter disregard for the injustice and anguish his words would cause, informed me that the president of the United States was determined to remove our peoples from the east and force them further west. He noted with the self-satisfied air of one who believes they know everything, that their leader, the one they called Jackson, was likely to win a second term that year, so the removals would surely persist.[175]

There was a long silence, but then one by one, my friends reassured each other that that was impossible, and they soon resumed speaking of other things. Ha-na-tá-nu-maúk stepped from his pose to admire his portrait, of which he was clearly proud, for he had dressed extravagantly for it.[176] Some of my kâ-wâsihkopayicik friends had positioned themselves just behind Ha-na-tá-nu-maúk so that Catlin could not fail to see them. They posed first on one leg, then the other, going back to their lodges and returning with one fine adornment after another, hinting that they too wished to have their portraits painted.[177]

When Ha-na-tá-nu-maúk paused for a much-needed break to water the plants in the forest, a few jostled to take his place, and Catlin, with an excited smile, hastened to chalk in their outlines. But when the chief returned, he took great offence that Catlin would even consider bestowing the kâ-wâsih-kopayicik with the same honour as he would someone of high rank like himself. The kâ-wâsihkopayicik were accepted by their people but not regarded with the same prestige as warriors, so Catlin was made to erase them at once.[178] The kâ-wâsihkopayicik were devastated. They were easily more beautiful and meticulously appointed than any warrior or chieftain. Although they had no eagle feathers and bear claw trophies, their colourfully dyed partridge- and turkey-feathered plumage was understandably attractive to Catlin. They sulked in the background. Mistah-âmow, Big Bee, gossiped and made the others giggle about the warriors who Catlin had authorized into portraits—many of them ex-lovers, for our peoples loved who they chose.

"kahkiyaw nimiyik, he gave me all of it," I heard one say, pointing with his lips at Catlin's still-wet portraits of one of the warriors. I had taught them some nêhiyawêwin, for it was the best language for sexy teasing.

"Neeee, niwîsakawâw, I just pounded him!" giggled another.

Meanwhile, Catlin made a great fuss of soothing Ha-na-tá-nu-maúk, telling him, "I only wished to record the unusual and amusing costumes of these fainthearts and fops,[179] my most noble chief. Of course, their garments pale next to your elegant and gentlemanly figure, for any observer can see that your stylish robe is truly of great extravagance and beauty, the likes of which should be carefully depicted for posterity as suits a man so respected and worthy as yourself."[180] But the chief was not mollified, so they agreed to resume the next day.

We retired with my kâ-wâsihkopayicik friends to Catlin's earth-covered lodge,[181] where he showed us his many completed portraits. "You know that they call me Medicine White Man for my abilities to conjure up such likenesses!"[182] He flipped through piles of paper sketches and canvas paintings, finding at last what he was looking for.

"Here is my portrait of the Second Chief, Máh-to-tóh-pa, Four Bears. A hero of the highest order, no tragedian ever trod the stage, nor gladiator ever entered the Roman Forum, with more grace and manly dignity than he.[183] He even gave me his shirt, depicting the history of his battles. I shall display it in my Indian Gallery, which shall be the finest example of its kind in the world."[184] He showed me another. "Here I have painted

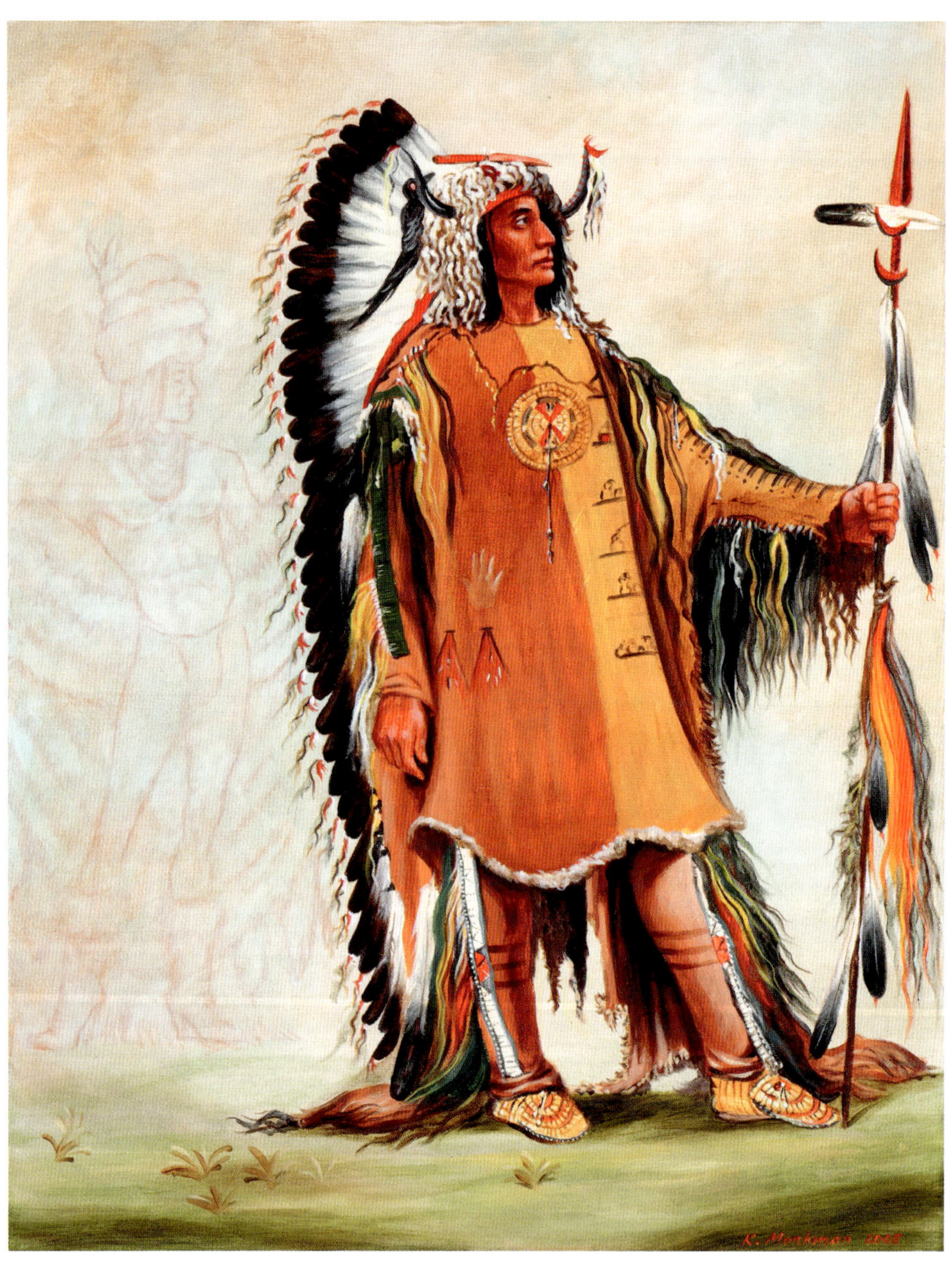

Some of my kâ wâsihkopayicik friends had positioned themselves just behind Ha-na-tá-nu-maúk so that Catlin could not fail to see them.

Máh-To-Tó-Pah (Four Bears) with Indian Dandy 19,233, 2008. Acrylic on canvas. 28 in. x 22 in.

my self-portrait, painting this very painting, surrounded by admirers." He thought the admirers were for him, but I knew Máh-to-tóh-pa personally. He had served his people well, they loved and respected him, and in truth many wished *he* were Head Chief.[185]

Máh-to-tóh-pa did not pay attention to Catlin, but walked past him to me. I held out my arms, with the folded oskitakosinokîsikowak feather robe draped over them to offer him. He nodded, took the robe, and inhaled sharply at its beauty. I had known he appreciated fine things. It was our way to give away our most precious belongings.

He smiled at Sak'wi-ah'ki, his daughter, who had married and had an okosisimâw, a son, with the fur trader who had brought Catlin here.[186] She came over to stand beside him, and he took the oskitakosinokîsikowak feather robe I had gifted him and placed it around her shoulders. I nodded at Máh-to-tóh-pa—it was fitting. As with so many of our women, she had guided, provided for, and many times saved her môniyâw husband and so many other newcomers' lives. They had been fools not to acknowledge her, but her own people understood her courage and strength.[187]

Catlin, of course, did not notice. He was repeating with great fervour the need to document our "proud and heroic elegance of savage society, in a state of pure and original nature, beyond the reach of civilized contamination,"[188] at which point he looked at me, and said, "Look, your honour dance. I painted it from memory while I was staying with the Sac and Fox, but I made it more authentic, you see."

After all of his boasting, I had been eagerly anticipating a resplendent representation, and when I gazed upon his canvas I saw what was clearly an oθaakiiwaki[189] who didn't look anything like my glamourous self. Catlin had underestimated me and assumed I wouldn't know the difference—and even worse, he had neglected my majesty and disguised my glorious body in clothing that did not fit my personal style at all. He had taken a dance of fierce beauty drenched in sexiness, and covered everything up in what looked like heavy dark buckskin. I don't dress to cover up—I dress to celebrate every part of myself!

"ê-nâpêhkâsot, bully, show-off, I honoured you by bringing you into my dance," I said, parting my painted ruby lips into a broad smile. I was angered, but as is our way I did not want him to see that he had vexed me. I batted my long lashes without looking directly at him. "Do you not have eyes to see? I am magnificent in my nakedness! And what do you mean 'authentic'? I made this outfit myself"—gesturing at my dreamcatcher bra and my loincloth, a wisp of pink gauze fluttering from a waist belt of small colourful beads that barely concealed my prodigious mitakay. "How much more authentic can you get?! êkosi, that's it!" I flashed him an even more dazzling smile in an attempt to veil my indignation, and strode abruptly out of the lodge into bright sunlight, my kâ-wâsihkopayicik friends following behind me, flouncing in shared outrage.

I needed to cool down and be out of sight of this môniyâw who called himself a painter. I left the village in a huff, accompanied by my kâ-wâsihkopayicik friends, and made for the waterfall nearby, one of my favourite places to relax and connect with my mihdeke,[190] niwîcêwâkanak pikwâwiyak kâ-sâkihâcik, and niwîcêwâkanak pikwîsi kâ-isi-wîkicik. They worked hard at shifting me out of my dark mood, and knowing me well, they succeeded. They re-enacted, in exaggerated pantomime, the various positions and combinations of wild group sex positions with the warriors from the village, each *tableau vivant* growing more complex and outrageous until they all collapsed under the physical strain of a gyrating human pyramid of arms, legs, and rainbow-coloured plumage. I laughed until I couldn't breathe, and my sides ached for days after. That was our way.

In the moment, I didn't know that this would be the last time I would see many of them, for misi-omikîwin would soon sweep through our lands yet again. But I cannot think of that now—I have lived too long, loved too deeply, and lost too many. There is grief enough in my tale.

When we returned to the village that night, I made it a point to snub Catlin entirely. Underneath his fine words it was clear that he had a disregard for that which he did not understand.

Catlin knew he had offended me, and the next day he arrived at the lodge bearing many lavish gifts of silver for each of my kâ-wâsihkopayicik friends, and presented me with the most opulent of the gifts, a large silver medallion. Naturally I rejected it, refusing to extend my hand. Suddenly, without asking me whether he could touch me, he slipped the ribbon over my head. The gleaming silver pendant drew enthusiastic whoops and cheers from the group, but cool reserve from me.

Catlin attempted to mollify me with the same honeyed promises he'd made Ha-na-tá-nu-maúk, flattering me that I was unique in his travels. He was always lavish with his praises—excessively so. I would come to learn that he was extremely thin-skinned and could be vicious when his ego was even mildly affronted. He was a narcissistic egomaniac of the worst variety, twisting words to flatter the one to whom he spoke, making sure he was advantaged in every situation. At this point, I knew him well enough not to trust him fully, but I admit that my present human form caused me to feel human pleasures and fall prey to human weaknesses—he seduced me with his promises.

He had grand plans to tour his paintings all over America and Europe. He envisioned a "Berdashe" performing as a curiosity in his "Indian Gallery." If I would be that creature, he assured me, he would paint me properly to make up for the homely portrait that had caused me such offence. The good people of London and Paris would be honoured to meet me, and he might even be able to arrange an audience with the King.[191]

I knew that perhaps his sincerity was questionable, but why shouldn't I believe these wondrous things about myself? Besides, this could be an opportunity to convey to the King the violence with which our peoples were being pushed aside as his subjects moved west across these lands. Perhaps, in speaking to him, I could bring about some positive change—or at least slow the rapacious incursions of the môniyâwak.

But I would not travel by ship. I could not stomach the long dreary voyage, and I suffer terribly from seasickness on these artificial ways of crossing the big waters. kinanâskomitin to Kisê-manitow I'm a shapeshifter, so I never have to vomit inside a bucket trapped in a wooden vessel tossed about on the rough seas. I told Catlin I would meet him in London—if and when it suited me.

ᐁᑯᐢᐱᕽ ᑲᑮ ᐃᑐᐦᑌᐦᐅᔮᐣ ᐄᑕ ᑲ ᐅᐦᒌᒋᐠ ᐅᐢᑭ ᐅᑭᔮᑫᐘᐠ

When I Travelled to the Newcomers' Homelands

After leaving Mitu'tahakto's, my Numakiki friends, and that irksome painter Catlin, I returned to my own people and any ideas of visiting London quickly faded from my mind. We began to hear more disturbing reports of our relatives to the south being forced from their lands, the ᏣᎳᎩ ᎠᏰᏟ,[192] Mvskoke,[193] Chahta, Chikasha,[194] and yat'siminoli. We heard fragments from traders that could not be believed—entire nations being forced to leave their territories.

Deeply disturbed, I walked into the forest, found a wide, smooth rock, and let myself connect to askiy. I called to the kaskaskacîscacayak, the sparrows that belonged to this land, not the ones the newcomers had brought. As they had travelled from north to south, they had witnessed terrible things. They told me of great lines of our peoples being forced to walk. They told me how the people were starving and how those that could go no further were left at the side of the road, even the children—especially the children.

After the kaskaskacîscacayak left, I stayed in the forest a long time, alone. askiy felt different—the energy I would normally feel in connection with the land was muffled, weaker. I felt myself weaker as well, for we were all connected. Were so many of our people no longer able to pray? Or worse, were so many no longer in this world?

What was missing in these European nations that allowed them to impose their will upon other nations and commit such cruelty? The challenges I had foreseen were now upon us. nistês, my elder brother, had told me that I might not be able to alter what was to be, but perhaps understanding the newcomers' ways could aid me in helping my people? iyiniwak, Indigenous peoples, still held power in our territories, but the settlers were encroaching more and more. I thought again about Catlin's offer to join his troupe in Europe. If I could travel there to better understand these Europeans, perhaps I could help my people face their fearsome onslaught?

I began my journey across kihcikamîhk, the ocean, at the mouth of misti-sîpîhk, Kaniatarowanénhne, which the newcomers had named the St Lawrence River. I whistled to a team of passing dolphins, who agreed to pull me through the turbulent sea foam on a giant scallop shell, but being free creatures accustomed to play, not work, they quickly tired of this. For some time, I enjoyed the thrill of my aquatic chariot, but when they whistled a joke in their language that I was heavier than a blue whale I abruptly released the reins, my vanity mildly affronted. Resignedly, I assumed the shape first of my brothers, the kihcikamêwi-kinosêwak—the cod—my swift, silver body slicing through the water like a hot knife through moose fat. Where once there was so much cod that our Beothuk relatives had only to dip baskets into the waters and haul out enough fish to feed a village, our kihcikamêwi-kinosêwak relatives were now much depleted. In assuming their form, I absorbed their collective memory. It was to be the first lesson of my journey to the lands of the Europeans: first the Vikings, then the Basques, then the Portuguese, the French, and now the English, had taken millions of our cod relatives to fuel their global trade empires.

As I swam east, I ran into net after net dangling from English boats. To escape being ensnared, I transformed into a blue whale, chuckling to myself now at the dolphins' joke, finding a pod to swim with for a while. They sang their joyful songs to me, and I answered in their language. Humans had much to learn from them. They changed their course to join me in my journey across the ocean. I revelled in the deep interconnected wâhkôhtowin that the whales had with one another. Constantly communicating, they knew immediately when one was in distress and were able to help me avoid any trouble. I sank into the freedom of their culture, leaving the human cares aside for the journey, knowing I would face them again soon enough.

As I approached the English shores, the water became brown, mixed with filth of all kinds. To avoid it, I leapt out of the water, transforming in mid-air to a peregrine falcon so that I might survey the stinking muddle of stone and grime that was the city of London—the largest city in the world—from the grey clouds above. I got as close as I could before I choked on the foul air and careened into a secluded alcove where I could shift again into human form.

Once transformed, I emerged, coughing on the smoke from a million brick chimneys blackening the sky, and leaned against a sooty wall, taking a moment to compose myself. I had attired myself in my best attempt at recreating the nondescript dress of the women of these lands. I quite liked the silhouettes but the tightly laced stays and heavy layers of starched petticoats were a hindrance to movement and breathing, which was already difficult. I had toned down my usual flair and finery, as I wished to observe these creatures before they remarked upon me.

This grey citadel was the centre of the creeping pestilence of colonization. They called it the centre of civilization, but to me it was a sprawling mess of mud. All around me were fine buildings surrounded by small hovels. My senses were assaulted by a cacophony of chaos. The stench of rotting refuse that seemed to ooze from every corner. The constant hammering as more buildings were added to this warren of dark streets, and the clatter of gold and silver carriages and tradesmen's-cart wheels on the cobblestones. All of it under the soot-laden fog that hung heavy and dank, blocking the sun.[195] I tried to feel the vibrations of the earth under the slippery surface beneath my shiny black heels, but the echoes of ancient buried cities blocked the connection. mwêstas, I heard that over a thousand people died every week in this town, and I could well imagine it.[196] I had only been there a few days and already I ached for the open skies and spruce-scented air of home.

People as numerous as mosquitoes, in all manner of dress—elegant and ragged—rushed about.[197] Rich women in their many fine and many-layered costumes seemed weak and fragile compared to the iskwêwak I knew; they seemed only able to walk assisted by men or servants, their little dogs prancing behind them.[198] Uncaring, they walked past wretched mothers who begged in the streets with their children, living in conditions we would have considered unfit for our dogs. I had never seen such callous selfishness! In our lands, those who had food to give would share and be respected for it. To hoard while others suffered was a shameful act.

As for the men, they barked at each other, shouting aggressively to all beneath their station. And they looked even stranger now seeing so many of them all together, "they [did] not shave the upper part of their mouths, but let the beards grow long, and this [made] them look fierce and savage like our . . . dogs when carrying black squirrels in their mouths."[199] At every second street corner drunken louts gathered in restless groups, singing or fighting. I was told that there were eighty thousand common wives trading pleasure for coins in this city of commerce.[200] Some said they were there to ensure the safety of married women, but I could not fathom that men would take from women what they did not wish to give. I had been here not one day and already I was much confounded; everything was backwards here—instead of relationships, they had transactions.

The city was divided by a dirty river which stank of the shit from over a million arses. It was horrifying to witness nipiy, the source of all life, defiled in this way. I sat on the stone-enforced bank to let my tears drop into her dark, oily surface as an offering to help clean and heal her spirit.[201]

I finally chanced upon handbills for "Catlin's North American Indian Collection with their war dances, songs, games and war-whoops" at the Egyptian Hall, Piccadilly. I inquired the way and, enjoying being in two-legged form again, walked—or rather wobbled—there, in my high heels, across the unfamiliar surface of the cobblestone streets; I was excited to see iyiniwak from home. When I got there, instead of being comforted by the people, languages, and creatures of my faraway land,

I was heartbroken to see an iron cage near the entrance imprisoning two of the most woebegone maskwak I had ever seen. Ribs showed through the bears' dull and dirty fur, and they barely raised their glassy eyes as they sniffed at the air when I approached.[202]

"maskawisîk niwîcêwâkanak, be strong, my friends," I whispered. "namôya kinwês êkwa ta-pêhoyêk pâmwayês kwayask kinosêwak êkwa mînisa ta-mîciyêk, you won't have to wait much longer before you can eat all the fish and berries you want." I scratched their thick and matted necks. They grunted in recognition, imploring me to leave this grey and cursed land at the first opportunity before life was drained out of me too.

I followed the strange moaning and an irregular drumbeat coming from the hall, and stepped inside. Blending in with the crowds at the back, I saw Catlin dressed as a Sac warrior and his ginger-haired nephew as a Sioux chief disguised with copper skin paint, along with some twenty scruffy English men and "round-faced boys, wearing long wigs" and bizarre clothing.[203] They were making a confounding, horrendous racket, like weasels having their balls cut off, and prancing about in some ridiculous burlesque manner. A modest crowd of fine gentlemen and ladies looked upon this dreary spectacle, believing it to somehow be a representation of our most noble cultures.[204]

Catlin was overjoyed to see me. "You've been sent to save me! You're a huckleberry above the persimmons here! What fresh excitement!"[205]

That evening, I dined with Catlin over yet another meal of stewed calves' feet and baked potatoes that made me homesick for paskwâwi-mostosowiyâs, buffalo meat. The sight of Catlin and his self-serving ways immediately made me feel that coming here was a mistake, but I would do what I had set out to do, then return to my people. He told me his woes with sobs and self-pity over the ensuing days. He owed a great deal of money to his father and others, and attendance to his "Indian Gallery" was waning.[206] The sorry spectacle had played itself out. mwêscasês, Catlin packed up his three hundred and ten paintings, the crate loads of iyiniwak clothing, the precious belongings he'd taken from our peoples,[207] and sent the ailing bears to the Zoological Gardens, where they soon passed over ahcâhko-sîpiy, the river of spirits in the night sky, finally free.

Catlin had received a letter from Maungwudaus, a Mississauga Nishnaabeg, who had been educated by, and adopted the ways of, those who believed in the man on the cross. The English called him George Henry. Like me, he wished to build compassion and understanding for his people amongst the Europeans, who had been impacting his people far longer than mine. He thought that, by studying Catlin's exhibit, he could make his own show to earn money to help his people.[208] Like me, he also thought that if he showed our ways to the Europeans and created a shared understanding, it might open their eyes and halt their relentless onslaught.

Catlin wanted to remount his "Indian Gallery" with me, Maungwudaus, and the rest of his family participating as living paintings, *tableaux vivants*, in Paris. He told me that he thought the show would be much more successful with "genuine Indians," and wished us to perform some sort of play-acting of councils, pipe-smoking, war dances, scalping, and such. I was not at all sure about this endeavour, or my involvement in it, but I had come here to learn their ways, and learn I would. I also yearned to escape this damp, claustrophobic warren and would go anywhere to further that end.

When Maungwudaus, his wife Uhwessiggzhiggookwe, Woman of the Upper World, and his family arrived,[209] it was a huge relief to be amongst iyiniwak once more. Maungwudaus had great intelligence, an ease of manner, and was tall and handsome, which did not hurt either.

Before leaving for Paris, we accompanied Maungwudaus's half-brother Kahkewāquonāby, who the Europeans called Peter Jones, to petition the newly crowned young Queen Victoria in her big stone lodge, Windsor Castle, to give their people official title to their own land.[210] Kahkewāquonāby's young niece Nahnebahwequa, who the English called Catherine Bunch Sonego, also attended.[211] I could not see why they must come to this leader to ask for a piece of paper saying what we all knew to be true, that their territory was their own, but the Anishinaabe

Nation in the east had dealt with the Europeans far longer than my people had, so I heeded their council.

The young Queen was not the handsomest of women, but she had a great many warriors standing guard with swords and guns.[212] She also had a tall, elegant German man by her side—her husband, Albert. More than once during our meeting I caught her stealing lustful glances at him. We were briefly introduced to the couple's young children: a little toddling girl and an oskawâsis not yet old enough to walk. The baby stared at me, his hazel eyes curious and bright as an attendant explained that he was Prince Albert Edward, heir to the throne. The Queen hardly looked at us, or her own children as they were brought out, nor when they were quickly ushered back out of the hall by their nursemaids. She only had eyes for her consort.[213] He was sufficiently handsome for a European I suppose, but I remembered kihêw's counsel long ago and refused to become distracted, at least not now.

I told the Queen of the encroachment of her people onto nêhiyânâhk and the way her people were harvesting animals as if they were some kind of commodity, something that could be owned and sold instead of being respected like relatives with whom we were in wâhkôhtowin. I explained this all as patiently as I could, for these newcomers were like children; even their leaders had no understanding of the most basic concepts of manitow wiyasiwêwina, the sacred agreements with the waters, land, animals, and one another, including those not yet born. Her eyes held mine for a brief moment before returning to rest upon Albert, but she said only, "We have heard you. Next."

Maungwudaus then told the Queen how her people, British settlers, were increasingly encroaching upon and cutting down timber around the Credit River; these new arrivals were not respecting the pre-existing laws of our lands, or even the agreements they had made with Maungwudaus's people when they reached a decision to share them.[214] Nahnebahwequa stood beside him, silent and watchful, for in a few years she would be back with petitions of her own. Stifling a yawn, and with a little wave of her hand, the Queen said only, "We have heard you. Next."

Maungwudaus, Nahnebahwequa, Kahkewāquonāby, and I left Windsor Castle unsure of whether or not our words had been heard—or what, if any, change would come from our efforts. "I will try again," Kahkewāquonāby said. "We are the keepers of our lands and laws, they must understand." I took note of how little respect our laws were given, or even mutually agreed-upon covenants between our peoples and theirs. I would need to warn my people to be vigilant in their dealings with these nations, for their thinking was foreign to us, as was ours to them, although very few of them seemed to note it, much less care.

mwêscasês, I accompanied Maungwudaus and his family to the docks at Dover. On our way, Maungwudaus spotted what he thought were mêmêkwêsiwak, little people, in a hedgerow along the side of the road, and whispering, he pointed his lips in their direction. They dressed differently here, and were bolder, since they revealed themselves to him so easily. They motioned for us to follow them, but I cautioned Maungwudaus that faeries—as that is what they were, not mêmêkwêsiwak—were not to be trusted. I put down some coins for them and we continued on our way.

After sending Maungwudaus and his family off on the ship to Calais, I took note of the sailors loitering by the docks. Normally, I might dally awhile and seek out some rough caresses, but I still could muster no joy in this blighted nation. I stepped into the shadows, transformed into a gull, and flew to join my companions in Paris, where I hoped there would be more light, and success with my quest.

When I reached Paris, I circled, surveying the city spread out beneath me. It had been more artfully designed than London's haphazard sprawl, but was still an overwhelming place. As I flew lower, I choked on the smoke from a million coal stoves and saw that, like in London, people threw their filth into the streets that ran "zig-zag and abut against each other as if they did not know which way to run."[215]

I landed and quickly fashioned myself in the style of the Parisian ladies I saw strolling about. Dressed again in discomfort, but with more elegance this time, I adjusted once more to the loudness of cities, my ears assaulted by the rattling of the cabs and other vehicles over the rough stones, and the rumbling of the omnibuses.[216] Traders shouted at me from all sides, offering me fish, flowers, money, or pleasure . . . As I walked amongst the people, I noticed several loud crowds milling around places they called cafés. It was in these cafés that news circulated, and public opinion formed, and that kings were expelled, and others were set up on their thrones.[217] I heard voices openly criticizing their rulers, something I had not noticed in England, where people seemed more ground down by the grim machinery of industrialization.

I reunited with Maungwudaus, his family, and Catlin in the rooms they had rented outside the centre of town. It was so good to see Maungwudaus that when I scooped him into my arms I plucked him right out of his moccasins, and he let out a loud fart that made us all laugh. What joy and relief to be amongst my own people again in these strange lands. Warm embraces were exchanged with his wife, Uhwessiggzhiggookwe—their number included four friends, Saysaygon, Keecheussin, Michimaung, and Aunimuckwuh-um, as well as their six sons.[218]

Catlin had also hired additional Anishinaabe performers, including Not-een-a-akm, a handsome young half-Anishinaabe, half-French translator who was the occasional dancer and dandy of the troupe.[219] In addition, Catlin had brought along an Iowa family who had travelled here from across the sea. Among them was a broken-hearted young couple, Shon-ta-yi-ga and O-kee-wee-me; they were mourning the loss of their two children who had died during this European journey.[220] Catlin's obsessive ambition and disregard for others was astonishing. I heard him complain to his nephew Burr about losing not only the children, who had attracted the biggest audiences, but also their parents, who had taken time off performing to grieve.[221]

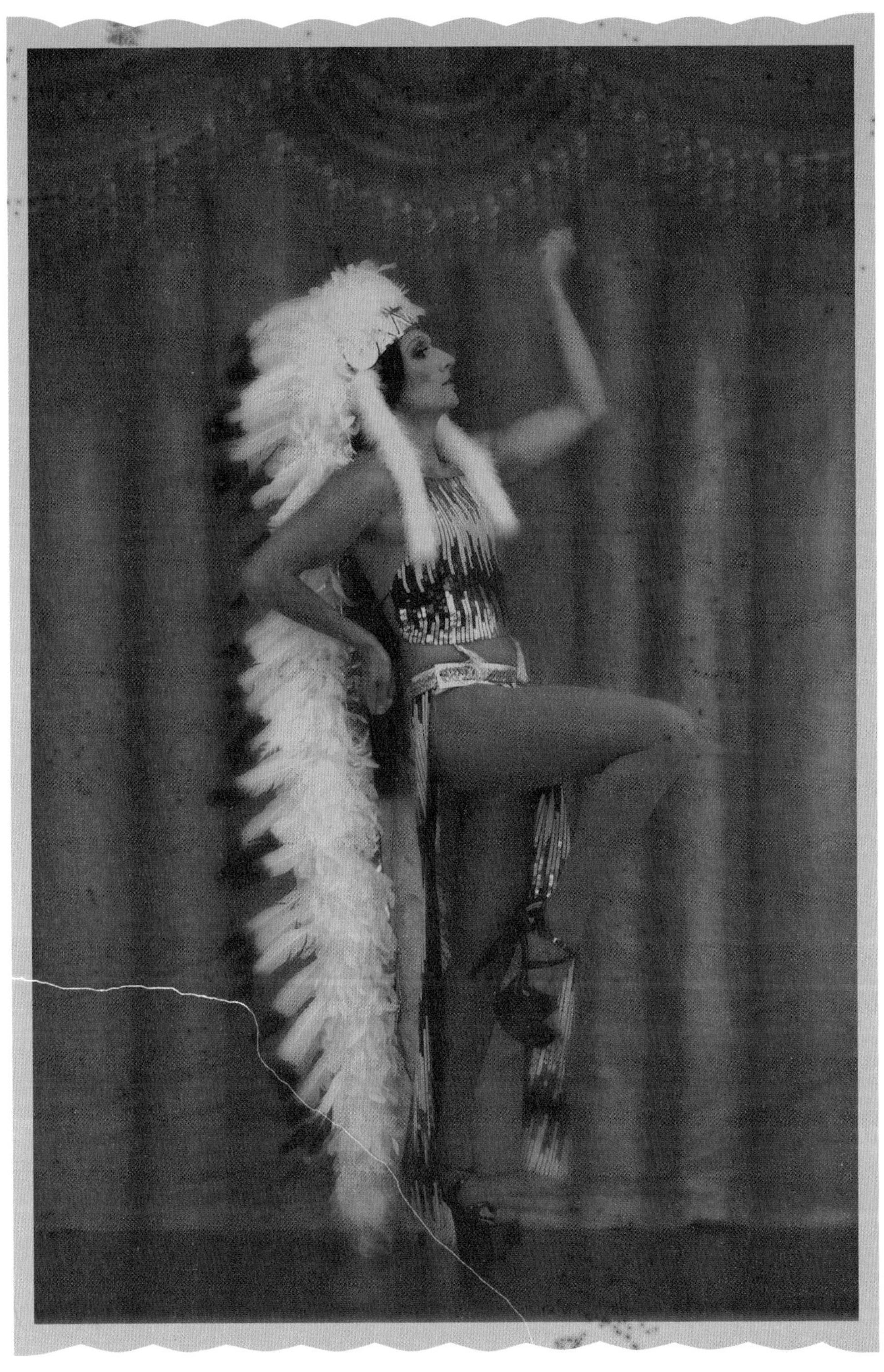

Molly, my Penawapskewi sister, exchanged clothes with me, for we each admired the other's style.

Kent Monkman in collaboration with photographer Chris Chapman and makeup artist Jackie Shawn. *Miss Chief as Vaudeville Performer* from the series *The Emergence of a Legend* (4/5), 2006. Series of five photographs, chromogenic prints on metallic paper. Photo size 4.5 in. x 6.5 in., framed size 16 in. x 13.25 in.

Catlin's show was every bit as awful as it had sounded when he described it to me in London, but Maungwudaus was there, so we could laugh together at the ridiculousness of the performance. I focused my mind on what I was here to do and carefully watched the audience, learning more about their ways night after night. I hoped that this knowledge would translate to a better understanding and fair treatment of my people back on miskinâhk-oministik. I also enjoyed the company of Not-een-a-akm, whom the Europeans called Alexander Cadotte or Strong Wind. He and I had hearty and frequent encounters between performances, sometimes incorporating the costumes of Catlin's shows into our re-enactments of his re-enactments. But ours, of course, were much more enjoyable.

Catlin presented me as the main attraction, "The Mysterious Exotic Berdashe from the Wilds of North America," and Maungwudaus and I laughed at the image of me on the posters he pasted about town. Catlin was unrelenting in his attempts to get me into more "traditional" attire. He heaped flattery, but by now I could see through his lavish praises. I knew they were but thin ruses to get me to wear the beautifully crafted, heavily beaded ceremonial Lakota woman's dress he had traded for baubles in one of the villages he had visited,[222] but I made my own outfits and did what pleased me, as always. I was firm, and his star attraction, so he eventually did not push it further.

When it came to the actual performances, we followed the lead of Maungwudaus to make sure we did not break any ceremonial protocols. We performers cobbled together what we had seen of the hokey pokey and ballroom dance with our own steps, giggling to ourselves the whole while. But the French exclaimed at the "authenticity" and applauded with gusto every night. It wasn't just the supposed authenticity that enticed audiences to our show, however; they also assembled there for the pleasure of receiving shocks and trying their nerves . . . all looked on with amazement and pleasure.[223]

One night, an extravagantly jolly gentlewoman in the flush of admiration and desire unclasped her own necklace and many other rather costly

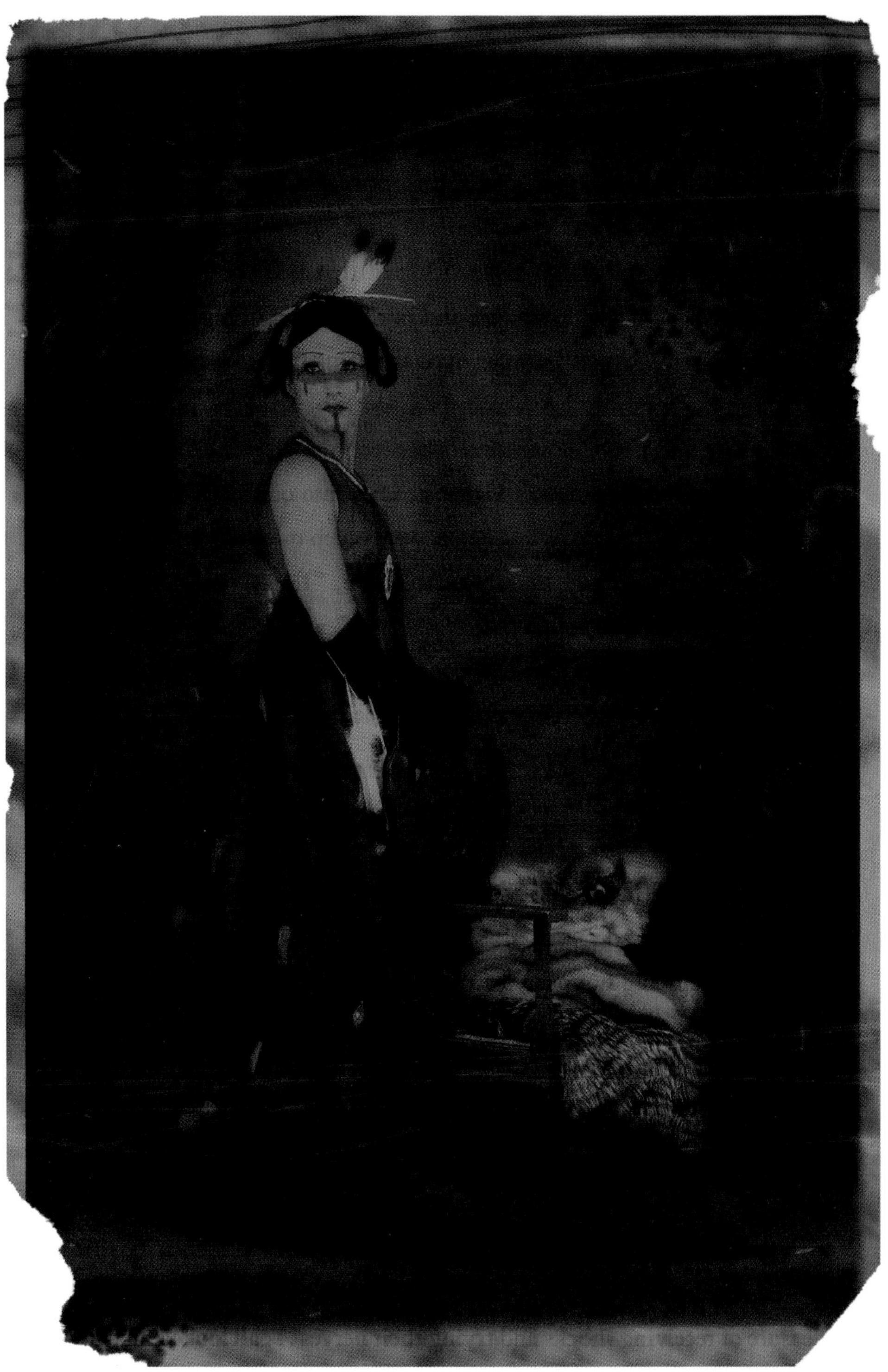

Molly taught me some of her act, but we both found it drained our souls to be here in these cities of stone and soot, so long disconnected from the lands that nurtured our spirits.

Kent Monkman in collaboration with photographer Chris Chapman and makeup artist Jackie Shawn. *Miss Chief as the Trapper's Bride* from the series *The Emergence of a Legend* (5/5), 2006. Series of five photographs, chromogenic prints on metallic paper. Photo size 4.5 in. x 6.5 in., framed size 16 in. x 13.25 in.

adornments and pressed them upon Not-een-a-akm.[224] In a flutter of excitement, many other ladies of similar wealth and stature began to do the same until Not-een-a-akm was draped with all manner of finery.[225] Not-een-a-akm indulged the women with winning smiles, flirtatious looks, and over-the-top flattery,[226] and then later met up with some of their more fashionable husbands in a discreet location.

As for me, I had my pick of elegant lovers lined up after each performance. In my dressing room, I bathed and deloused the heavily perfumed filthy creatures before allowing them to introduce me to their more delectable depravity, some of which exceeded even my own far-reaching limits in the art of lovemaking. But these distractions were keeping me from more important encounters.

I eventually made my way to the court of King Louis Philippe and made a strong case for my people. He listened, but threw up his hands in the air, telling me in aggrieved tones that it was no longer him that I needed to talk to, but rather the frigid Queen across the channel. She had thwarted his advances and his hold on New France had long since faded. I politely assured him that the Queen was by no means frigid, but perhaps her rejection was of him, as was, after all, her choice—upon which he became irate and screamed for the guards to escort me out. They promptly did so.

As my heels clacked down the long palace hallway, I attracted the attention of certain circles, including the rather intense, passionately moustached poet Charles Baudelaire, who flirted shamelessly with me once we were outside the palace gates. He was soon followed by another, the painter Eugène Delacroix who pulled me aside, whispering, "Baudelaire is a fine poet, but take him not into your bed, for he has the great pox, and has already infected half of our number."[227] I paid him heed, for our people were plagued enough by European diseases, and although I am immortal, I did not wish to risk being the cause of bringing more sickness to our shores and my people.

Delacroix would come and sketch us sometimes, and invited me to his studio to sit for him.[228] He spoke of the philosophies of the Europeans

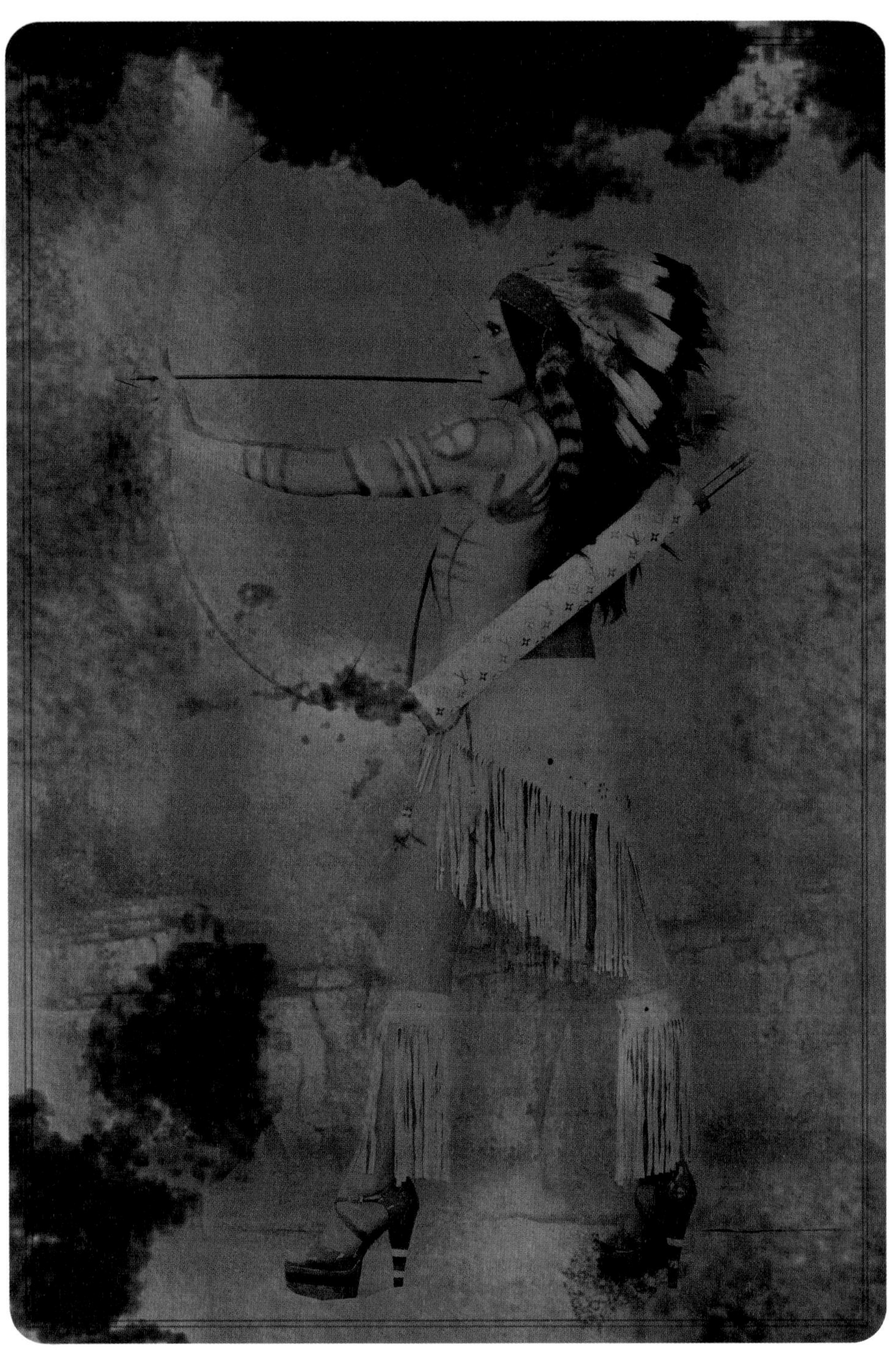

We all knew that Catlin was exploiting us in his fanciful depictions of "the dying race," but we all had our own reasons for being here. And although many of our people would be lost, we would survive.

Kent Monkman in collaboration with photographer Chris Chapman and makeup artist Jackie Shawn. *Miss Chief as Performer, Catlin's Sharp Shooter* from the series *The Emergence of a Legend* (1/5), 2006. Series of five photographs, chromogenic prints on metallic paper. Photo size 4.5 in. x 6.5 in., framed size 16 in. x 13.25 in.

and I told him how we viewed the world—of miyo-pimâtisiwin, living in balance and harmony with all around us, and how that was under siege by those from his nation and others. We discussed how our different systems of laws and governance worked and agreed that greed was indeed the most destructive of human vices. Interludes like these made Paris more bearable, but I missed my niwîcêwâkanak pikwâwiyak kâ-sâkihâcik lovers, and the skies of home that went on forever.

I was becoming fed up with Catlin's incessant self-serving ambitions, and was unconvinced that performing pantomimes for the Europeans led to any greater understanding between our cultures—in fact perhaps the opposite, for the majority regarded us as not much more than curiosities or circus animals. That scribbler, Dickens, insulted the Anishnaabeg who had visited England before us, calling their ceremonial dances "miserable jigs after their own dreary manner" and much worse.[229] And the French were no better. The main attraction, at Catlin's direction, was always the scalping. I refused to re-enact something that was not my custom, but the others did as Catlin asked, for they were desperate to earn enough money to send home to their people and to return home themselves.[230]

To see how other iyiniwak survived here, I shifted forward through time slightly to visit Molly Spotted Elk, a fearless Penawapskewi sister on whom I modelled some of my performance attire.[231] Like me, she found it drained her soul to be in these cities of stone and soot so far from the lands that nurtured our ahcâhk-iskotêwak, our soul flames. She dealt with the strangeness by studying at the Sorbonne and earning money to send back home to her family. She taught me some of her act and we exchanged clothes, for we each admired the other's style, but in these cities, disconnected from the lands that nurtured our spirits, we were losing our strength and purpose.

When Catlin later asked us to walk the streets in clothing pieced together from here and there, as advertisements for his show, I tantalized the most handsome of passers-by with a most alluring dance Molly had taught me, which elicited many interested glances and winks in the direction of the park from certain admirers in the audience as they tossed silver coins. When Catlin tried to take the coins from me, I snatched them back, shouting at him that they were for our people. The hornswoggler callously told me not to bother, for in his view we were to soon face "the doom that would almost seem to be fixed" for our "unfortunate race."[232] In outrage, I told him that as long as one of us was living there was no doom, despite the best efforts of his countrymen, but he would not stop. He continued to belittle us as "an interesting race of people, who are rapidly passing away from the face of the earth."[233] I remembered our laws of tolerance and attempted to remain calm, but when he called me a "champion of the mere remnant of a poisoned race,"[234] I struck him with my bejewelled handbag and blackened his eye.

The time to leave was growing closer. One day I looked into the eye of an anguished man slumped against a wall in the shadows. In his hollow eyes I saw the north reflected—he was far from home. Two wet tracks down his burnt umber, sun-hardened cheeks. I sat down beside him. He told me that he was from the northeast of miskinâhk-oministik and he'd been persuaded to bring his family to be part of an exhibit, like a zoo animal, with other human beings from different lands. They had not been inoculated from smallpox as was the law at that time and his two youngest children had just died. "Leave while you still can," I begged him, as I gently tucked a roll of francs into his sealskin bag. He stared out without seeing me. "It's too late." I hoped that he was wrong, but later I found out that he had taken ill and passed over to the other side along with his wife and their other children.[235] The weight of his pain sickens me still.

The plagues of Europe took so many of us. One of those who helped us when we most needed it was the strong, wise writer who understood our situation better than most, George Sand. She was niwîcêwâkanak pikwîsi kâ-isi-wîkicik, one of us. She came to visit Shon-ta-yi-ga's wife O-kee-wee-me when she fell gravely ill with consumption, a disease that would ravage my people later, in the children's work camps—but I get ahead of myself.[236]

George brought O-kee-wee-me the flowers she loved best, white cyclamen, and sat with her to give her comfort in her last days.[237] Sweet O-kee-wee-me battled her sickness as best she could, while her husband, Shon-ta-yi-ga, stayed by her side day and night—singing, praying, and burning cedar, for there were none of her traditional medicines here. But the illness was deep in her lungs, and after losing her children earlier on this ill-fated voyage, she no longer had the will to cling to life.[238]

As O-kee-wee-me began her journey to ahcâhko-sîpiy, I held Shon-ta-yi-ga close and cried with him, but he was inconsolable. I saw O-kee-wee-me's ahcâhk-iskotêw hover a moment, mingling with the sweet plumes of cedar smoke, the smell that connected to home, before slipping through the open window towards the stars.

The people of Paris had fallen in love with the tragic romance of O-kee-wee-me's story, and paid for an elaborate Catholic funeral in Montmartre.[239] Shon-ta-yi-ga had lost all will, so he allowed her to be buried, encased in a stone house in a land to which she did not belong. He took a cab through the winding roads of the city to sit by her grave every day and leave her offerings.[240] He longed to depart the country that had caused him so much pain, but doing so would mean leaving his dear wife's burial place behind.

Most of Maungwudaus's party had fallen ill with misi-omikîwin, and soon Saysaygon, Michimaung, and Aunimuckwuh-um would also cross over ahcâhko-sîpiy.[241] So many of our number sickened and died in those crowded, grey European cities, just as they were dying back on our lands. And there would be more to come.

I was crushed by the sadness of these losses in the confines of this strange place, but I determined to stay and try to keep Maungwudaus's spirits somewhat buoyed until he could return home. I was suffocating living amongst so many thousands and these child-like women and big-stomached, strawberry-nosed men who cared only for extracting more from their workers so they could further line their pockets.[242]

Then, one afternoon, I idly picked up a journal of Catlin's that he had forgotten in the tearoom of our lodgings. I was curious about his journals, for he was always drawing and scribbling about us, so I glanced through the pages. He had some quick sketches of me, but no paintings because, in order for him to paint me he kept insisting I wear some Salish dress, or a Sioux shaman's ceremonial headdress—sacred items he should not even be touching, let alone have in his possession.

His exoticization of us had become more and more desperate as revenues fell, and he began resorting to greater extremes to pay the bills and find fame. As I deciphered his scrawl, I read his most offensive ideas for putting us—the original people of miskinâhk-oministik—into some sort of park, as a monument to his memory in which "refined citizens" could view "for ages to come," a "nation's Park, containing man and beast, in all the wild and freshness of their nature's beauty."[243] I drew a breath. I should have known such a thing was possible for a man like him to imagine. To him, we were as specimens in a museum or zoo, and I was done with it!

Furious, I flipped through more pages and found the most vile descriptions of me, written by Catlin, whom I now knew to be the most two-faced of villains. To my face, he flattered me, for I was his most lucrative performer, but in his journal he described my glorious honour dance as "one of the most unaccountable and disgusting customs in Indian country . . . I wish that it might be extinguished before it is fully recorded."[244] I was outraged, not at his petty lack of understanding and disapproval—he was, after all, too shallow to comprehend the complex sexualities and gender spectrums accepted by our nations—but that he had been flattering me falsely all this time and I had allowed it. I could blame no one but myself, which was even more infuriating.

I flipped through further pages, seeing more of his usual self-aggrandizing comments about him saving a dying race through his gallery. I threw the journal back on his desk. Out fell a handbill, promoting Mr. Catlin's forthcoming lecture. He was always going on ad nauseam about representing our "truly lofty and noble race," saving "the Red Man," and railing against the evil Europeans who were settling on our lands, displacing us and driving our nations to extinction, but this handbill was promoting his lecture on the "advantages of emigrating to the Valley of the Mississippi, with accounts of the Gold Regions of California, illustrated by Colossal Maps and Paintings."[245] He had even scribbled in the margins "a dying nation," "cruel savages!"[246] He was, in fact, interested in us only as far as we could make his fortune. Now he had found a more lucrative avenue: hastening our demise himself.

I opened Maungwudaus's door. He was sitting in the dark with his curtains drawn, staring at the wall—his body was alive but his dreams and reason for living were no more. His wife and three of his children—including their youngest, still a baby—had all left him for the ahcâhko-sîpiy.[247] Maungwudaus's ahcâhk-iskotêw had left with them, and he was but a shell of his former self. I sat down beside him. "It is over. This place is not for us, even to visit. It is time to go home." He nodded, his body clenched and heaving, crying without making a sound for a very long time.

I held him into the night, and the next morning I used some of the money that I had found in Catlin's room and booked Maungwudaus and his remaining children passage on a boat that would take them home to the land to which they belonged,[248] but I worried for their safe passage. I had seen how the merchant boats sailing to miskinâhk-oministik were full of the wretched hordes of Europe's outcasts, including criminals escorted directly from prisons who shuffled on board while still shackled. These were the people Danny had warned me about. I did not understand the concept of prisons until much later. I would see how they could break even the strongest of our people, and do worse than that to our children.

ᒥᑐᓂ ᐲᑐᐢ

ᑮᑳᐧᔭ

ᑳᑮ ᐃᓯ ᐚᐸᐦᑕᒫᕽ

Our Ways of Seeing Were So Different

I was anxious to leave these strange lands inhabited by people who valued money over the kinship of wâhkôhtowin, but before I left, I wanted to say goodbye and properly thank some of those who had shown kitimâkêyihcikêwin, compassion, to us in Paris. So after seeing Maungwudaus and his children off at the docks, I called on George Sand to thank her again for her kindness to O-kee-wee-me in her last days. George's warmth and good spirits were a balm to my grief and she convinced me to visit her salon that very afternoon. My spirits were low and I was tired of this place, but George coaxed me—"You have come all this way," she said, "and still have not met the most interesting people in Paris." She had one of the finest salons in the city of light and had invited many fine and artistic souls who might actually have the compassion to hear, and the minds to understand, the plight of my people. Some would also have the means.[249]

In her elegantly appointed apartment that afternoon, I was overjoyed to see Antoine and Stewart amongst the varied and colourful guests George had assembled for a lunch of tartare, caviar, and escargot. They had returned to Stewart's estate in Scotland to settle some affairs and then come to Paris to visit old friends, buy more costume silks and finery, and hire another painter. They were planning to attend another Rendezvous and Miller had refused to return.[250] They implored me to join them, but I told them I must decline as I had more urgent matters to attend to.

"Teach your people," I urged Stewart. "You have seen and understood our ways. Tell them that the lands are to be cared for, not stripped bare. These actions of your countrymen will have stark consequences for their descendants if they do not learn."

Stewart held my eyes and inclined his head. "I will try with all my conviction, I assure you. For if they do not learn, they will destroy us all." He turned to Antoine, who had been listening sombrely, for he understood more than Stewart what was at stake.

"They are like dangerous children," said Antoine softly in nêhiyawêwin, with an undertone of sadness and anger in his voice. I nodded.

It was not only how these Europeans regarded the land and all creatures as theirs to command—they also believed they could command how their people loved. If they were ever discovered, Stewart and Antoine could be killed for loving one another.

Antoine pinched my ass to break the seriousness and, teasing each other, we began to reminisce about our playful days in the mountains. We were soon squealing with laughter as Antoine told the most lewd and sexual jokes—the ones that sound harshly vulgar in English or French, but are joyfully hilarious in Cree.[251] I switched to French to share my encounter with Mistâpêw, mixing in nêhiyawêwin for the juiciest details. George Sand blushed and dabbed sweat from her forehead with her handkerchief, while Antoine's eyes widened with incredulity until I could no longer restrain my laughter. Not knowing if I was serious, he stared hard at me, then started to laugh so hard he attracted the attentions of a rather intense, passionately moustached Frenchman. I recognized him from my time performing with Catlin; it was the poet Baudelaire. As he strode over to join us, I quickly whispered to Stewart and Antoine of his affliction, hoping to spare them and their many lovers back on our shores from yet another disease.

Baudelaire begged to know what we had found so hilarious just moments before. Antoine warned me not to even try to explain, but I valiantly attempted to translate. Antoine almost wet his trousers, laughing even harder than he had laughed before as I tripped over the juicy, joyful innuendos of nêhiyawêwin with the harsh crudeness of English and French. My feeble attempts to convey the playfulness embedded in our language to a now mortified Baudelaire only produced another eruption of hysterical laughter from Antoine and giggles from me. Baudelaire stared hard at me, unable to comprehend my meaning, then changed the subject, proceeding to dog me with questions about Catlin, art, and representation. Stewart and Antoine soon lost interest and, sighing loudly with exaggerated boredom, beckoned the butler for more absinthe. I too wilted under the onslaught of direct questioning and soon made my excuses. My laughter with Antoine had been healing for my soul, and helped me put aside my grief for a few moments. This was our way.

I shifted the web of our world and folded it to step forward through time and bring back with me someone I knew should be there—Heȟáka Sápa, or as the English-speakers called him, Black Elk.[252] He was a wičháša wakȟáŋ, a medicine man or holy man, and heyókȟa, sacred clown, of the Oglala Lakota people.[253] He was from a time two generations or so yet to come, and while one has to be careful when folding the web of time and space—both for the delicate nature of the spatial and temporal dimensions, and the frailty of the individual experiencing the travel—Heȟáka Sápa was unperturbed, for he had travelled much in ceremony. Being a wise man of great vision and interests, he was very much at home with the artists and intellectuals at the salon. He enjoyed meeting George Sand immensely, and told her of the winkte, people of his nation who had been designated as boys at birth but lived as women, and how they were considered sacred by his people.[254] With one eyebrow raised and a long puff on her cigar, George remarked that she wished her nation was as advanced as his, and then, dropping her voice an octave, inquired whether he had any stories about Mistâpêw.

Very few of them understood our meaning when we spoke of spirit, but perhaps through a greater understanding of physics they might come to see the wâhkôhtowin of all things and therefore treat the earth and all our relations with kistêyihtamowin, respect. Thinking that perhaps I could help their science to catch up with ours before it was too late, I introduced Heȟáka Sápa to another of George's guests, William Huggins, a scientist in the field of astronomy. A cherubic-looking man with a far reaching mind, he listened to Heȟáka Sápa with deep interest, recognizing him as a person of great knowledge. Heȟáka Sápa described to him how everything is alive, with a spirit, and how we are all related to all of creation, including plants, rocks, water, and the land. Huggins's eyes widened as Heȟáka Sápa explained how human beings came from behind what Huggins knew as the Pleiades. We are all of the stars, and all connected by that same material to one another.

Huggins later became a founder of the field of astrophysics; this conversation with Heȟáka Sápa led him to conclude that stars are made up of elements also found in life on earth, and that there is a "common chemistry" to the universe.[255] Huggins was one of the few scientists of his time to be open to new—actually very old—ways of seeing the world, but based on his work, others with flexible thinking would eventually be able to catch up to the elders among our peoples.[256] But I am getting ahead of myself.

mwêscasês, Eugène Delacroix sought me out to tell me that he had made a new drawing of one of our performances, and asked me if I would like to visit his studio to see it. By the way he arched his left eyebrow slightly and placed his hand on the small of my back, I knew where this invitation to "view his drawings" would lead. "Are you still using that weary old line, Delacroix?" remarked a rich, wry voice. I turned to take in a striking man with a shock of coal black hair standing behind us, dressed even more flamboyantly than Stewart in a waistcoat as green as the sea draped with massive golden chains, and a robe of deep purple.

"I believe I acquired it from you, did I not, Dumas?" Delacroix answered with a harder than necessary cuff to the man's shoulder. I winked at Delacroix's twinkly eyed, tawny-skinned friend, turned to Delacroix and told him I should be very happy to peruse his drawing the very next day. "Meet Alexandre Dumas, irrepressible republican, generous friend, fashion-forward rake, and hero of all the romantic readers of Paris!"[257] toasted Delacroix, holding his champagne glass high in the air. Dumas had an astounding breadth of knowledge; with detailed knowledge of medicine, he told me of the recent cholera outbreak in his city. Dumas's most amusing anecdotes were about his rival, Honoré de Balzac.

Delacroix's studio was temporarily housed in the horse stable behind his new apartment on the rue de Furstenberg. He had recently been commissioned to decorate the chapel at Saint-Sulpice. With the horses and central skylight, it reminded me of the Numakaki lodges where the glittering kâ-wâsihkopayicik had presented themselves to Catlin. Seeing in his paintings of Moroccan street scenes how entranced Delacroix was by colourful and inventive attire, I was certain that, if he could accompany me to our lands, he would find the elaborate flamboyance of kâ-wâsihkopayicik fascinating subjects for his paintings. We spoke about this, and also about the centralization of power of the European systems, and the riches they were pulling out of what they called their colonies, including our land, miskinâhk-oministik. I told him that his people and the English had no idea of the value of what they were destroying in the process. We were of the same mind that greed was indeed the most destructive of human vices.

I asked him why the Europeans were so passionate about painting images of the world and interpreting them in this flat, empty way, as if in an attempt to capture our lands and make them theirs. I mused aloud to him that perhaps some of our shamans were right—perhaps the paintings did rob something of our lands and souls[258]—but his cool cleverness could not parse my meaning. His brooding eyes frowning intently, he continued to talk of artistic inspiration, and what he called the "classics" and the concept of the ideal while he railed against his rival Jean-Auguste-Dominique Ingres's pursuit of Neoclassical perfection.[259] I told him that to us, the surface of things held little meaning and Romantic or Neoclassical styles meant even less. We appreciated beauty, but it was the spirit in everything that took precedence. Delacroix's eyes widened excitedly as he began a rebuttal, but rather than talk endlessly about the perfection of symmetry versus the spirit, I threw down a challenge: each should paint his own interpretation of

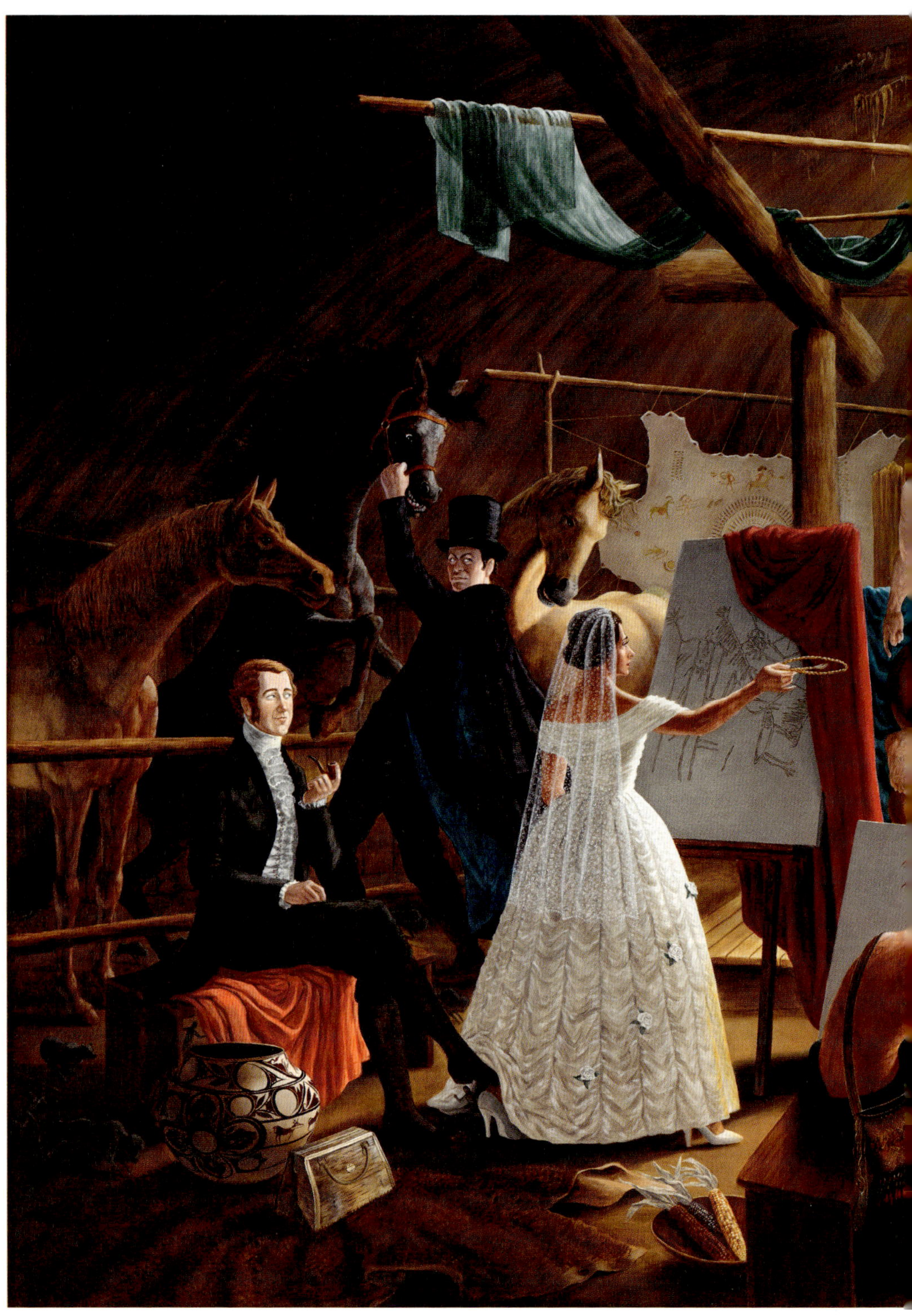

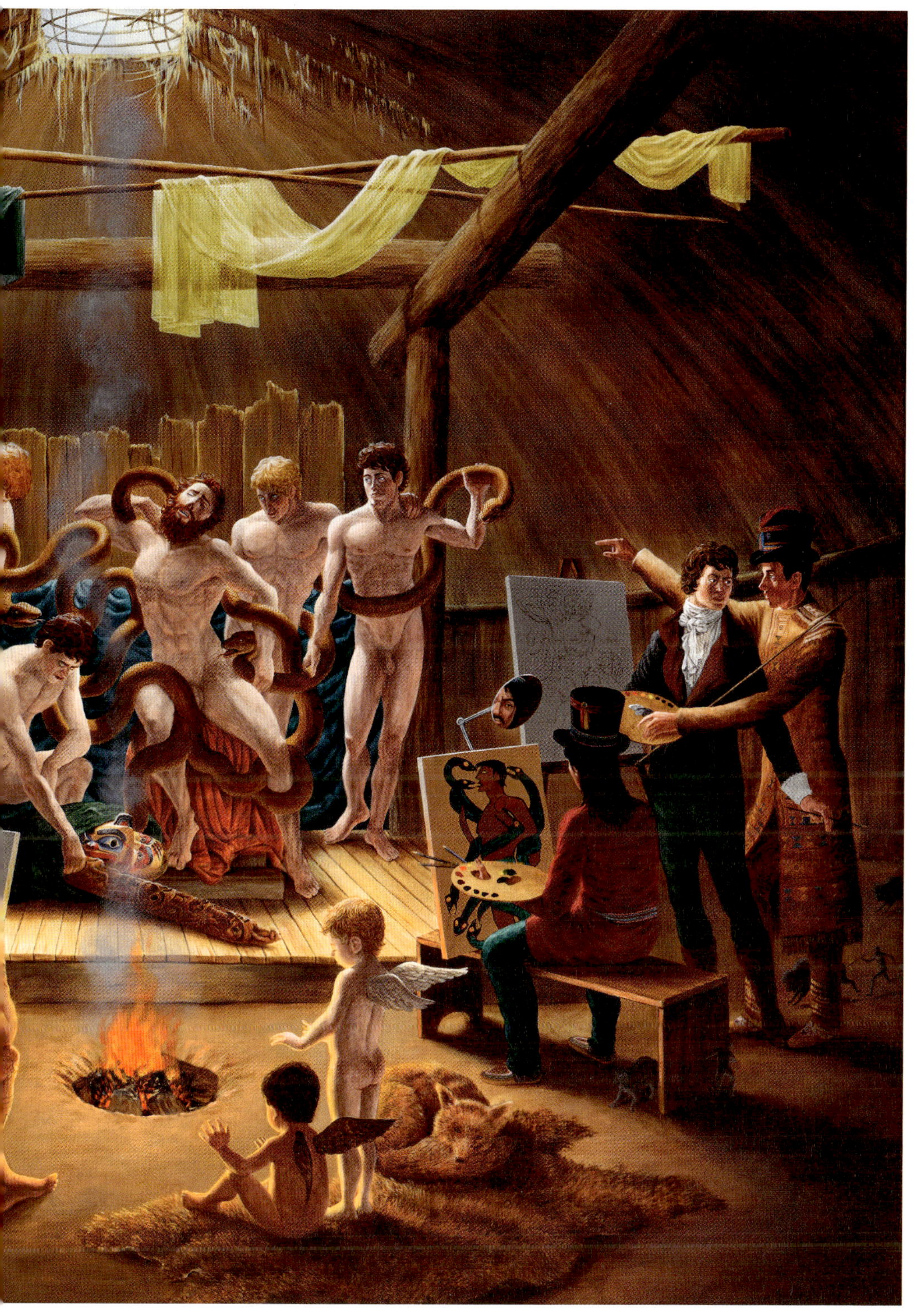

I threw down a challenge to Delacroix: each should paint his own interpretation of the same scene, and at the end we would let the paintings argue amongst themselves.

The Academy, 2008. Acrylic on canvas. 72 in. x 108 in.

the same scene, and at the end we would let the paintings argue amongst themselves.

For our artistic experiment, I again lightly parted the veils of time, and brought back Caillou, the delectable model the sculptor Auguste Rodin would use for his Adam a few years hence.[260] Antoine and Stewart then arrived, and with them they brought some muscular Basque fishermen and French sailors they had found while "promenading" on the wharves.

We passionately debated about how to best pose our magnificent models but I eventually acquiesced to Delacroix, it was his land, after all. He was obsessed with art made thousands of generations ago, especially Laocoön, a sculpture made by the Roman Nation. He wished to recreate the sculpture's pose, one that he claimed was the classical ideal of human agony. But he and I had our own interpretations. I had seen the misery of my own people, which held no beauty for me. And my people's spirits were not constrained like those of the men Delacroix now posed. To me, the twisted struggle of their pose seemed to capture the repressed and tortured spirits of so many môniyâwak living in Paris and London.[261]

To make our challenge more interesting, I invited through the folds of time one of our great artists who would in the future capture spirit with his brush, Miskwaabik Animiiki, Copper Thunderbird, or, as some knew him, Norval Morrisseau.[262] Like Heȟáka Sápa, he was no stranger to travelling in the middle worlds. "Boozhoo, Miss Chief!" he grinned, blew me a kiss, then focused on his work, his brush making serpentine lines on his canvas.

I'd brought in my helpers, the mêmêkwêsiwak, the little people from our forests, whom Delacroix adoringly called "sweet putti." Attracted by the openings in time, Wîsahkêcâhk had looked in with wry amusement. It was good to see nistês again, in coyote form. He watched for a while then yawned, licked his paws, and curled up for a nap. Stewart observed from the corner with wry amusement how shamelessly his love, Antoine, flirted with us all.

Delacroix had the tricks of a conjuror. He was able to capture, on a flat surface, the shadows and curves of flesh and bone, and especially the full, luscious lips of the bearded Zeus. Miskwaabik Animiiki, our visionary, on the other hand, had captured that which only he could see. For him the group did not matter, only the central man and his struggle with his demons. He saw himself in the writhing mass of muscle and tissue, devoured in the most complete way by serpents, for in our peoples' way of seeing the world, sex is part of everything and everywhere, as natural as breathing.

I smiled to myself thinking of how the next time I travelled back to the period long before the visitors arrived on miskinâhk-oministik, I would carve this scene currently before me at the place we leave our messages, art, and stories—onto the rocks at apisci-sîpîsisîhk, Milk River. I often left my artworks as signposts there, and at other places. For those who could read them, it would help them navigate their strange and wondrous future.

I focused on capturing the môniyâwak's spirits in paintings, as I had so often done on rock. I had seen how artists could wield great power over their subjects. If I could also harness this power, perhaps this was one more way to help with my intercourse with the môniyâwak. If they could feel what we felt through my art, perhaps this understanding would reduce the harm they were inflicting on miskinâhk-oministik.

I painted directly from spirit, but Delacroix's mastery of the light and shadow was impressive—it lifted the men's bodies from his canvas, but it did not hold their ahcâhkwak, their souls, as Miskwaabik Animiiki's and my paintings did. With my brushstrokes, I captured the sound of their souls, but only Wîsahkêcâhk could hear them. If the newcomers could truly look at our artworks, they would see deep beyond this plane into the truth of existence.

Delacroix was not able to understand what I or Miskwaabik Animiiki were painting, but he declared the competition a draw, for he had the grace to recognize depths of art beyond what he could comprehend.

As we painted, Delacroix and I had been exchanging glances. The challenge and the intensity with which we both worked in the sexually charged atmosphere of scrutinizing the nude male bodies had created an unrestrained lust in both of us.[263] Wîsahkêcâhk, always attracted to such rousing emotions, lingered after the others had left. "Enjoy your diversion, nîcimos, my sweetheart, but don't linger too long, for your place is back on our lands, and this is but a distraction." He was right and I had already stayed longer than I had intended to, but I would be leaving soon.

After Wîsahkêcâhk left, I waited until Delacroix bolted shut the door, then he led me to a dark corner and I disrobed, my lace gown catching on my cimasowin as it slid to the dirt floor. He ran his hands greedily all over my body as he kissed me passionately. His body was lean and hairy in all the right places, and his skin alabaster, almost blue, below the neck. He was unwashed, as Europeans most often were, and his sharp spice intoxicated me. I allowed him to use my body and mitakay as he wished, smacking his taut buttocks in return. At the moment of his release, he let out a joyful contagious laugh that broke through the overly serious impression I had previously held of him. I accepted his grateful kisses; they tasted like mitakay, tobacco, and somewhat of piss, but in my ardour I cared not.

The sun was setting over the rooftops of the Parisian skyline when we emerged from the warm peaty darkness of the stable. As I plucked some straw from my hair and straightened my dress, Delacroix pressed a small mahogany box of Winsor and Newton watercolour paints and a fine sable brush into my hands. "These are for you to continue your studies of the European male." His eyes were teary when we kissed one last time. I would not see Delacroix again, although we would write to each other about painting. I had learned all I wanted to learn about the Europeans, and perhaps they had learned a little from us, but I needed to go now—I had been hearing that the numbers of Europeans were increasing evermore on miskinâhk-oministik, Turtle Island, that their power was centralizing, and soon there would be no room for us on our own lands.[264]

ᑳᐃᐧ ᐃᑐᐦᑌᐃᐧᐣ

ᐃᓯ

ᒥᐢᑭᓈᕽ ᒥᓂᐢᑎᑯᕽ

Return to

miskinâhk-

ministik

Flying back over kihcikamîhk was exhilarating after the cramped and polluted confines of Paris and London. The tiny warbler form I had taken was small, but had stamina and strength enough to take me home. I felt the soot and sadness of Europe fall away with each flap of my tiny wings. I had no need of rest, flying for days until I neared the shores of miskinâhk-oministik again.[265] Quickening my pace, despite the exhaustion of the long journey, I collapsed on the shore, tasting sweet askiy once more and gaining strength.

The view towards home further inland was not the same, and as I flew westward in the direction of my people, I was alarmed how the môniyâwak settlements had spread like a cancer in these years I had been away, and how few iyiniwak villages now remained intact. Heavy clouds of soot like those I had seen smothering London and Paris hung over the sprawling new settlements on the banks of the great river Kaniatarowanénhne and great lakes, just as they did over Europe. I landed far from the settlement they called Fort William,[266] transformed into human form, and hearing the sweet welcoming whispers of the grasses and trees all around me, sank to my knees. I put my hands and face to the earth and inhaled deeply the sweet, fecund smell of askiy. As tears rolled down my face, I put down tobacco and sang her song until my voice was hoarse.

I had been away for far too long.

When I returned to the village of my dear Numakaki kâ-wâsihkopayicik friends, it had changed much more than I could have imagined. Sometime after my last visit to Mitu'tahakto's, a steamboat belonging to the American Fur Company had brought the devastating misi-omikîwin into the villages.[267] Even before I approached the village, I had been warned, but the silence as I drew near filled me with dread. No gay laughter hung in the air.

Those I saw were downcast and dressed poorly, in ragged clothing. A young woman with a deeply scarred face who was gathering firewood recognized me. In a strangely flat voice, as though these horrors had happened to someone else, Minéekeesúnkteka[268] told me of the devastation

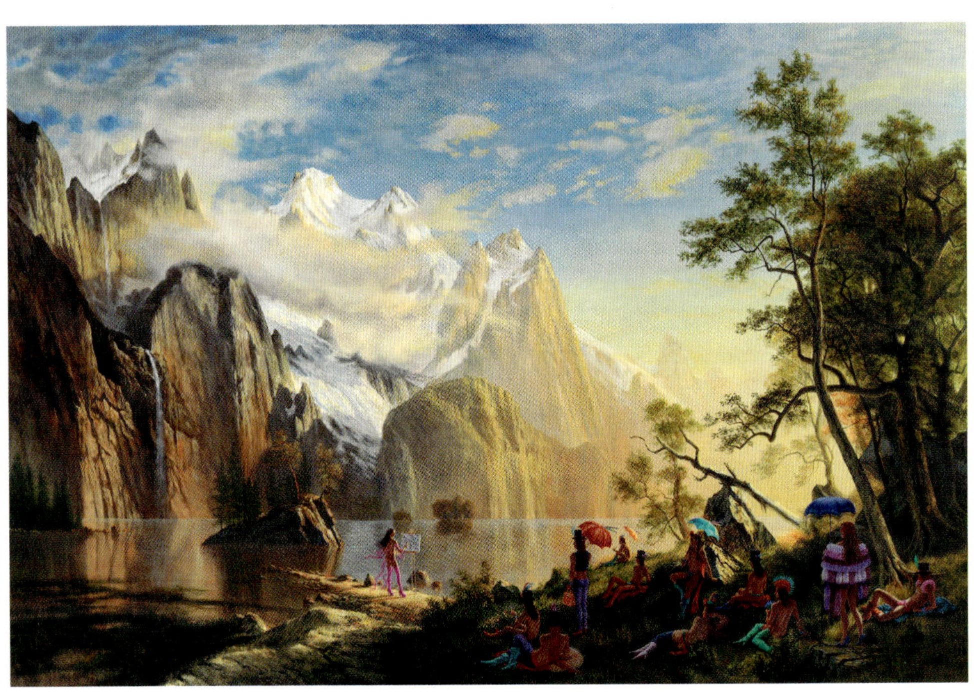

To celebrate the gifts of sun and life Kisê-manitow had given us, I proposed that the kâ wâsihkopayicik, old and young, join me at the river to paint and honour their true selves as Catlin had not done twenty years before.

Sunday in the Park, 2010. Acrylic on canvas. 72 in. x 96 in.

the disease had wrought. During the worst of it, ten of my dear friends had passed to ahcâhko-sîpiy, the river of spirits, every day.[269] There had been no survivors to bring water or care for the sick, no one to hunt or trade, no one to mourn for or to bury the dead. When I had last visited, there had been over two thousand souls living in this and the neighbouring Numakaki village. Now, the woman told me, there remained a little over one hundred survivors.[270] The immensity of the loss overwhelmed me and I could not speak.

"We all lost everyone," Minéekeesúnkteka said quietly. "But there is one of your companions still alive. Those of us who remain are now living in Like-a-Fishhook Village with the Minitari, who also lost many to the disease.[271] Come, I will take you."

Numbly, I followed her. misi-omikîwin had swept across miskinâhk-oministik many times since it was first brought here by the Europeans, each time taking with it more than half of any village, sometimes almost every soul.[272]

As Minéekeesúnkteka led me to the village, I saw my dear friend, the one I had nicknamed Big Bee, Mistah-âmow, for the size of his stinger, step out from between the dome-shaped earth lodges. He let out a strangled cry and ran towards me. We clung to each other for a very long time in an embrace that held our grief. He had been my lover thirty years ago, but we each still had the body-memory of the other and knew without speaking that we needed that reminder of life and love if we were to survive this loss. Our love-making that night was soft and sad, but we knew each other in a way no one else did, and that connection helped bring us both some peace.

Afterwards he turned to me and said, "I helped him pass to ahcâhko-sîpiy, you know."[273] I looked at him intently. He must be talking about his true love—they had been together since they were young boys. I waited for him to speak further if he wished. "His skin had erupted all over in the pustules, so that in his greatest weakness he could find no way of lying down that did not cause him agony. When the pain got so bad that he could not stop screaming, he begged me to kill him. I could not deny him!" Mistah-âmow started sobbing, releasing for the first time the weight he had carried for so long. I wrapped his soft, now-frail body in my arms and held him tightly for the rest of the night.

In the morning, we went to visit some of those in the village who lived also as niwîcêwâkanak pikwîsi kâ-isi-wîkicik. We had a feast, honouring those we had lost. I shared the food I had brought, and handed out gifts to the elders. We spoke of what was happening across miskinâhk-oministik. The skies were darkening over all of our nations. The new diseases had ravaged our peoples. Where was Wîsahkêcâhk? I searched for his ahcâhk-iskotêw, but he was hiding it, not wanting to be found. Our peoples were being threatened from all directions, and I needed his counsel. I knew that he would repeat to me that this human business was their own, that we should not get involved in their affairs, only guide them, but had he ever imagined the scale of this loss? I needed him by my side.

We continued to talk for a long while, then someone started singing. We sang together, then the stories started. It wasn't long before they had me laughing at an outrageous account about one of the warriors Catlin had painted so many years earlier. The warrior who had managed to make love to all of them in one night had been given a plant root to keep him hard so he wouldn't sôhkêpayiw, shoot fast.

"takahkipayihow—he moved well," one seasoned but still magnificent kâ-wâsihkopayicik recalled with a raised eyebrow. "niwîsakahok, he just nailed me. So hard and so well that I had to find some other root to soothe my micisk, asshole, the next day!" he said, massaging his buttock to loud laughter. I asked where to get the root they spoke of. "Which one? for your mitakay or your micisk?"

"Both!" I exclaimed. We all laughed until we cried. This was how we survived. Laughter was our medicine.[274]

The next day was warm and bright. I wanted to celebrate the gifts of sun and life Kisê-manitow had given us, so I proposed that the kâ-wâsihkopayicik, old and young, join me at the river to paint and honour their true selves, as Catlin had not done twenty years before. We always gave when we took something—something the Europeans had yet to learn. In exchange for them allowing me to capture their gloriousness on my canvas, I gave them the gifts I had shipped from Paris with the only trader I met at the Rendezvous that I trusted, a Frenchman I knew well: top hats made from the very beavers their uncles had trapped, silks, peacock feathers, ostrich feathers, suede boots, and parasols. I hoped that these small pleasures might aid in easing their grief.

They spent the morning getting themselves ready for our outing, then we walked to the river, where I set up my easel and the paint box Delacroix had given me. After surviving so much, it was good for them to feel proud, beautiful, and very much alive. Some still carried the scars from smallpox, but that only made them more beautiful to me. I painted them in all their power. It was my winter count,[275] a way to tell our story as we wanted it told. I would render us as we were, not as those who did not understand us saw us. In this painting, the Dandies and the spirits of our dear friends who had left us would forever shine as the bright acâhkosak they were born to be. I stayed with Mistah-âmow for as long as I could.

ᑲᑮ ᒪᑕᐠ

ᐅᓃᑳᓂᐦᑳᐤ

My Intercourse with the Crown

nipahi mwêstas, a great deal later, I transformed into kêh-kêhk form to fly east. Spreading my strong hawk wings wide, I coasted on the wind, letting the undulating currents wash over me, soothing my grief over whom and what we were losing, and focusing my intention.

Following the rivers until I recognized the land I loved so well, I flew over the sites some of my sisters camped at this time of year until I saw their mîkiwâhpa, tipis. Niska's was the most artfully made and easy to see from up in the clouds. I landed, and shifted back into human form, calling out to prevent startling someone who might want to put an arrow through the heart of an intruder.

Niska answered my call and ran towards the forest to the place we always met at, under the poplar trees. "tânisi, nimis, hello, how are you, older sister?" she greeted me. Before I had a chance to reply, she had grabbed me in a bear hug and squeezed me so hard I let out a huge fart. She had always been strong, and was almost as tall as I. In the years since I'd seen her, she had become even more gorgeously ample. With more weight to anchor her, she was stronger than I expected. I gasped for breath as she knocked me off balance with a gleeful roar. She let go and steadied me, still laughing as I recovered. Her laughter was so contagious it was impossible to resist joining in, even though it was at my expense. "Eeee, you've become a delicate flower, haven't you, nîcimos? pê-mîciso, come eat. Let's get some meat on your scrawny ass!" It was good to be home.

Kimiwan and the one everyone still called Minôsis—even though they were all ohkomimâwak, grandmothers, now—joined us. We ate moose stew together and regaled each other with stories of our Rendezvous days. Minôsis's sex stories were even better now she was an ohkomimâw, always so filthy and outrageously hilarious in nêhiyawêwin, but too shocking for me to tell you in English.

They first gave an accounting of who was still with us and who had passed on to ahcâhko-sîpiy. With each new wave of smallpox, measles, influenza, tuberculosis, or any of the other new diseases for which we had no immunity, we lost half to three-quarters of our people. Kimiwan, the eldest, had the misfortune to have outlived almost all her family. Her four children had passed over, and of nine grandchildren, only one remained. Just like the villages of my dear Numakaki kâ-wâsihkopayicik from her grandmother's time until now, the sicknesses had swept through every few years until only one in ten in each village remained living. After we had all shared our memories of each of those who had left this world, we were silent for a long while. The only sound was the crackling of the fire and the soft *sshhhhh* as Niska pulled on her pipe.

Kimiwan then spoke of how, with all the nations so weakened by these losses, they were barely able to hunt and feed their people, let alone defend their territories. Even the mighty Iron Confederacy could not hold off the settlers now flooding by the millions onto the Plains. I shared with my sisters what I'd seen in the European cities, how disconnected these people were from their own lands, and how their brokenness was reflected in the strangeness of what they valued. They listened open-mouthed, exclaiming at each example as I described how the European leaders ignored those in need—sitting on furniture of gold while their own people starved in the street. This was unfathomable to us: a leader not taking care of their people, or someone of means not sharing food, would bring shame and immediate loss of status in our communities.

"Eh, these newcomers are like children, they have no manners!" Niska said. They barely believed me when I told them story after story describing the hubris of that ê-nâpêhkâsot Catlin wanting to put us in floating museums, and meanwhile dressing himself up in buckskin and performing the "dances" of his own invention to eager European audiences. All three frowned when I told them he had our sacred red pipestone, mihkospwâkan, named after himself, as if he had not had the pipestone shown to him! They looked at me with bewilderment when I explained how he had also spent time in a debtors' prison in Europe.

"What is a prison?" Minôsis asked. I did my best to explain what the prisons were, and all three women shook their heads in silence, struggling to understand the impact prisons would have on human beings. Little did we all know then how their grandchildren and great-grandchildren would one day find themselves locked up behind bars in numbers far greater than the millions of settlers who were invading our lands.

"These môniyâwak showed up and talked about land belonging to them," agreed Minôsis. "Our children are wiser than them!"

"Speaking of môniyâwak with no manners," interrupted Niska, for she loved to tease and gossip, "did you hear that Simpson's môniyâw wife has passed? Maybe he'll want one of us for a new wife—maybe you, eh Minôsis? But then he'll leave you like he left his âpihtawikosisân wîkimâkana, country wife!" We laughed, for we all knew stories about him and his kind, abandoning their country wives when they no longer needed them, leaving them to raise their children alone.[276] Niska laughed the hardest, for it had happened to her twice. She laughed so hard that she choked on the succulent moose nose she'd been slurping on. Minôsis hoisted her onto her feet and smacked her between the shoulder blades. Out popped the tasty morsel, right into Kimiwan's open mouth.

"Mmmm, wihkasin, ever delicious!" Kimiwan said without missing a beat. Minôsis laughed so hard she peed herself and had to run over to the bushes.

We laughed again when Minôsis came back, pretending nothing had happened, but underneath the laughter we were all pretending not to feel uneasy. They told me that my paskwâwi-mostos sisters and brothers were now almost gone from our territory, their numbers so diminished that our hunting parties had to ride deeper and deeper into Siksika territory for a successful hunt, but even so, our hunters were struggling to feed and clothe our people.[277]

The British were pressuring our leaders to sign paper treaties. Some were resisting, but many in the east had already signed, some long ago;[278] two generations ago, Chief Peguis had signed with the Scotsman, Selkirk, to give his people the land they had just taken from our people. I had been at some of the signings and knew that the spoken agreement between our leaders and the British was often not what was written on the paper. And even if the words "cede, surrender and forever give up title to the land" had been translated, they would have been meaningless to leaders of all of our nations, for the very concept of land "ownership" was unfathomable. But once the agreements were made and the pipe smoked, the môniyâwak became our kin, kiciwâminawak, our cousins. We expected them to abide by the laws of this land,[279] just as we did.

For our peoples, the spoken words were everything, the môniyâw paper agreements were only indulged to respect the newcomers' ways. For us, to break an agreement was shameful, and to break one made with Kisê-manitow, unthinkable.[280] Kimiwan, Niska, and Minôsis knew that the British would also one day come to our people with their delegations and their paper treaties, and feared what that would mean for us.

When the time came, ceremony would be done to seek counsel.[281] Kimiwan's eyes filled with tears. "All I wish," she said softly, "is for our children and grandchildren who remain, and their children and grand-children, to be able to live in miyo-pimâtisiwin,[282] to be able to live in connection and harmony with this land which sustains them. I pray that they have that future. That they have a future." There was no answer to that but a slow nod and silence.

"The Kanien'kehá:ka have a lot to say about these newcomers coming here and imposing their rules on miskinâhk-oministik," said Minôsis.

"It is true," I agreed. Even with the mighty Rotinonhsyón:nih that the Kanien'kehá:ka had with the Onöndowàga, Goyogohó:no, Onöñda'gega, Onyota'a:ka, and Skarù:rę, promises the settlers made to them were still broken.[283]

Kimiwan told us that a Kanien'kehá:ka relative of hers was going to try to speak to the British Crown directly when the Queen's son, who they called Prince, came to Montréal for a visit in the summer. She suggested that I also go to listen and observe.[284] I remembered this Prince, for I'd met him—young Albert Edward—as a baby in the home of his formidable mother. "He must be eighteen or so now. Old enough to hear our concerns, negotiate with us, and perhaps for other things too," I said, winking at them.

"Young enough to keep three ohkomimâwak happy!" Niska said. "Four if we include you!" She pointed her lips at me.

"tâpwê, true, this dried-up old amisk needs a juicy young cimasowin!" Kimiwan chuckled, throwing her heels up in the air and panting, tongue out, eyes rolled back.

"It would have to be a misicimasowin to satisfy this dried up amiskosis!" Minôsis wiggled her hips. "This old mîkiwâhp is already too roomy and leaky!"

We laughed well into the night as I regaled my friends with greatly exaggerated stories and re-enactments—of how the Queen had lusted after her tall young husband with her tongue hanging out, and how she had licked his face, and grabbed his mitakay through his pants when she thought we weren't looking. Minôsis had to run to the bush again for she couldn't hold her sikiwin, urine, after having thirteen awâsisak, children.

After visiting my dear friends, I made my way to Tiohtià:ke.[285] It was a long time since I had last been there. In just over seven generations, it had gone from a fortified Kanien'kehá:ka village of fifty longhouses with three thousand people surrounded by cornfields to an imposing centre of colonial power, with tall buildings of stone—much more like the cities I had seen in Europe than the muddy city of Tkaronto was.

The young prince was supposed to be inaugurating a new bridge named after his mother, so I made my way there. It was astonishing to see the span of iron and stone across the Kaniatarowanénhne.[286] The newcomers could build in ways that changed the land and waters. It was remarkable, but it sent a cold shiver of fear through my body for what that meant for the land.

I had made a new oskitakosinokîsikowak feather robe, more dazzling than the one I gave to Máh-to-tóh-pa. As I glided through the crowd, it parted way for me with hushed murmurs. The môniyâwak did not know me, but they assumed by my carriage and attire that I was associated in some way with royalty. The mayor of Montréal was there, along with other môniyâwak dignitaries I did not recognize. Among their number I spotted the Hudson's

Bay Company man, Simpson. He looked me up and down as I wove my way amongst the throng gathered to see the prince, but I returned his look coldly, for I knew how he treated the "wives" he took from our people, how his obsession with making the numbers in his ledgers favourable for his company created hardship for my people, and how he refused to listen to counsel. I pointedly ignored him despite his vain attempts to catch my eye.

One of their leaders, a bulbous-nosed man with bushy hair sprouting haphazardly from the sides of his head, was so intoxicated that he vomited in front of everyone, but rather than slink away in shame, he made light of it and continued speaking.[287] I was shocked that even a môniyâw would have such little self-respect to behave so in public, much less at a formal gathering, and astonished that any authority was given to a man like this. I had a flash of a half-formed plan on how to perhaps exert some influence, for who would be easier to get close to than a fool such as this? He was repulsive, to be sure, but his words were clever, if not wise, and the other môniyâwak clearly afforded him some degree of respect. First, however, I would assess the prince that had travelled far to be here, and see what influence I could wield over him. He was more powerful, and infinitely more attractive.

I stopped to confer with the Kanien'kehá:ka dignitaries, one of whom had worked on the bridge.[288] As this was their territory, I asked them for their permission for me to be here on their lands, for their assistance and their counsel. They had come to speak to the prince about two hundred years of agreements which had been eroded by first the French king, then the Jesuits, and now the British Crown. They had already given up much, and were now limited to living on their former hunting grounds as vast swaths of land had been taken by the church and government, who wanted still more.[289]

I listened carefully as the Kanien'kehá:ka dignitaries began their eloquent entreaties, for what they said was true and clear, but the prince's eyes glazed over, and he scanned the crowd for someone who might hold his interest. At the end of their speech, he smiled with only his mouth and said, with a complete lack of sincerity, that he would consider their words carefully.[290] A finely dressed older man at the prince's side then cleared his throat and stepped forward. He explained that he was the Duke of Newcastle and a secretary to the Queen, and that earlier that year he had ordered an investigation into the Indian Department. "My dear men," he declared, "I will speak to the Great White Mother and see to it that your grievances are most satisfactorily addressed."[291]

As the duke stepped back, a stiff-shouldered young man who had been hanging back sulkily during the speeches quickly advanced. He whispered something in the duke's ear and narrowed his eyes at the Kanien'kehá:ka dignitaries. The duke glanced back at them too, his face suddenly darkening as he retreated with the young man to speak privately.

I could see the Kanien'kehá:ka leader working to control his anger. "That one is the head of their Indian Department," he said quietly through clenched jaws. "Last year he broke treaty with the Batchewana and forced them to sell their lands. If the English are listening to him, they are not listening to us, and there is no honour in their treaties."[292] He turned his head to look me directly in my eyes to make sure I had heard and understood. I nodded, conveying that I would heed his words and act accordingly. He and his companions then left, walking stiffly as they controlled their anger, but projecting a deceptive mask of calm to the newcomers.

I stepped forward. If the young prince would not listen to the plain facts of his own law and honour treaties his people had made in his mother's name, I would try a different tactic. As I approached the plinth on which he sat, I caught his gaze. I held contact with his brilliant hazel eyes long enough to see the twinkle of a stylish playboy who was bored—nikâhcitinâw, I caught him. I reached down and gently touched the young prince's calves as I stroked downwards to his boots. As I tugged on his laces, the soldiers moved to block my action, but were stayed by the prince's hand before they could remove me.

"Welcome, Eddie," I said, shocking the môniyâw dignitaries behind the prince with my familiar address and even more familiar caresses as I unlaced his boots. "Allow me to wash the dust off your tired appendages and gently rub the cares from your aching muscles."

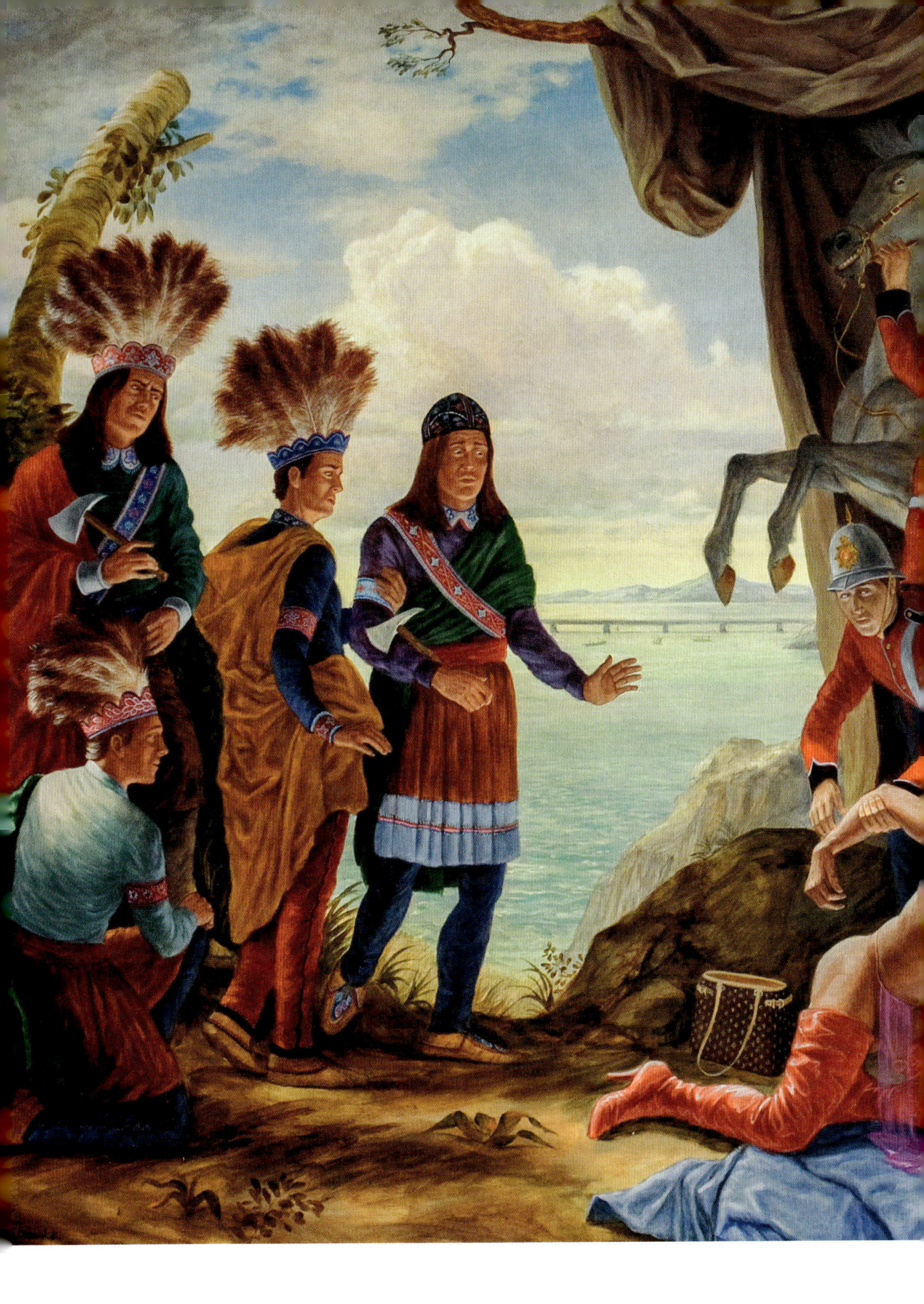

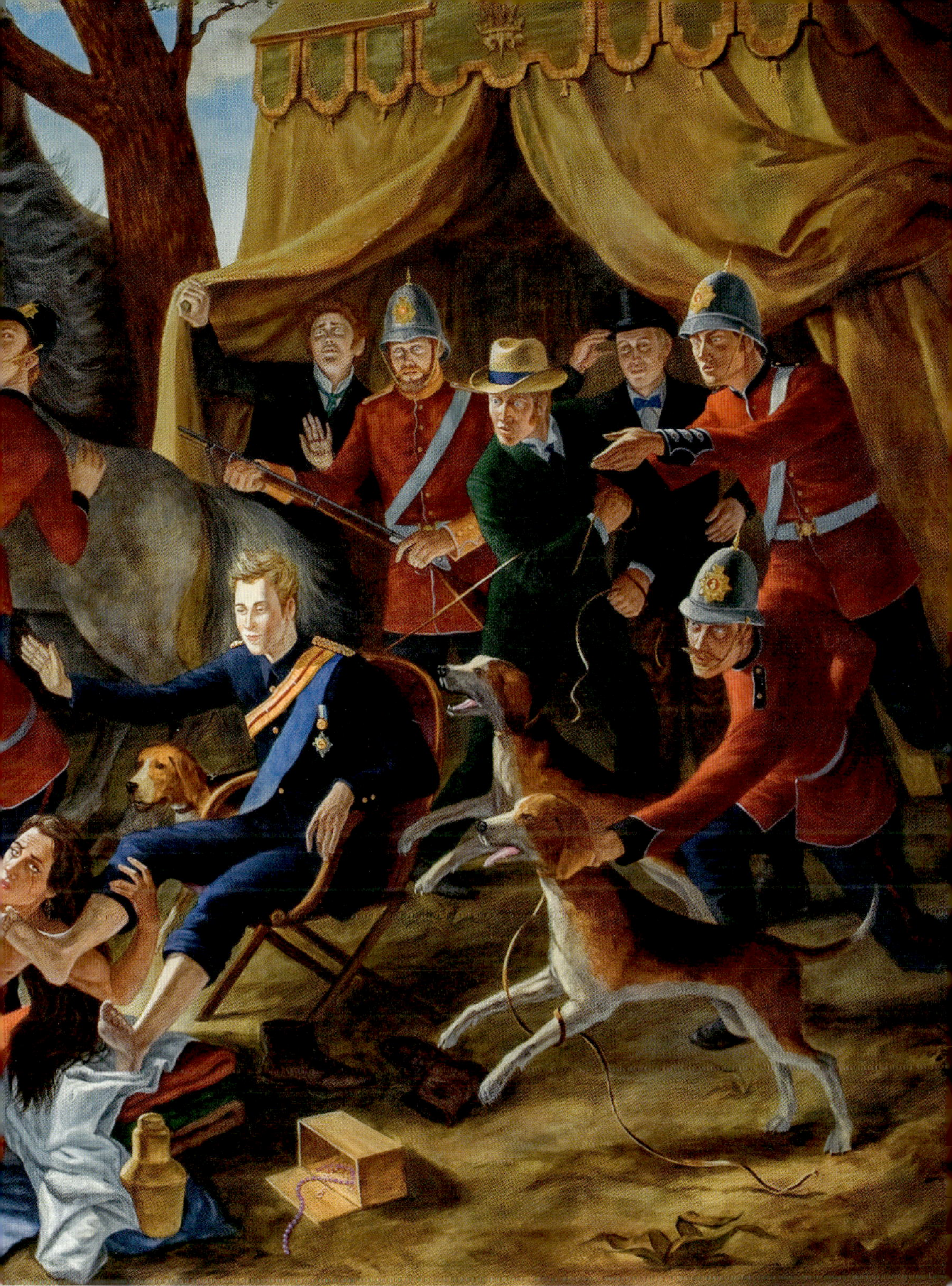

I told the young prince that I had come as someone concerned about all the Cree Nations, from the forests and muskegs of winipêk to the plains and valleys of the far west, upon whose lands his people now encroached.

My Treaty is With the Crown, 2011. Acrylic on canvas. 60 in. x 96 in.

He raised his eyebrows and smiled at me. "For who might you be, to so boldly welcome us to our own land?"

I snorted at his ridiculousness. "I am Miss Chief, sent here to love and help my people the iyiniwak who have belonged to these lands since before your ancestors even thought of existing, let alone bothering us.

"I come as someone concerned about all the Cree Nations, from the forests and muskegs of wînipêk to the plains and valleys of the far west upon whose lands your people now intrude. Our buffalo herds are dwindling and the illnesses brought to us by your people have devastated our nations. To find paskwâwi-mostoswak our hunters must encroach more and more on our neighbours' territory, leading to wars, which we do not want and for which we do not have the resources.[293] We need assurances that any treaties made with our peoples be made in accordance with our laws, never to be broken, and that these settlers of yours will not intrude on our farming, fishing, or hunting grounds." I massaged his lean and furry calves as I continued to talk and bathe his upper feet with my hair, letting my words sink into his body, mind, and spirit.

The prince invited me to join him later in his private chambers to speak further about what was happening to the people of this land. After sending his valet and attendants away, we spoke at length in other ways that did not involve words. At the sight of his cimasowin, I giggled openly, thinking of how I would share, with some exaggerations perhaps, details of the length and girth of his mitakay with Niska, Minôsis, and Kimiwan.

"Is it not sufficient enough for you, madame?" the prince inquired about my laughter.

"Oh no, it's more than enough, your royal highness," I said, stroking his ego and the mitakay that would sire the future of the British Crown.

After our intimacies, when he was relaxed and open, I gently traced his upper thigh and whispered in his ear, "Your people have an obligation to honour the treaties signed with our peoples, but even more than that you must understand our laws." He listened, but I could see that he did not understand our concepts, so instead I related the injustices being done in his mother's name. He was quiet for a while, then told me there were other things he wished to understand. He was still a child—charming and dangerously innocent. But he would not stay innocent much longer.

His eyelids drooped, so ninôhkwâtâw, I licked him and tugged playfully on his silky hair to focus his attentions. "You must not interfere with the animals, rock, and waters, for we are of these lands, and they are our sacred responsibility." I could see that he did not understand our way of thinking about the world so instead related the injustices being done in his mother's name again, but this time in more tactile detail.

takahkipayihow, he moved well, and kahkiyaw nimiyik, he gave me all of it. I chuckled to myself again—the next time Kimiwan, Niska, and Minôsis called me the queen mother they wouldn't be entirely wrong. Far better it was I who was receiving the royal seed than them—at least there wouldn't be any royal bastards—but then, what better way to leverage the Crown for my people! How amusing the thoughts that can cross one's mind while in the throes of passion.

We spent the next three nights in his apartment, where his highly sexed nature proved him to be an avid student of the many lessons he wished to learn and I was glad to teach him.[294] nitôminâw, I greased him up, and then nisâkaskinahâw, I filled him up. In between satisfying his begging for more and educating him about our laws and our peoples, I taught him everything he needed to know for his future exploits, nicîhcîkinâw isi mitoni ka-miywêyihtahk, I scratched him exactly as he liked it. I also took this opportunity to coax promises from the young prince in his most vulnerable and greedy moments, restraining his climaxes, êkosi nimiyâw âpihtâw piko. I only gave him half of it until I had him begging me and moaning assurances that his mother, the powerful Queen, would negotiate fair and equitable treaties with the peoples of this land going forward.

During the days, we enjoyed the many distractions the prince's hosts had organized for him. Eddie was particularly eager to take a trip in a canoe, so the Hudson's Bay Company governor George Simpson arranged for such a venture to take place by his summer manor on an island across from

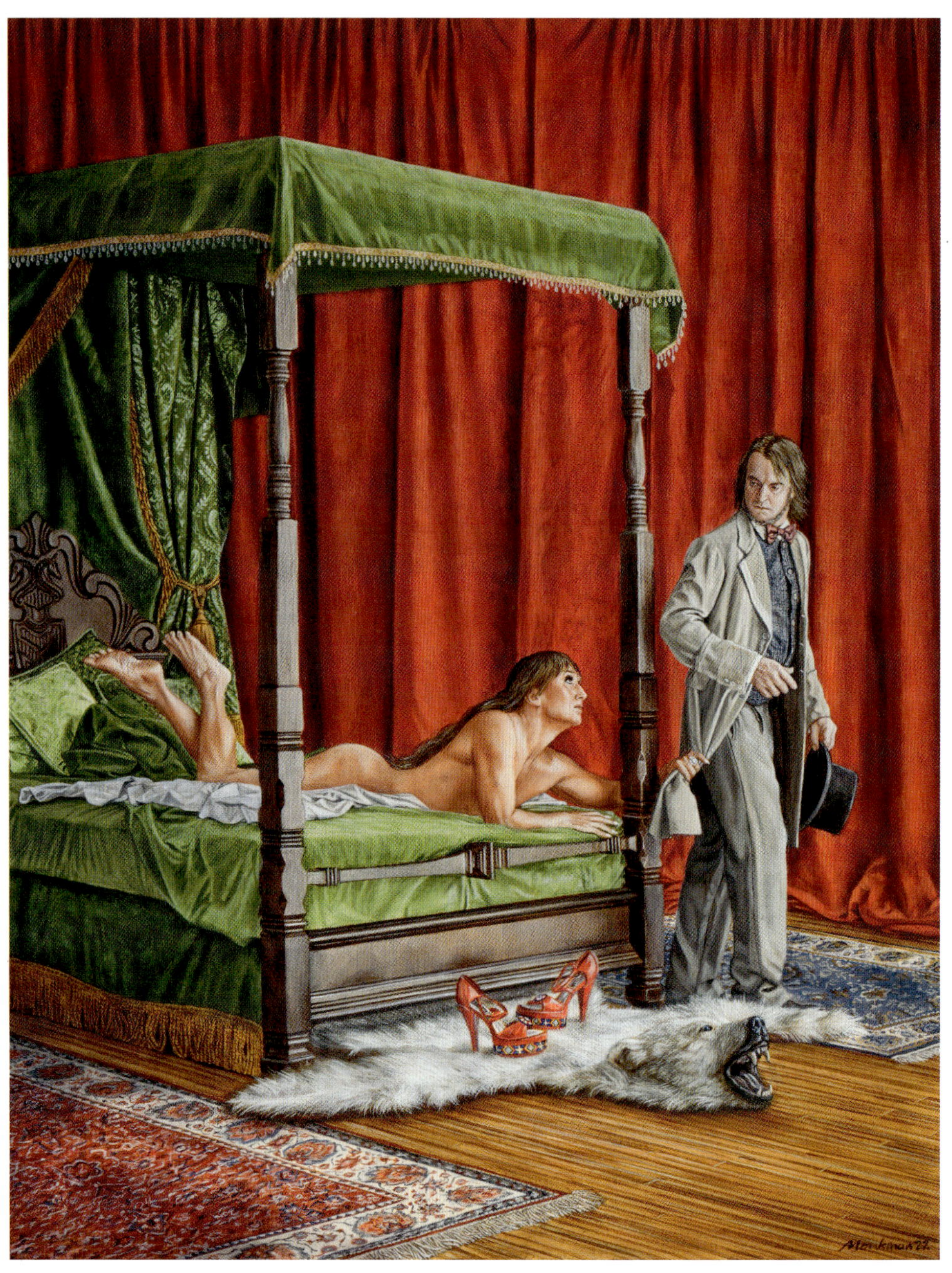

I focused my attentions on coaxing the prince to moan assurances that his mother, the powerful queen, would negotiate fair and equitable treaties with the peoples of this land going forward.

Study for Fate is a Cruel Mistress (Potiphar's Wife), 2022. Acrylic on canvas. 27 in. x 21 in.

Kahnawà:ke. Simpson harangued one hundred Kanien'kehá:ka canoeists into performing a synchronized routine in the waters of Kaniatarowanénhne. He waved his arms to guide the canoes, but the paddlers were experts who executed the complicated manoeuvres flawlessly without him. The prince laughed with delight at the display, but I wondered if he ever spared a glance at the village of Kahnawake across the water, whose territory was becoming ever smaller with every encroachment of the prince's people.

After this display, the prince and his attendants retired to enjoy a lavish luncheon at Simpson's home. Simpson was a man of great ambition, so he had been sure to seat himself close to the prince. When he wasn't showering Eddie with compliments and stories, Simpson was trying to catch my eye, but my full attentions were on young Eddie. I accepted one of his point blankets, however, for one never knew which relationships might be useful one day.

As he handed me the blanket, his hand lingered on mine, and I could hear Simpson's heart hammering in his chest. I locked eyes with him and Simpson blinked in confusion. With my sensitive ears, I heard his blood pounding through his veins with alarming pressure. I later learned that Simpson died shortly after that meeting. Some assumed that the strain of hosting a royal visit had been onerous for him. But most likely the thrill of meeting me was more than he could bear.[295]

The next day I parted ways with the prince, who went on to visit the rest of the land his family was calling Canada.[296] To my great disappointment, the attentions I'd lavished upon him yielded little noticeable benefit for my people in the years to come.[297] He had been open to our plight, and was more progressive than most around him, but he offered only hollow sympathies and empty words. He lacked interest in political or state affairs, and remained a playboy, overindulging in many vices such as iskotêwâpoy, strong drink. I had thought to influence the Crown,[298] for that is with whom our peoples had signed the treaties. I was discouraged, but would find another way. Even if young Eddie had had the inclination or the capacity to move his mother, which it was now clear he did not, the power in these lands was soon to shift.

ᓂᑮ ᑭᐢᑭᔨᐦᑌᐣ
ᐊᓂᑭ ᑭᑲ ᑭᒧᑎᐘᐟ
ᑲᐦᑭᔭᐤ ᑮᒁᔭ

I Learned
That They Would
Steal Everything

After another failure to petition the Crown for my people I was discouraged. I stayed apart from human beings for a time, going deep into the bush to mourn those we'd lost since the newcomers had arrived, and grieving for those whose loss was still to come. I called out for Wîsahkêcâhk, but he did not come. The poplar trees tried to comfort me, whispering that even though their blood might stain the earth, our peoples would survive.

After several days, one of the mêmêkwêsiwak who had been watching me tentatively approached me. Looking into my eyes to see if his presence was welcome, he sat down beside me and wrapped his hand around my little finger. He didn't speak, but the lightness of his spirit helped me focus my mind and gave me strength. I would go among the newcomers and do what I could to help teach them our laws—and if they did not listen, to undermine those who were causing harm on our lands. Every action, no matter how small, would help alleviate the suffering of my people.

I made my way to the Kitchissippi, one of the main rivers used by the voyageurs, who called it the Ottawa River, and sat down on the bank. I gently traced my fingers over the art carved into asiniy that told ancient stories of creatures no longer here on askiy. While I waited, I traded gossip with some sîsîpak. The ducks liked to talk. I was still upset with Wîsahkêcâhk for not answering my call, so hearing their stories about how they had outwitted him yet again made me laugh harder than usual.

mwêscasês, a party of voyageurs in several large trading cîmâna, canoes, came to shore with an âkayâsîwiskwêw, an English woman, in the bow. The canoes being of birchbark, they had to disembark in the water, and as she did so, I noticed that she took special care to hold high what I recognized to be a very similar set of paints to the one my friend Delacroix had given me. I set up my paints on a flat grandfather rock, still warm from the sun in a grove of birch and oak trees, and waited for her. Sure enough, she soon appeared, paints and sketchbook in hand.

She told me that her name was Frances Anne Hopkins. Her husband was an official with the Hudson's Bay Company, undertaking duties under the orders of George Simpson.[299] She remembered my unforgettable entrance in my oskitakosinokîsikowak feather robe at Simpson's luncheon in Montréal for the prince, despite not having had the good fortune to be introduced to me.

While the voyageurs set up camp, we painted together and talked. Frances spoke of how her people were fighting political battles between themselves for power over our lands;[300] I told her what these battles and the expansion of the settlements was doing to our peoples. She was inside the circles of power, but her extensive travels with her husband and the voyageurs had given her a greater understanding of, and fellow feeling for, our situation than most of her people held.

Frances answered my questions about the structures of power in this British colonial world, and said she would help me if she could. I told her how we pitied them for the strange pre-occupation they had—not at how much one could give, like the most respected in our communities, but in how much they could take and hoard for themselves. She gave a little snort, then remained quiet for a while. "I do see," she said. "We are even more senseless than we know." I met her eyes for a moment, then we both returned to our painting.

After a while, she held up her watercolour sketch, and, satisfied, signed her initials to it. "I doubt my paintings will sell if people find out that a woman made them," she explained. "So, I use only my initials in my signature. But there are other ways to leave your mark." She pointed at the female figure she had added to her landscape, clearly meant to represent herself.[301] I understood her point very well.

As we painted, I asked her how she could travel through the bush, sleeping rough, while wearing all those layers, the petticoats and the corsets. She laughed and said she'd never known anything else, and inquired about my heels. I explained that my shoes were not like the shoes of human beings. They contained power, and to me felt like moccasins; besides,

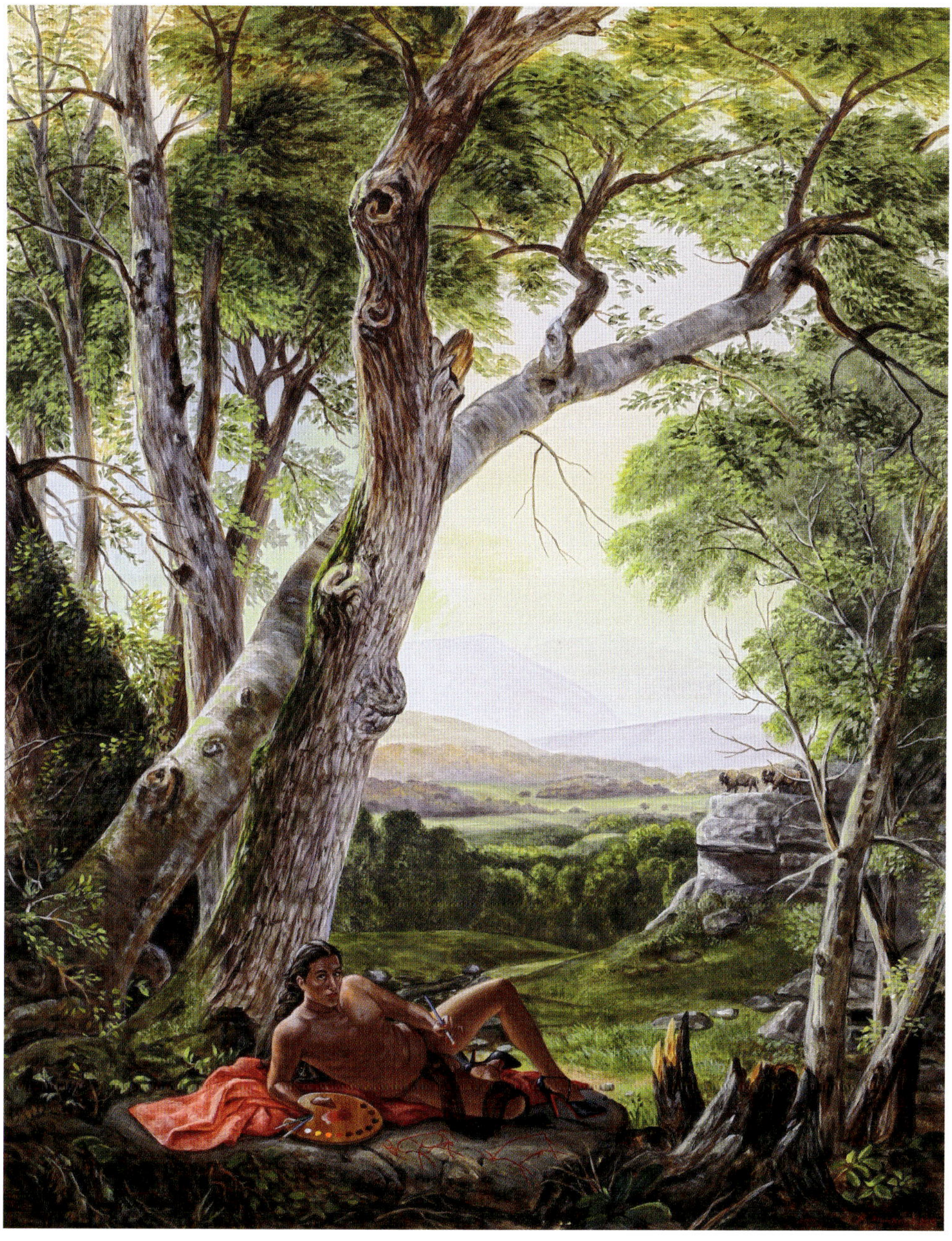

"Representational painting is over," I told Frances. "I am painting the past and the future."

The Allegory of Painting, 2015. Acrylic on canvas. 48 in. x 38 in.

I liked the pink on the bottom, like the paw pads of my dear elder brother Wîsahkêcâhk.

Frances painted things much more as they truly appeared than Catlin or some of the other European painters who painted our lands empty of our presence. "Your work is quite good," I told her, "but representational painting is over. I am painting the past and the future. You will live long enough to see an artist copy me as he claims to invent a new way of seeing, but all he is doing is playing with the physical lines we use to represent spirit. We inspired modernism when the future was our past."[302]

Frances and I stayed in touch, and that winter she invited me to a winter ball in the town built over the Haudenosaunee villages Ganatsekwyagon and Teiaiagon, now called Toronto by the settlers.[303] It was to be a masquerade ball, hosted by an artist by the name of Kane, whom she said was a serviceable artist who had painted a great deal of the country, including many of my people.[304] She was friendly with his wife, Harriet, who was also a painter, although not as adventurous as Frances.

Harriet had helped her husband produce his book *Wanderings of an Artist among the Indians of North America*, which Frances found interesting, but as she had travelled a great deal amongst us, she felt some sections to be quite fanciful, and told me as much.[305] I was curious to see how this painter, Kane, saw my people, and it would be useful for me to understand what plans the settlers had for us. But, more than that, this would give me a chance to wear my new arctic fox robe sent to me by an admirer in Paris.

---

mwêscasês, outfitted with a sled and luggage from the prince and fine sled dogs from my cousin the Fur Queen,[306] I made the voyage to Tkaronto.[307]

It was a long journey, but the dogs were happy to be in the bush, and I felt bathed in the heady scent and strong spirits of cedar and spruce as the trees blurred past. The air was sharp and crisp. I pulled my winter fox robe around me and laughed out loud with the deep connected happiness of travelling through our lands once more. I felt the joy returned to me from the trees, rocks, and the earth under its blanket of snow, and listened with pleasure to the low sweet concert only the old ones and I could hear: the hum of askiy and the silvery songs of the trees. I hummed along with them for the rest of my journey.

We came upon Yonge Street around the region of Zhooniyaang-zaaga'igan, Of the Silver Lake,[308] which the newcomers called Lake Simcoe, and then turned south. We passed through the lands that were now cleared of the forests where our peoples had hunted, trapped, canoed, and roamed freely since the beginning. The more the land was divided into rectangles bordered by fences, and dotted with farmhouses, saw-mills, and churches, the more subdued the soft hum of askiy and the whispered songs of the trees became. The exhilaration I'd felt earlier in my journey faded along with their voices. I passed the concession line of Bloor Street and entered the city.

Tkaronto was a small muddy town compared to London or Paris, with buildings crowded against one another and taverns on almost every corner. It had none of the grand style of the European cities, but all of the stink. I found accommodation at the Red Lion Inn and asked the stablehand to look after the dogs. After freshening up, I paused to inhale the mingled scents still lingering in my fox robe fur and smiled, remembering his sweet caresses, then stepped out to walk to the ball.

The last time I'd been here, the thriving village of Teiaiagon was still on the banks of Cobechenonk river, which the settlers had renamed the Humber River,[309] and that of Ganatsekwyagon still stood on the Katabokokonk, now called the Rouge River.[310] Those villages and their farmlands that had fed thousands of our Haudenosaunee relatives were now gone, replaced by the settler farms and mills, but our relatives were still here.

Our peoples assumed the dress of the Europeans of York, but adorned their clothes with details, beadwork, buttons, and flashes of colour that set them apart with style. The city was full of newcomers, mostly European—but others from each corner of askiy with rich hues of skin, and aspects far more pleasing to the eye than those of the pallid Europeans, now also bustled through the streets.

Above the city hung the heavy soot I had seen in London and Paris as well as the stench of mêyi. The smell of shit was far worse than any I'd known before. Pigs from Europe were now bred here to be killed for the people of the city to eat. In the world of the newcomers, all living beings were currency. There were tens of thousands living in this crowded city, and the divisions among them were just as harsh as they had been in London and Paris. I still could not fathom the disregard those with riches displayed as they walked by those in need.

I passed through neighbourhoods with wooden shacks and boarding houses, where the roads were still dirt that turned the snow to brown mush. Hungry-looking children, blue from the cold, crouched in the shadows, their clothes in tatters. I quickly went back to my rooms and fetched the warmest shawls I had for them. They stared at me, not being accustomed to such attentions, then grabbed at the shawls with a muttered thanks in Gaeilge and ran away.

As I approached the centre, the slushy streets gave way to stone and my heels clicked loudly, attracting curious stares and interested looks. I walked past large stone houses on a street named Jarvis, where the roads were paved and lit with gas lamps. Here all who passed by were elegantly dressed and walked on specially built sidewalks in order that their feet should never endure the indignity of dirt.[311] As I drew closer to Wellesley Street, where Kane lived, there were still pockets of land where no buildings yet stood, and in the shadows I thought I saw a dark shape slink behind a tree.

It was early evening and the sun was just sinking behind the tops of the white cedar and sugar maple trees in the heavily wooded neighbourhood. Generous brick homes, fancifully appointed with gingerbread balusters and arches, were nestled in large deep lots, the smoke from their chimneys hanging in the frosty air. There was a trail of footprints in the snow into a wooded ravine that led away from the sidewalks and slushy roads still bustling with horse-drawn sleighs.

In the twilight of the crisp evening I could see dark silhouettes of men moving down the trail, and I followed them deeper into the woods, my heels sinking into the snow. In the ravine it was much darker, but I could see men walk close to each other, nod, then one would follow the other down a well-packed trail, disappearing from view. I recognized the body language and immediately understood. Even the coolness of winter did little to dampen the corporeal passions of men seeking their own kind.

It wasn't long before I followed suit, approaching a tall handsome man in a frock coat and top hat, with shiny patent boots. He was dressed as a môniyâw but had a more streamlined cut to his clothing, with embroidered flowers on his lapels and a beaded hat band. I caught the sweet scent of tobacco and drew closer to him, smelling as well the smoked moosehide strips that tied his braids. He pulled me closer, the warm steam of his breath hanging in the cold air.

As I unbuttoned his trousers in the thicket of cedars, he moaned and uttered in Anishinaabemowin. I looked up into his handsome face as I wrapped my lips around his warm brown mitakay. When we were done, he told me his name was M'iingan,[312] tipped his hat, and slipped away quietly in the opposite direction, takahkipayihow. I noticed some mêmêkwêsiwak peering out below the snow laden branches of a cedar, pointing at me with their small brown lips and giggling. I reached into my pocket and laid a handful of hard candy on the snow near their tiny footprints and walked away. I glanced back and smiled as the little silhouettes scooped up the candy and disappeared into the darkness of the forest.

As I made my way out of the trail to the street I saw a few more niwîcêwâkanak pikwâwiyak kâ-sâkihâcik on their way in. One gave me an appreciative up-and-down appraisal and a low whistle. "Well, it's not every day that the queens of Molly Wood's Bush see the likes of you!"[313] I blew them a kiss, and tossed my hair back flirtatiously, and told them that if they were here when I got back, I would make the wait worth their while.

The acâhkosak were shining brightly by the time I entered the ball, fashionably late, slightly ruffled, but with a lovely glow. All heads turned.

The socialites of York whispered amongst themselves, trying to guess what or who my "costume" was. But who else could I be? There is only one Miss Chief, and what I wear is never a costume!

A petite woman in a tall bouffant powdered wig, with rouged cheeks and lips, squeezed her opulent silk hoop skirt through the crowded room to take my hand. "Welcome, Miss Chief!" she said, beaming.

"Frances! Eeeee, tâpwê!" It was good to see her, for I had missed our talks on painting and politics.

She led me through Kane's sprawling brick manse to peruse his paintings, which were hung on every available surface of the richly coloured flocked wallpaper or perched on wooden easels. I could hardly contain myself—what a fabulist he was! Such liberties he took in his paintings—in one he had placed an obviously Stl'pulmsh mother with a Chinook baby and cradleboard.[314]

In painting after painting, I saw geographies, peoples, and clothing belonging to different regions, all jumbled together—many works depicted village life in a completely romantic and western light, with no understanding of how powerful and essential our women are—only an outsider man could not see that our women ran everything. I also recognized my dear friend Maungwudaus among the portraits, though at first I had not known him, as Kane had changed his features to fit his own preferences. Delacroix would have done so much better! With a lump in my throat, I kissed my finger and touched the canvas nonetheless.[315]

Frances could see that I was becoming agitated, so she quickly introduced me to an elegant young Haudenosaunee man who was just about to leave for England to study medicine. Oronhyatekha had a charming, confident manner about him, and even though he was still a very young man, it was already abundantly clear that his powerful personality would smash through the bigotry that surrounded him. I shared with him my critiques of Kane's paintings, and he arched one eyebrow and said, "I then wholeheartedly advise you not to go into the drawing room. I've tried to reason with him . . ."[316]

With a nervous-looking Frances trailing behind me, I strode directly into the drawing room and immediately my mood darkened even more. Like Catlin, Kane had a fetish for collecting our most sacred and beautiful belongings. Everywhere I turned were spirits calling to me, lonely and untended from our many nations. I saw pipe stems with intricate carvings displayed unwrapped in glass boxes. A Haida whale-tooth amulet emanating great power was mounted in a curiosity cabinet, alongside ivory letter-openers from the lands across the ocean and an old carved Celtic cross from Ireland, his birth country. Sacred masks were hung on the walls as if they were decorations. There was even a medicine bundle, half broken open, displayed for all to see on a side table.[317] What had happened to the keepers of these ceremonial items? Who knew how they should be wrapped? Who knew their songs? Our sacred belongings had spirits that needed to be cared for. I felt sickened and angry all at once. I stood trembling, my heart racing, barely able to breathe.

Just then I realized someone was talking to me, and had been for a while. A man with an explosion of unruly hair, great bushy eyebrows, and the gleam of a zealot in his eyes. Apparently his name was Ryerson. He was lecturing me on the educational power of Kane's paintings and "his" "objects." Still processing what I was seeing, and reeling a little from the shock, I could not fully absorb the words he was saying. By objects, did he mean our sacred belongings, these spirits?[318] Undeterred, he continued pontificating—assuming, I suppose, that I was one of his own people in fancy dress. He explained that he had recently undertaken a study of "Indian schools" and planned to create a comprehensive system just for the benefit of the Indian children, that they might be assimilated and become useful members of society.[319]

With a self-congratulatory smile, he said they planned to remove the children from their families to boarding schools hundreds of miles away, so their families could not visit—to better remove the language and cultural ties. They would be forced to work and take classes in English. At first I did not believe what I was hearing. How could anyone think that our children were not being taught by their families everything they needed to know to be good iyiniwak? How could anyone take a child from their mother? Paralyzed by the implications of what Ryerson's horrific plan would do to my people, I could not move, let alone speak. Take our children? This could not be possible. It was all much, much worse than I could have imagined. No, this would not happen, I would not let it!

Thinking my silence meant a lack of understanding, he proceeded to explain his ideas once more. I was now shaking with rage, my voice breaking with emotion—the room was closing in on me. "Our children are the most precious gifts to us, loaned to us by Kisê-manitow—raising them well, miyo-ohpikihâwasowin, good child rearing, is one of our most sacred laws![320] What could this do but destroy a people!? atimocisk!" I shouted in his face, making heads turn and the chatter of the party fall silent.

He sputtered and took a step backwards. Before he could answer, Frances came upon me and clamped both of her small moist hands over my trembling fists. The hallway to the front door was blocked with guests, so she quickly pulled me into the darkened library, thick with tobacco smoke. She shut the door behind her, using her Japanese paper fan to cool her reddening face and heaving breast. "Miss Chief, I'm so sorry to have brought you here. Ryerson is merely a buffoon who says the most outrageous things to try to gain power—no one takes him seriously." Frances looked pained. Being a woman of her station, she had been taught to avoid conflict.

"Frances, is that you, my dear?" chuckled a loud gravelly baritone in a continental accent. My hackles went up—something about this performative tone was reminiscent of Catlin's pompous airs. "And to whom and for what are you so sorry, pray tell?"

Frances reeled around and her face sank. "Merciful almighty father in heaven! Paul! You scared the living daylights out of me! Oh my nerves!" she stammered, fanning madly. "It's me—Frances." In attempting to divert confrontation she had led me into the very lion's den. In the corner of the room, ensconced on a tufted leather parlour chair, sat a man of about fifty, with a thick shock of wavy hair and a full greying beard. He was mismatched, attired in a Hunkpapa Lakota war shirt, Crow moccasins, and the leggings of an Anishnaabe trapper,[321] and his friend was wearing a Klallam shaman's mask and not much else, his white fish-belly glowing in the darkened room. Frances fumbled with the door knob behind her back, which did not cooperate. "Miss Chief, may I present to you our host, Paul Kane, and er . . ." Frances gestured weakly at the nearly naked mônîyâw seated in a matching chair.

Paul Kane took a long inhalation on a ceremonial Lakota pipe, blowing smoke rings into the air, and passed it to his friend, who removed the shaman's mask to inhale from the pipe. "A pleasure to make your acquaintance, Miss Chief." Kane sipped his brandy and stood up, gesturing to his friend. "Ladies, this is my dear friend, the intrepid explorer John Henry Lefroy."[322] Kane took a step across the thickly woven rug towards me to fully take me in, his eyes travelling from my head down to my winter heels. His mouth flopped open as if he were a dead fish at market, then snapped shut. "Wonderful costume!" he pronounced. "My dear Frances, is this dusky beauty a Bengali princess or—"

Before he could finish, Frances stepped in between us, attempting a distraction. "Mr. Kane, wouldn't you like to paint my dear friend, Miss Chief Eagle Testickle? Who is of the Cree tribe, I mean niheyow-way . . . um nehay-yo-way-in . . ." Frances stammered, shrinking back against the wall and fumbling with the door latch.

Before I could voice my objection and unleash my fury, Kane scoffed, "No, no thank you! My dear lady, I paint only authentic, real North American Indians, uncontaminated by their contact with us Europeans. I travel far through the wild and pathless forest to find them and study their Native manners and customs." He turned to me. "Here in the town of Toronto, your people are no longer to be seen. All traces of their footsteps are fast being obliterated from their once-favourite haunts."[323]

This insult—by a thief of our most sacred belongings, a middling painter of romantic mythologies—was too much on top of the other

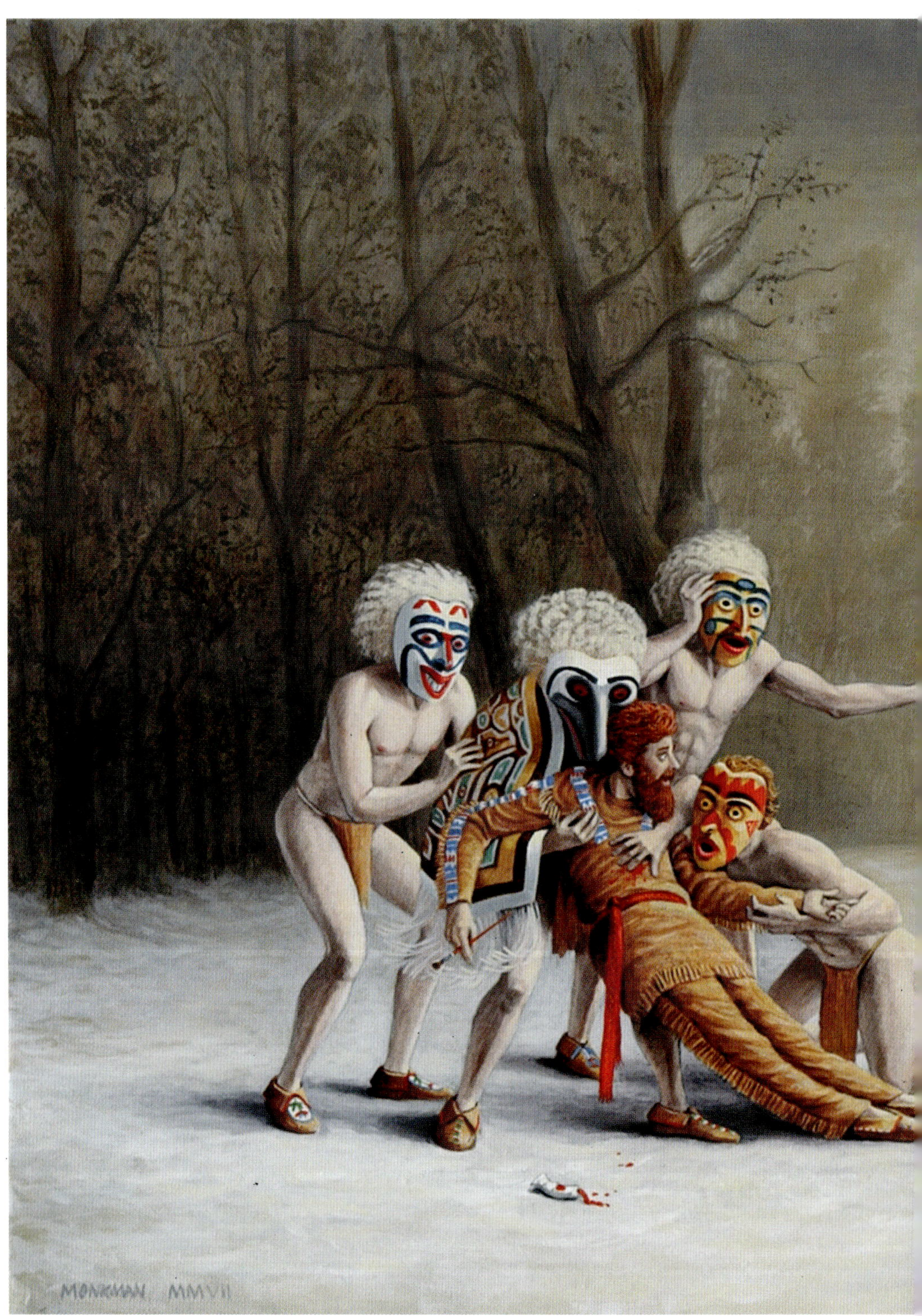
MONKMAN MMVII

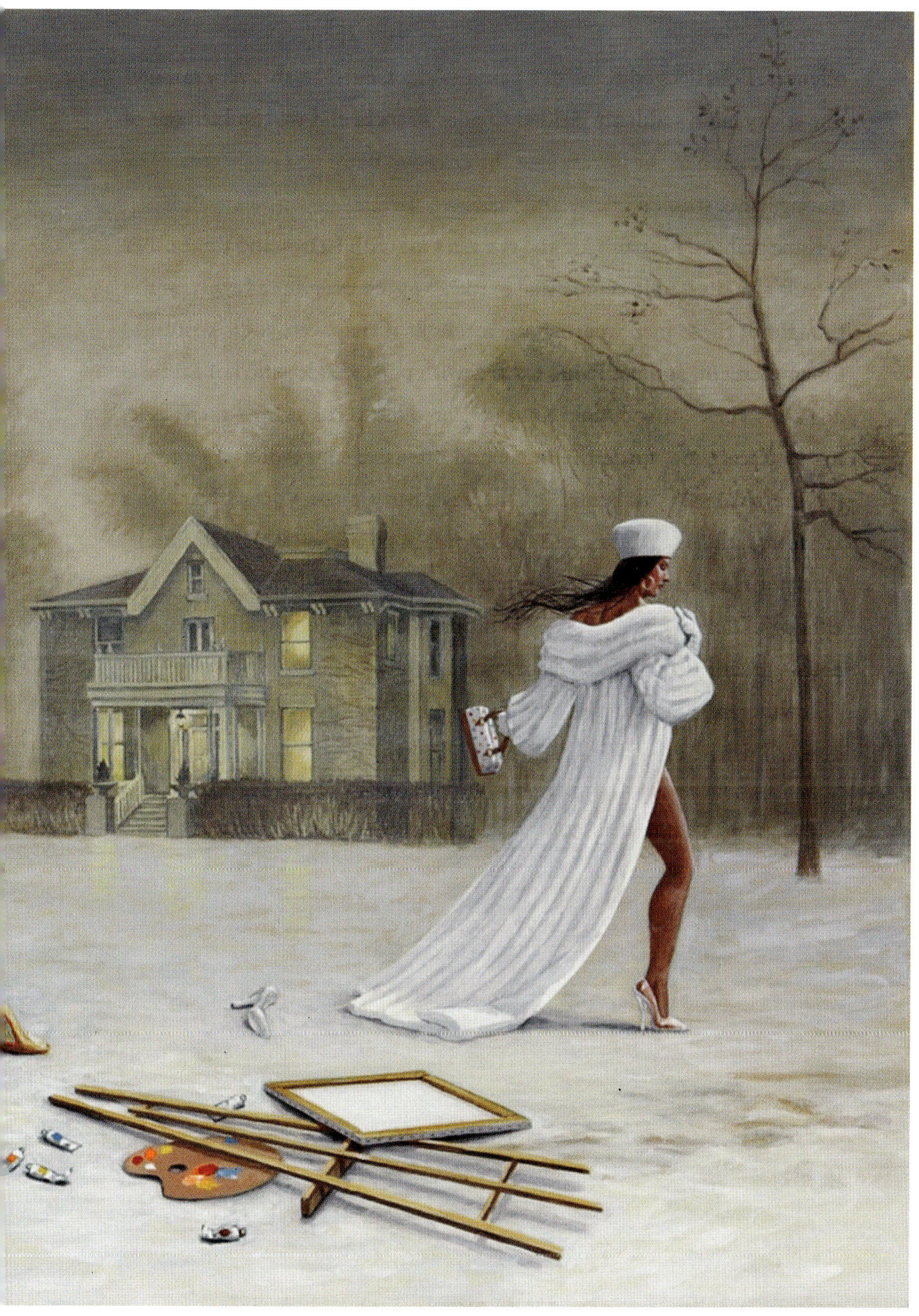

I swung my handbag with the full force of my fury and knocked him down. I'd had enough of this pretender who dared to tell me I was inauthentic!

Duel After the Masquerade, 2007. Acrylic on canvas. 20 in. x 30 in.

offences. I challenged Kane to a painters' duel, outside, this very minute! The sticky latch suddenly yielded to poor Frances and we tumbled out of the suffocation of the library into the crowded hallway. I pushed past the throngs of costumed guests and made my escape.

Kane grabbed his paint kit and ran after me with Lefroy and three other friends also dressed in ceremonial masks.[324] I grew ever more furious at the thought of these men wearing the masks as if they were mere costumes for amusement, and not living entities with power undreamed of by these dog asses, these atimociskak! Kane implored me to stay calm—then, seeking to placate me, made the inane and offensive suggestion of painting me dressed in an "authentic" Haudenosaunee woman's dress. Kane was another Catlin! The hubris and foolishness of these men knew no bounds. I am not Haudenosaunee and certainly not a woman! I am nêhiyaw, and although I dearly love my iskwêwak sisters, I am all genders, all forms, and nothing that can be defined by one word in any language.

I swung my handbag with the full force of my fury and knocked him down. I'd had enough of this pretender who dared to tell *me* I was inauthentic!

I would be back for those masks in the morning.

I slept not a wink, for I spent the night steaming with rage. When I returned soon after dawn, Kane was still sleeping off his hangover, his servant told me. I stormed past the quivering man and into Kane's living room. "Where are the masks?!" He had no idea of what I spoke and was clearly terrified. Not wanting to punish the poor man for his master's sins, I softened my tone. "The masks worn last night at the masquerade."

"Master Lefroy took them, sir—I mean madame! He left just a quarter of an hour ago, headed northwest."

I hitched my fine atimwak to my sled, urging them to run hard, and caught up to Lefroy within the hour. He was wearing the garb of a Métis hunter, and travelling with a toboggan pulled by a motley trio of European mutts.[325] I knocked his sled over with one crack of my whip. "I'll take those," I told him.

Lefroy began to stammer some kind of objection, but I had long run out of patience. I seized the masks. "It matters not how you got them, but these were made for ceremony. I will take them back home, to the medicine people who know how to take care of them."

I cracked my whip once more and was away. I needed to be out of this muddy town and back amongst my people. My head was still spinning with what I had seen and heard. That man, Ryerson . . . taking our children—that could not be possible. He was a madman, no one would do that. But I felt uneasy.

I travelled west until there was no more snow, then, as spring break-up was well underway, unharnessed the dogs—they would find their way back to the Fur Queen. mwêscasês, I would return the medicine masks to their homes on the west coast. Little did I know then that in a few decades, while the European nations were carving up continents to steal their spoils, they would be banning all our ceremonies across these lands, including potlatches in our western coastal nations.[326] All ceremonial items, including these masks, would be seized, sold, traded, and scattered—along with the rest of their plunder—to be imprisoned in glass cases all across the world, with no one to wrap them or sing their sacred songs.[327]

From kihcikamîhk, Lake Superior, I took the Pigeon River out west, connecting from river to river until I reached nêstawê'ya—Three Points, the Forks—at the place that the môniyâw called Fort Garry.[328] I then took the Assiniboine River and linked up with âpakosîs-sîpîhk, the Souris River, travelling to the land of my southern kin. I eventually left the river to travel by land to Mitu'tahakto's.

I knew that these lands had always been rich in paskwâwi-mostoswak. I hoped to meet a herd as I travelled so that I might ask about what my sister had told me, but I saw not a single paskwâwi-mostos along the whole journey, which filled me with a cold fear.

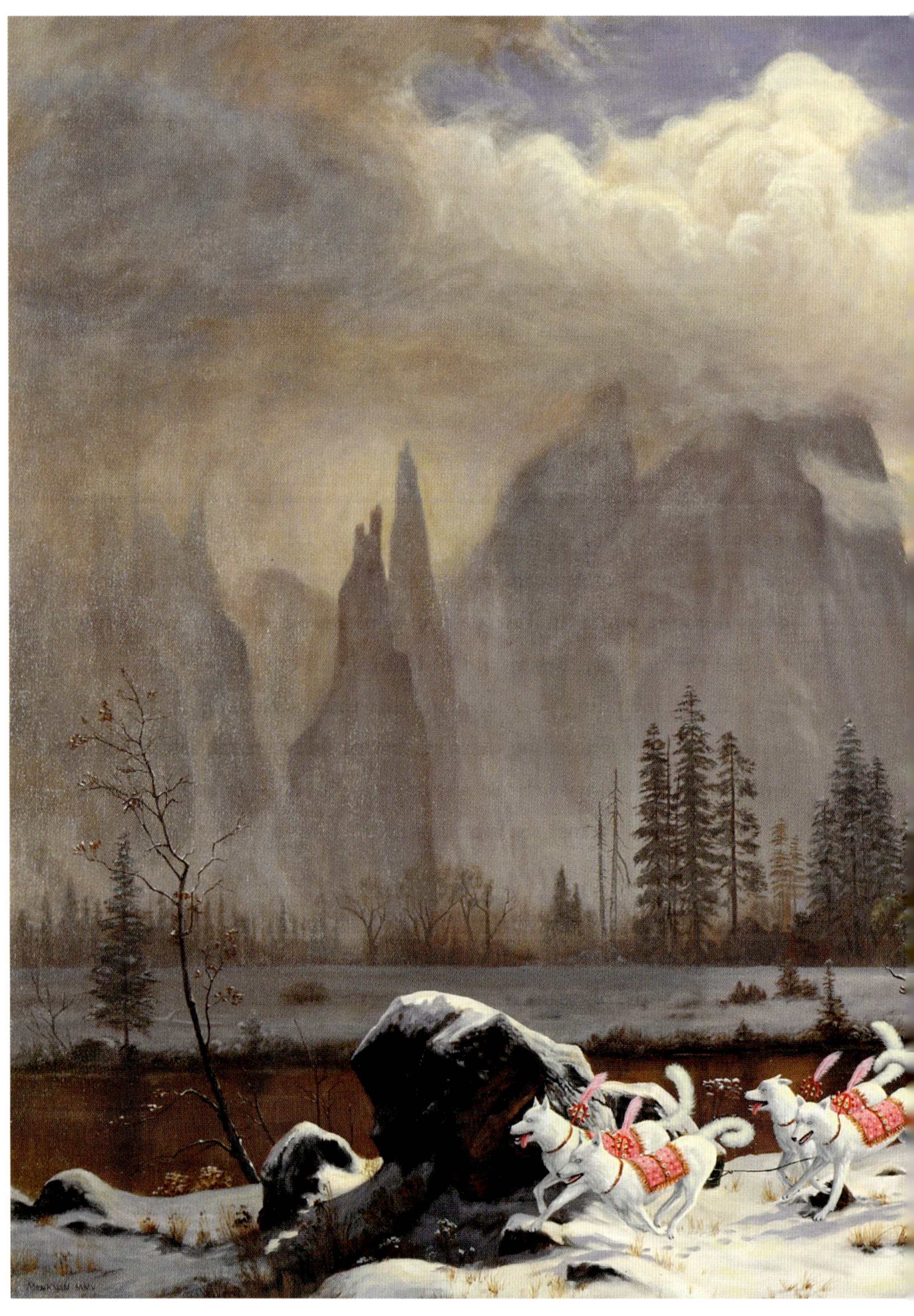

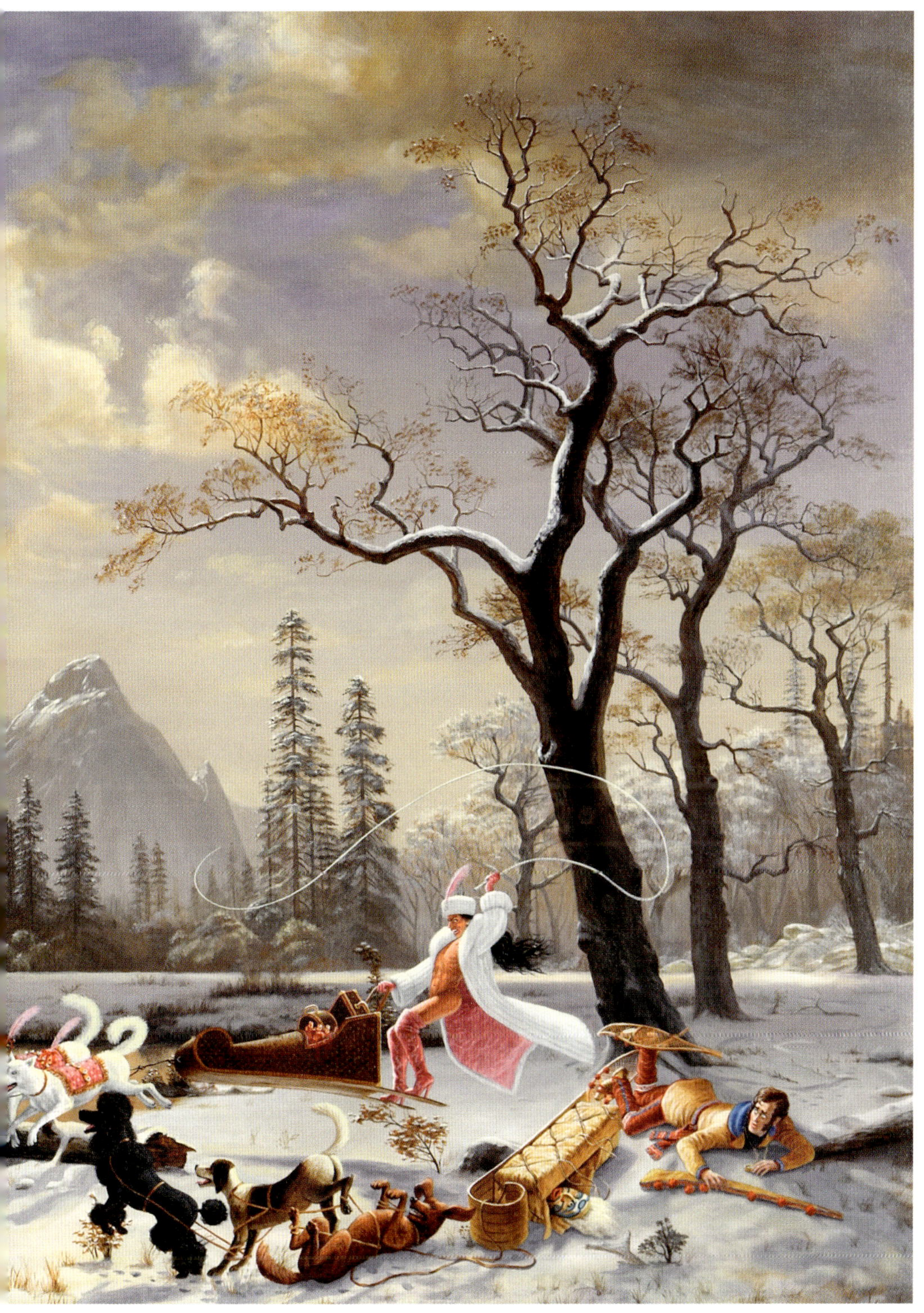

I hitched my fine atimwak to my sled, urging them to run hard, and caught up to Lefroy within the hour.

Charged Particles in Motion, 2007. Acrylic on canvas. 48 in. x 72 in.

ᑕ ᐋᐧᒋᐦᐊᑯᐠ ᓂᑖᔨᓯᓃᒪᐠ ᓂᑮ

ᐅᓯᐦᐋᐤ ᐅᑭᒫᐢᑫᐧᐤ ᐁ ᑮ

ᐊᐱᒋᔭᑭᐠ ᐊᓂᑭ ᐅᐢᑭ

ᐅᑭᔩᑫᐘᐠ ᐅᑑᑭᒫᒥᐚᐘ

To Help My People I Made Mischief with the Newcomers' Leaders

A few years after the prince's visit, I had another opportunity to try to influence those laying claim to our lands. I discovered that the newcomers' leaders were meeting in the place known to the Mi'kmaq as Booksak, but the newcomers called it Charlottetown.[329]

Through my networks of animals, plants, and traders, I learned that in this meeting a great game for power was being played between the leaders of the British settler colonies on our lands. The provincial leaders recognized the wisdom of the Haudenosaunee Confederacy structure and were trying to emulate it to form a government, but they did not understand its deep roots in askiy and spent their time squabbling instead. Their ragtag governments were fighting amongst each other for territory and influence, and couldn't even agree where to establish the seat of power for these lands over which they had no legal, moral, or spiritual authority. But they had a greater threat that was forcing them to unite. The Americans had taken control of our hunting grounds in the south and were embroiled in their own civil war, and these British colonials feared that the Americans would come up and claim these territories for themselves, just as the British and French had done to us.

No one had invited any of us, the original inhabitants of these lands, for we were obstacles to their railroads and their settlements, so I invited myself. My people needed an ally in power, and I had my ways of getting a seat at the table.

I walked through the empty streets draped only in the Hudson's Bay blanket George Simpson had given me. There were two meetings of clowns and actors going on in the small city of Charlottetown this week, but most inhabitants were only concerned with one. The whole town was at Slaymaker and Nichols' Olympic Circus, watching a troupe of acting dogs, comical monkeys, clowns, and the learned trick horse Pegasus. I would be at the other.

When I arrived at their big house with its columns copied from old Europe, these old colonial drunks had been arguing and drinking for days and were already kîskwêpêwin, besotted with liquor. Down on the wharves I'd heard talk of how these men had brought with them a

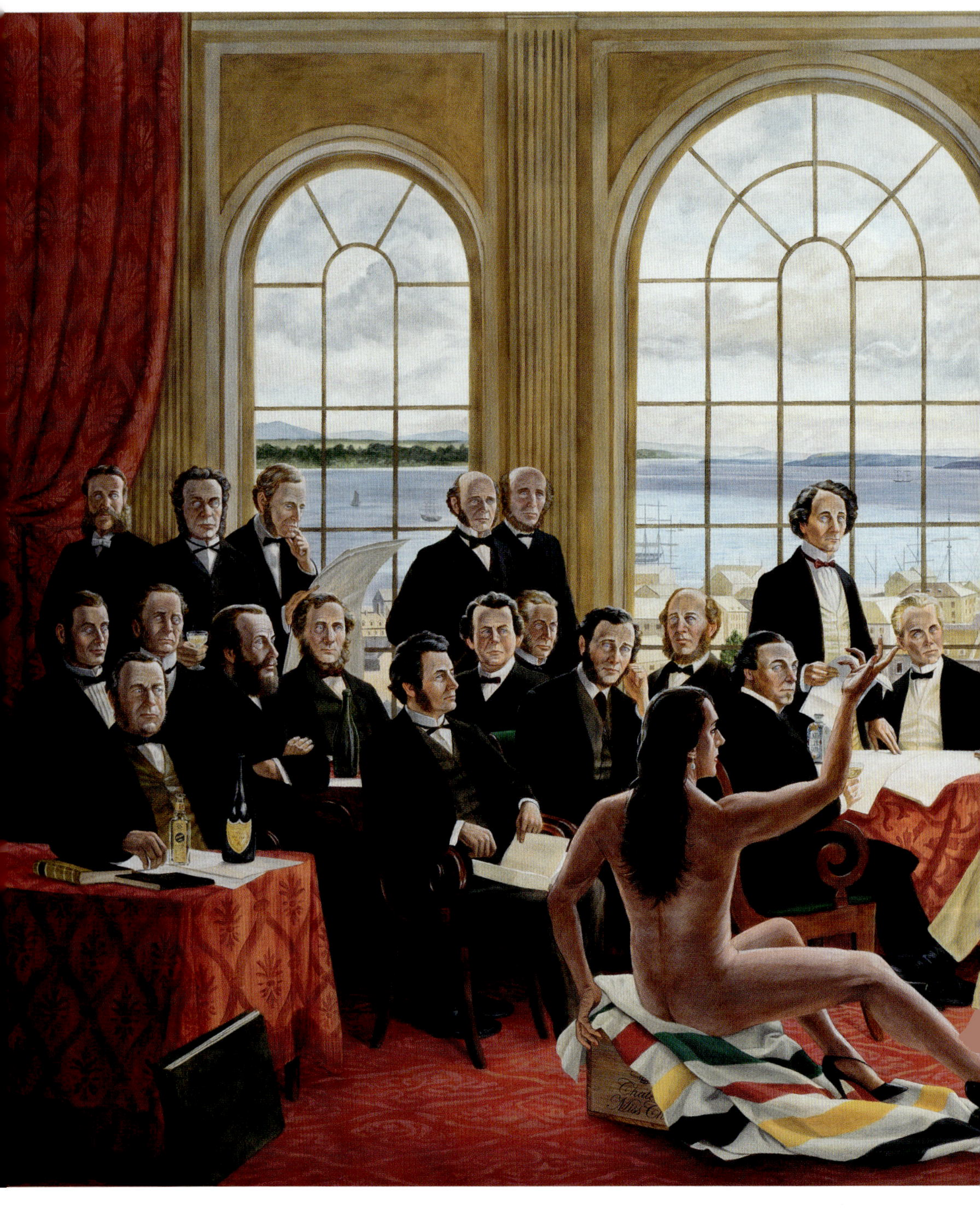

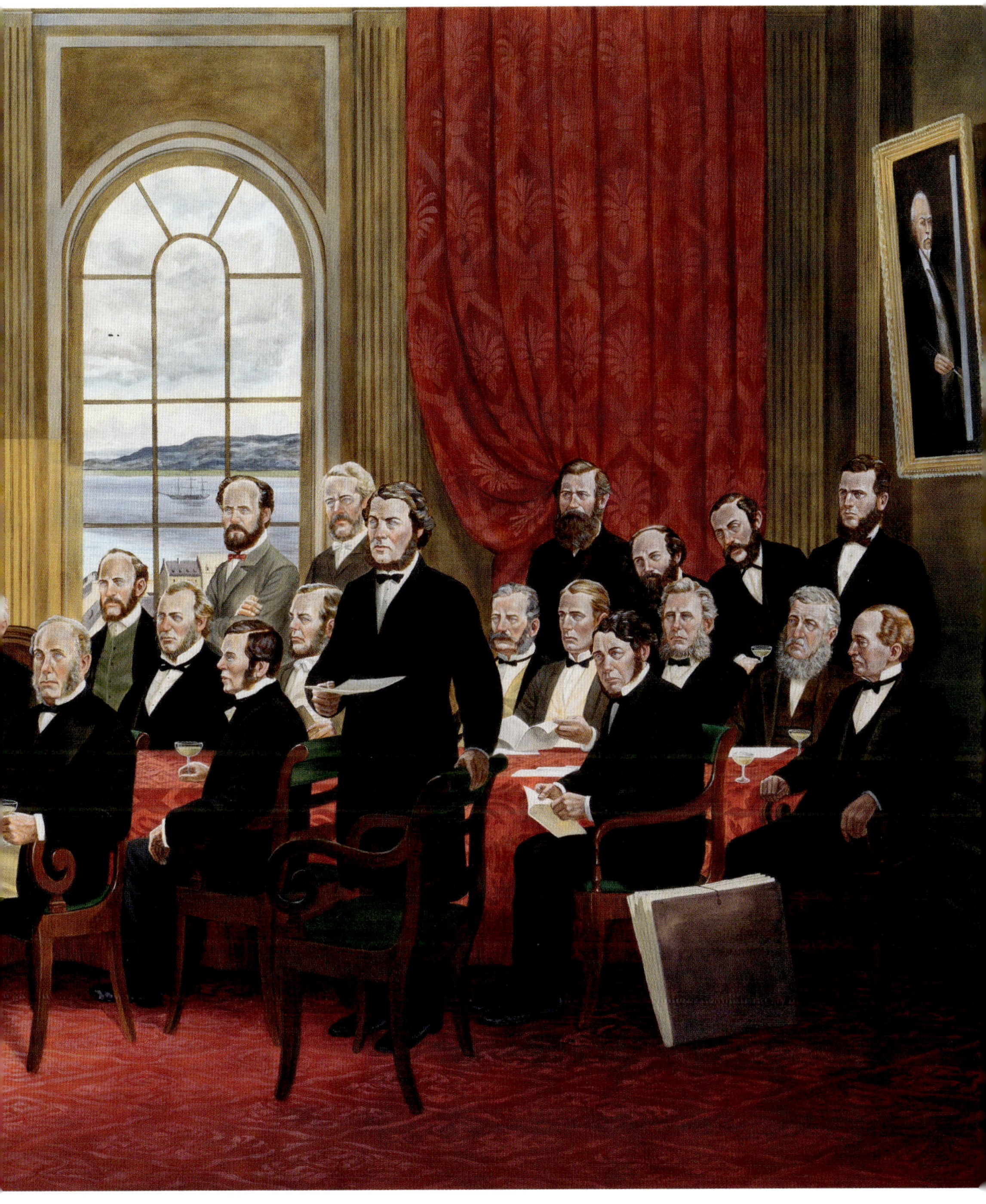

No one had invited any of us, the original inhabitants of these lands, for we were obstacles to their railroads and their settlements, so I invited myself. My people needed an ally in power, and I had my ways of getting a seat at the table.

The Daddies, 2016. Acrylic on canvas. 60 in. x 112.5 in.

steamship hold's worth of champagne. By the time I arrived, they had already made a significant dent in it.[330] They were shouting so loudly at one another they didn't notice when I stepped in, but once I dropped my blanket and seated myself in my natural glory in their midst, the room fell silent. I, in my magnificence, was the one thing upon which they could focus all of their attentions. Naked, I am at my most powerful.

They stared at me, mouths wide open. In a clear, strong voice I told them they needed to stop their expansion and listen to the land. We had agreed to share it with them, but our laws of miyo-wîcêhtowin needed to be respected. They looked in my direction, but it was hard to tell if any were listening, or if they were merely gaping at my generous offering dangling before them.

Once I stopped speaking, there was a heavy silence until they once again started shouting and talking over one another—some seeming to be thinking about what I had said, but the red-faced, most drunken ones dismissing what they referred to most offensively as the romantic notions of a dying race. When they resumed their arguing, I observed them, trying to discern which one might have the most power and would be the best for me to target with all of my skills.

One of them, Cartier, had dark, deep-set eyes underneath bushy brows, with hair combed back tightly on his scalp. He spoke so loudly and passionately, hardly letting his companions get a word in. A man so confident and talkative could be useful in making sure our laws were known amongst his people, but would he ever stop talking to allow me the time to teach them to him?[331]

Another man on the edge of the discussions had been looking around the room with a surly expression. His long, narrow face was flanked by prominent sideburns that ran all the way down to his chin. George Brown. My talents would be wasted on one so dour and stiff, and I was doubtful I could channel influence through someone who seemed to dislike so many of the others in the room. I noticed how he kept shooting hostile glances at one of the men in particular.[332]

The target of Brown's disdain was John A. Macdonald. I remembered this shameless old okîskwêpêsk, this drunkard, from when I met Prince Eddie at Tiohtià:ke (Montréal). In complete disregard of the formality of this meeting, Macdonald was so sodden that in the middle of berating George Brown, he lost his balance and fell backwards—only to be pushed upright once more by those behind him and continue on. Despite his inebriation, he remained eloquent, and it was clear that he was a wily politician, able to manoeuvre around the others with ease. I could see that he had the fervour and ambition of someone who wanted to win at any cost. What he and others at the table wanted was to join their various settler colonies into a united country that one of them would control.

In Europe, I had learned that men like him were so simple, blinded by greed; they saw the world only as that from which they could profit. The okîskwêpêsk was clearly of this sort. And while his lumpy, large-nosed face was not to my liking, and his sour-milk body odour and alcohol- and vomit-tinged breath quite repulsive, his relationship with the bottle was a weakness I could perhaps exploit to help my people. It would be easy to let a man like this think I was giving him what he wanted, and perhaps in time shift his thinking, for he had power to influence others of his kind.

I remained at the champagne-soaked gathering for the next few days, listening, observing, and luring. The okîskwêpêsk asked me to dance at the ball, but he was so pickled, I had to hold him upright.[333] Fortunately, I had twenty times his strength and even in my heels was steadier on my feet. My strength and elusiveness intrigued him, and by the end of this gathering, he had become enamoured of me, and I became his country wife, married à la façon du pays.

We would continue to have discreet visits, and our liaisons carried on for the next few years in what was to be my greatest acting achievement—although thankfully, the okîskwêpêsk's steady drinking incapacitated him by every evening, so our relationship was never consummated.

While the okîskwêpêsk seemed to admire my many attributes, he also saw in me a chance to connect to the powerful trapper Cree and

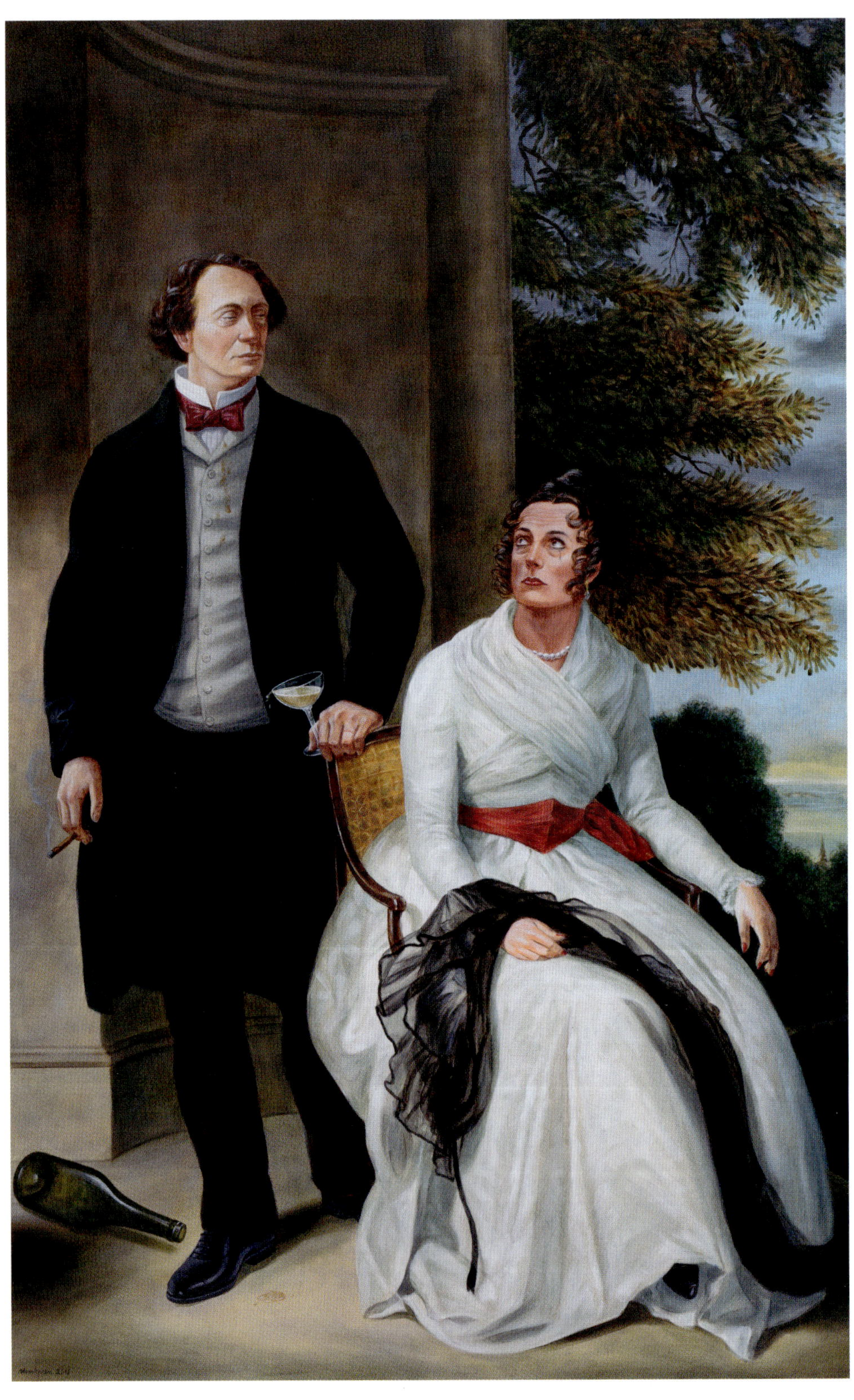

When the stakes are high and our enemies mighty, we must do what we can in order to tip the scales in our favour.

A Country Wife, 2016. Acrylic on canvas. 60 in. x 36 in.

Métis communities. Yet his interest was only for his gain—his pattern of thought about our peoples was vile. He said to me one day, "We have been pampering and coaxing the Indians. We must take a new course—we must vindicate the position of the white man, we must teach the Indians what law is . . ."[334] Too angry to speak, I threw him over my lap and spanked him thoroughly, only to discover that the atimocisk—the confounding dog ass actually was enjoying it! I pushed him to the floor in disgust.

With this wîcêwâkanihtowin, this alliance, I had hoped to influence Macdonald for the benefit of our peoples. But he was enamoured with his own ideas, focused on creating his nation in the way he wanted, and determined to take the highest offices for himself. "I don't care for office for the sake of money," he slurred to me one evening, "but for the sake of power, and for the sake of carrying out my own views of what is best for the country."[335]

His views, and those of the other môniyâwak who had seized power through influence and bribery, were almost always to do with taking our lands. They held meetings across the country attempting to unite their own leaders and settle their affairs, but the only mention of our peoples was how to remove and control us. These meetings became increasingly focused on iyiniwak lands. When I spoke to the okîskwêpêsk of our laws, of the necessity for balance and only taking what we needed, he dismissed me as if I were a child. "I would be quite willing, personally, to leave that whole country a wilderness for the next half-century," he said, clumsily patting me as though trying to soothe me—or silence me. "But I fear if Englishmen do not go there, Yankees will.[336] There is no maxim which experience teaches more clearly than this, that you must yield to the times.[337] Besides, there are even greater advantages for us all in view. By going west, we will become a great nation . . ."[338] I tried to cajole him into saying more, to find out how he intended to go west, that I might warn and prepare the nations in his path, but he had already succumbed to the drink and was snoring on the table.

One night he almost set fire to the humble cabin we used for our liaisons. After several bottles of wine, he fell asleep with candles still lit. His nightshirt and bedsheets caught fire, and he suffered painful burns on his hands and forehead.[339] More of him would have burned if I had not woken up in time to douse him with his own chamber pot. There would be many days when I would wonder how our futures might have been different if I had not saved him that night, but another of his ilk would have surely taken his place, and besides, Kisê-manitow had not sent me from the acâhkosak to this askiy to cause harm, even to this vile soul.

I attempted to override my revulsion towards him by focusing more intently on how I could influence him to honour our peoples. Many times, I made him promise not to listen to the odious recommendations made by Ryerson and others to mould our children so they would acquire the habits and modes of thought of white men. In the evenings, he agreed, but like every addict, he remembered nothing by the morning.[340] I often got close to softening his rhetoric about our peoples, but like many men who hide their true feelings, outwardly he became more cruel and patronizing to distract from and compensate for his secret life. Eventually it became clear that although he had power, he would not use it to help our peoples, and his attraction to me as an individual did not, as I had hoped, translate into respect or care for iyiniwak.

After three years of suffering his hubris, I accompanied the okîsk-wêpêsk to one last meeting of the "Canadian" alliances—what they called "Confederation." There were still none of our people present. Once more I spoke eloquently and forcefully about the agreements and understandings between our peoples and the settlers, and their need to respect our relationship to the land and its laws, but they merely nodded and made a show of listening. When they wrote their paper for Confederation, they mentioned us only once in their British North America

Act, in a line that said that the new Canadian government would have control over our affairs.

I had been able to control my growing rage, but then Cartier began to speak and I lost all self-restraint. He told the others about the economic and trade advantages to be had by "purchasing" Rupert's Land for the equivalent of trinkets from the Hudson's Bay Company in Britain.[341] Brown concurred, declaring that Rupert's Land was their birthright.[342] Infuriated, I screamed, "Purchase? How can you purchase what cannot be sold?" My voice shook. "By what possible means can this fur trading company in another country, or any entity for that matter, claim any ownership over these lands to which thousands of our nations belong!?" They stared at me blankly. My dissent was ordered struck from the record.

This vast expanse of prairie, bush, rivers, lakes, and forests that they called Rupert's Land, one-third of the area that would come to be called Canada—prairie, bush, rivers, lakes, and forests on which my iyiniwak people, the nêhiyawak, and the Nakoda, Anishinaabe, Nakawē, Dene, Omàmiwininiwak, Očhéthi Šakówiŋ, Siksika, Tsuut'ina, Innu, Naskapi, and Inuit, had been living, hunting, and trapping since they were first placed here by Kisê-manitow[343]—were being "sold" by the Hudson's Bay Company to this one-year-old country of these old drunkards' imagination: the Dominion of Canada. Not one of these nations—or the Métis, with whom we shared the lands—was being consulted or considered in this transaction.

The okîskwêpêsk wanted all the lands clear from sea to sea so he could build the railroad he had promised to the western provinces if they agreed to join his Dominion. His was a dream forged by fools and built on a lie. The concept was unfathomable; the arrogance of presuming to own what is the Kisê-manitow's only, unthinkable. When our leaders had signed agreements with the early newcomers, such as the one Chiefs Peguis, Mache Wheseab, Mechkaddewikonaie, Kayajieskebinoa, and Ouckidoat made with the man called Selkirk, we made space so that his poor Scots could share our land. These settlers were welcomed as kiciwâminawak, in the spirit of nikwatisowin êkwa mâtinamâkêwin.

This sale meant more money to the Hudson's Bay Company and another blow to our peoples. Since their arrival on miskinâhk-oministik, we had kept those that worked for them and their competitors alive. They had disrupted our alliances, pushed almost every community towards hunting and trapping for trade with them rather than sustenance, and almost wiped out our brothers and sisters—the amiskwak, beavers, and the paskwâwi-mostoswak. We had changed our systems and cultures to adjust to their ways, but despite my best efforts, not enough of them had seen that they also needed to change their systems and cultures to the ways of our lands.

Their policies would kill my people. It was as the elders had foretold: drinkers of dark liquids would come upon our land, speaking nonsense and filth.[344]

My fury got the better of me. I pulled out a case of what they thought was their champagne. But it was an effervescent drink that my maskwak brother and sisters had taught me to make from fermented juniper, tamarack, and misâskwatômina. It would open up these grey souls, so that their true natures might be revealed. I poured them each a generous glass of my "champagne," but abstained myself.

They did not suspect me, for to them, I was the okîskwêpêsk's lowly and disposable country wife, and while they had their prejudices, their authentic selves opened like putty in my hands.

I led them outside, tearing off the dull and restrictive clothing I'd worn in that exhausting role and revealing myself as I am. These self-appointed leaders of stolen land gaped, hypnotized by my true self. Under the influence of my presence and their libations, they revelled in the first moments of freedom and abandon they had known since early childhood. I summoned my maskwak to help coax them even further back to their authentic natures. They blossomed, squealing with terrified glee, running like rabbits from a fox as I cracked my whip. Oh, how Niska, Kimiwan, and Minôsis would laugh when I regaled them with this tale.

I could not interfere or change human business, but I could help in my way. Perhaps these leaders of the new country would be better humans after tasting liberation and freedom. Or perhaps it merely made me feel better to unleash some of my fury in a way that did not harm the pathetic creatures, but caused me much pleasure.

I had used up all my patience. It was time to move on. Us âtayôhkanak usually pay little attention to dates, but I do remember the day I left the okîskwêpêsk, July 1, 1867, for the birth of Canada was no celebration for us.

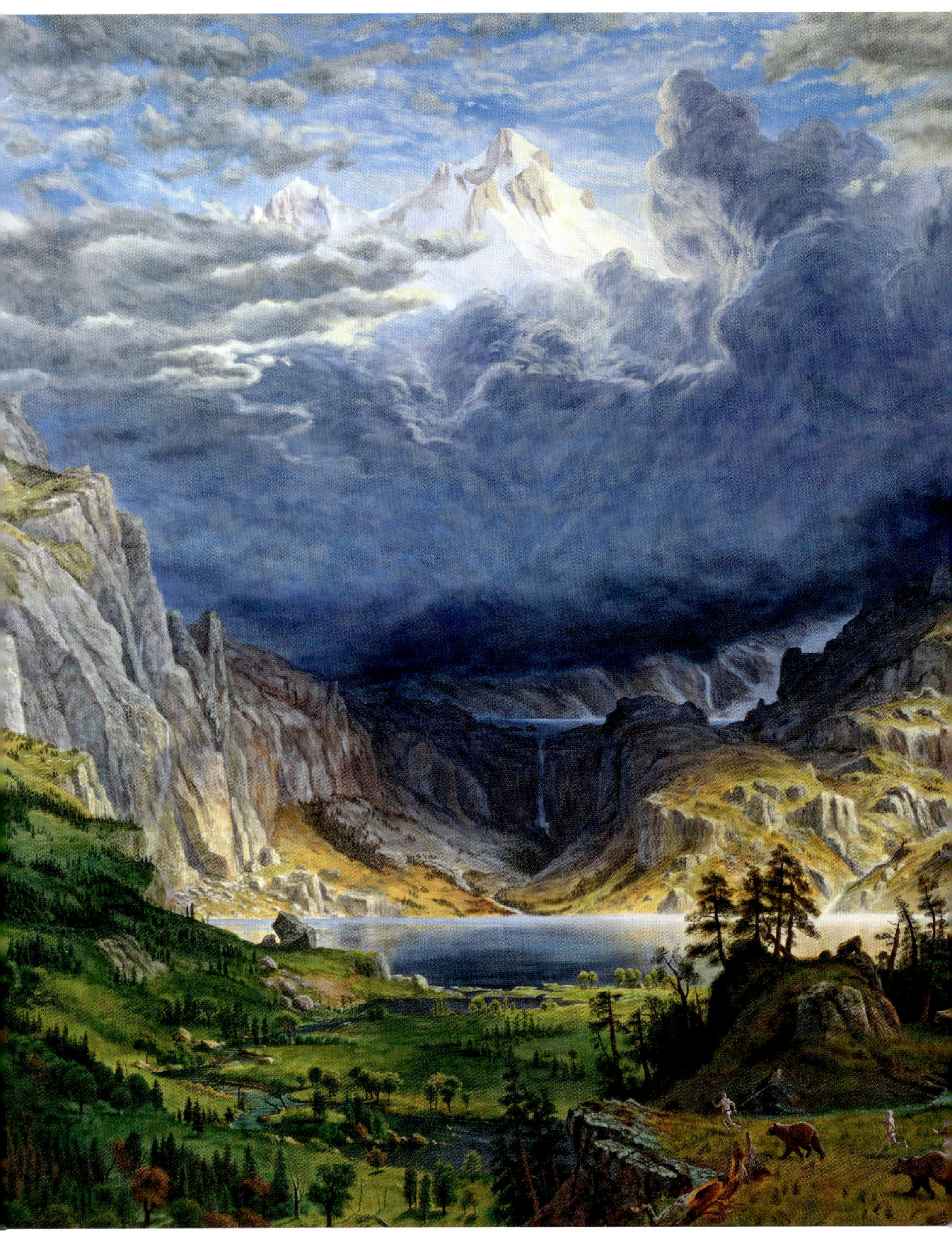

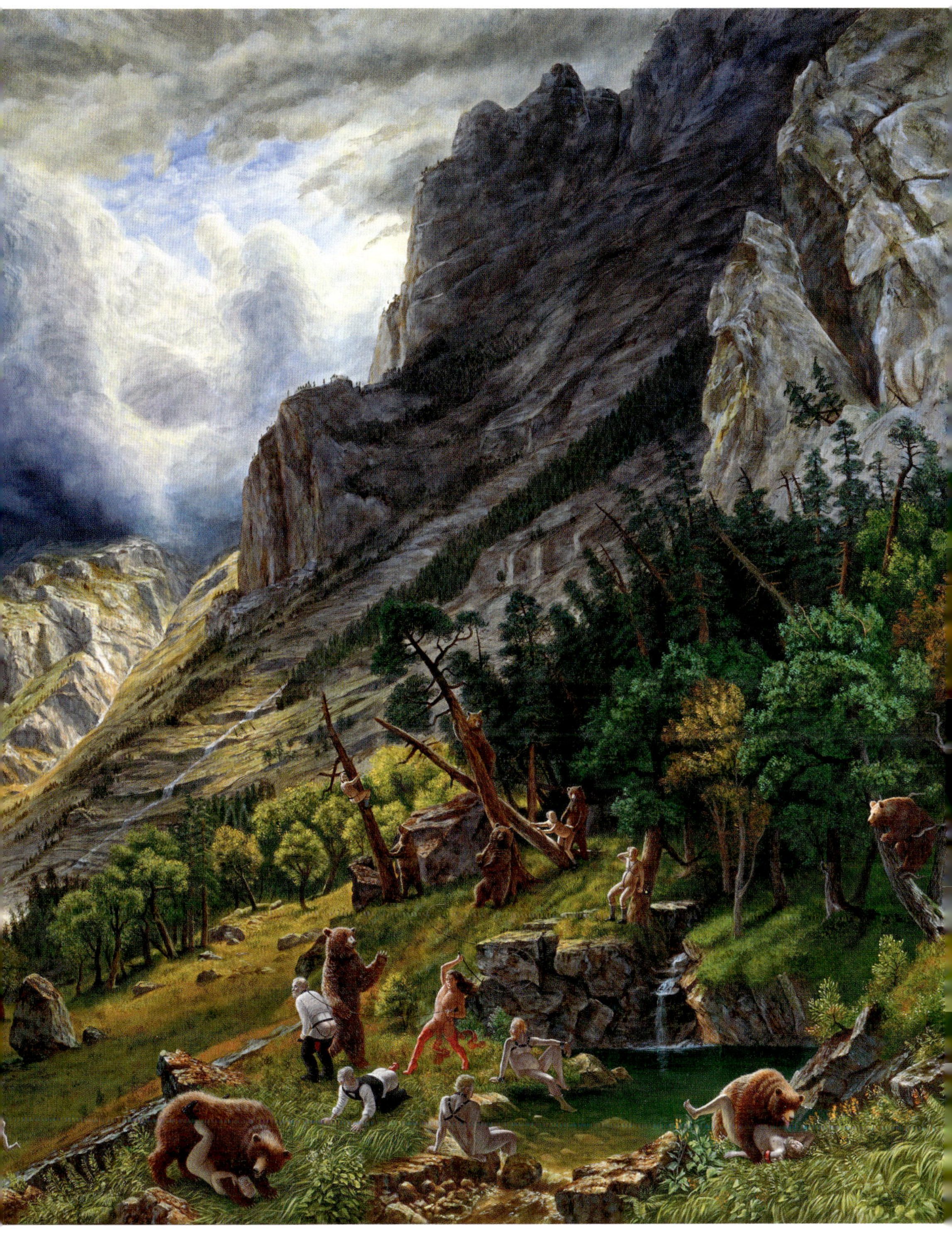

I would teach them what it was to be subjugated!

The Bears of Confederation, 2016. Acrylic on canvas. 76 in. x 132 in.

NOTES

A Star is Born

1 kinanâskomitin to Floyd Favel for inspiring this chapter title (Floyd Favel, interview by Gisèle Gordon, August 2018).

2 This description of the beginning of the universe is based on a passage by Cree lawyer and scholar Sylvia McAdam, or Saysewahum (Sylvia McAdam, *Nationhood Interrupted: Revitalizing Nêhiyaw Legal Systems*, Saskatoon: Purich Publishing Limited, 2015, p. 37). Floyd Favel says that Kisê-manitow created themselves "through a thought . . . through an impulse" (Floyd Favel, audio interview by Gisèle Gordon, October 2, 2018).

3 "In Native science," explains Blackfoot scholar Dr. Leroy Little Bear, "we are about energy waves. In other words, you and I are simply combinations of different energy waves that make for our existence." According to Indigenous worldviews, the universe is in flux, and everything is part of an "ecological relational network" (Leroy Little Bear, "Blackfoot Metaphysics: 'Waiting in the Wings,'" lecture at the Oils and Science Symposium, Calgary, November 23, 2016).

4 Wîsahkêcâhk is sometimes referred to as a "trickster" (Louis Bird, "Legend of Wiisaakechaahk," *Our Voices*, February 12, 1993, transcript, p. 1). According to Cree writer John G. Hansen, stories about Wîsahkêcâhk "[impart] a unique, indirect understanding of how one ought to interact with the world . . . I was always struck with how intelligent or foolish he could be about his decision making" (John G. Hansen, "The Autonomous Mind of Wasekchak," *The Quint* 11, no. 1, December 2018, p. 19).

5 Cree scholar Edward Ahenakew describes "the legend of Pe-ya-siw (Thunderbird), the name we give to the Great Birds that are usually invisible, enormous in size, the rulers of the universe, from whose eyes come the flashes of lightning, and from whose throats the thunder that rumbles or tears the firmament" (Edward Ahenakew, *Voices of the Plains Cree*, ed. Ruth M. Buck, Regina: University of Regina, 1995, p. 70).

6 The actual Cree creation story is sacred knowledge, and telling it in its entirety requires specific protocol and takes many days (Floyd Favel, audio interview by Gisèle Gordon, October 2, 2018).

7 Here Miss Chief is referring to the sacred site of petroglyphs at masinasin, Alberta (in Plains Cree Y dialect the word for petroglyphs would be spelled masinâpiskahikêwin), which is called

Áísínai'pi in Blackfoot and Writing-on-Stone in English. It is located along what the Cree call apisci-sîpîsis, the Blackfoot call Kinàksisahtai, and the English call Milk River (Writing-on-Stone Provincial Park, "Blackfoot Glossary," https://www.albertaparks.ca/parks/south/writing-on-stone-pp/education-interpretation/blackfoot-glossary/; Algonquian Dictionaries Project, Blackfoot Dictionary, 2020, https://dictionary.blackfoot.atlas-ling.ca; Miyo Wahkohtowin Community Education Authority, Online Cree Dictionary, https://www.creedictionary.com).

8 Cree thought and stories are diverse; regarding the creation story, "We have many stories, given to us at different times by different people. I myself know three creation stories. The principle of oral stories is that all are correct" (Floyd Favel, conversation with Gisèle Gordon, February 18, 2023).

9 In Cree astronomy, the constellation of Wîsahkêcâhk points to pakonî-kîsik, the Hole in the Sky. European scientists call these constellations Orion and the Pleiades respectively. Cree astronomer Wilfred Buck designates pakonî-kîsik as a "spatial anomaly, a wormhole" through which kîsikokak, or beings of light, came to askiy, or the earth, and founded humanity. Star Woman, also called Sky Woman, was the first spirit being to come to askiy "to experience, learn, teach, and explore" (Wilfred Buck, "Cree Mythology Written in the Stars," interview by Rosanna Deerchild, *Unreserved*, CBC Radio, August 12, 2016, audio, 9:14; Wilfred Buck, *Tipiskawi Kisik: Night Star Stories*, Winnipeg: Manitoba First Nations Education Resource Centre Inc., 2018, pp. 12–14).

10 As stellar spectroscopist Dr. Kim Venn notes, "heated hydrogen gas can glow pink, from recombining protons and electrons; when they recombine the electron will lose energy as it becomes attached to the proton to make a new hydrogen atom, and some of that energy will be released as pink light" (Dr. Kim Venn, personal correspondence with Gisèle Gordon, March 11, 2019).

11 As Adrienne Mayor writes, "there were stories to explain the remains of huge animals in the Northeast. The Algonquians, for example, referred to the 'bones found under the earth' as ancient monsters killed by their culture hero Manabozho" (Adrienne Mayor, *Fossil Legends of the First Americans*, Princeton: Princeton University Press, 2005, p. 9).

12 While *bison* is considered to be the more scientifically correct term, this story uses the word *buffalo*, which is preferred by many Indigenous people (Tasha Hubbard, "The Call of the Buffalo: Exploring Kinship with the Buffalo in Indigenous Creative Expression," PhD diss., University of Calgary, 2016, p. 1).

13 Equus species evolved on Turtle Island 4 million years ago and are believed to have crossed about 3 million years ago into Eurasia, where the modern horse evolved (Ben Singer, "A Brief History of the Horse in America: Horse Phylogeny and Evolution," *Canadian Geographic*, 2005; Kathleen Hunt, "Horse Evolution," The TalkOrigins Archive, January 4, 1995).

14 Sylvia McAdam writes on Cree elders' teachings about soul flames and the Creator's flame, or manitow-iskotêw. Every human being has a soul flame drawn from the same manitow-iskotêw, according to elder Barry Ahenakew (quoted in McAdam, *Nationhood Interrupted*, pp. 27–29).

When I Dreamed What Was to Come

15 According to Cree scholar Dr. Belinda Daniels, mamahtâwisiwin is the act of "tapping into the great mystery or channelling capabilities to [a] source that makes anything and everything possible . . . As Indigenous beings we can tap into this spiritual vortex for solutions, protection, guidance, strength" (Dr. Belinda Daniels, email to Gisèle Gordon, January 6, 2019). Cree elder and scholar Willie Ermine describes how "*mamatowisowin* is the capacity to connect to the life force that makes anything and everything possible" (Willie Ermine, "Aboriginal Epistemology," in *First Nations Education in Canada: The Circle Unfolds*, ed. Marie Battiste and Jean Barman, Vancouver: University of British Columbia Press, 1995, p. 110).

16 Turtle Island is a modern pan-Indigenous term. As Miss Chief experiences time differently, this is the term she uses. Métis writer Chelsea Vowel says that "Growing up, I always associated the term 'Turtle Island' with the Haudenosaunee . . . I knew it wasn't our term . . . Nonetheless, many indigenous scholars and activists have taken to using this term and it has become somewhat ubiquitous even among non natives when referring to indigenous issues" (Chelsea Vowel, "Pan-Indianism, Pan-Métisism," *âpihtawikosisân*, May 2, 2011, https://apihtawikosisan.com/2011/05/pan-indianism-pan-metisism/).

17 Borrows observes that in the Cree worldview, truth and justice are gifts given to human beings by Kisê-manitow, and "the only way they can find these gifts is if they look inside their hearts, only the bravest and purest of hearts would be able to do so" (quoted in McAdam, *Nationhood Interrupted*, p. 38).

18 Cree-Métis archaeologist Dr. Paulette Steeves argues that "mapping Pleistocene sites in the Eastern and Western Hemispheres paints a picture of human occupation across diverse environmental niches as early as 130,000 C BP [centuries before present] and possibly earlier than 200,000 C BP in the Western Hemisphere" (Paulette F. C. Steeves, *The Indigenous Paleolithic of the Western Hemisphere*, Lincoln: University of Nebraska Press, 2021, p. 127).

19 Cree-Métis scholar Dr. Keith Goulet speaks about the historical knowledge embedded in the Cree language regarding the Ice Age and kîwêtin, the north wind (Keith Goulet, "Keewetin (North Wind)," directed by Danis Goulet, 2015, video, 3:45, https://youtu.be/MmpvRjlDY5A, accessed June 20, 2019).

20 Indigenous stories of the piyêsiwak, thunderbirds, and misi-pisiwak or misi-kinêpik, great lynxes or water monsters, have been linked to extinct creatures such as dinosaurs and mastodons. As Adrienne Mayor writes, "Many stories refer to battles between sky or thunder beings and water monsters. In the Great Plains, the idea of primal conflicts between water monsters and giant birds was influenced by discoveries of the striking remains of huge flying reptiles, *Pteranodons* whose wings spanned twenty feet, lying in the ground . . ." (Mayor, *Fossil Legends*, p. 211).

21 There is some evidence that Indigenous Polynesian explorations may have reached the Americas prior to Columbus's arrival (Andrew Lawler, "Beyond *Kon-Tiki*: Did Polynesians Sail to South America?" *Science*, vol. 328, no. 5984, June 11, 2010, pp. 1344–47).

22 The Great Law of Peace is the agreement that unites the nations of the Haudenosaunee Confederacy (Haudenosaunee Confederacy, "The League of Nations," 2021, https://www.haudenosauneeconfederacy.com/the-league-of-nations/).

23 O'seronni'ón:we is the Kanien'kehá:ka name for the French, and translates literally to "the original/real axe head makers" (Kanien'kéha Endangered Language Initiative Mohawk Dictionary, "French, from France," https://kanienkeha.net/people/other-peoples/oseronnionwe/).

24 The Algonquin endonym is Omàmiwininiwak (Algonquins of Pikwakanagan First Nation, "Culture," 2018, https://www.algonquinsofpikwakanagan.com/culture/).

25 The Montagnais endonym is Innu (Les Entreprises Essipit, "Our History," 2021, https://vacancesessipit.com/en/innu/).

26 *Ratiristón:ni*, which means "iron makers," is the Kanien'kehá:ka term for the Dutch (Kanien'kéha Endangered Language Initiative, "Dutch," https://kanienkeha.net/people/other-peoples/ratiristonni/).

27 Tekeni Teiohate—also known as Guswenta, Kaswentha, or the Two Row Wampum treaty—was an agreement established between the Haudenosaunee and the Dutch in 1613 (Teyotsihstokwáthe Dakota Brant, "Law of the Land," *Trent Magazine*, December 14, 2017).

28 Jérôme Lalemant described a smallpox epidemic that struck the Kanien'kehá:ka (Mohawk) and Onyota'a:ka (Oneida) in 1662, which "wrought sad havoc in their Villages and has carried off many men, besides great numbers of women and children; and, as a result, their Villages are nearly deserted" (Jérôme Lalemant, "Relation of 1662–63," in *The Jesuit Relations and Allied Documents: Travels and Explorations of the Jesuit Missionaries in New France, 1610–1791, Vol. XLVIII: Lower Canada, Ottawas: 1662–1664*, ed. Reuben Gold Thwaites, Cleveland: The Burrows Brothers Co., 1899, p. 78).

My First Encounter with a Newcomer

29 According to Floyd Favel's interpretation, the Cree term môniyâw, plural môniyâwak—which refers to non-Cree people and is generally used to specifically describe a white person—came from the Cree pronunciation of *Montréal* (Favel, interview, August 2018).

30 The Hudson's Bay Company's charter proclaimed its control over 1.5 million square miles of land around Hudson Bay, or over 40 per cent of the area that would eventually come to be called Canada (Hudson's Bay Company, "The Royal Charter," HBC Heritage, 2016, https://www.hbcheritage.ca/things/artifacts/the-royal-charter).

31 In the seventeenth and eighteenth centuries, Britain used North America as a penal colony: courts would send convicted felons—some of whom would otherwise have been sentenced to death—to the colonies to work off their sentences as indentured servants. This was seen as a more merciful punishment that would in addition "yeild [sic] a profitable service to the Comon Wealth in parts abroade [sic]," according to a 1615 commission by King James I (quoted in Abbot Emerson Smith, "The Transportation of Convicts to the American Colonies in the Seventeenth Century," *The American Historical Review*, vol. 39, no. 2, January 1934, pp. 233–34).

32 Starting in the early seventeenth century, working-class migrants came to Turtle Island under arrangements whereby they repaid their debt through labour in the colonies. Over time, the labour force of white indentured servants came to be replaced by enslaved, unpaid Africans

(David W. Galenson, "The Rise and Fall of Indentured Servitude in the Americas: An Economic Analysis," *The Journal of Economic History*, vol. 44, no. 1, March 1984, pp. 3–4, 10–12).

33 During the entire history of the transatlantic slave trade, Europeans are estimated to have transported more than 12.5 million Africans as enslaved people, with about 2 million dying from the horrific conditions they were subjected to during crossings (James Williford, "Gross Injustice: The Slave Trade by the Numbers," *Humanities* vol. 31, no. 5, September/October 2010). As Elikia M'bokolo writes, Africa still suffers from the damage caused by the Atlantic slave trade (Elikia M'bokolo, "The Impact of the Slave Trade on Africa," *Le Monde Diplomatique*, April 1998).

34 In a statement recorded in the 1753 Treaty of Carlisle, Haudenosaunee chief Scarrooyady said to a Pennsylvania commission, "The Rum ruins us. We beg you would prevent its coming in such Quantities, by regulating the Traders . . . We desire it may be forbidden, and none sold in the Indian Country . . . When these Whiskey Traders come, They bring thirty or forty Cags [kegs], and put them down before us, and make us drink; and get all the Skins that should go to pay the Debts we have contracted for Goods bought of the Fair Traders . . . In short, if this Practice be continued, we must be inevitably ruined" (Benjamin Franklin, Isaac Norris, and Richard Peters, "Treaty of Carlisle, 1 November 1753," *Founders Online*, National Archives, https://founders.archives.gov/documents/Franklin/01-05-02-0026).

The Massacre of Our Beaver Relatives Foreshadowed What Was to Come

35 Trees have a complex system of roots similar to a nervous system. Recent research shows that trees in Turtle Island forests are covered in fungi with which they have a symbiotic relationship known as a "mycorrhizal network." Through this system, trees can share nutrients and even send stress signals to each other through their roots (Valentina Lagomarsino and Hannah Zucker, "Exploring the Underground Network of Trees—The Nervous System of the Forest," *Science in the News, Harvard University*, May 6, 2019, https://sitn.hms.harvard.edu/flash/2019/exploring-the-underground-network-of-trees-the-nervous-system-of-the-forest/, accessed February 28, 2021).

36 The number of beavers on Turtle Island prior to European contact is estimated to have ranged from 60 million to 400 million (Frances Backhouse, "Rethinking the Beaver," *Canadian Geographic*, December 1, 2013; Calvin Martin, *Keepers of the Game: Indian-Animal Relationships and the Fur Trade*, Berkeley: University of California Press, 1978, p. 173).

37 The power struggle over diminishing beaver resources in the seventeenth century culminated in the Beaver Wars between the Haudenosaunee Confederacy and nations allied with the French, such as the Wendat. These conflicts were further aggravated by major smallpox epidemics. The Wendat were dispersed from their homeland by the mid-1600s, creating far-reaching repercussions for the fur trade as a whole (Timothy P. Foran, "Economic Activities: Fur Trade," Canadian Museum of History, Virtual Museum of New France, 2018; Olive Patricia Dickason, *Canada's First Nations: A History of Founding Peoples from the Earliest Times*, Toronto: McClelland and Stewart Inc., 1993, pp. 130–35).

38 European involvement in the fur trade had a highly negative impact on beaver populations. Due to the new demands for fur as well as the introduction of firearms to Turtle Island, the beaver was depleted in the St. Lawrence region (Kaniatarowanénhne) by 1635 (Ann M. Carlos and Frank D. Lewis, "Indians, the Beaver, and the Bay: The Economics of Depletion in the Lands of the Hudson's Bay Company, 1700–1763," *The Journal of Economic History*, vol. 53, no. 3, September 1993, p. 467).

39 After his voyage of 1497, John Cabot alerted the rest of Europe to the cod-rich waters of the new world. Cod became one of the many resources to be extracted by European nations (Mark Kurlansky, *Cod: A Biography of the Fish That Changed the World*, Toronto: Vintage Canada, 1998, p. 51). By the early twentieth century cod had been depleted in the North Sea, and by the end of the century it had become rare in the waters off North America (ibid., pp. 20–32, 144, 186).

40 The Beothuk lived in present-day Newfoundland. As Métis historian Olive Dickason writes, European settlers intruded onto Beothuk land and eventually targeted and killed the Beothuk outright; the Beothuk also suffered from tuberculosis introduced by settlers (Dickason, *Canada's First Nations*, pp. 95–96). Shawnadithit, the last known Beothuk, died of tuberculosis in June 1829, although Mi'kmaq oral evidence indicates that some survivors may have integrated with other Indigenous nations (James A. Tuck and David Joseph Gallant, "Beothuk," *The Canadian Encyclopedia*, June 20, 2019).

41 It is estimated that in 1630, 46 per cent of the land today called the United States was covered in forests, and since then, about 256 million acres of trees have been logged or cleared since the arrival of Europeans ("Land and Forest Area," in *U.S. Forest Resource Facts and Historical Trends*, ed. Sonja N. Oswalt and W. Brad Smith, United States Department of Agriculture, 2014, p. 7). Britain, having already depleted its own forests, wanted the great pines of Turtle Island to increase its navy, essential to the building of the British Empire (Eric Rutkow, *American Canopy: Trees, Forests, and the Making of a Nation*, New York: Scribner, 2012, pp. 14–15).

42 European diseases such as influenza, smallpox, and bubonic plague inflicted the Americas in waves so rapid and devastating that some Indigenous communities could not recover and were lost (Alexander Koch et al., "Earth System Impacts of the European Arrival and Great Dying in the Americas after 1492," *Quaternary Science Reviews*, vol. 207, March 1, 2019, p. 21). By the end of the seventeenth century, over 90 per cent of the Indigenous population in southwestern Turtle Island had died, according to the estimates of one Jesuit missionary (Elizabeth Fenn, *Pox Americana: The Great Smallpox Epidemic of 1775–82*, New York: Hill and Wang, 2001, p. 125).

The Newcomers Had Much to Learn

43 Historical buffalo ranges prior to 1800 spread from the Columbia Plateau in present-day Oregon to as far east as the Appalachians (J.A. Allen, "The American Bisons, Living and Extinct," in *Memoirs of the Geological Survey of Kentucky, Volume 1*, ed. N.S. Shaler, Cambridge: Welch, Bigelow & Co., 1876, p. 87; Louis Trouvelot and N.S. Shaler, "Map of North America: To Illustrate Facts of Geological Distribution," *Kentucky Geological Survey*, 1876).

44 *Bison latifrons* is an extinct species of bison that lived on Turtle Island until about 22,000 years ago. Very large in size, it stood at about eight feet tall at the shoulder and weighed over 2,200 pounds, with its horns sometimes spanning over seven feet (San Diego Zoo Wildlife Alliance, "Extinct Long-horned Bison & Ancient Bison (*Bison latifrons* and *B. antiquus*) Fact Sheet," San Diego Zoo Wildlife Alliance Library, 2009, https://ielc.libguides.com/sdzg/factsheets/extinctlonghorned-ancientbison).

45 The total pre-contact buffalo population on Turtle Island is estimated to have been 60 million (Russell Thornton, *American Indian Holocaust and Survival: A Population History Since 1492*, Norman: University of Oklahoma Press, 1987, p. 52). The size of historical herds could be immense, and it could take days for an entire herd to pass by an observer. Kâ-kîsikâw-pîhtokâw (Coming Day) recalled oral history that described how "for a distance of some ten miles the earth was not visible, as the buffalos covered it" (quoted in Leonard Bloomfield, *Plains Cree Texts: Volume XVI*, New York: G.E. Stechert & Co., 1934, p. 103). Colonel Richard Irving Dodge remembered seeing a herd in 1871 that stretched twenty-five miles across and fifty miles long (James H. Shaw, "How Many Bison Originally Populated the Rangelands?" *Rangelands*, vol. 17, no. 5, October 1995, p. 148).

46 The Indigenous death toll of the late eighteenth century smallpox epidemic was devastating. Fur trader Samuel Hearne estimated that the 1781 wave killed nine-tenths of the Chipewyans northwest of Hudson Bay; a North West Company servant estimated that three-fourths of the Indigenous population of the Plains was lost to the epidemic (Fenn, *Pox Americana*, p. 28). Data from around Cumberland House during this period suggests a mortality rate of up to 95 per cent (C. Stuart Houston and Stan Houston, "The First Smallpox Epidemic on the Canadian Plains: In the Fur-Traders' Words," *The Canadian Journal of Infectious Diseases*, vol. 11, no. 2, March–April 2000, p. 113). William Walker wrote in 1781 that "the small pox is rageing [sic] all round Us with great Violence, sparing very few that take it. We have received the News of above 9 tents of Indians within here, all Dead, the tents left Standing and their bodies left Inside Unburied" (quoted in ibid., p. 14). Matthew Cocking wrote in a 1781 York Factory journal entry that "the whole tribe of U'Basquia Indians are deceased except one young Child . . . the many different Tribes of Southern Assinne Poet and Yatchithinue Indians are also almost wholly extinct as I am assured by Messrs Tomison and Longmoor for they say that they really believe of young and old not one in fifty of those Tribes are now living" (ibid., p. 14).

47 In the last years of his life, Meriwether Lewis was noted to take pills containing opium on a regular basis, the purpose of which he claimed was to stave off the ill-effects of fever (Stephen Ambrose, *Undaunted Courage: Meriwether Lewis, Thomas Jefferson, and the Opening of the American West*, New York: Simon and Schuster, 1996, p. 558). Lewis also struggled with alcohol abuse in the last years of his life (ibid., pp. 460–73).

48 Meriwether Lewis and William Clark became close friends while undertaking military service as young men. When President Thomas Jefferson selected Lewis in 1803 to lead an expedition into the lands west of the Mississippi, Lewis personally chose Clark to be his co-captain. Lewis often referred to Clark as "my dear friend" and "friend and companion" (William Benemann, "My Friend and Companion: The Intimate Journey of Lewis and Clark," *We Proceeded On*, vol. 41, nos. 1 and 2, 2015).

49 Two years after the Corps of Discovery's expedition, Lewis spent a short period with Clark and Clark's new wife Julia in a rented house. Lewis soon departed from the house at Julia's instigation (Stephen Ambrose, *Comrades: Brothers, Fathers, Heroes, Sons, Pals*, New York: Simon and Schuster, 1999, p. 119). In his analysis of Lewis and Clark's relationship, William Benemann speculates that Julia saw Lewis as an unwelcome rival for her husband's attention (Benemann, "My Friend and Companion").

50 Lewis's mental and emotional well-being deteriorated in the years following the 1804–1806 expedition, particularly after he left Clark's residence (Ambrose, *Comrades*). Lewis's longing for Clark's presence was apparent when Lewis committed suicide on October 11, 1809. Earlier that day, Lewis had told his servant John Pernier that Clark was coming to help him with his current emotional troubles (Ambrose, *Undaunted Courage*, p. 571). That night, Lewis refused to sleep in a bed, preferring to have bear skins and buffalo robes laid out on the floor to mimic his sleeping arrangements during the western expedition he had taken with Clark a few years earlier (Benemann, "My Friend and Companion").

51 Newe is the name the Shoshone Nation use to refer to themselves in their own language (Christopher Loether, "Shoshones," *Encyclopedia of the Great Plains*, 2011; Herman Viola, "Indian Country: Native Peoples, Lewis and Clark, and Mapmaking," Smithsonian Institution, 2000. http://www.edgate.com/lewisandclark/indian_country.html).

52 Nuxbaaga is the name the Hidatsa Nation use to refer to themselves in their own language (James P. Ronda, *Lewis & Clark Among the Indians*, Lincoln: University of Nebraska Press, 1984, p. 70; Buffalo Bill Center of the West, "Land of Many Gifts," https://centerofthewest.org/tag/land-of-many-gifts/).

53 Clark acknowledged that Sacagawea was "of great service to me as a pilot through this country" (William Clark and Meriwether Lewis, *Original Journals of the Lewis and Clark Expedition, 1804–1806, Vol. 5.*, ed. Reuben Gold Thwaites, New York: Dodd, Mead & Company, 1904, p. 260). Lakota scholar Vine Deloria, Jr. states that "Sacagawea proved to be the deciding factor between success and failure of the expedition. Her memory was so extraordinary that we often do not understand it . . . This kind of memory is peculiar to North American Indians and is a talent far above mere retention of data" (Vine Deloria, Jr., "Frenchmen, Bears, and Sandbars," in *Lewis and Clark Through Indian Eyes: Nine Indian Writers on the Legacy of the Expedition*, ed. Alvin M. Josephy, Jr., and Mark Jaffe, New York: Alfred A. Knopf, 2006, p. 20).

54 In a journal entry on April 7, 1805, Lewis stated that the expedition was "now about to penetrate a country at least two thousand miles in width, on which the foot of civillized [sic] man had never trodden" (Clark and Lewis, *Original Journals . . . Vol. 1*, p. 284).

55 As Bill Yellowtail points out, Lewis and Clark did not enter a vacant western wilderness but a populated, diverse region with complex social and trade networks (Bill Yellowtail, "Meriwether and Billy and the Indian Business," in Josephy and Jaffe, *Lewis and Clark Through Indian Eyes*, p. 72). Lewis and Clark met many nations during their expedition, which are named in the following notes (Clark and Lewis, *Original Journals . . . Vol. 1*; Victor Temprano, "Native Land," Native Land Digital, https://native-land.ca/, accessed 2019; Center for Digital Research in the Humanities, "Identification of Western Indians" and "Identification of Eastern Indians," *Journals of the Lewis & Clark Expedition*, 2007).

56 Numakaki is the name the Mandan Nation use to refer to themselves in their own language (Elizabeth Fenn, *Encounters at the Heart of the World: A History of the Mandan People*, New York: Hill and Wang, 2014, p. 15).

57 Wahzhazhe is the name the Osage Nation use to refer to themselves in their own language (Phil Konstantin, "Tribal Names and the Lewis and Clark Corps of Discovery," *On This Date in North American Indian History*, 2002, https://studylib.net/doc/7576714/mandan----on-this-date-in-north-american-indian-history).

58 Tsétsêhéstâhese is the name the Cheyenne Nation use to refer to themselves in their own language (Chief Dull Knife College, *Cheyenne Dictionary*, 2017, http://cdkc.edu/cheyennedictionary/index.html).

59 Apsáalooke is the name the Crow Nation use to refer to themselves in their own language (Crow Tribe Executive Branch, "Crow Tribe of Indian," Crow-NSN.gov; Viola, "Indian Country").

60 Sahnish is the name the Arikara Nation use to refer to themselves in their own language (Hunter Old Elk, "The Mandan, Hidatsa, and Arikara People," Buffalo Bill Center of the West, February 28, 2019, https://centerofthewest.org/2019/02/28/the-mandan-hidatsa-and-arikara-people/; Konstantin, "Tribal Names").

61 Séliš is the name the Flathead or Salish Nation use to refer to themselves in their own language (Julie Cajune, "The Salish and Pend d'Oreille of the Flathead Indian Reservation," Honoring Tribal Legacies [online resource], n.d.; Konstantin, "Tribal Names").

62 Niimi'ipuu is the name the Nez Percé Nation use to refer to themselves in their own language (Haruo Aoki, *Nez Perce Dictionary*, Berkeley: University of California Press, 1994; PBS, "The Native Americans," Lewis and Clark: The Journey of the Corps of Discovery, n.d., https://www.pbs.org/lewisandclark/native/index.html).

63 Sqeliz is the name the Spokane Nation use to refer to themselves in their own language (Northwest Portland Area Indian Health Board, "Our Member Tribes," NPAIHB.org, 2015; Viola, "Indian Country").

64 Mamachatpam is the name the Yakama Nation use to refer to themselves in their own language (Northwest Portland Area Indian Health Board, "Our Member Tribes"; Konstantin, "Tribal Names").

65 Wanapum is the name the Wanapum Nation use to refer to themselves in their own language (Konstantin, "Tribal Names"; Wanapum Heritage Center, 2023, Wanapum.org; Wanapum Scholarship, "Wanapum History," 2023, https://wanapumscholarship.org/wanapum-history/).

66 Waluulapam is the name the Walla Walla Nation use to refer to themselves in their own language (Marianne Mithun, *The Languages of Native North America*, Cambridge: Cambridge University Press, 2001, p. 477; Konstantin, "Tribal Names").

67 Watɬlala is what the Shahala or Cascade Nation call themselves in their own language (Ronda, *Lewis & Clark Among the Indians*, p. 205; Si Matta, "About," Gathering the Stories, 2022, https://www.gatheringthestories.org/; Kristopher K. Townsend, "The Watlalas," Discover Lewis & Clark, 2023, https://lewis-clark.org/native-nations/chinookan-peoples/watlalas/).

68 Očhéthi Šakówiŋ is the name the Sioux Nation use to refer to themselves in their own language, and includes the Lakȟóta (Lakota)—Thítȟuŋwaŋ (Teton Sioux)—the Dakhóta—Sisíthuŋwaŋ (Sisseton), Waȟpéthuŋwaŋ (Wahpeton), Waȟpékhute (Wahpekute), and Bdewákhaŋthuŋwaŋ

(Mdewakanton)—and Nakhóta speakers—Iháŋktȟuŋwaŋ (Yankton Sioux) and Iháŋktȟuŋwaŋna (Yanktonai) (Christopher Pexa, *Translated Nation: Rewriting the Dakhóta Oyáte*, Minneapolis: University of Minnesota Press, 2019; PBS, "The Native Americans"; Viola, "Indian Country"; Center for Digital Research in the Humanities, "Identification of Eastern Indians").

69 Ñút^achi, Jiwére, and Báxoje are the names the Missouri, Otoe, and Iowa Nations use to refer to themselves, respectively (Jimm G. Goodtracks, "Ioway, Otoe-Missouria Language," Ioway Otoe Language, February 2006, https://iowayotoelang.nativeweb.org/; Konstantin, "Tribal Names").

70 Kathlamet and Wahkiakum are the names that the Kathlamet and Wahkiakum of the Chinook Nation use to refer to themselves in their own language (Konstantin, "Tribal Names"; Chinook Indian Nation, "The Chinook Indian Nation," n.d., https://chinooknation.org/who-we-are/).

71 Skilloot is the name that the Skilloot Nation use to refer to themselves in their own language (James Drake, "Lewis and Clark: Native American Tribes," Lewis and Clark Expedition, http://www.lewis-and-clark-expedition.org/lewis-clark-native-american-tribes.htm).

72 Nehalem is the name the Tillamook Nation use to refer to themselves in their own language (Barry Pritzker, *A Native American Encyclopedia: History, Culture, and Peoples*, New York: Oxford University Press, 2000, p. 207; PBS, "The Native Americans").

73 Tlatskanai is the name the Clatskanie Nation use to refer to themselves in their own language (Konstantin, "Tribal Names").

74 Multnomah is the name the Multnomah Nation use to refer to themselves in their own language (Konstantin, "Tribal Names").

75 Piikani is the name the Piegan Nation use to refer to themselves in their own language (Orrin Lewis and Laura Redish, "Indian Tribes and Languages of North America," Native Languages of the Americas, 2015, http://www.native-languages.org/north-america.htm).

76 Nakoda is the name the Assiniboine Nation use to refer to themselves in their own language (Temprano, "Native Land"; PBS, "The Native Americans").

77 Umo^{n}ho^{n} is the name the Omaha Nation use to refer to themselves in their own language (Marisa Miakonda Cummings, "Fighting the Colonizer Inside," *Omaha Magazine*, February 13, 2019; Ronda, *Lewis & Clark Among the Indians*, p. 14).

78 Chaticks si Chaticks is the name the Pawnee Nation use to refer to themselves in their own language (Pawnee Nation of Oklahoma, "2013 Annual Report: A Report to the Pawnee People," PawneeNation.org, 2013; Viola, "Indian Country").

79 Gaigwu is the name the Kiowa Nation use to refer to themselves in their own language (Konstantin, "Tribal Names").

80 Hinono'eino is the name the Arapaho use to refer to themselves in their own language (Lewis and Redish, "Indian Tribes and Languages"; Ronda, *Lewis & Clark Among the Indians*, p. 126).

81 Aaniihnén is what the White Clay People, called Gros Ventre, use to refer to themselves in their own language (Konstantin, "Tribal Names"; Randall Werk, "We call ourselves Aaniihnén . . .", Facebook, April 20, 2020).

82 Kiikaapoi is the name the Kickapoo Nation use to refer to themselves in their own language (Kansas Kickapoo Tribe, "History," https://www.ktik-nsn.gov/history; Konstantin, "Tribal Names").

83 Pan'akwati and Schitsu'umsh are the names the Bannock and Coeur d'Alene Nations use in their own languages to refer to themselves, respectively (Lewis and Redish, "Indian Tribes and Languages"; Northwest Portland Area Indian Health Board, "Our Member Tribes"; Konstantin, "Tribal Names").

84 Wasco is the name the Wasco Nation use to refer to themselves in their own language (Konstantin, "Tribal Names"; Warm Springs Community Action Team, "People of the River," n.d., https://wscat.org/community/history/).

85 Ita'xluit is the name the Wishram Nation use to refer to themselves in their own language (Ronda, *Lewis & Clark Among the Indians*, p. 170; PBS, "The Native Americans").

86 La'k!elak is the name the Clatsop Nation use to refer to themselves in their own language (Patricia Roberts Clark, *Tribal Names of the Americas: Spelling Variants and Alternative Forms, Cross-Referenced*, Jefferson: McFarland & Company, 2009, p. 124; Viola, "Indian Country").

87 Sts'ailes is the name the Chehalis Nation use to refer to themselves in their own language (Konstantin, "Tribal Names"; Sts'ailes, "We Are Sts'ailes," Sts'ailes.com, n.d.)

88 Atfalati is the name the Wappatoo Nation use to refer to themselves in their own language (Lewis and Redish, "Indian Tribes"; Konstantin, "Tribal Names and Languages").

89 Ql'ispé is the name the Pend d'Oreille Nation use to refer to themselves in their own language (Cajune, "The Salish and Pend d'Oreille of the Flathead Indian Reservation"; Konstantin, "Tribal Names").

90 Guithla'kimas is the name the Clackamas Nation use to refer to themselves in their own language (Clark, *Tribal Names of the Americas*, p. 76; Konstantin, "Tribal Names").

91 Stl'pulmsh is the name the Cowlitz Nation use to refer to themselves in their own language (Lewis and Redish, "Indian Tribes and Languages"; Drake, "Lewis and Clark: Native American Tribes").

92 Ksanka is the name the Kootenai Nation use to refer to themselves in their own language (Clark, *Tribal Names of the Americas*, p. 117; Konstantin, "Tribal Names").

93 Kuitsch and Siuslaw are the names the Lower Umpqua Nation and Siuslaw Nation use to refer to themselves in their own languages, respectively (Lewis and Redish, "Indian Tribes and Languages"; Konstantin, "Tribal Names"; Confederated Tribes of Coos, Lower Umpqua and Siuslaw Indians, "History," 2022, https://ctclusi.org/history/).

94 Hanis is the name the Coos Nation use to refer to themselves in their own language (Clark, *Tribal Names of the Americas*, pp. 54, 80; Center for Digital Research in the Humanities, "Identification of Western Indians").

95 Qwulhhwaipum is the name the Klickitat Nation use to refer to themselves in their own language (Konstantin, "Tribal Names").

96 Wusi is the name the Alsea Nation use to refer to themselves in their own language (Lewis and Redish, "Indian Tribes and Languages"; Drake, "Lewis and Clark: Native American Tribes," p. 8).

97 Liksiyu is the name the Cayuse Nation use to refer to themselves in their own language (Haruo Aoki, *A Cayuse Dictionary Based on the 1829 Records of Samuel Black, the 1888 Records of Henry W. Henshaw and Others*, the Confederated Tribes of the Umatilla Indian Reservation, 1998; Konstantin, "Tribal Names").

98 Imatalamłáma is the name the Umatilla Nation use to refer to themselves in their own language (Ronda, Lewis & Clark Among the Indians, p. 167; Confederated Tribes of the Umatilla Indian Reservation, "Imatalamłá," Umatilla Language, 2023, https://dictionary.ctuir.org/uma/imatalamla/).

99 Palus is the name the Palouse Nation use to refer to themselves in their own language (Konstantin, "Tribal Names").

100 K^{w}ínaył is the name the Quinault Nation use to refer to themselves in their own language (Northwest Portland Area Indian Health Board, "Our Member Tribes"; Konstantin, "Tribal Names").

101 Siletz is the name the Siletz Nation use to refer to themselves in their own language (Confederated Tribes of Siletz Indians, "A Siletz History: Part II—Early Contact," CTSI, n.d., https://www.ctsi.nsn.us/early-contact/).

102 Wyam is the name the Tenino Nation use to refer to themselves in their own language (Temprano, "Native Land"; Center for Digital Research in the Humanities, "Identification of Western Indians").

103 Kaw is the name the Kansa use to refer to themselves in their own language (The Kaw Nation, "Kanza People," Kaw Nation: People of Southwind, 2019, https://kawnation.com/?page_id=72).

104 Pó^{n}ka is the name the Ponca Nation use to refer to themselves in their own language (Center for Digital Research in the Humanities, "Pó^{n}ka," *Omaha & Ponca Digital Dictionary*, n.d.; Center for Digital Research in the Humanities, "Identification of Eastern Indians").

105 oθaakiiwaki is the name the Sac or Sauk Nation use to refer to themselves in their own language (Temprano, "Native Land"; Center for Digital Research in the Humanities, "Identification of Eastern Indians").

106 meškwahki·haki is the name the Fox or Meskwaki Nation use to refer to themselves in their own language (Temprano; Center for Digital Research in the Humanities, "Identification of Eastern Indians"; "Meskwaki Tribe," Milwaukee Public Museum, 2019, http://archive.mpm.edu/research-collections/botany/collections/ethnobotany/meskwaki).

107 Ndee is the name the Apache Nation use to refer to themselves in their own language (Lewis and Redish, "Indian Tribes and Languages"; Pritzker, *Native American Encyclopedia*, p. 22).

108 Nʉmʉnʉʉ is the name the Comanche Nation use to refer to themselves in their own language (Comanche Nation, "About Us," https://comanchenation.com/our-nation/about-us; Center for Digital Research in the Humanities, "Identification of Eastern Indians").

109 Núuchi-u is the name the Ute Nation use to refer to themselves in their own language (Talmy Givón, *Ute Reference Grammar*, Philadelphia: John Benjamins Publishing Company, 2011, p. 17; Center for Digital Research in the Humanities, "Identification of Eastern Indians").

110 Kitikiti'sh is the name the Wichita Nation use to refer to themselves in their own language (Wichita and Affiliated Tribes, "In the Beginning: 1540–1750," https://wichitatribe.com/history/in-the-beginning-15.40-1750.aspx; Center for Digital Research in the Humanities, "Identification of Eastern Indians").

111 Anishinaabe is the name the Ojibwe Nation use to refer to themselves in their own language (Center for Digital Research in the Humanities, "Identification of Eastern Indians").

112 Lenape is the name the Delaware Nation use to refer to themselves in their own language

(Brice Obermeyer, *Delaware Tribe in a Cherokee Nation*, Lincoln: University of Nebraska Press, 2009, p. 40).

113 Sawano is the name the Shawnee Nation use to refer to themselves in their own language (Shawnee Tribe Cultural Center, "Shawnee: Sawano," Shawnee Culture, 2019, https://www.shawneeculture.org/; Center for Digital Research in the Humanities, "Identification of Eastern Indians").

114 Kalapuya is the name the Kalapuya Nation use to refer to themselves in their own language (Center for Digital Research in the Humanities, "Identification of Western Indians"; Five Oaks Museum, "This IS Kalapuyan Land: Tribes and Languages Map," 2023, https://fiveoaksmuseum.org/this-is-kalapuyan-land-tribes-and-languages-map/).

115 qʷidiččaʔa·tx̌ is the name the Makah Nation use to refer to themselves in their own language (Melissa Peterson-Renault and the Makah Cultural and Research Center, "Makah Tribe History and More," https://makah.com/makah-tribal-info/; Center for Digital Research in the Humanities, "Identification of Western Indians").

116 The Awathi is called the Missouri River in English. Nuxbaaga (Hidatsa) elder Hazel Blake notes the importance of the river as a lifeline to the Hidatsa of Lewis and Clark's time (Hazel Blake, "Creation Story," Discover Lewis and Clark, https://lewis-clark.org/native-nations/three-affiliated-tribes/).

117 The term kâ-wâsihkopayicik literally translates to "the ones who shine" in Cree. When visiting the Mandan in Mitu'tahakto's in 1832, George Catlin used the term *dandy* to describe the men he saw "strutting and parading around the villages in the most beautiful and unsoiled dresses" (George Catlin, *North American Indians: Being Letters and Notes on Their Manners, Customs, and Conditions, Written During Eight Years' Travel Amongst the Wildest Tribes of Indians in North America, 1832–1839*, London: George Catlin, 1880, p. 128). Note that kâ-wâsihkopayicik is not a historical term but rather Miss Chief's personal name for her friends who have a spectacular sense of style (Gail Maurice's suggestion, email to Gisèle Gordon, February 14, 2019).

118 Métis members of the Corps of Discovery included Sacagawea's husband Toussaint Charbonneau; Pierre Cruzatte, a navigator, interpreter, and skilled fiddle player; and George Drouillard, a talented hunter and interpreter who knew many languages, including Plains Indigenous Sign Language (Lawrence Barkwell, "The Metis Men of the Lewis and Clark Expedition," Louis Riel Institute, 2011, pp. 1–5). York, a Black man, had been enslaved by William Clark for his entire life, and demonstrated good hunting skills on the mission (Irving Anderson, "The Corps," Lewis and Clark: The Journey of the Corps of Discovery, n.d., https://www.pbs.org/lewisandclark/inside/idx_corp.html).

119 Lewis and Clark considered Sacagawea integral for signalling peaceful intent and the expedition's "only dependence for a friendly negotiation" with the Shoshone (William Clark and Meriwether Lewis, *Original Journals of the Lewis and Clark Expedition, 1804–1806, Vol. 2*, ed. Reuben Gold Thwaites, New York: Dodd, Mead & Company, 1904, pp. 111, 163). Sacagawea helped in other crucial ways as well: she maintained camp by hauling water and wood, foraging for food and medical plants, and mending clothes, all while carrying her baby on her back ("Sacajawea: Her Story, by Her People," *Idaho Statesman*, 2003). On one notable occasion she calmly rescued valuable paper documents from a river (Clark and Lewis, *Original Journals . . . Vol. 2*, p. 39).

120 Some Indigenous nations attempted to avoid the expedition. When travelling to the Three Forks of the Missouri in July of 1805, the Corps spotted what appeared to be a smoke alarm created by an Indigenous community to warn others of the approaching expedition. As Lewis and Clark moved through this region, they only came across abandoned camps (Clark and Lewis, *Original Journals . . . Vol. 1*, pp. 254–328).

121 Though no member of the Corps of Discovery was ever killed by a bear, Lewis and other men were chased by them on several occasions (Clark and Lewis, *Original Journals . . . Vol. 2*, pp. 24, 34, 109, 122, 156–57, 186, 204; William Clark and Meriwether Lewis, *Original Journals of the Lewis and Clark Expedition, 1804–1806, Vol. 5*, ed. Reuben Gold Thwaites, New York: Dodd, Mead & Company, 1904, p. 204). Vine Deloria, Jr. writes that the bears "saw the members of the expedition as food, not friends . . . Did the bears see vulnerability in the white men they could not detect in the Indians? The Indians of all tribes had a long-standing and complex relationship with bears . . . Could the bears have foreseen the coming chaos on the plains represented by the presence of the expedition, when waves of settlers would bring a commercial civilization to what had been an unrestricted commons?" Deloria speculates that "in the case of Lewis and Clark, we find aggressive bears that proclaim their mastery of the land, fear nothing, and take steps to repel invaders" (Deloria, "Frenchmen, Bears, and Sandbars," pp. 15–17).

122 Though some nations were suspicious of the expedition, the Corps were otherwise welcomed by the Sahnish (Arikara), Numakaki (Mandan), Niimi'ipuu (Nez Perce), and Chinook (Ronda, *Lewis & Clark Among the Indians*, pp. 208–9, 64–65, 59). Otis Halfmoon states that when the expedition met his Niimi'ipuu ancestors, they had relationships that resulted in two children, one being the son of Clark, and the other the son of York (Otis Halfmoon, "Lewis and Clark Through Nez Perce Eyes," Discovering Lewis & Clark, 2001, https://www.lewis-clark.org/article/984).

123 Lewis's expedition journal entry for August 11, 1806 makes reference to receiving a wound from a gunshot accidentally fired by party member Pierre Cruzatte while out hunting elk. Lewis describes the bullet entering his "left thye about an inch below my hip joint" and "across the hinder part of the right thye"—or rather, across the buttocks (Clark and Lewis, *Original Journals . . . Vol. 5*, p. 240).

Many Trappers Sought Freedom in Our Forests

124 pimîhkân, or pemmican, dried and pounded buffalo meat mixed with equal parts buffalo fat and sometimes berries, has four times the caloric value of fresh meat. Packed into ninety-pound hide bags, it kept for years without spoiling and allowed buffalo hunting brigades, trappers, and voyageurs to survive long periods and travel great distances (Bill Waiser, *A World We Have Lost*, Markham: Fifth House Limited, 2016, pp. 234–35). The Hudson's Bay Company and the North West Company vied for dominance of the manufacture and storage of pemmican as the extent of the pemmican supply determined the extent of colonial expansion and company profit (ibid., p. 315).

125 The fur trade in the North American west was marked by fierce competition between various companies, namely the Hudson's Bay Company, the American Fur Company, the North West

Company, and the Rocky Mountain Fur Company. The rivalry between the North West Company—whose members were mostly Highland Scots and Catholic French Canadians—and the Hudson's Bay Company—which consisted primarily of Protestant English and Scottish members—was especially intense (David A. Morrison, "The North West Company, 1779–1821," *The Canadian Encyclopedia*, March 4, 2015; Jennifer S.H. Brown, *Strangers in Blood: Fur Trade Company Families in Indian Country*, Vancouver: University of British Columbia Press, 1985, p. xiv).

126 In the first few decades following the establishment of the Hudson's Bay Company in 1670, the London Committee of the Company prohibited its employees from having relationships with Indigenous women (Sylvia Van Kirk, *"Many Tender Ties": Women in Fur-Trade Society, 1670–1870*, Norman: University of Oklahoma Press, 1983, pp. 14–15, 46–52).

127 *Country wife* was the term for the Indigenous wife of a male European trader, as these kinds of partnerships were called marriage à la façon du pays (in the custom of the country) (ibid., pp. 36–37).

128 When the French entered the North American fur trade, many became involved romantically with Indigenous women. In addition to providing companionship, such marriages also helped establish valuable kinship ties within the Indigenous networks of the fur trade (ibid., pp. 161–63; Dickason, *Canada's First Nations*, pp. 170–71). Unlike the English, French traders were encouraged by colonial powers to pursue "intermarriage with the Indians and the exchange of children to create kinship bonds with the eastern tribes," as Vine Deloria, Jr. writes (Deloria, "Frenchmen, Bears, and Sandbars," p. 8).

129 The Métis culture arose in fur trade communities in the region known today as western Canada. The Métis were historically recognized by other Indigenous and European societies as a distinct Indigenous nation (Canadian Geographic, "Identity," *Indigenous Peoples Atlas of Canada*, Ottawa: The Royal Canadian Geographic Society, 2018, pp. 8–9). Otipemisiwak, a Michif term meaning "the people who own themselves," is what the Métis Nation calls themselves (Chelsea Vowel, email to Gisèle Gordon, August 24, 2022). Métis writer Chelsea Vowel explores the deeper contemporary conversations around Métis identity in Canada in her essay, "You're Métis? Which of Your Parents Is an Indian?" (in *Indigenous Writes: A Guide to First Nations, Métis and Inuit Issues in Canada*, Winnipeg: Highwater Press, 2016, pp. 36–54).

130 Nakawē is the name the Saulteaux call themselves (Federation of Saskatchewan Indian Nations, "Cultural Responsiveness Framework," 2013; Jessica Gordon, "Community Based Planning," Pasqua First Nation, 2010, https://www.pasquafn.ca/fileadmin/user_upload/PFN_CommunityPlan_31May2010_sm.pdf).

131 The Iron Confederacy was an alliance that gained prominence on the Plains during the nineteenth-century fur trade (Lawrence Barkwell, "The Iron Confederacy (Nehiyaw Pwat)," Louis Riel Institute, September 20, 2013, p. 1, https://www.scribd.com/document/169615628/Iron Confederacy Nehiyaw Pwat). The Iron Confederacy included the following bands: Pembina Band, Little Shell Band, Turtle Mountain Band, St. François Xavier Saulteaux/Métis, Nakawiniul (Wilkie's) Band, Big Bear's Band, Poundmaker's Band, Crazy Bear Band, Canoe Band of Nakota, Four Claws (Gordon) Band, Nekaneet Band, Carry the Kettle Band, Rocky Boy's Band, Montana Band, Muscowequan Band, Beardy's Band, One Arrow's Band, Carlton Stragglers Band,

Petaquakey Band of Muskeg Lake, Dumont's Band, Piapot's Band, Red Stone Band, Maski Pitonew Band, Piche (Bobtail) Band, Moose Mountain group of White Bear Band, Striped Blanket Band, Prison Drum Band, Crooked Lakes group of Cowessess Band, Ochapowace Band, Pasqua Band, Kahkewistahow Band, and Sakimay Band (Dibaajimowin, "Nehiyaw-Pwat: The Iron Confederacy," August 15, 2018). Together, these nations formed a kinship network as well as a partnership in political, military, trade, and hunting matters (Barkwell, "The Nehiyaw Pwât (Iron Alliance) Encounters with the Dakota," Louis Riel Institute, July 24, 2019, p. 2).

132 Lord Selkirk's plan to settle Scottish immigrants in Canada emerged from the dispossession of Scottish people following the Highland Clearances. Beginning in the mid-eighteenth century, thousands of Highlanders were evicted from their homelands by land-owning lords in order to make way for large-scale sheep farming (Committee for the Bicentenary of the Red River Selkirk Settlement, "Lord Selkirk's Settlers," Manitoba Historical Society, October 19, 2011, http://www.mhs.mb.ca/info/selkirk/settlers.shtml; Terry Stewart, "The Highland Clearances," Historic UK, https://www.historic-uk.com/HistoryUK/HistoryofScotland/The-Highland-Clearances/). In 1811, Selkirk purchased from the Hudson's Bay Company 116,000 acres of land in the Forks region of the Red River, where the first of Selkirk's settlers arrived in the autumn of 1814 (The Lord Selkirk Association of Rupert's Land, "The Founding of the Selkirk Settlement at Red River," http://www.lordselkirk.ca/the-settlers/; Albert Edward Thompson, *Chief Peguis and His Descendants*, Winnipeg: Peguis Publishers, 1973, pp. 9–10).

133 According to Albert Edward Thompson, the great-great-grandson of Peguis, the Selkirk settlers had no access to supplies from the Hudson's Bay Company and had not planted any crops when they first arrived in the area. During their early years of settlement, Peguis provided them with food (Thompson, *Chief Peguis*, pp. 9–10, 18).

134 The Selkirk Treaty was signed in the Red River region in 1817 by Lord Selkirk and Cree and Saulteaux chiefs, including Chief Peguis, Mache Wheseab, Mechkaddewikonaie, Kayajieskebinoa, and Ouckidoat (Daniel Wilson, "Reviews—Red River and Assiniboine Explorations," in *The Canadian Journal of Industry, Science, and Art Vol. VI*, ed. E.J. Chapman, Toronto: Lovell and Gibson, 1861, pp. 181–82; Selkirk et al., *Selkirk Treaty*, July 18, 1817, Hudson's Bay Company Archives E.8/1 fo. 9d). As Anishinaabe academic Niigaan James Sinclair has emphasized, by signing the treaty, Peguis and the other chiefs "offered a partnership in a family" to the European signatories (Niigaan James Sinclair, "The History of the St. Peters Band Removal," lecture, Canadian Mennonite University, Winnipeg, MB, January 12, 2018). Selkirk's commitment to paying "quit rent," the term he used in the treaty, implied Indigenous ownership of the land; according to the feudal European tradition of quit rent, a tenant paid rent on land occupied by a feudal lord (Adam Gaudry, "The Selkirk Treaty, 1817," *Library and Archives Canada Blog*, July 20, 2017).

135 Miles MacDonell, the governor of the Selkirk colony, issued a proclamation on January 8, 1814 stating that "It is hereby ordered, that no persons trading in furs or provisions within the Territory . . . shall take out any provisions . . . procured or raised within the said Territory . . . The provisions procured and raised as above shall be taken for the use of the colony." Those who disobeyed MacDonell's orders would be prosecuted and their goods confiscated (quoted in A. Amos, *Report of Trials in the Courts of Canada, Relative to the Destruction of the Earl of*

Selkirk's Settlement on the Red River, with Observations, London: John Murray, 1820, pp. 61–62). MacDonell's proclamation became known as the Pemmican Proclamation, and it greatly angered the Métis and North West Company. The resulting conflict would become known as the Pemmican Wars.

136 Cuthbert Grant's Cree name was Wappeston, or White Ermine. An employee of the North West Company and a military leader of the Iron Confederacy, Grant led the Métis faction during the Pemmican Wars of the 1810s (Lawrence Barkwell, "Battle of Seven Oaks," *The Canadian Encyclopedia*, July 18, 2018).

137 Olive Dickason notes that "a [Métis] sense of identity had crystallized with the troubles that developed after the coming of the Selkirk settlers in 1812," pinpointing the Battle of Seven Oaks as the definitive event in the rise of the Métis Nation (Dickason, *Canada's First Nations*, p. 263).

138 During the Pemmican Wars, Selkirk settlers and Cree allies moved to Norway House for safety (Thompson, *Chief Peguis*, pp. 10–13; Dr. Keith Goulet, interview by Gisèle Gordon and Sadie MacDonald, November 14, 2019). According to Peguis's great-great-grandson Albert Edward Thompson, after the Battle of Seven Oaks on June 19, 1816, Peguis and his followers buried the bodies of those killed and provided food to the fleeing settlers (Thompson, *Chief Peguis*, pp. 12–13).

139 Cree academic Dr. Alex Wilson defines mino-pimâtisiwin as the responsibility "to live in conscious connection with the land and living things in a way that creates and sustains balance—or, as my father translates from our dialect, to live beautifully" (Alex Wilson, "Our Coming In Stories: Cree Identity, Body Sovereignty, and Gender Self-Determination," *Journal of Global Indigeneity*, vol. 1, no. 1, 2015, p. 1).

140 William Benemann speculates on how the early nineteenth century North American fur trade attracted gay men because of its insular community and the lack of white women in fur-trapping regions. Harsh sodomy laws in Britain likely also contributed to this community-building in the American wilderness (William Benemann, *Men in Eden: William Drummond Stewart and Same-Sex Desire in the Rocky Mountain Fur Trade*, Lincoln: University of Nebraska Press, 2012, pp. 6–20).

141 William Drummond Stewart was a Scottish lord enchanted by the adventure offered by the North American fur trade in the first half of the nineteenth century. He had a fondness for fine dress and was noted to have a pair of tartan trews. William Benemann's research shows that Stewart had open (for the time) romantic and sexual relationships with other men. His story is told in detail by Benemann in *Men in Eden*. Stewart attended each of the rendezvous from 1833 to 1838 (Carl P. Russell, "Wilderness Rendezvous Period of the American Fur Trade," *Oregon Historical Quarterly*, vol. 42, no. 1, March 1941, pp. 35–36).

142 American artist George Catlin first studied to be a lawyer before choosing to pursue an artistic career in 1823. While travelling the American west, he carried a sign that said "G. Catlin, Artist" (Peter Matthiessen, "Introduction," in *North American Indians*, ed. Peter Matthiessen, New York: Penguin Classics, 1989, pp. ix–x).

143 Catlin stated that he set out on his travels with "the determination of reaching, ultimately, every tribe of Indians on the Continent of North America, and of bringing home faithful portraits of their principal personages . . . views of their villages, games, etc. and full notes

on their character and history. I designed, also, to procure their costumes, and a complete collection of their manufactures and weapons, and to perpetuate them in a *Gallery unique*, for the use and instruction of future ages." Never shy of extolling his own perceived virtues, he believed in "the originality of such a design, as I was undoubtedly the first artist who ever set out upon such a work," and was convinced that, by doing so, he was "snatching from a hasty oblivion what could be saved for the benefit of posterity" (Catlin, *North American Indians*, pp. 3–4).

144 Catlin described his mission as an "arduous and perilous undertaking" (ibid., p. 4).

145 Rendezvous were annual trading gatherings of Indigenous trappers and European traders in the Rocky Mountain region and took place from 1825 to 1840 (Brenda D. Francis, "Introduction," in *The Fur Trade & Rendezvous of the Green River Valley*, ed. Brenda D. Francis and Fred R. Gowans, Pinedale: The Sublette County Historical Society and The Museum of the Mountain Man, 2016, pp. 11–13).

146 Antoine Clement was a handsome trapper of Cree and French background, renowned for his hunting skills. Alfred Jacob Miller described Antoine as "our best hunter" who was known to undertake tasks "in his own peculiar fashion, that is, he would have as much fun as possible" (Alfred J. Miller and Michael Bell, *Braves and Buffalo: Plains Indian Life in 1837*, Toronto: University of Toronto Press, 1973, p. 84). Stewart and Clement met at the 1833 rendezvous, and the two entered a long companionship. Benemann writes on Stewart's romantic relationship with Clement in *Men in Eden* (pp. 87–91).

147 This description of Antoine having a "temper" that "when aroused, was uncontrollable" comes from Alfred J. Miller's account (Alfred J. Miller and Marvin Chauncey Ross, *The West of Alfred Jacob Miller (1837): From the Notes and Water Colors in the Walters Art Gallery, With an Account of the Artist*, Norman: University of Oklahoma Press, 1951, p. 36).

148 James "Jim" Beckwourth was one of the original members of "Ashley's Hundred" and was present at the first Rocky Mountain rendezvous in 1825. Born into slavery, Beckwourth was freed as an adult and became involved in the western fur trade, eventually being adopted into the Crow Nation (James Pierson Beckwourth and T.D. Bonner, *The Life and Adventures of James P. Beckwourth, Mountaineer, Scout, Pioneer, and Chief of the Crow Nation of Indians*, London: T. Fisher Unwin, 1902; Charles G. Leland, "Preface to the New English Edition," ibid., p. 7).

149 This description of the "mirth, songs, dancing, shouting, trading, running, jumping, singing, racing, target-shooting, yarns, frolic, with all sorts of extravagances that white men or Indians could invent" is provided by James Beckwourth in his discussion of the 1826 Rocky Mountain rendezvous (Beckwourth and Bonner, *Life and Adventures*, p. 105).

150 George Simpson was governor of the Hudson's Bay Company from 1821 to 1860 and became known as the "Little Emperor" for his ruthless management style that focused on acquiring maximum profits above all else (John S. Galbraith, "Simpson, Sir George," *Dictionary of Canadian Biography, Vol. 8*, University of Toronto/Université Laval, 1985; James Daschuk, *Clearing the Plains: Disease, Politics of Starvation, and the Loss of Indigenous Life*, Regina: University of Regina Press, 2013, p. 59; CBC, "The Emperor Makes His Cuts," *Canada: A People's History*, 2001).

151 The fur trade nearly collapsed completely during the Pemmican Wars (see notes 135 to 138 in "Many Trappers Sought Freedom in Our Forests") due to the combined forces of armed warfare, disease, famine, and climate change. As a result, the Hudson's Bay Company and the North West Company merged in 1821, creating a monopoly (John Douglas Belshaw, *Canadian History: Pre-Confederation*, Victoria, BCcampus, 2015, https://opentextbc.ca/preconfederation/).

152 Meriwether Lewis's death on October 11, 1809 at the homestead of Priscilla Grinder in Tennessee is considered by many historians to have been a suicide (Benemann, "My Friend and Companion"). That night, according to the account given to Alexander Wilson by Grinder, Lewis "said he would sleep on the floor, and desired the servant to bring the bear skins and buffaloe robe" (Alexander Wilson to Alexander Lawson, May 28, 1811, in "The Death of Meriwether Lewis: Investigating an American Mystery Through Primary Sources," ed. Norman Anderson, *Biographies of the Nation*, June 2011, p. 13). James Neelly, who travelled with Lewis shortly before his death, wrote a letter to Thomas Jefferson stating, "It is with extreme pain that I have to inform you of the death of His Excellency Meriwether Lewis, Governor of Upper Louisiana who died on the morning of the 11th Instant and I am sorry to say by Suicide . . ." (James Neelly to Thomas Jefferson, October 18, 1809).

I Summoned My Admirers to Honour Me

153 The honour dance to Miss Chief is based on a sketch by George Catlin, who during his time with the Sac and Fox witnessed what he called a "dance to the berdashe" (George Catlin, *North American Indians*, ed. Peter Matthiessen, New York: Penguin Classics, 1989, p. 445; George Catlin, *Dance to the Berdash*, 1835–1837 [painting], Smithsonian American Art Museum).

154 niwîcêwâkanak pikwâwiyak kâ-sâkihâcik is the term Miss Chief uses to describe her friends who have sexual and/or romantic relationships with those of the same gender. It is not a historical term, but rather was created in consultation with our advisors Dr. Belinda Daniels and Gail Maurice.

155 niwîcêwâkanak pikwîsi kâ-isi-wîkicik is the term Miss Chief uses to describe her trans friends, gender-fluid friends, and those who do not live or present according to western cisgender/cissexual gender binary norms. It, too, is not a historical term, but rather was created in consultation with our advisors Dr. Belinda Daniels and Gail Maurice.

156 Catlin described the Meskwaki honour dance he saw in the 1830s as follows: "a feast is given to him annually; and initiatory to it, a dance by those few young men of the tribe who can, as in the sketch, dance forward and publicly make their boast" (George Catlin, *Letters and Notes on the Manners, Customs, and Condition of the North American Indians: Vol. II*, New York: Wiley and Putnam, 1842, p. 215). The Wichita Two Spirit Society says that "It is clear from the way the Sioux and the Sac and Fox are treating this member of their community that they respect him. It is also clear that Catlin does not" (Wichita Two Spirit Society, "Pre-Colonial History," ICT2SS.com, 2013).

157 As Sylvia McAdam writes, Cree women "would have been consulted regarding the land, because authority and jurisdiction to speak about land resides with the women. The water ceremonies belong to the women . . . their connection is based on the understanding that the earth is female and the authority stems from this" (McAdam, *Nationhood Interrupted*, p. 55).

158 James Beckwourth observed that trappers at the 1825 rendezvous consumed whisky "as freely as water" (Beckwourth and Bonner, *Life and Adventures*, p. 79).

159 Many free and formerly enslaved Black men were drawn to the free trapper lifestyle. James Beckwourth, the son of an enslaved Black woman and a white planter, acquired notoriety and prosperity as a Rocky Mountain fur trader (see note 148 in "Many Trappers Sought Freedom in Our Forests"). Other known Black trappers in the North American west include Edward Rose, Auguste Janisse, Polette Labrosse, and the Bonga brothers (Leland, "Preface," p. 7; William W. Gwaltney, "Beyond the Pale: African-Americans in the Fur Trade West," *Lest We Forget*, January 1995).

160 Drawing from Captain Benjamin Bonneville's account of his travels in the Rocky Mountains, Washington Irving provides the following description of a typical free trapper—an independent trapper unaffiliated with the fur trading companies: "A hunting-shirt of ruffled calico of bright dyes, or of ornamented leather, falls to his knees; below which, curiously fashioned leggins [sic], ornamented with strings, fringes, and a profusion of hawks' bells, reach to a costly pair of moccasins of the finest Indian fabric, richly embroidered with beads. A blanket of scarlet, or some other bright color, hangs from his shoulders, and is girt round his waist with a red sash, in which he bestows his pistols, knife, and the stem of his Indian pipe, preparations for peace or war. His gun is lavishly decorated with brass tacks and vermilion, and provided with a fringed cover, occasionally of buckskin, ornamented here and there with a feather" (Washington Irving, *Captain Bonneville*, New York: G.P. Putnam's Sons, 1890, pp. 93–94).

161 Stewart brought velvet Renaissance costumes to a lavish 1843 gathering he hosted in Shawnee territory during the post-rendezvous period. Stewart and his company wore these costumes in performances put on for their own entertainment (Benemann, *Men in Eden*, pp. 236–50).

162 Stewart carried "imported delicacies" from Europe to the 1837 rendezvous (ibid., pp. 193–201).

163 Between 1800 and 1860, over two hundred men were convicted for sodomy in Britain. More than fifty were executed during this period (Kieran McCarthy, "'*Peccatum Illud Horribile Inter Christianos Non Nominandum*': The Prosecution of Homosexuality in English and Irish Law 1533–1993," *University College Dublin Law Review*, vol. 12, 2012, pp. 1–37).

164 The arrival of European diseases in North America devastated many Indigenous nations. (See note 42 in "The Massacre of Our Beaver Relatives Foreshadowed What Was to Come" and note 46 in "The Newcomers Had Much to Learn".) Epidemics were sometimes used to European advantage; during Pontiac's uprising of 1762, the British commander-in-chief Jeffrey Amherst suggested distributing smallpox-infected blankets amongst the involved Indigenous nations. Although smallpox had struck the Plains in the late eighteenth century, Miss Chief here alludes to the waves of epidemics that ravaged the Plains nations from 1837 to 1870 (Dickason, *Canada's First Nations*, pp. 183, 200–211).

165 Catlin described his series of Indigenous portraits as "a fair and just monument to the memory of a truly lofty and noble race," a phrase he often used (Catlin, *North American Indians*, p. 3).

166 Catlin referred to the Indigenous individuals he met as "specimens"; when describing his journeys to the west, he claimed that "the finest specimen of Indians on the Continent are in these regions" (Catlin, *North American Indians*, p. 25). When he met Cree people, he wrote, "Their customs may properly be said to be primitive, as no inroads of civilised habits have been as yet successfully made amongst them" (ibid., p. 65). Catlin spoke of his painting Indigenous people as having "flown to their rescue . . . of their looks and their modes . . . phoenix-like, they may rise from the 'stain on a painter's palette,' and live again upon canvass [sic], and stand forth for centuries yet to come" (ibid., p. 11).

167 Catlin notes that there was a class of "dandies or exquisites" amongst the Mandans in the village he visited. These individuals paid "the strictest regard to decency, and cleanliness and elegance of dress" (ibid., p. 93). According to Catlin, "these clean and elegant gentlemen . . . attire themselves . . . with swan's down and quills of ducks, with braids and plaits of sweet-scented grass and other harmless and unmeaning ornaments . . ." (ibid., p. 110–12).

168 George Catlin often dressed as an oθaakiiwaki (Sac or Sauk) warrior when he presented his "Indian Gallery" of paintings and gave lectures on Indigenous culture (Christopher Mulvey, "George Catlin in Europe," in *George Catlin and His Indian Gallery*, ed. George Gurney and Therese Thau Heyman, Washington, D.C.: Smithsonian American Art Museum, 2002, p. 85). He wears a European-styled buckskin outfit in a sketch he made of himself painting the Mandan chief Máh-to-tóh-pa (George Catlin, *Catlin Painting the Portrait of Mah-to-toh-pa—Mandan*, 1861–1869 [painting], National Gallery of Art, Washington, D.C.).

169 Catlin saw European influences as contaminating Indigenous cultures. He portrayed Wi-jun-jon, an Assiniboine chief, in a portrait contrasting the chief's traditional clothes with a flamboyant European-style outfit Wi-jun-jon had purchased for himself on a visit to Washington, D.C. Catlin seems to have hoped that this apparent change in authenticity would be seen with dismay (*Wi-jún-jon, Pigeon's Egg Head (The Light) Going To and Returning From Washington*, Smithsonian American Art Museum, https://americanart.si.edu/artwork/wi-jun-jon-pigeons-egg-head-light-going-and-returning-washington-4317).

170 Catlin described western Turtle Island as "trackless forests and boundless prairies" in which Indigenous people were "melting away at the approach of civilisation" (Catlin, *North American Indians: Being Letters and Notes*, p. 17).

171 Catlin's travels brought him to the territories of many nations (Royal B. Hassrick, *The George Catlin Book of American Indians*, New York: Promontory Press, 1981, pp. 18–19, 145). Siksika is the endonym of the Blackfoot (Siksika Nation, "About Siksika Nation," SiksikaNation.com).

172 Catlin wrote about how the Mandan village gathered to watch him paint (Catlin, *North American Indians*, p. 105).

173 The name the Seminole use for themselves is yat'siminoli (Seminole Tribe of Florida, "Indian Resistance and Removal," Semtribe.com, accessed May 14, 2021).

174 The English name for the Chahta is Choctaw (Choctaw Nation, "About Choctaw Language," ChoctawNation.com, accessed May 14, 2021).

175 The Trail of Tears refers to the brutal state-sanctioned mass removals of the Cherokee, Muscogee, Choctaw, Chickasaw, and Seminole from their homelands to a designated "Indian Territory" west of the Mississippi during the nineteenth century. President Andrew Jackson signed the Indian Removal Act into law in 1830. An estimated 14,000 people died due to disease, starvation, exposure, and abuse from the soldiers forcibly escorting them west (Shelle Stormoe, "The Trail of Tears in Arkansas: Learning About Indian Removal Through Mapping Landscapes," Arkansas Historic Preservation Program, 2015, pp. 14–19).

176 Catlin describes the outfit worn by Ha-na-tá-nu-maúk, the head Mandan chief of a village Catlin visited in 1832, as "one of great extravagance" and described Ha-na-tá-nu-maúk as having a "haughty" personality (Catlin, *North American Indians*, p. 87).

177 To Catlin, those he called the dandies seemed to express "hopes that I would select them as models, for my canvass [sic]"; one carefully groomed hopeful model was said to hover near Catlin's lodge in expectation, shifting his weight from "one leg [to] the other" (ibid., pp. 110–12).

178 According to Catlin, the dandies did not take hunting or warrior roles but "generally remain about the village, to take care of the women" and wear beautiful clothing which, in Catlin's opinion, had "no other merit than they themselves have, that of looking pretty and ornamental" (ibid.). When Catlin attempted to paint one of the "gay and tinselled bucks" of the Mandan village, he encountered the displeasure of the chiefs and medicine men whose portraits he had already painted. The headmen considered the dandies to be of lower rank in their society and therefore unfit to be subjects of paintings alongside themselves. Catlin had created a chalk outline of one of the dandies, but as the drawing has not survived, it is possible that the artist destroyed it (ibid., pp. 111–12).

179 Catlin used the terms "fainthearts" and "fops" to describe those Miss Chief refers to as kâ-wâsihkopayicik (ibid., pp. 110–11).

180 Catlin often described the Indigenous leaders he met in flattering terms. When writing of the chief Máh-to-tóh-pa, he declared, "This, readers, is the most extraordinary man, perhaps, who lives at this day, in the atmosphere of Nature's noblemen" (Catlin, *North American Indians: Being Letters and Notes . . .*, p. 104). He also seems to have lavished flattery on a distrustful medicine man named Mah-to-he-hah in order to win him over; Catlin writes of his conversation with Mah-to-he-hah, in which he complimented the medicine man on his "extraordinary" history, commended "his character and standing in his tribe as worthy of my particular notice," and explained that he had only delayed in making a portrait of him out of a desire to practise upon other subjects first before doing "justice" to Mah-to-he-hah (Catlin, *North American Indians*, p. 108).

181 Catlin wrote that the Mandan lodges in Mitu'tahakto's were "built entirely of dirt; but one is surprised when he enters them, to see the neatness, comfort, and spacious dimensions of these earth-covered dwellings. They all have a circular form, and are from forty to sixty feet in diameter" (ibid., p. 75).

182 In his published records of the time he spent with the Mandans, Catlin states that they called him Te-ho-pe-nee Wash-ee, or Medicine White Man. Catlin claimed that "the

operations of my brush are *mysteries* of the highest order to these red sons of the prairie." (ibid., pp. 104, 20).

183 Catlin's classically inspired description of Máh-to-tóh-pa is a direct quote from the artist: "No tragedian ever trod the stage, nor gladiator ever entered the Roman Forum, with more grace and manly dignity than did Máh-to-tóh-pa enter the wigwam . . ." (Catlin, *North American Indians*, p. 164).

184 Máh-to-tóh-pa indeed did give Catlin a shirt like the one described here; however, Catlin used a replica in his exhibition, which he likely cobbled together using Cree rather than Mandan materials (Joan Carpenter Troccoli, "Illustrated Commentary," in Gurney and Heyman, *George Catlin and His Indian Gallery*, p. 157).

185 Catlin recognized that Máh-to-tóh-pa was "undoubtedly the first and most popular man in the nation" (Catlin, *North American Indians*, p. 87).

186 James Kipp was an American Fur Company agent who ran operations near Mitu'tahakto's and acted as interpreter for Catlin. He was married four times, twice to Mandan women, who taught him how to speak their language (W. Raymond Wood, "James Kipp: Missouri River Fur Trader and Missouri Farmer," *North Dakota History*, vol. 77, nos. 1 and 2, 2011, pp. 8–9; Catlin, *North American Indians*, pp. 121, 166).

187 James Kipp married his first wife shortly after he arrived in Mitu'tahakto's, and through her he became the first white settler to speak the Mandan language fluently (Wood, "James Kipp," pp. 8–9). James W. Schultz described Sak'wi-ah'ki, Kipp's second Mandan wife, as "a woman of most noble character and kindly disposition. I cannot speak too highly of her" (James W. Schultz, *Friends of My Life as an Indian*, Boston: Houghton Mifflin Company, 1923, p. 79). Kipp eventually abandoned Sak'wi-ah'ki and their child for his white family back east, though he occasionally returned to visit them (Wood, "James Kipp," pp. 15–25; Barton H. Barbour, *Fort Union and the Upper Missouri Fur Trade*, Norman: University of Oklahoma Press, 2002, p. 130).

188 This description is taken from a quote by Catlin ("The Red Kings Beyond the Frontiers," *The North American Magazine*, vol. 2, no. 12, October 1833, pp. 387–88).

189 Here Miss Chief is looking at Catlin's work *Dance to the Berdash* [sic], which depicted an oθaakiiwaki (Sac and Fox) ceremony.

190 Mihdeke is the Mandan term for a Two-Spirit person (George F. Will and Herbert Joseph Spinden, *The Mandans: A Study of Their Culture, Archaeology, and Language*, Cambridge: Peabody Museum of American Archaeology and Ethnology, 1906, p. 210; David J. Wishart, *Encyclopedia of the Great Plains Indians*, Lincoln: University of Nebraska Press, 2004, p. 324).

191 Catlin made four expeditions to various Indigenous nations from 1830 to 1836, during which he produced a vast catalogue of paintings and sketches. At the end of 1839, Catlin travelled to England, launching a tour of his gallery over Europe that would last until 1846 (Elizabeth Broun, "Preface," in Gurney and Heyman, *George Catlin and His Indian Gallery*, p. 9; Brian W. Dippie, "Green Fields and Red Men," ibid., p. 27).

192 The Cherokee endonym is ᏣᎳᎩ ᎠᏰᏟ (Cherokee Nation, Cherokee.org, 2021).

193 Mvskoke is the name the Muscogee call themselves. This Nation is also called the Creek by English speakers (The Muscogee Nation, Muscogeenation.com, 2016).

194 The Chikasha are known as the Chickasaw in English (The Chickasaw Nation, "Chikasha Poya 'We Are Chickasaw,'" Chickasaw.net, 2021).

195 Maungwudaus (George Henry) was an Anishinaabe Methodist missionary from Credit Mississauga territory noted for his skill as an interpreter (Donald B. Smith, *Mississauga Portraits: Ojibwe Voices from Nineteenth-Century Canada*, Toronto: University of Toronto Press, 2013, pp. 128–63). When writing about his experiences of London in 1845, Maungwudaus noticed that "many ladies and gentlemen ride about in carriages" that were "covered with gold and silver." He also observed that "most of the houses are rather dark in color on account of too much smoke" (Maungwudaus, *An Account of the Chippewa Indians*, Boston: Maungwudaus, 1848, p. 3).

196 Maungwudaus stated that there were "about 900 berths [sic] and about 1100 deaths every week in this city alone" (ibid., pp. 3–4).

197 Maungwudaus, when describing the people of London, compared them to "musketoes [mosquitos] in America in the summer season . . . in their numbers, and biting one another to get a living." He also noted that "many [were] very rich, and many [were] very poor" (ibid., p. 3).

198 Maungwudaus speculated that wealthy English women were unable to "walk alone," as they "must always be assisted by the men" in the streets. He also saw people walking in the parks, "the servants leading little dogs behind them" (ibid., p. 4).

199 Maungwudaus described the moustaches of European men: "They do not shave the upper part of their mouths, but let the beards grow long, and this makes them look fierce and savage like our American dogs when carrying black squirrels in their mouths" (ibid., p. 4).

200 Maungwudaus recounted being told about the "eighty thousand common wives" (referring to the sex workers of the time) that "[walked] in the streets every night for the safety of the married women" (ibid., p. 5).

201 The pollution of the Thames reached horrific levels during the mid-nineteenth century, eventually culminating in the "Great Stink" of 1858 (Michelle Elizabeth Allen, *Cleansing the City: Sanitary Geographies in Victorian London*, Athens: Ohio University Press, 2008, pp. 55–58). In 1858, *The Illustrated London News* lamented that the Thames had "by sheer neglect on the part both of the people and the Government, become a foul sewer, a river of pollution, a Stream of Death, festering and reeking with all abominable smells, and threatening three millions of people with pestilence as the penalty of their ignorance and apathy" (*The Illustrated London News*, "The Purification of the Thames," July 24, 1858).

202 Catlin brought two grizzly bears with him on his 1839 voyage to England. The bears were highly agitated during the sea journey, with Catlin noting their "pitious howlings, and then their horrid growls . . . the gnashing of their teeth, and their furious lurches, and bolts, and blows against the sides of their cage" (George Catlin, *Catlin's Notes of Eight Years' Travels and Residence in Europe, with his North American Indian Collection, Vol. 1*, London: George Catlin, 1848, https://archive.org/details/catlinsnoteseigo2catlgoog/pagen8). The bears continued to suffer throughout Catlin's

1840 tour of England; their "howls and growls" drew crowds to their cage, and Catlin's assistant Daniel "had to stand between the crowd and his pets, to save them from the peltings and insults of the crowd" (ibid., p. 25). Catlin eventually sold the pair to the Zoological Gardens in Regent's Park, where they "seemed daily to pine" and died within a few months (ibid., pp. 32–33).

203 When he first began giving lectures in London in 1840, Catlin hired and trained local English actors to impersonate Indigenous warriors, with "round-faced boys, wearing long wigs" playing Indigenous women. Catlin professed that with these actors, "I had succeeded in presenting the most faithful and general representation of Indian life that was ever brought before the civilized world." Catlin and his nephew Burr Catlin often dressed in Indigenous clothes and headdresses to add effect to his performances (ibid., pp. 94–95, 70–78; Mulvey, "George Catlin in Europe," p. 66).

204 Catlin had a tendency to exaggerate and misrepresent the histories of Indigenous peoples to attract greater audiences. When describing a knife that had belonged to Máh-to-tóh-pa, Catlin claimed that it had been "several times plunged to the hearts of his enemies" (Catlin, *North American Indians*, p. 231). He also fabricated some items, such as a shirt he had created using Cree quillwork and his own pictographs, represented as one worn by Mah-to-toh-pa, who was Mandan (Troccoli, "Illustrated Commentary," p. 157; see note 184 in "The Painter Who Could Not See").

205 Catlin wrote about the arrival of the "Ojibbeways . . . a party of nine wild Indians from the backwoods of America" in London: "I hope [the reader] will find fresh excitement enough" (Catlin, *Catlin's Notes of Eight Years' Travels . . . Vol. I*, p. 103).

206 During his lifelong quest for money-making schemes, Catlin frequently found himself plagued with numerous debts which caused him to continuously search for new sources of income. At the start of his European journey, Catlin owed over $6,000 to his father and other lenders, which made him anxious to recoup costs with the Indian Gallery. Costs mounted despite his show's initial success, and the gallery's popularity dwindled until the introduction of nine Anishinaabe (Ojibwe) performers in 1843, which revived public interest in Catlin's shows (Mulvey, "George Catlin in Europe," pp. 63–76).

207 Catlin's Indian Gallery consisted of 310 oil portraits of Indigenous people as well as 200 other oil paintings, many drawings, and numerous Indigenous belongings, some of which were sacred (Matthiessen, "Introduction," p. xiii).

208 In 1844, when faced with financial difficulties, Maungwudaus recruited his family members to perform with him in an "Indian show," touring Europe and the United States for the next several years. Maungwudaus's troupe met George Catlin in Paris in 1845 and became part of his Indian Gallery show (Smith, *Mississauga Portraits*, pp. 128–63).

209 Maungwudaus's wife Uhwessiggzhiggookwe (Woman of the Upper World) was also known as Anna (Smith, *Mississauga Portraits*, p. 131). Names of Maungwudaus's family members and friends have been determined with the assistance of Jonathan Ferrier and Maungwudaus's descendant Waawashkeshi Luke Henry (Jonathan Ferrier, Mississaugas of the Credit First Nation, family history teaching, email communication, October 28, 2021).

210 Peter Jones, or Kahkewāquonāby, was a Methodist reverend from the Credit River Band and a staunch advocate for his people's land rights. In 1838, he travelled to London to petition

Queen Victoria about the grievances facing the Credit River Mississauga. He also travelled to Paris in 1845 during the period when Maungwudaus and his family were performing in Catlin's show (Donald B. Smith, *Sacred Feathers: The Reverend Peter Jones (Kahkewaquonaby) and the Mississauga Indians*, Toronto: University of Toronto Press, 2013). Kahkewāquonāby shared a mother with Maungwudaus, but his father was a white man (ibid., p. 187).

211 Nahnebahwequa's English married name was Catherine Sutton (James Rodger Miller, "Petitioning the Great White Mother: First Nations' Organizations and Lobbying in London," in *Reflections on Native-Newcomer Relations: Selected Essays*, Toronto: University of Toronto Press, 2004, p. 225). She was not present when Maungwudaus met Queen Victoria, but as a thirteen-year-old she accompanied Kahkewāquonāby on his 1837 visit to London (Donald B. Smith, "Nahnebahwequay," in *Dictionary of Canadian Biography*, vol. 9, University of Toronto/Université Laval, 2003). As an adult, Nahnebahwequa would go back to London to petition Queen Victoria herself—she made an impression on the Queen, enough to prompt investigations into the Indian Department during the 1860 royal tour of the Prince of Wales, Albert Edward (Ian Walter Radforth, *Royal Spectacle: The 1860 Visit of the Prince of Wales to Canada and the United States*, Toronto: University of Toronto Press, 2004, pp. 229–30). While Nahnebahwequa succeeded in obtaining title to her land, colonial authorities ultimately failed to enact the change Nahnebahwequa sought for her people as a whole. Outraged that others in her band had lost their lands without redress, she denounced the government for its "wholesale robbery and treachery" throughout her life (Miller, "Petitioning the Great White Mother," pp. 225–26).

212 Maungwudaus, who met Victoria during his 1845 travels in England and observed the many guards she had around her, stated that while she was "handsome," "there are many handsomer women than she is" (Maungwudaus, *An Account of the Chippewa Indians*, p. 4).

213 Queen Victoria was not a maternal person and disliked babies, though she and Albert had an active sex life; she once lamented that pregnancy had made her "miserable" and that marriage would be happier without pregnancy involved (Paula Bartley, *Queen Victoria*, New York: Routledge, 2016, pp. 75–81; Donald Spoto, *The Decline and Fall of the House of Windsor*, New York: Simon & Schuster, 1995, p. 8).

214 During the 1820s and 1830s, the Credit River band struggled to have their land rights recognized as they faced encroaching white settlement on their lands and the subsequent loss of timber and fishing resources. By 1836, Lieutenant Governor Francis Bond Head sought to remove all Anishinaabe people to Manitoulin Island, and succeeded in removing the Saugeen Ojibwa's tract. Peter Jones (Kahkewāquonāby), who believed that securing title deeds would enable the Mississauga to keep their lands, travelled to Britain in 1837 to bring his community's case to colonial secretary Lord Glenelg and Queen Victoria. Both promised to grant title deeds. Unfortunately, lieutenant governor George Arthur failed to act and continued to ignore petitions that Jones and the other Credit River Mississauga sent him. In 1847, the Credit River band, facing mounting pressure to leave their lands, resettled in the Six Nations reserve (Smith, *Sacred Feathers*, pp. 205–6, 163–78, 212).

215 American traveller John Sanderson visited Paris in the mid-1830s, and described it in unflattering terms: "Paris is a wilderness of tall, scraggy, and dingy houses, of irregular heights and

sizes . . . The streets run zig-zag, and abut against each other as if they did not know which way to run" (John Sanderson, *The American in Paris*, London: Henry Colburn, 1838, pp. 28–30).

216 John Sanderson was also overwhelmed by Paris's "unceasing racket—this rattling of the cabs and other vehicles over the rough stones, this rumbling of the omnibuses . . . the chaos of these streets is perpetual from generation to generation; it is the noise that never dies" (ibid., pp. 28–30).

217 Observer John Sanderson noted the political activism in Paris cafés when he visited the city in the 1830s: "these houses serve, in addition to their province of eating and drinking, as places of conference, or clubs; it is here that men communicate on political subjects, that news is circulated, and public opinion formed; and that kings are expelled, and others are set up on their thrones" (ibid., p. 109).

218 Maungwudaus travelled to England with his family: his wife Uhwessiggzhiggookwe and sons Awunnwabe, Waubuddick, Ujejock, Noodinnokay, and Minnissinnoo. Two more children, Dennis and Hannah, were born during the family's travels abroad. Maungwudaus also invited four Anishinaabe friends from Walpole Island to join the troupe: Saysaygon, Kecheussin, Aunimuckwuh-um, and Mishimaung (Smith, *Mississauga Portraits*, pp. 140, 146; Maungwudaus, *An Account of the Chippewa Indians*, p. 7; Catlin, *Catlin's Notes of Eight Years' Travels . . . Vol. II*, p. 279).

219 Alexander Cadotte, or Not-een-a-akm (Strong Wind), acted as interpreter for an Anishinaabe (Ojibwa) troupe that performed in Catlin's Indian Gallery shows in England from 1843 to 1844. "A young man of fine personal appearance and address," Cadotte was very popular among the female members of the audiences (Catlin, *Catlin's Notes of Eight Years' Travels . . . Vol. I*, pp. 110, 155–75).

220 O-kee-wee-me and Shon-ta-yi-ga were members of the Iowa group that performed in Catlin's European tour from 1844 to 1845. One of their children died during the Atlantic crossing, and while in Scotland, their young son Corsair died of a fever in his father's arms (Catlin, *Catlin's Notes of Eight Years' Travels . . . Vol. II*, p. 170)

221 While grieving the loss of their son, O-kee-wee-me and Shon-ta-yi-ga abstained from performing in Catlin's show; during their absence from the Indian Gallery, Catlin complained about losing "not only the exciting interest of the tiny Ioway [sic] child, but also the services of the father, Little Wolf and of the wife, for [some] length of time, if not altogether" (Benita Eisler, *The Red Man's Bones: George Catlin, Artist and Showman*, New York: W.W. Norton and Company, 2013, pp. 321–22).

222 One of the dresses that Catlin displayed in his Indian Gallery was a "dress of deer-skin . . . ornamented with brass buttons and beads" belonging to Wi-lóoh-tah-eeh-tcháh-ta-máh-nee, a Lakota woman whose portrait Catlin painted (George Catlin, *A Descriptive Catalogue of Catlin's Indian Collection, Containing Portraits, Landscapes, Costumes, &c., and Representations of the Manners and Customs of the North American Indians*, London: George Catlin, 1848, p. 15; Catlin, *North American Indians*, p. 252).

223 "This exciting scene, with its associations, had like to have been too much for the nerves and tastes of London people; but having evidently assembled here for the pleasure of receiving shocks and trying their nerves, they soon seemed reconciled, and all looked on with amazement and pleasure . . ." (Catlin, *Catlin's Notes of Eight Years' Travels . . . Vol. II*, p. 33).

224 One particular fan, dubbed "the jolly fat dame" by Catlin, came to see the show several times in order to talk to the handsome performer Not-een-a-akm and give him gifts such as "a very splendid bracelet" (Catlin, *Catlin's Notes of Eight Years' Travels . . . Vol. I*, pp. 157–63). Catlin described her lavish gift-giving: "As her heart was more smitten, her hand became more liberal: she had come this night loaded with presents, and dealt them out without stint to the whole party . . ." (ibid., p. 168).

225 The "jolly fat dame" sparked a gift-giving frenzy at Catlin's shows: "During the excitement thus produced by the distribution of her trinkets, some female in the midst of the crowd held up and displayed a beautiful bracelet 'for the first one who should get to it' . . . Many ladies were offering them their hands and trinkets" (Catlin, *Catlin's Notes of Eight Years' Travels . . . Vol. I*, p. 168).

226 Catlin provided this description of how women in his audiences reacted to the young Anishinaabe men in the show: "The excitement and screaming and laughing amongst the women in that part of the room made kissing fashionable, and every one who laid her hand upon his arm or his naked shoulders (and those not a few) got a kiss, gave a scream, and presented him a brooch, a ring, or some other keepsake, and went home with a streak of red paint on her face" (ibid., p. 119).

227 Baudelaire had syphilis and gonorrhea (Frederick William John Hemmings, *Baudelaire the Damned: A Biography*, London: Hamish Hamilton, 1982, pp. 34, 50).

228 Delacroix was known to have visited Catlin's Parisian show in 1846. He greatly admired the Indigenous performers as artistic subjects and drew sketches of them from the audience (Smith, *Mississauga Portraits*, p. 146; Tom Prideaux, *The World of Delacroix*, New York: Time Incorporated, 1966, p. 148).

229 In a racist article dedicated to dismissing the idea of the "noble savage," author Charles Dickens made extremely derogatory comments about the Anishinaabe performers in Catlin's show, insulting their dances as mentioned here as well as calling them "mere animals" and "wretched creatures" (Charles Dickens, "The Noble Savage," *Household Words*, vol. 8, no. 168, June 1853, p. 337).

230 Near the end of the Iowa group's travels in France, Catlin noted their anxiety to return to "their friends and affairs in their own humble villages," and how they collected money and gifts to bring home to their loved ones (Catlin, *Catlin's Notes of Eight Years' Travels . . . Vol. II*, pp. 273–74).

231 Molly Spotted Elk, whose birth name was Mary Alice Nelson, was a Penobscot scholar and entertainer who travelled around the United States and Europe in the 1920s and 1930s performing traditional dances for audiences. She also acted in several Hollywood films and was a dedicated writer, recording traditional Penobscot stories and creating a Penobscot dictionary, later published as the book *Katahdin: Wigwam's Tales of the Abnaki Tribe* (Penobscot Cultural & Historic Preservation, "Mary Alice Nelson Archambaud (Molly Spotted Elk)," Penobscot Culture, 2019, https://www.penobscotculture.com/molly-spotted-elk; "Molly Spotted Elk, From Poverty in Old Town, Maine, to Fame in Paris—and Back," New England Historical Society, 2018, https://newenglandhistoricalsociety.com/molly-spotted-elk-from-poverty-old-town-maine-fame-paris-back/).

232 When writing about Indigenous people, Catlin said that "the Great Spirit . . . alone can avert the *doom* that would almost seem to be fixed for their unfortunate race" (Catlin, *North American Indians,* p. 394).

233 Catlin also described Indigenous people as "an interesting race of people, who are rapidly passing away from the face of the earth" (ibid., p. 3).

234 This is the phrase Catlin used to describe the chief Kee-an-ne-kuk, when visiting the Kiikaapoi (Kickapoo) (ibid., p. 361; Kansas Kickapoo Tribe, "History").

235 In 1880, Carl Hagenbeck convinced two Inuit families from Labrador—Abraham Ulrikab, his wife Ulrike, their two young daughters Sara and Maria, and their nephew Tobias; as well as Terrianiak, Paingo, and their daughter Noggasak—to travel to Europe to be performers in human zoos across Germany (Hartmut Lutz et al., "Introduction," in *The Diary of Abraham Ulrikab: Text and Context*, Ottawa: University of Ottawa Press, 2005, p. xviii). Abraham kept a diary during their time abroad and wrote of their miserable experiences. He described how the Inuit travellers were often ill and suffered from terrible homesickness, and detailed the ridicule of the audiences and Hagenbeck's cruelty. Every single Inuk individual died of smallpox while in Europe (Lutz et al., "Introduction," pp. xxiii–xxiv).

236 For generations, tuberculosis has had a devastating effect on Indigenous people. The rampant rates of tuberculosis at residential institutions are part of a pattern of deliberate neglect and colonial violence (Jeremy Appel, "Researchers Say that TB at Residential Schools Was No Accident," *Alberta Native News*, July 17, 2021). In the mid-twentieth century, tuberculosis killed 8,000 out of every 100,000 children in residential institutions, one of the highest rates ever reported worldwide ("Fighting for Breath: Stopping the TB Epidemic," Museum of Health Care at Kingston, 2021, https://www.museumofhealthcare.ca/explore/exhibits/breath/).

237 George Sand was moved by O-kee-wee-me's tragedy during her tour in Paris; Sand is said to have brought O-kee-wee-me white cyclamen on a deathbed visit (Eisler, *The Red Man's Bones*, p. 329; Catlin, *Catlin's Notes of Eight Years' Travels . . . Vol. II*, p. 272).

238 O-kee-wee-me eventually died in Paris in June 1845 at the age of twenty-seven (Catlin, *Catlin's Notes of Eight Years' Travels . . . Vol. II*, p. 272; Eisler, *The Red Man's Bones*, p. 329).

239 Hundreds of Parisians attended O-kee-wee-me's funeral (Catlin, *Catlin's Notes of Eight Years' Travels . . . Vol. II*, p. 272).

240 When writing of Shon-ta-yi-ga's reaction to O-kee-wee-me's death, Catlin described how "the poor heartbroken noble fellow, the Little Wolf, shed the tears of bitterest sorrow to see her, from necessity, laid amongst the rows of the dead in a foreign land." Shon-ta-yi-ga visited her grave every day during the troupe's time in Paris (ibid., p. 272).

241 Saysaygon, Aunimuckwuh-um, and Mishimaung died of smallpox in Belgium. Only six of the thirteen members of Maungwudaus's group survived to return home (Eisler, *The Red Man's Bones*, pp. 321–40; Jessica L. Horton, "Ojibwa Tableaux Vivants: George Catlin, Robert Houle, and Transcultural Materialism," *Art History*, vol. 39, no. 1, February 2016, p. 135; Maungwudaus, *An Account of the Chippewa Indians*, p. 7; Smith, *Mississauga Portraits*, p. 149).

242 Maungwudaus's account offers unflattering descriptions of English people: "Many of the Englishmen have very big stomachs, caused by drinking too much ale and porter. Those who

drink wine and brandy, their noses look like ripe strawberries" (Maungwudaus, *An Account of the Chippewa Indians*, p. 5).

243 Catlin hoped that he would acquire "the reputation of having been the founder of such an institution," and stated that a park would be an ideal "monument to my memory" (Catlin, *North American Indians,* p. 263). Catlin proposed that regions of Turtle Island (specifically, areas that were "sterile" and "of no available use to cultivating man") be "preserved in their pristine beauty and wildness, in a *magnificent park*, where the world could see for ages to come, the native Indian in his classic attire, galloping his wild horse . . . amid the fleeting herds of elks and buffaloes. What a beautiful and thrilling specimen for America to preserve and hold up to the view of her refined citizens and the world, in future ages!" (ibid.).

244 Catlin dismissed nonbinary Indigenous gender identities as "one of the most unaccountable and disgusting customs that I have ever met in the Indian country . . . I should wish that it might be extinguished before it be more fully recorded" (ibid., p. 445).

245 When Catlin was struggling financially in England during the later years of the 1840s, he began promoting English emigration to Turtle Island. One London handbill advertises an April 9, 1850 lecture by Catlin in which he would speak about "the Valley of the Mississippi, and its advantage to emigration, with some account of the gold regions of California." The success of these lectures led to his being hired by the Texas department of a colonization company. In addition to becoming an active participant in the displacement of Indigenous people, something he had previously claimed to lament, Catlin also engaged in dishonest business practices to recruit settlers (Mulvey, "George Catlin in Europe," pp. 75–77; Brian W. Dippie, *Catlin and His Contemporaries: The Politics of Patronage*, Lincoln: University of Nebraska Press, 1990).

246 In the late 1840s, while living in London, Catlin published a pamphlet called *Notes for the Emigrant to America*, in which he called Indigenous people "cruel savages" (Mulvey, "George Catlin in Europe," pp. 75–76).

247 The three youngest of Maungwudaus's seven children—Minnissinno, Dennis, and Hannah, a newborn—died while the family was touring Scotland in 1847. Maungwudaus's wife Uhwessiggzhiggookwe died shortly afterwards in England (Maungwudaus, *An Account of the Chippewa Indians*, pp. 8–9; Smith, *Mississauga Portraits*, 149–150; Catlin, *Catlin's Notes of Eight Years' Travels . . . Vol. II*, pp. 298–99).

248 Even after the loss of his loved ones, Maungwudaus had to continue travelling and performing to raise money. He parted from Catlin shortly after the deaths of his Walpole Island friends, and finally returned to Turtle Island with his surviving children in 1848 (Smith, *Mississauga Portraits*, pp. 149–50).

Our Ways of Seeing Were So Different

249 France had an active tradition of salon gatherings, in which academics and artists met to discuss intellectual subjects. In the 1840s, George Sand, her lover Frédéric Chopin, and Eugène Delacroix lived in the same neighbourhood, and frequently visited each other (Prideaux, *The World of Delacroix*, pp. 85, 130, 147).

250 After touring the United States for several years, William Drummond Stewart was compelled to return to Scotland in 1839 following the death of his childless older brother and Stewart's subsequent inheritance of the family estate and title. Antoine Clement accompanied Stewart to Scotland, ostensibly as Stewart's valet, though Benemann has written that the two were in a long-term intimate relationship by this point (Benemann, *Men in Eden*, pp. 219–26).

251 Cree writer Tomson Highway has written about the sexiness of the Cree language, and how its sexual humour does not always translate well into English: "In English, it is horrifying. It makes your hair stand on end. Your spine freezes, and something inside you goes dead. The politically correct would string me up by the balls and hang me dry for having said it. In Cree, among friends, it is hysterically, thigh-slappingly, gut-bustingly funny" (Tomson Highway, "Why Cree Is the Sexiest of All Languages," in *Me Sexy*, ed. Drew Hayden Taylor, Vancouver: Douglas & McIntyre, 2008, pp. 33–40).

252 Highly respected Oglala Lakota *wičháša wakȟáŋ* (holy man) Black Elk was active from the late nineteenth century to 1950. He travelled to Europe in the 1880s as part of Buffalo Bill Cody's Wild West Show (Clyde Holler, "Black Elk, Nicholas (1866–1950)," *Encyclopedia of the Great Plains*, ed. David J. Wishart, 2011). As Vine Deloria, Jr. notes, "Black Elk shared his visions with John Neihardt [the editor and co-author of his memoirs] because he wished to pass along to future generations some of the reality of Oglala life and, one suspects, to share the burden of visions that remained unfulfilled with a compatible spirit" (Vine Deloria, Jr., "Introduction," in *Black Elk Speaks: Being the Life Story of a Holy Man of the Oglala Sioux*, ed. John G. Neihardt, Lincoln: University of Nebraska Press, 1995, p. xiii).

253 *wičháša wakȟáŋ* is the Lakota term for a holy man or spiritual leader. The word *heyókȟa* means "thunder dreamer," referring to those who receive visions of the thunder beings. Black Elk stated that his responsibility as a *heyókȟa* was to "[present] the truth of his vision through comic actions" (Lakota Language Consortium, *Lakota Dictionary Online*, 2018; Black Elk and John G. Neihardt, *The Sixth Grandfather: Black Elk's Teachings Given to John G. Neihardt*, ed. Raymond J. DeMallie, Lincoln: University of Nebraska Press, 1985, p. 232).

254 According to Lakota academic Marjorie Anne Napewastewiñ Schützer, the term *winkte* is drawn from the old Lakota word *winyanktehca* and means "to be as a woman." It describes Two-Spirit people, who are revered in Lakota society (Marjorie Anne Napewastewiñ Schützer, "Winyanktecha—Two Souls Person," paper presented at *Conference of the European Network of Professionals on Transsexualism, Manchester, England, August 1994*, Amsterdam: The Gender Team, 1994).

255 William Huggins is considered to have founded stellar astrophysics. Using spectroscopy to analyze the chemical makeup of stars, Huggins determined that the same chemicals existed both in space and on earth (Malcolm S. Longair, *The Cosmic Century: A History of Astrophysics and Cosmology*, Cambridge: Cambridge University Press, 2015, pp. 18–19).

256 Floyd Favel suggests that Black Elk may have influenced European scientists: "the explosion of physicists in Germany, and France, and England in the . . . 1860s, 1870s, 1880s . . . that's when people started to listen to Indians talking in wild west shows. I'm sure Black Elk influenced somebody in his lectures and talks . . . as he talked about their Lakota worldview. Because if you translate a lot of our worldviews . . . how we talk in Cree . . . into English, if

you try to translate physicists' concepts into Indian language, it makes sense" (Floyd Favel, interview by Gisèle Gordon, August 2018).

257 Dumas and Delacroix were friends, with both men running in the fashionable salon crowd of Parisian society. A republican in his politics, Dumas's work was popular with young, romantic readers of the day. He was noted to be a generous host and entertained visitors lavishly (Mike Phillips, "Black Europeans: A British Library Online Gallery feature by guest curator Mike Phillips," The British Library, n.d., pp. 3–7, https://www.bl.uk/onlinegallery/features/blackeuro/pdf/coleridge.pdf).

258 Catlin wrote that some women and medicine men of the Mandan village he visited were suspicious of his art's powers; according to Catlin, they claimed that his process of creating lifelike portraits of chiefs would "take a part of the existence of those whom [he] painted, and carry it home with [him] amongst the white people, and that when they died they would never sleep quiet in their graves" (Catlin, *North American Indians*, p. 106).

259 Delacroix was a notable Romantic painter but still had a high respect for classicist ideals (Prideaux, *The World of Delacroix*, p. 11). Delacroix had an infamous rivalry with Jean-Auguste-Dominique Ingres, a Neoclassicist artist (ibid., p. 128).

260 The model for Auguste Rodin's *Adam* was a carnival strongman named Caillou, who had the muscular, "Michelangelesque" figure that Rodin hoped to capture in his sculptures (Ruth Butler, *Rodin: The Shape of Genius*, New Haven: Yale University Press, 1996, p. 159).

261 The models in *The Academy* are posed to evoke the Laocoön sculpture, an ancient Roman work that shows the moment in which Laocoön and his two sons are strangled by snakes sent by vengeful gods. This work has been upheld as a classical Western sculptural ideal since it was rediscovered in 1506 (Maria H. Loh, "Outscreaming the Laocoön: Sensation, Special Affects, and the Moving Image," *Oxford Art Journal*, vol. 34, no. 3, 2011, p. 396).

262 Inspired by traditional petroglyph art and stories as well as his own dream visions, Morrisseau sought to communicate spiritual power through his work and rekindle Anishnaabe cultural pride (Cheryl Petten, "The One and Only, Norval Morrisseau," *Windspeaker*, February 18, 2017; Nokomis, "Norval Morrisseau: Grandfather of Canadian Native Art," *Native Art in Canada: An Ojibwa Elder's Art and Stories*, 2015, https://www.native-art-in-canada.com/norvalmorrisseau.html; Carmen Robertson, *Norval Morrisseau: Life and Work*, Toronto: Art Canada Institute, 2016, p. 5).

263 In his journal on September 17, 1850, Delacroix commented, "Laurens tells me that Ziegler is making a great number of daguerreotypes, including some of nude men. I must ask him to lend them to me" (Eugène Delacroix, *The Journal of Eugène Delacroix*, ed. Hubert Wellington, Oxford: Phaidon Press Ltd., 1980, p. 136).

264 The population of Upper Canada and Lower Canada increased from approximately 1.5 million in 1848 to 2.5 million by 1861 (Statistics Canada, "The 1800s (1806 to 1871)," Statcan.gc.ca, August 26, 2015). The United States' population increased from approximately 23 million to more than 31 million during the same period (United States Census Bureau, "1990 Population and Housing Unit Counts: United States," Census.gov, 1990).

265 Blackpoll warblers are capable of flying non-stop for up to three days, covering an average 1,800 miles over the Atlantic Ocean (Cornell Lab, "Blackpoll Warbler," All About Birds, 2019, https://www.allaboutbirds.org/guide/Blackpoll_Warbler/overview).

266 Fort William is part of Thunder Bay today (Charnel Anderson and David D. Kemp, "Thunder Bay," *The Canadian Encyclopedia*, July 24, 2019).

267 As recorded by fur trader Francis A. Chardon, smallpox was brought to Mitu'tahakto's by an American Fur Company steamship, *St. Peters*, in June 1837 (Francis A. Chardon, *Chardon's Journal at Fort Clark, 1834–1839*, ed. Annie Heloise Abel, Pierre: State of South Dakota Department of History, 1932, p. 118).

268 Catlin painted a portrait of a young Mandan woman named Minéekeesúnkteka in 1832, describing her as "a Beautiful Girl" (George Catlin, *Mi-néek-ee-súnk-te-ka, Mink, a Beautiful Girl*, 1832 [painting], Smithsonian American Art Museum, Washington, D.C.).

269 Francis A. Chardon was present during the smallpox epidemic, and in August 1837 wrote that "8 and 10 die off daily" from the disease (Chardon, *Chardon's Journal*, p. 131).

270 As recorded by Catlin, nearly all of the Mandans in the village he visited died in a smallpox epidemic in the summer of 1837 (Catlin, *North American Indians*, p. 487). Catlin estimated that of 2,400 people in the Mandan villages, only 31 survived (Dippie, "Green Fields and Red Men," p. 53).

271 In September 1837, many of the Mandan survivors of the smallpox epidemic left Mitu'tahakto's. Some of the departed Mandan survivors moved to Crow villages, while others became nomadic. In 1845, the Minitari (Hidatsa) of the Upper Missouri River—who had also been devastated by the epidemic, losing half of their population—invited the Mandan survivors to build a new village together, which became known as Like-a-Fishhook (Chardon, *Chardon's Journal*, pp. 137–40; Jayne Reinhiller, "Holding on to Culture: The Effects of the 1837 Smallpox Epidemic on Mandan and Hidatsa," *Butler Journal of Undergraduate Research*, vol. 4, 2018, p. 207; Fenn, *Encounters at the Heart of the World*, pp. 327–29).

272 See note 42 in "The Massacre of Our Beaver Relatives Foreshadowed What Was to Come" and note 46 in "The Newcomers Had Much to Learn" for descriptions of smallpox death tolls. Smallpox struck Indigenous peoples in continuous waves of highly deadly epidemics (C. Stuart Houston and Stan Houston, "The First Smallpox Epidemic on the Canadian Plains: In the Fur-Traders' Words," *The Canadian Journal of Infectious Diseases*, vol. 11, no. 2, March 2000, p. 112).

273 Francis A. Chardon, a witness to the 1837 epidemic, recorded cases of Mandan smallpox victims committing suicide or mercy-killing their loved ones out of desperation to end their pain and suffering. On August 19, he wrote in his journal that "a Mandan and his Wife Killed themselves yesterday, to not Out live their relations that are dead" (Chardon, *Chardon's Journal*, pp. 129–33).

274 Several Indigenous writers have commented on the use of humour as a survival mechanism. As Thomas King observes, "We say of Native humour that it's about survival, that the only way Native people have been able to endure the array of oppressions that have been visited on us is through humour" (Thomas King, Performing Native Humour: The Dead Dog Café Comedy Hour," in *Me Funny*, ed. Drew Hayden Taylor, p. 169–186, Vancouver: Douglas & McIntyre,

2005). In 1969, Vine Deloria, Jr. stated that "When a people can laugh at themselves and laugh at others and hold all aspects of life together without letting anybody drive them to extremes, then it seems to me that that people can survive" (Vine Deloria, Jr., *Custer Died for Your Sins: An Indian Manifesto*, New York: Avon Books, 1972, p. 168).

275 Cheyenne artist Delwin Fiddler describes winter counts as a method for passing down history through the generations, with most communities painting on hides as a record (Delwin Fiddler, Jr., "Winter Count, then and now," *Native Hope*, 2021, https://blog.nativehope.org/winter-count-then-and-now). Aaniihnén curator George P. Horse Capture likens winter counts to a symbolic calendar created by a community historian (George P. Horse Capture, "From Museums to Indians: Native American Art in Context," in *Robes of Splendor: Native American Painted Buffalo Hides*, New York: The New Press, 1993, p. 82).

My Intercourse with the Crown

276 While some of the Indigenous–European relationships established during the fur trade were mutually loving and long-lasting, other Europeans, such as George Simpson, treated these relationships as disposable (Van Kirk, *"Many Tender Ties,"* pp. 161–63).

277 Charles "Buffalo" Jones estimated that there were about 15 million buffalo in January 1865, and 14 million by 1870 (Charles Jesse Jones, *Buffalo Jones' Forty Years of Adventure*, London: Sampson Low, Marston and Company Limited, 1899, p. 255). This number was down from 40 million at the start of the nineteenth century, and 20 million in 1850 (Thornton, *American Indian Holocaust and Survival*, p. 52).

278 Treaties signed between the Crown and Indigenous people during the mid-nineteenth century include the Bond Head Treaty with the Odawa Miniss (Manitoulin Island) Anishnaabeg in 1836, the Robinson Treaties with the Anishnaabe of Lakes Superior and Huron in 1850, the Douglas Treaties with the Salish and Kwakwaka'wakw of Vancouver Island in 1850–1854, the Saugeen Peninsula Treaty with the Saugeen Anishnaabe in 1854, and the Pennefather Treaty with the Batchewana in 1859 (Terry Debassige, "The Treaties of 1836 and 1862," Black's Bay Lodge, n.d., http://blacksbay.ca/aboriginals/treaty_series_part_1.htm; *Canadian History*, "1850—The Douglas Treaties," 2018, https://canadianhistory.ca/natives/timeline/1850s/1850-the-douglas-treaties; *Canadian History*, "1850—The Robinson Treaties," 2018, https://canadianhistory.ca/natives/timeline/1850s/1850-the-robinson-treaties; Government of Canada, "Treaty Texts—Upper Canada Land Surrenders," Canada.ca, 2016).

279 "When treaties became binding, it became a ceremonial covenant of adoption between two families. kiciwâminawak, our cousins: that is what my elders said to call you. In nêhiyaw law, the treaties were adoptions of one nation by another . . . We became relatives. When your ancestors came to this territory, kiciwâminawak, our law applied. These kinship relationships were active choices, a state of relatedness or connection by adoption" (McAdam, *Nationhood Interrupted*, p. 41).

280 As Sylvia McAdam writes, "Everything in creation has laws and these are called *manitow wiyinikêwina*." She states that "*manitow* means Creator, *wiyinikêwina* means an act similar to a type of weaving. The weaving describes all of creation as bound together, having been given

laws" (ibid., p. 38). When referring to Treaty 6, Cree scholar Dr. Paulina R. Johnson states that "our Treaty was not only made with the British Crown but with Manitow as well." This understanding is inherent in the procedures used in Treaty 6: "When we negotiated with Treaty, our pipes were our connection to Kisê-manitow, and we believed that the presence of the bible was the Môniyâwak's connection to their god" (Paulina R. Johnson, "E-kawôtiniket 1876: Reclaiming Nêhiyaw Governance in the Territory of Maskwacîs through Wâhkôtowin (Kinship)," PhD diss., University of Western Ontario, 2017, pp. 123–24).

281 The reference to a ceremony before negotiations refers to the role of the Cree women's council, or okihcitâwiskwêwak, who would conduct such ceremonies before treaties such as Treaty 6 (McAdam, *Nationhood Interrupted*, p. 31).

282 Sylvia McAdam writes that "each nêhiyaw child has a birth right that is steeped in the history of the land and their kinship with all of creation. They are born into responsibilities and obligations that will guide them from cradle to death" (ibid., p. 36).

283 By the nineteenth century, the Haudenosaunee confederacy, or Rotinonhsyón:nih, consisted of the Six Nations: the Kanien'kehá:ka (Mohawk), Onöndowàga (Seneca), Goyogohó:no (Cayuga), Onöñda'gega (Onondaga), Onyota'a:ka (Oneida), and Skarù:rę (Tuscarora) (Jeremy Green, "Kanyen'kéha: Mohawk Language," *The Canadian Encyclopedia*, May 4, 2018).

284 In 1860, Albert Edward, the future King Edward VII and then eighteen years old, undertook a lavish "royal tour" of Canada, with one important stop being Montréal, where he was to represent the Crown at the inauguration of the Victoria Bridge (Ruth B. Phillips, "Making Sense Out/of the Visual: Aboriginal Presentations and Representations in Nineteenth-Century Canada," *Art History*, vol. 27, no. 4, September 2004, pp. 594–95).

285 The Kanien'kehá:ka name for Montréal is Tiohtià:ke or Otsira:ke (Karonhí:io Delaronde and Jordan Engel, "Tiohtià:ke tsi ionhwéntsare," *The Decolonial Atlas*, February 4, 2015, https://decolonialatlas.wordpress.com/2015/02/04/montreal-in-mohawk/).

286 Kaniatarowanénhne is the Kanien'kehá:ka name for the St. Lawrence River (ibid.).

287 It is said that John A. Macdonald, following a night of "heavy drinking," once vomited in public while listening to a member of the opposition give a speech (Julia Skelly, "The Politics of Drunkenness: John Henry Walker, John A. Macdonald, and Graphic Satire," *Canadian Art Review*, vol. 40, no. 1, 2015, p. 79).

288 Kanien'kehá:ka labourers from Kahnawá:ke were involved in the construction of the Victoria Bridge (Ian Radforth, "Performance, Politics, and Representation: Aboriginal People and the 1860 Royal Tour of Canada," *The Canadian Historical Review*, vol. 84, no. 1, March 2003, p. 4).

289 In 1850, as Montréal grew and settlers encroached further on Kahnawá:ke, the Act for the Better Protection of Lands and Property of the Indians in Lower Canada determined that Indigenous lands, including Kahnawá:ke, would fall under the authority of the Province of Canada; Kahnawakehro:non leaders were not consulted (Joan Holmes, "Kahnawake Mohawk Territory: From Seigneury to Indian Reserve," National Claims Research Workshop, Ottawa, November 9, 2006, http://www.joanholmes.ca/KahnawakePaper.pdf).

290 Albert Edward showed little interest in Indigenous people and the political issues concerning them during his 1860 tour. His descriptions of his meetings fixated on costumes he described as quaint, and he wrote to his mother that he had experienced nothing of interest, despite the

fact that he had witnessed ceremonies put forth by the Six Nations Haudenosaunee of Brantford (Radforth, *Royal Spectacle*, p. 209).

291 In response to Nahnebahwequa's 1860 petition to protect Indigenous land rights (see note 211 in "When I Travelled to the Newcomers' Homelands"), Queen Victoria ordered the Duke of Newcastle to accompany Prince Albert Edward on his tour and investigate the status of Indigenous people. While in Canada, the duke asked Richard Pennefather to carry out the inquiry, but as Superintendent-General of Indian Affairs, Pennefather was a biased observer (Radforth, *Royal Spectacle*, pp. 229–32). Newcastle presented Pennefather's report to the queen with the following comment: "'I hope that the Advocates of the Indians in this Country who have frequently called on you and have written . . . are now persuaded that there really is not much to complain of in Canada'" (Nathan Tidridge, *The Queen at the Council Fire: The Treaty of Niagara, Reconciliation, and the Dignified Crown in Canada*, Toronto: Dundurn, 2015, p. 86).

292 Anishinaabe scholar Carol Nadjiwon points out that during his time as Superintendent-General of Indian Affairs in the Province of Canada, Richard Pennefather actively tried to impede Indigenous attempts to seek justice (Carol Nadjiwon, "1850 Huron Robinson Treaty & 1859 Pennefather Treaty Research," Batchewana First Nation, February 2011, https://batchewana.ca/about/treaties). According to Haudenosaunee doctor Oronhyatekha, Pennefather prevented the Haudenosaunee community of Grand River from meeting with Prince Albert Edward during his visit to Toronto, even though a meeting had been approved beforehand (Keith Jamieson and Michelle A. Hamilton, *Dr. Oronhyatekha: Security, Justice, and Equality*, Toronto: Dundurn, 2016).

293 After 1850, due to dwindling buffalo populations and rising European encroachment, Plains Nations increasingly had to hunt on one another's traditional territory in order to feed their people, leading to increased conflict (John S. Milloy, *The Plains Cree: Trade, Diplomacy, and War, 1790 to 1870*, Winnipeg: University of Manitoba Press, 1988, pp. 107–14).

294 Albert Edward was notorious for his sexual affairs. The first was with actress Nellie Clifden, whom he met while attending a military training course in 1861. He would go on to have many mistresses throughout his life, to the extent that upon his ascension to the throne, writer Henry James would dismiss him as "Edward the Caresser" (Katherine Graber, "'One Whirl of Amusements': Examining the Evolving Role of the Royal Mistress from Lillie Langtry to Alice Keppel," *Lucerna*, vol. 3, 2008, pp. 99–102).

295 George Simpson died shortly after hosting Albert Edward during the prince's Montréal visit (Radforth, *Royal Spectacle*, p. 221). Writing on Simpson's death later in life, former Hudson's Bay Company factor Henry John Moberly noted that he "had been extremely weak for some time, and the excitement of receiving the Prince of Wales, afterward King Edward VII, on his visit to Montréal, had proved too much for him" (Henry John Moberly, *When Fur Was King*, Toronto: J.M. Dent and Sons Limited, 1929, pp. 108–9).

296 The name Canada has a long history in the colonization of Turtle Island. Jacques Cartier wrote down the name "kanata" after the Haudenosaunee of Stadacona told him their word for "town" or "village." It was then applied to a colony of New France, and became a common

European name for the New France region in general. The British, after their conquest of the region, began calling the North American colonies Upper and Lower Canada after 1791, with the two sometimes being referred to as the Canadas. The colonies merged into the Province of Canada in 1841; the two regions were officially designated as Canada East and Canada West, though the Upper and Lower distinctions remained in use. After Confederation in 1867, the country was called the Dominion of Canada (Alan Rayburn, *Naming Canada: Stories about Canadian Place Names From Canadian Geographic*, Toronto: University of Toronto Press, 1994, pp. 11–16; James Maurice Stockford Careless and Richard Foot, "Province of Canada 1841–67," *The Canadian Encyclopedia*, March 4, 2015).

297 Albert Edward had a short reign as king from 1901–1910, and did not effect great positive change for the Indigenous peoples of Turtle Island during that time. In 1906 Sa7plek (Sahpluk), or "Joe Capilano," travelled to London to meet Albert, now Edward VII, to get him to stop land encroachments; Edward VII said he would help, but little was done afterwards (Dorothy Kennedy, "Chief Joe Capilano," *The Canadian Encyclopedia*, October 26, 2021). Edward VII was also the monarch represented in the Numbered Treaties 9 and 10 ("The James Bay Treaty—Treaty No. 9 (Made in 1905 and 1906) and Adhesions Made in 1929 and 1930," Ottawa: Queen's Printer and Controller of Stationery, 1964; "Treaty No. 10 and Reports of Commissioners," October 14, 1907, Ottawa: Queen's Printer and Controller of Stationery, 1966).

298 "The Crown" refers to the British government as represented by the royal sovereign. Legally, the Crown holds executive authority over Canada (Carolyn Harris and Andrew McIntosh, "Crown," *The Canadian Encyclopedia*, March 18, 2021).

I Learned That They Would Steal Everything

299 Frances Anne Hopkins was a British artist who practised in Canada in the mid-nineteenth century. She travelled with her husband Edward Hopkins, an employee of the Hudson's Bay Company, on trader canoe routes several times during the 1860s, creating paintings and sketches of voyageur life (Philip Shackleton, "Beechey, Frances Anne (Hopkins)," *Dictionary of Canadian Biography, Vol. XIV*, University of Toronto/Université Laval, 1998).

300 Canada West (Ontario) and Canada East (Québec) experienced deep internal political conflict in the early 1860s. In Canada West, for example, the Conservatives under John A. Macdonald clashed with the Clear Grits under George Brown (P.B. Waite, "Confederation," *The Canadian Encyclopedia*, October 29, 2019). An 1856 article in Brown's paper, *The Globe*, professes the interest of the Canadian public in the Hudson's Bay Company's territories: "we are looking about for new worlds to conquer." The writer claimed that "the colony is fully entitled to possess whatever parts of the great British American territory she can safely occupy" (*The Globe*, "The Great North West," December 10, 1856).

301 Hopkins faced discrimination as a female artist, and did not experience wide success during her lifetime. She signed her works with her initials in order to hide her identity as a woman but

also frequently inserted figures of herself into the subject matter of her paintings (CBC News, "Photographer Embarks on Canoe Trip into 19th Century," CBC.ca, June 19, 2018; Hudson's Bay Company, "Frances Anne Hopkins," HBC Heritage, 2016, https://www.hbcheritage.ca/people/women/frances-anne-hopkins).

302 Pablo Picasso, like other modernist artists, was influenced by Indigenous art (Susan Hiller, "Editor's Introduction," in *The Myth of Primitivism*, ed. Susan Hiller, London: Routledge, 1991, pp. 3–4).

303 A 1680 map by Abbé Claude Bernou shows the Haudenosaunee villages Ganatchekiagon (Ganatsekwyagon) and Teyoyagon (Teiaiagon) near the site of present-day Toronto, with present-day Lake Simcoe labelled as Lac de Taronto (Abbé Claude Bernou, "Map of the Great Lakes" 1680, Map and Data Library, University of Toronto; Alan Rayburn, "The Real Story of How Toronto Got Its Name," *Canadian Geographic*, September/October 1994). Teiaiagon, on the Humber River, was a major Seneca village around the period of contact, with an estimated 5,000 inhabitants (Diane Boyer, "Cultural Commotion at the Toronto Carrying Place Trail," *Muséologies*, vol. 4, no. 2, 2010, p. 97; Jon Johnson, "The Indigenous Environmental History of Toronto, 'The Meeting Place,'" in *Urban Explorations: Environmental Histories of the Toronto Region*, ed. L. A. Sandberg et al., Ontario: Wilson Institute for Canadian History, 2013, p. 62). Kanien'kehá:ka scholar William Woodworth notes that Teiaiagon was destroyed by fire and the people killed by the French (quoted in Victoria Freeman, "'Toronto Has No History!': Indigeneity, Settler Colonialism and Historical Memory in Canada's Largest City," PhD diss., University of Toronto, 2010, p. 303). Ganatsekwyagon, located on the Rouge River, was another important Haudenosaunee village in the region and was heavily populated up to the mid-seventeenth century (Toronto Historical Association, "Ganatsekwyagon," Toronto History, 1998, http://www.torontohistory.net/ganatsekwyagon/). The Seneca here were later displaced by ongoing French raids (James H. Marsh, "Toronto Feature: Teiaiagon Seneca Village," *The Canadian Encyclopedia*, July 2, 2015; Victor Konrad, "An Iroquois Frontier: The North Shore of Lake Ontario During the Late Seventeenth Century," *Journal of Historical Geography*, vol. 7, no. 2, 1981, pp. 141–42).

304 Paul Kane was an Irish-born artist active in Toronto during the mid-nineteenth century. He made a successful career creating portraits of Indigenous people and sacred items, the subjects of which were drawn from Kane's travels along western trade routes used by the Hudson's Bay Company. Kane was inspired by George Catlin, whose Indian Gallery he may have seen in London in 1842; like Catlin, Kane had a patronizing view of Indigenous peoples and believed he was saving vanishing cultures. He also inaccurately depicted Indigenous people and sacred belongings, combining cultures to create romanticized paintings such as *Flat Head Woman and Child, Caw-wacham* and *Medicine Mask Dance* (see notes 314 and 324) (Arlene Gehmacher, *Paul Kane: Life & Work,* Toronto: Art Canada Institute, 2014, pp. 3–8).

305 Harriet Clench, the wife of Paul Kane, was an award-winning artist and art teacher (Gehmacher, *Paul Kane*, p. 4; "Kane, Harriet Clench," Canadian Women Artists History Initiative Database, updated August 2022).

306 The Fur Queen is a character from Tomson Highway's book *Kiss of the Fur Queen* (Toronto: Anchor Canada, 2005). Thank you to Tomson for granting his permission to us to reference her here.

307 *Tkarón:to* is a Kanien'kehá:ka word meaning "where there are trees standing in the water" or "tree in the water there" (Karonhí:io Delaronde and Jordan Engel, "Haudenosaunee Country in Mohawk," *The Decolonial Atlas*, February 4, 2015, https://decolonialatlas.wordpress.com/2015/02/04/haudenosaunee-country-in-mohawk-2/).

308 The Anishinaabemowin name Zhooniyaang-zaaga'igan means "of the Silver Lake" and refers to Lake Simcoe (Charles Lippert and Jordan Engel, "Nayaano-nibiimaang Gichigamiin," *The Decolonial Atlas*, April 14, 2015, https://decolonialatlas.wordpress.com/2014/12/01/the-great-lakes-in-ojibwe/).

309 The river that the Anishinaabe called Cobechenonk, or "leave the canoes and go back" river, is called the Humber River today (Smith, *Mississauga Portraits*, p. 15).

310 In 1799, David William Smith recorded the name Katabokokonk as meaning "river of Easy Entrance"; late nineteenth-century academic Henry Scadding recorded the name as Atatabahkookong, or "grassy entrance." Smith also wrote down Ketche Sepee or "Great River" as the name for the river that became known as the Rouge (Henry Scadding, "Canadian Local History: The First Gazetteer of Upper Canada, with Annotations," in *First Gazetteer of Upper Canada*, Toronto: Copp, Clark & Co., 1876, pp. 5–6).

311 The need for railway labourers brought waves of poor Irish immigrants into Toronto in the 1840s and 1850s. Richer neighbourhoods like those on Jarvis and Spadina had paved streets, sidewalks, and piped water, while immigrants living in the shacks of Cabbagetown had to grow cabbages in their yards for food (Barbara Sanford, "The Political Economy of Land Development in Nineteenth Century Toronto," *Urban History Review*, vol. 16, no. 1, June 1987, pp. 23–24; Betty I. Roots, Donald A. Chant, and Conrad E. Heidenrich, *Special Places: The Changing Ecosystem of the Toronto Region*, Toronto: UBC Press, 1999, pp. 81–82).

312 *M'iingan* means "wolf" in Nishnaabemwin, the Odawa and Eastern Ojibwe dialect of Anishinaabemowin (Mary Ann Naokwegijig-Corbiere and Rand Valentine, "M'iingan," Nishnaabemwin: Odawa & Eastern Ojibwe Online Dictionary, 2022).

313 Molly Wood's Bush is an early nineteenth-century nickname for the region that would later become the Church and Wellesley neighbourhood, better known as Toronto's gay village. The historical name was derived from the derogatory slang word *molly*, which referred to a gay man, and city magistrate Alexander Wood, who was embroiled in a same-sex scandal in 1810 and purchased the region's land in the 1820s (Church/Wellesley Village BIA Monument Committee).

314 Kane inaccurately combined depictions of two Indigenous individuals to create his romanticized painting *Flat Head Woman and Child*, Caw-wacham; the real woman in the portrait was Caw-wacham, a Stl'pulmsh (Cowlitz) woman, while the baby was Chinook (Diane Eaton and Sheila Urbanek, *Paul Kane's Great Nor-West*, Vancouver: UBC Press, 2011; Curators of the University of Missouri, "Cowlitz," Database for Indigenous Cultural Evolution, 2015; Gehmacher, *Paul Kane*, p. 25; Kane, *Wanderings of an Artist*, p. 205; Kane, *A Child in the Process of Having Its Head Flattened*, 1847 [painting]).

315 Kane created two portraits of Maungwudaus around 1850 in which he altered Maungwudaus's features to appeal to European tastes (Smith, *Mississauga Portraits*, p. 154).

316 Oronhyatekha, a Kanien'kehá:ka (Mohawk) doctor, graduated from the Toronto School of Medicine in 1867 (Ethel Brant Monture, *Famous Indians: Brant, Crowfoot, Oronhyatekha*,

Toronto: Clarke, Irwin & Company Limited, 1960, pp. 139–40). During the 1870s Oronhyatekha served as consulting physician for Tyendinaga and later for the Oneida of the Thames (Michelle A. Hamilton, "Canada's First Indigenous Physician? The story of Dr. O (1841–1907)," *Canadian Journal of Surgery*, vol. 60, no. 1, February 2017, pp. 8–10).

317 Kane acquired many Indigenous belongings on his travels, such as Kwagiulth and Nuxalt masks, and may have had the Hudson's Bay Company send artifacts to him in Toronto upon his return (Eaton and Urbanek, *Paul Kane's Great Nor-West*, p. 104; Royal Ontario Museum, "Paul Kane: Collector," Paul Kane: Land Study, Studio View [online resource], 2000).

318 In their work with the Royal Ontario Museum on exhibitions like *Being Legendary*, Leslie McCue, Sara Roque, and Kristy McInnis have worked to shift museum language around Indigenous collections, emphasizing that *objects* should be called *sacred belongings* (meetings, correspondence, and personal conversations with Gisèle Gordon, September to October 2022).

319 Adolphus Egerton Ryerson was an education reformer and the Chief Superintendent of Education for Canada West from 1844 to 1876. In 1847 he was commissioned by the Indian Affairs Branch to produce a report on the residential institution education method for Indigenous children. Ryerson recommended an industrial school model managed by religious organizations and overseen by the government, in which Indigenous children would be trained to be "working farmers and agricultural labourers, fortified of course by Christian principles, feelings and habits." Ryerson emphasized the goal of culturally assimilating Indigenous children through religious interference, claiming that "the North American Indian cannot be civilized . . . except in connection with . . . religious instruction and sentiment . . . This influence must be superadded to all others to make the Indian a sober and industrious man" ("Report of Dr. Ryerson on Industrial Schools," in *Statistics Respecting Indian Schools with Dr. Ryerson's Report of 1847 Attached*, Department of Indian Affairs, Ottawa: Government Printing Bureau, 1898, pp. 73–74). Ryerson's recommendations eventually founded the basis for the residential institution system in Canada (Neil Semple and Katrine Raymond, "Egerton Ryerson," *The Canadian Encyclopedia*, 2017).

320 Sylvia McAdam writes that "one of the most important laws that speak to raising a nêhiyaw child is miyo-ohpikinâwasowin or ohpikinâwasowin. Miyo- means good, ohpikinâwasowin means child-rearing or raising. miyo-ohpikinâwasowin directs parents to raise their children to become lawful nêhiyaw citizens for their respective nêhiyaw nations" (McAdam, *Nationhood Interrupted*, p. 29).

321 In two different photo portraits taken around 1850 to 1860, Kane is dressed in buckskin and furs ("Paul Kane," c. 1850 [photograph], M.O. Hammond Collection, National Gallery of Canada, Ottawa; "Paul Kane," c. 1860 [photograph], Archives of Ontario).

322 John Henry Lefroy, director of the Toronto Magnetic Observatory, undertook an expedition in 1843–44 to determine the location of the magnetic north. Kane painted his portrait in 1845 (see note 325 below), and Lefroy in turn wrote a letter of support for Kane so that the artist could win HBC governor George Simpson's approval to travel west (Gehmacher, *Paul Kane*, pp. 16–17).

323 In his book *Wanderings of an Artist*, Kane stated: "I had been accustomed to seeing hundreds of Indians about my native village, then Little York, muddy and dirty, just struggling into existence, now the City of Toronto . . . But the face of the red man is now no longer seen. All traces of his

footsteps are fast being obliterated from his once favourite haunts, and those who would see the aborigines of this country in their original state, or seek to study their native manners and customs, must travel far through the pathless forest to find them" (Kane, *Wanderings of an Artist*, p. vii).

324 The masks in *Duel After the Masquerade* are based off of those depicted in the Kane painting *Medicine Mask Dance*. They are sourced from different nations and locations, but grouped together in one fictional scene in Kane's painting (Paul Kane, *Medicine Mask Dance*, 1849–1856 [painting], Toronto, Royal Ontario Museum; Paul Kane, *Medicine Masks, Northwest Coast B.C.*, 1847 [painting]).

325 Lefroy's outfit and dog-sled in *Charged Particles in Motion* are based on Kane's 1845 portrait of Lefroy, which shows the explorer with his winter equipment and team of dogs in the foreground (Kane, *Scene from the Northwest: Portrait of John Henry Lefroy*, c. 1845–1846 [painting], Art Gallery of Ontario, Toronto).

326 In 1885, the Canadian government, seeking to eliminate Indigenous cultures, banned the potlatch ceremony and did not remove the ban from the legal code until 1951. Potlatches continued during the ban, with some Indigenous people being arrested for organizing or attending them, such as Dan Cranmer and his Kwakwa̱ka̱'wakw community in 1921 (U'mista Cultural Society, "Potlatch," Living Tradition: The Kwakwaka'wakw Potlatch of the Northwest Coast, 2019, https://umistapotlatch.ca/potlatch-eng.php).

327 The Indian Act led to government seizures of sacred belongings, with many prosecuting officials selling those ceremonial items to museums or collectors, or keeping them in their own private collections (Dan Eshet, *Stolen Lives: The Indigenous Peoples of Canada and the Indian Residential School,* Facing History and Ourselves, 2016, p. 38; U'mista Cultural Centre, "The History of the Potlatch Collection," Umista.ca, 2021).

328 The Forks refers to where the Red River and Assiniboine River meet in present-day Winnipeg and was historically called nêstawê'ya, or Three Points; it acted as a trading centre for centuries (Joseph Burr Tyrrell, *Algonquian Indian Names of Places in Northern Canada*, Toronto: The University Press, 1915, p. 220; Niigaan Sinclair, "New Name for Historic Space," *Winnipeg Free Press*, September 14, 2018).

To Help My People I Made Mischief with the Newcomers' Leaders

329 In 1902, Reverend Silas T. Rand wrote that the Mi'kmaq name for the Charlottetown Harbour was Booksāk, which means "narrow water-passage between broken cliffs" (Silas T. Rand, *Rand's Micmac Dictionary*, Charlottetown: The Patriot Publishing Company, 1902, p. 34).

330 The Canadian delegates' alcohol consumption during confederation reached extraordinary levels. The steamer on which they travelled to Prince Edward Island purportedly contained $13,000 worth of champagne (CBC, "The Charlottetown Conference," Canada: A People's History, 2001, https://www.cbc.ca/history/EPCONTENTSE1EP8CH4PA1LE.html). While attending a ball that took place during the Québec conference of October 1864, Frances Elizabeth Owen Monck, the sister-in-law of governor-general Charles Stanley Monck,

reported that there was "drunkenness, pushing, kicking, and tearing" and that the "supper room floor was covered with meat, drink, and broken bottles" (Frances Monck, *Monck Letters and Journals, 1863–1868: Canada from Government House at Confederation*, ed. W.L. Morton, Toronto: McClelland and Stewart, 1970, p. 155).

331 George-Étienne Cartier, a major figure in Confederation due to the political alliance he formed with John A. Macdonald, was a talkative, confident speaker (CBC, "George-Étienne Cartier," Canada: A People's History).

332 George Brown, the dour, Protestant founder of the newspaper *The Globe* and leader of the Reform Party, had expressed his criticisms of Confederation openly before participating in confederation procedures directly during the 1860s ("George Brown," Canada: A People's History; Daniela Rochinski, "'Wild' vs. 'Mild' West: A Binary or Symbiotic Unit? The Complexity of the Mythic West Reimagined from a Canadian Perspective, 1870–1914," MA thesis, University of Saskatchewan, 2002, p. 41).

333 During the Québec conference proceedings, Frances Monck commented in her diary that Macdonald "is always drunk now, I am sorry to say, and when some one went to his room the other night, they found him in his night shirt, with a railway rug thrown over him, practising Hamlet before a looking glass" (Monck, *Monck Letters and Journals*, pp. 158–59).

334 In a speech to the House of Commons on July 6, 1885, Macdonald said, "I can show to you, not only that they have been well treated, but . . . that the Indians had no wrongs to redress . . . that we have been pampering and coaxing the Indians; that we must take a new course, we must vindicate the position of the white man, we must teach the Indians what law is" (John A. Macdonald, "Speech Before the House of Commons, July 6, 1885," in *Debates of the House of Commons*, 5th Parliament, 3rd Session, June 6, 1885–July 20, 1885, Ottawa: Maclean, Roger & Co., 1885).

335 Macdonald once said to newspaper editor Samuel Thompson, "I don't care for office for the sake of money, but for the sake of power, and for the sake of carrying out my own views of what is best for the country" (Samuel Thompson, *Reminiscences of a Canadian Pioneer for the Last Fifty Years: An Autobiography*, Toronto: Hunter, Rose & Company, 1884, p. 319).

336 In an 1865 letter, John A. Macdonald wrote "I would be quite willing, personally, to leave that whole country a wilderness for the next half-century but I fear if Englishmen do not go there, Yankees will" (John A. Macdonald, "Letter to Sir Edward W. Watkin, March 27, 1865," Sir John A. Macdonald Fonds, 511, 9-11, reel C-24, Library and Archives Canada.).

337 In an address to the House of Commons on November 10, 1854, Macdonald declared, "There is no maxim which experience teaches more clearly than this, that you must yield to the times" (*The Globe*, "Article 1," November 10, 1854).

338 While in Halifax on September 12, 1864, Macdonald, when speaking of the effects that building a railway to the west would have on trade and commerce, stated, "But there are even greater advantages for us all in view. We will become a great nation . . ." (John A. Macdonald, "Toast to Colonial Union, Halifax, September 12, 1864," Macdonald-Laurier Institute, 2014).

339 Macdonald once accidentally set a London hotel room on fire after falling asleep while leaving a candle lit. It is likely that he had been drinking before this incident (Ged Martin, "John A.

Macdonald and the Bottle," *Journal of Canadian Studies*, vol. 40, no. 3, Fall 2006, pp. 162–185; Susanna McLeod, "John A.'s Close Call with Fire," *The Kingston Whig Standard*, January 3, 2017).

340 In a House of Commons debate on May 3, 1880, Macdonald stated: "It is quite true that to civilise an Indian you must commence with the child. I hope that we shall have a system by which the children may be, as it were, withdrawn from the parents as much as possible, and brought under the influence of civilised Indians" (John A. Macdonald, "House of Commons, May 3, 1880: Supply—Concurrence," in *Debates of the House of Commons of the Dominion of Canada, Vol. IX*, Fourth Parliament, Second Session, April 6, 1880–May 7, 1880, Ottawa: T.J. Richardson, 1880, p. 1945).

341 In the mid-nineteenth century, both Canada and the British Crown were keen to obtain the vast territory known as Rupert's Land, over which the Hudson's Bay Company had claimed ownership for nearly two centuries. The territory's resources and potential for settlement were promising to the Canadian government, especially in regards to its agricultural fertility, which was confirmed by the Hind-Dawson expedition of 1857. It was also hoped that Canadian acquisition of the territory would circumvent the United States' expansionist ambitions and lead to the development of a cross-continental railroad. The HBC was reluctant to sell Rupert's Land, but pressure from the British government eventually forced the company into negotiating a sale with Canada. George-Étienne Cartier represented Canada in the talks, which lasted for six months from 1868 to 1869. For £300,000 and retainment of title over 5 per cent of Rupert's Land, the HBC surrendered the territory in November 1869, with Rupert's Land being formally annexed to Canada in June 1870 (Shirlee Anne Smith, "Rupert's Land," *The Canadian Encyclopedia*, March 4, 2015; J.C. Bonenfant, "Cartier, Sir George-Étienne," *Dictionary of Canadian Biography, Vol. X*, University of Toronto/Université Laval, 2003; Lewis H. Thomas, "Confederation and the West," *Revista de Historia de América*, no. 65/66, 1968, pp. 35–40; Rochinski, "'Wild' vs. 'Mild' West,'" pp. 43–44).

342 In the decade prior to Confederation, George Brown made vocal arguments in favour of expansion into western lands occupied by the HBC (Thomas, "Confederation and the West," p. 35). In a December 10, 1856 article published in his newspaper *The Globe*, Brown wrote, "The question which presents itself to us in Canada relates to the best method of taking possession of the vast and fertile territory which is our birthright, and which no power on earth can prevent us occupying" ("The Great North West," *The Globe*, December 10, 1856, p. 2).

343 The vast region known to the English-speaking world as Rupert's Land encompassed the traditional territory of the Nakoda (Assiniboine), nêhiyaw (Cree), Anishinaabe, Nakawē (Saulteaux), Dene, Omàmiwininiwak (Algonquin), Očhéthi Šakówiŋ (Sioux), Siksika (Blackfoot), Kainai (Blood), Piikani (Peigan), Aaniihnén (Gros Ventres), Tsuut'ina, Innu, Naskapi, Inuit, and Métis (Temprano, Native Land Digital).

344 Zuni elders foretold that "Drinkers of dark liquids will come upon the land, speaking nonsense and filth" (The Zuni People and Alvina Quam, *The Zunis: Self-Portrayals*, Albuquerque: University of New Mexico Press, 1972, p. 3).

ᓇᓈᐢᑯᒥᑫᐏᓇ

ACKNOWLEDGEMENTS

This book would not have been possible without the generous support of Canada Council for the Arts' Creating, Knowing and Sharing Program. We are also grateful for the support of essential publishers Kegedonce Press, *Brick: A Literary Journal*, Koyama Press, and Second Story Press through the Ontario Arts Council's Recommender Grants for Writers program.

We owe immense gratitude to Jared Bland, former Publisher of McClelland & Stewart. For most of the six years we've been working on this book, he has been Miss Chief's champion. As two novice book writers, we could not have asked for a greater protective and supportive force. The whole team at M&S was amazing—we owe huge thanks to Scott Sellers for having the bravery to be immediately open to the idea of Miss Chief's Memoirs. We thank Thomas King for his early advice on the world of publishing and for his introduction to our wonderful agent Jackie Kaiser, who helped us navigate this literary world with honesty and kindness. Meg Masters helped us shape the narrative into something readable in the early stages when it was sprouting off in all directions, so that Miss Chief's story could shine. Thanks to M&S Senior Managing Editor Kimberlee Kemp, Publishing Manager Joe Lee, and Editorial Assistant Rebecca Rocillo, as well as to Production Manager Christie Hanson and Ebook Production Coordinator Asher Nehring, for their firm hands and eagle eyes in pulling this complex project together so expertly on a tight deadline; Andrew Roberts for his gorgeous design befitting Miss Chief; copy editor Gemma Wain whose razor sharp skills and quick grasp of ideas made our writing so much clearer and stronger; and to current M&S Publisher Stephanie Sinclair for guiding this book out into the world with insight and care.

We are grateful for the huge support we've had from the team at Penguin Random House Canada from Chief Executive Officer Kristin Cochrane, who has been in Miss Chief's corner since day one. We thank the stellar audiobook team of Audio Book Director and Engineer Zak Annette, Manager of Audio Production Sonia Vaillant, and Producer Kathleen Jones (and Michael Nuyen's essential behind the scenes support). Special thanks to Gail Maurice who narrates the audiobook for bringing Miss Chief alive with warmth, power, and playfulness (and making our writing sound so much better). We also want to thank the team who worked so incredibly hard to bring Miss Chief to the world—Sarah Howland, Imprint Sales Director for McClelland & Stewart; Tonia Addison, Director, Marketing & Publicity; Erin Kelly, Group Director, Publicity & Marketing; and the person who started it all, Scott Sellers.

We are incredibly lucky to have worked with all of you.

We also extend massive thanks to Kent's studio team: the incredible painters who work with Kent; Creative Director Brad Tinmouth for his behind the scenes work on making the logistics work for the paintings; Nick Pittman for his attention to the design and colour; Studio Manager Adrien Hall for his thoughtful insight on sex and gender and for helping make space for the book with Kent's very busy studio schedule and his organizational support, always done with kindness and empathy. We are hugely indebted to Studio Archivist/Researcher Sadie MacDonald who tirelessly assisted us with historical research, author permissions, copyediting, tracking narrative continuity and structure, compiling the hundreds of endnotes, and helping keep everything together on this huge project over six years while caring for it so deeply—we could not have done it without you!

We thank every model who has worked with Kent in the works featured in these pages—they lend their power to make the paintings come alive.

We are deeply grateful to Cree professor and most patient human Dorothy Thunder and newly retired nêhiyawêwin expert Solomon Ratt, who helped make sure we didn't send bad Cree out into the world. Dr. Miriam McNab carefully reviewed our historical accounts to correct and clarify them and also gave us additional suggestions on language. Lightning fast Cree translator and professor Bill Cook helped us with the Cree syllabics and proofreading with additional editing help from Tessa Cook. Through Belinda Daniels, Willie Ermine's language teachings, especially in regards to mamahtâwisiwin, have enriched this book, as have Randy Morin's teaching on Cree terms for prayer and gratitude.

Lisa Jackson's early read-through when this book was a hot mess and her advice on structure and priorities is deeply appreciated, as is Chelsea Vowel's guidance on Otipemisiw (Métis) terms. Dr. Niigaanwewidam Sinclair was kind enough to share his extensive knowledge on the history of St. Peter's. Dr. Jonathan Ferrier contributed by consulting with Hereditary Knowledge Keeper Waawashkeshi Luke Henry, as well as Darren Wybenga and Margaret Sault, on our behalf, who shared knowledge of their ancestor Maungwudaus (George Henry) and his family. Zoe Hopkins's guidance on Mohawk names and terminology was also incredibly valuable.

This project involved a great deal of discussion on Two-Spirit identity and historical Cree gender identity with many language experts, historians, and queer scholars across the country. Thoughtful contributions were provided by Gail Maurice, Dr. Alex Wilson, Stan Wilson, Chelsea Vowel, Harlan Pruden, Dr. Belinda Daniels, and Edward Lavallee, with additional input from Laura St. Amant. We thank them for their contributions in conversations on these important and ever-evolving ways of thinking and naming.

We are grateful to Grandmother Pauline Shirt for her kindness to us over the years and for generously sharing her family history which helped shape the role of her ancestor Kâ-papâm-ahcâhkwêw in this story.

Discussions with Dr. Tasha Hubbard about buffalo and papamihaw asiniy helped drive home the importance of buffalo in the narrative. Dr. Nick Estes's conversations with us about water were a profound influence. Wilfred Buck's teachings on Cree and Anishnaabe star knowledge, Floyd Favel's traditional knowledge, and Dr. Kim Venn's deep knowledge of dark matter, physics and astronomy were invaluable to helping shape Miss Chief's origin story.

We'd also like to thank others whose conversations over the years have helped inform our thinking about telling this story: Jesse Wente, Danis Goulet, Kona Goulet, and Michael Greyeyes. We owe a huge debt to all the Knowledge Keepers, scholars, and thinkers whose research shaped the history and culture described in this narrative. Thank you for sharing your wisdom.

Thank you most of all to our families. Gisèle would like to thank her husband Archer Pechawis and their children Carson, and especially Miyoteh and Keewetin who have been waiting for half and their whole lives, respectively, for this book to be done. She would also like to thank Lynne, Kelley, and Sarah for being there. We are grateful to Kent's brother Don Monkman for keeping the family archives that inspired the second half of the book, which is loosely based on Kent's family history. We also thank Don for the time he took to share his in-depth knowledge of Winnipeg, its history, and its present with Gisèle. We honour the memory of Kent's grandmother Elizabeth Monkman, his great-aunt Margaret, and great-uncle Walter who were all survivors of Brandon Residential "School."

kinanâskomitinawâw kahkiyaw.

For more information and a complete list of works cited, see www.urbannation.com/TheMemoirsOfMissChief

CREE LANGUAGE GLOSSARY

nêhiyawêwin (Plains Cree Y dialect)

acâhkos (pl. acâhkosak)	star
acâhkos-iskwêw kîsik-iskwew	Sky Woman
âcimowin (pl. âcimowina)	a (true) story, a recounting of facts
âhâsiwimina	juniper berries
âhâw	okay
ahcâhk (pl. ahcâhkwak)	soul
ahcâhk-iskotêw (pl. ahcâhk-iskotêwa)	soul flame
ahcâhko-sîpiy	river of spirits, path to the spirit world (known in western astronomy as the Milky Way)
âhkamêyimo	don't give up
âkayâsiw (pl. âkayâsiwak)	one of the Cree terms for English people
âkayâsîwiskwêw	English woman
amisk (pl. amiskwak)	Beaver
amiskosis (pl. amiskosisak)	little beaver
amiskosoy	beaver tail
amiskowêsinâw	castor gland of a beaver
amiskwayânak (sing. amiskwayân)	beaver pelts
âpacihcikan	tool
âpakosîs-sîpîhk	Souris River (locative)
âpihtawikosisân (pl. âpihtawikosisânak)	half-sons (Métis)
apisci-sîpîsis (locative apisci-sîpîsisîhk)	Milk River
Apisciskôs	Little Bear (refers to the individual; not a literal translation)
asinîwaciya	the Rocky Mountains
asinîwipwât (pl. asinîwipwâtak)	Assiniboine
asiniy (pl. asiniyak)	rock
askiy	earth, the world
âstam!	come!
Atâhkakohp	Starblanket (refers to the individual)
âtayôhkan (pl. âtayôhkanak, dim. âcayôhkanis)	spiritual beings, spirit keepers, legendary beings

âtayôhkânis	a little sacred story
âtayôhkêwina	sacred stories
atim (pl. atimwak)	dog
atimocisk (pl. atimociskak)	dog ass
awahê	be careful, take care
awas!	go away!
awâsis (pl. awâsisak)	children (glowing sacred flames)
awiyâ!	ouch!
ay-hay	thank you
ayîkipîsim	Frog Moon, April
ayîkis (pl. ayîkisak)	frog
Âyimisîs	Little Bad Man (refers to the individual)
ayisiyiniwak	human beings
câpân	great-grandchild (also means great-grandparent)
cêskwa!	wait!
cêskwa pitamâ	wait a bit
cîmân (pl. cîmâna)	canoe
cimasowin	erection
ê-kîskwêpitât	his/her/their touches make him/her/them crazy, drives them into a frenzy
êkosi	that's it, done, enough
êkosi nimiyâw âpihtâw piko	I only gave him half of it
êkosi pitamâ	that's it for now
êkwa	and, then, also
ê-makwayikihkâtêk	filling his/her pants with a bulge
ê-nâh-napwêkinak	repeatedly folding him/her
ê-nânapwêkinât	as we folded him over and over into different positions
ê-nâpêhkâsot	bully, show-off
ê-tahkohcipayihot	jumped on top
ê-wâpanitêhtapit	ride all night
iskonikan (pl. iskonikana)	reserve "leftover land" (rejected by the government)
iskonikanânêwiyiniwak	people living on reserves
iskotêwâpoy	whisky; literally, "firewater"
iskotêwotâpânâsk	train
iskwêw (pl. iskwêwak)	woman
iyiniwak	Indigenous peoples
kahkiyaw nimiyik	he gave me all of it
Kamistatim	Baptiste Horse (refers to the individual)

kâ-kî-mâyahkamikahk	when bad things happened; "the troubles"; 1885 Resistance
Kâ-kîsikâw-pîhtokêw	Coming Day (refers to the individual)
ka-kî-wîcêwitin cî?	can I come with you?
Kâ-kîwistâhâw	He Who Flies Around (refers to the individual)
Kâ-miyêscawêsit	Beardy (refers to the individual)
Kâ-miyo-kîsihkwêw	Fine Day (refers to the individual)
Kâ-nîkânît	Foremost Man (refers to the individual)
Kâ-papâm-ahcâhkwêw	Wandering Spirit (refers to the individual)
Kâ-pwâtâmot	Sioux speaker (refers to the individual, Thomas Quinn)
kaskaskacîscacay (pl. kaskaskacîscacayak)	song sparrow
kaskitêwiyiniw (pl. kaskitêwiyiniwak)	Black person
kâ-wâsihkopayicik	literally: "the ones who shine," "the shiny ones" (Miss Chief's personal name for her friends who have a spectacular sense of style, sometimes historically referred to as Dandies)
kayâs	a long time ago
kayâsês	not that long ago
kêhkêhk (pl. kêhkêhkwak)	hawk
kêhtê-amisk	elder beaver
kêhtê-aya (pl. kêhtê-ayak)	Elder
kiciwâminawak	our cousins
kihcikamêwi-kinosêwak (pl.)	cod
kihcikamîhk	Lake Superior; also ocean (locative)
kihêw	Eagle
Kihêwin	Eagle (refers to the individual)
kikihci-âniskotâpân	your great-great-great-grandparent
kikî-wîcihitinân ta-miyo-pimâtisiyêk	we helped you have a good life
kimiwan	rain
kinanâskomitin (to one person) kinanâskomitinâwâw (to multiple people)	thank you; deep, profound gratitude
kinêpik oministikohk	Snake Island (locative)
kinosêwisîpîhk	Norway House (locative)
kisâkihitin (pl. kisâkihitinâwâw)	I love you
kisci-sîpiy	Nelson River
Kisê-manitow	the creator, the great spirit
kisêwâtisiw	she/he is kind and gentle

kisêwâtisiwin	kindness
kîsikâwi-pîsim	sun
kîsikokak	beings of light
kisiskâciwani-sîpiy	Saskatchewan River
kîskwêpêwin	intoxicated
kistahkisiw	the tree stands solid
kistêyihtamowin	respect
kistêyimowin	mutual respect
Kitahwahkên	Miserable Man (refers to the individual)
kitimâkêyihcikêwin	kindness of heart, compassion
kiwâhkôhmâkaninawak	our relatives
kîwêtin	the north wind
kîwêtin acâhkos	the North Star, the Going Home Star, Polaris (traditionally known as acâhkos êkâ kâ-âhcît, the star that does not move)
kohkom (pl. kohkomak)	your grandmother; sometimes used colloquially for his/her/their grandmother instead of the correct "ohkom"
Kohkominâhkîsîs	Grandmother Spider
kwîhkwîsiwak	blue jays
macan	it is evil, very bad
mamahtâwisiwin	a tapping into the great mystery
mâmawi-pimohâniwiw	the act of walking together
mâmawi-wîcihitowin	all beings helping one another
manâcihitowin	mutual respect, mutual veneration
manâcihtâ	treat with respect, treat delicately, treat carefully
Manicôs	Bad Arrow (refers to the individual)
manitow asiniy	spirit rock
manitow-iskotêw	creator's flame, soul flame
manitow-wâpow	straits of Manitou, the Great Spirit
manitow wiyasiwêwina	laws of everything in creation
masinâpiskahikêwin	petroglyphs, pictographs
masinasin	Writing-on-Stone, Áísínai'pi in Blackfoot (refers to the site)
maskawisîk niwîcewâkanak	be strong, my friends
maskêk	muskeg, grassy bog, low marsh
maskihkîwâpoy	bush tea
maskwa (pl. maskwak)	bear
mâtinamâkêwin	generosity, sharing
matotisân	sweat lodge

mêmêkwêsiwak (pl.)	sacred beings, little people that live near water; gentle, shy, skittish of humans
mêtawê	play
mêyi	shit
micisk	asshole
mihkospwâkan	red pipestone pipe
mihkwâkamîwi-sîpiy	Red River
mîkiwâhp (pl. mîkiwâhpa)	tipi
Minahikosis	Little Pine (refers to the individual)
minâtahkâwa	Cypress Hills
Minôsis	Kitten
misâskwatômin (pl. misâskwatômina)	saskatoon berry
misicimasowin	large erection
misi-kinêpik	sacred/legendary being; underwater horned serpent
misi-maskwa (pl. misi-maskwak)	great bear
misi-omikîwin	smallpox
misipâwistik	Grand Rapids
misipisiw (pl. misipisiwak)	large lynx; sacred/legendary being; underwater lynx
miskinâhk-oministik	Turtle Island (the continent of North America)
Mistah-âmow	Big Bee
mistahi-amisk (pl. mistahi-amiskwak)	giant beaver
Mistahi-maskwa	Big Bear
mistahi mwêstas	much later
mistahi-paskwâwi-mostos (pl. mistahi-paskwâwi-mostoswak)	great buffalo
Mistâpêw	sasquatch
mistatim (pl. mistatimwak)	horse
Mistatimwas	Sailing Horse (refers to the individual)
Mistawâsis	Big Child (refers to individual)
mistikôsiwak	French people, literally "wooden boat people." Sometimes applied generally to Europeans.
misti-sîpîhk	big river; St. Lawrence River (locative)
mitâhkay	vagina (side note: in the Cree language, vagina is considered animate)
mitakay	penis (side note: in the Cree language, penis is considered inanimate)
mitiy	ass
mîtos (pl. mîtosak)	tree (specifically a poplar, but often used for trees in general)

miyâhkasikan	sweetgrass, cedar, sage
miyawâtamowin	joyfulness, amusement, delight, enjoyment
Miyo-kîsikâw	good weather; Fine Day (refers to the individual)
miyo-ohpikihâwasowin	raising children well
miyo-pimâtisiwin	the good life, living life with conscious connection to the land in a way that creates and sustains balance
miyotêhêw	she/he is good-hearted, kind
miyotêhêwin	kindness of heart; openness, compassion
miyo-wîcêhtowin	balance, living in harmony, helping others
miywâsin (inanimate)	beautiful
Môci-kîsikâw	Happy Day (a name Miss Chief uses for Meriwether Lewis)
môniyâw (pl. môniyâwak)	white people, (thought to historically refer to "people from Montréal")
mostoswayân (pl. mostoswayâna)	buffalo robe
mwâkwa	loon
mwêscasês	a little later
mwêscasês kîsikâwa	a few days later
mwêstas	later
Nahpasê	Iron Body (refers to the individual)
namôya	no
namôya kinwês êkwa ta-pêhoyêk pâmwayês kwayask kinosêwak êkwa mînisa ta-mîciyêk	you won't have to wait much longer before you can eat all the fish and berries you want
namôya nânitaw	fine
namôya nânitaw, kiya mâka?	I am fine, and you?
nêhiyânâhk	Cree country
nêhiyaw (pl. nêhiyawak)	Cree people
nêhiyaw nâpêw (pl. nêhiyaw nâpêwak)	Cree man
nêhiyawêwin	language of the Plains Cree people
nêhiyaw-iskwêw (pl. nêhiyaw-iskwêwak)	Cree woman
nêhiyaw-pwât	Iron Confederacy
nêhiyaw wiyasiwêwina	Plains Cree laws applying to humans
nêstawê'ya	Three Points, the Forks; can also be spelled nistwayak
nicâpân	my great-grandfather, my great-grandchild
nicimasowin	my erection
nîcimos (pl. nîcimosak)	sweetheart
nicîstinâw isi mitoni ka-miywêyihtahk	I scratched him just exactly as he liked it
nikâhcitinâw	I caught him
nikamowin	song

nikosis	my son
nikwatisowin	sharing
nimâmâ	my mother
nimatâw	I fucked him/her
nimis	my older sister
nimosôm	my grandfather
ninêhiyawak	my Cree people
ninôhkwâtâw	I licked him
nipahi mwêstas	a great deal later
nipâkwêsimowin	Sun Dance
nîpisîhkopâwiyinînâhk	Beardy's (refers to the reserve)
nipiy	water
nipiy pimâtisiwiniwiw	water is life
nisâkaskinahâw	I filled him/her/them up (sexual connotation)
nisikos	aunt
nisîmis	my younger sibling
niska	goose
niskipîsim	Goose Moon, March
nistês	My older brother (Miss Chief often refers to Wîsahkêcâhk in this way)
nistim	my niece
nitahcâhk	my soul
nitânis	my daughter
nitânisihkâwin	my step daughter
nîtakay	my penis
nitâskinâw	spread, spread him/her/them wide open (sexual connotation)
nitêmak	my dogs, my horses
nitihkwatim	my nephew
nîtisân (pl. nîtisânak)	my sibling
nitisiyihkâson	I am called (my name is)
nîtominâw	I lubed/oiled/greased him
nitôtêm (pl. nitôtêmak)	my friend, my kinsperson
niwîcêwâkan (pl. niwîcêwâkanak)	my friend, my spouse, my companion, my partner
niwîcêwâkanak pikwâwiyak kâ-sâkihâcik	literally: "my friends who love whomever they want" (Miss Chief uses this term to describe her friends who have sexual and/or romantic relationships with those of the same gender)

niwîcêwâkanak pikwîsi kâ-isi-wîkicik	literally: "my friends who live however they want to live" (Miss Chief uses this term to describe her trans friends, gender-fluid friends, and those who do not live or present according to western cis-gender/cis-sexual gender binary norms)
niwîci âtayôhkanak	my fellow legendary beings
niwîsakahok	he just nailed me
niwîsakawâw	I just pounded him
nôcihitowipîsim	Rutting Moon, September
nohkom (pl. nohkomak)	my grandmother
nôsisim (pl. nôsisimak)	my grandchild, my great-grandchild
ocêkwi sîpiy	Fisher River
ohcinêwin	the breaking of laws against other beings
ohkoma	his/her grandmother
ohkomimâw (pl. ohkomimâwak)	grandmother
okihcitâwiskwêw (pl. okihcitâwiskwêwak)	women with authority over the land; law keepers of the Cree Nation whose role was to provide the legal "system" of the nêhiyaw people
okimâwaskwaciy	Chief Bear Hill
okîskwêpêsk	drunk (n.)
omosômiwâwa	their grandfather
Onîpawîhêw	Makes Him Stand (refers to the individual)
osâmipiy	drinking, abuse of the mind; literally: overdrink
oskâpêwis	ceremonial helper, a sacred helper who understands nêhiyaw laws
oskawâsis	baby (new child)
oskiciy	sacred pipe stem
oskitakosinokîsikow (pl. oskitakosinokîsikowak)	newcomer spirit being
otôtêmihtowin	respectful openness and acceptance of others; friendship, diplomacy
pahpahtêwastim	dappled horse
pakonî-kîsik	the hole in the sky; alternate spelling is pâkwan kîsik
Papamê-kîsik	Walking the Sky, Round the Sky (refers to the individual)
papâmihâw asiniy	flying rock
Papêwês	Lucky Man (refers to the individual)
paskowipîsim	the Moulting Moon, July
paskwâwihkwaskwa	sage
paskwâwi-mostos (pl. paskwâwi-mostoswak)	buffalo
paskwâwi-mostosowiyâs	buffalo meat

pâstâhowin	serious transgression or breaking of a nêhiyaw law against another human being
Payipwât	Hole in the Sioux (refers to the individual)
pê-mîciso!	come, eat!
Pêtâpan	Coming Dawn (refers to the individual)
pêyâhtakêyimowin	peace, taking care of each other and being respectful of each other
Pihêw ka-mihkosit	Red Pheasant (refers to the individual)
Pîhtokahânapiwiyin	Poundmaker (refers to the individual)
pikiskwêhkan mwêstas, sâkihiwê mêkwâc	talk later, be loving now
pimâtisiwin	life
pimicikamakohk	Cross Lake (locative)
pimîhkân	pemmican (a mixture of dried buffalo meat, fat, and berries that could be stored long-term and was essential to the fur trade)
pîsim	sun, moon, month
pîwâpiskowiw-sîpîsisihk	Iron Creek (locative)
piyêsiw (pl. piyêsiwak)	thunderbird
Piyêsiw-awâsis	Thunderchild (refers to the individual); also known as Kâpitikow
pwâtak	Sioux (Očhéthi Šakówiŋ)
sâkihitowin	love
sêmâk	right now
sikiwin	urine
sîkwan	spring
sîpêyihtamowin	patience
sîpiy	river
sîsîp (pl. sîsîpak)	duck
sôhkêpayiw	slang for "he shoots fast" (ejaculates)
sôniyâw	money
takahki	good, great
takahkipayihow	he moved well (sexual connotation)
takwâkin	autumn
tânisi	hello (how are you?)
tânisi niwîcêwâkan	hello (how are you?) my friend
tapahtêyimisowin	humility
tâpwê	true
tâpwêwin	truth, the act of telling the truth
tawâw	you are welcome; there is room

tipiskâwi-pîsim	moon
wâhkômâkanak kêyâpic kiwîcihikonawak	the ancestors still help us
wâhkôhtowin	the concept of kinship, including the people you are related to, in a wide sense
wahwâ!	wow, oh my!
wâpos (pl. wâposwak)	rabbit
Wappeston (wâpisihkos)	White Ermine (refers to the individual)
wâwiyêsiwi-pîsim	full moon
wêmistikôsiwak	French people
wîcêwâkanihtiwin (pl. wîcêwâkanihtiwina)	partnership, alliance
wîcihitowin	supporting and helping each other, interactive support
wihkasin	for inanimate, it's delicious
Wîhkaskokwasayin	Sweet Grass (refers to the individual); also known as wîhkasko-kisêyiniw, Old Man Sweetgrass
wîhkaskwa	sweetgrass
wîkimâkan	spouse
wînipêk	Hudson Bay, James Bay (refers to their "muddy waters")
wînipêk sâkahikan (locative wînipêk sâkahikanîhk)	Lake Winnipeg
Wîsahkêcâhk	a powerful nêhiyaw spirit being, sometimes called a trickster, often respectfully referred to as kistîsinaw (Elder Sibling), often called Elder Brother in English
wîskacân	whiskey jack bird
wîtaskîwin	peace, truce, alliance
wiyâtikosiwin	joy, happiness